About the Author

Victoria Purman is a multi-published, award-nominated, Amazon Kindle–bestselling author. She has worked in and around the Adelaide media for nearly thirty years as an ABC television and radio journalist, a speechwriter to a premier, political adviser, editor, media adviser and private sector communications consultant. She is a vice president of Romance Writers of Australia and a long-standing member of the Writers SA Board. She is a regular guest at writers' festivals, has been nominated for a number of readers' choice awards and was a judge in the fiction category for the 2018 Adelaide Festival Awards for Literature. Her most recent novel, *The Three Miss Allens*, was published in 2016.

Also by Victoria Purman

The Boys of Summer series:
Nobody But Him
Someone Like You
Our Kind of Love

Only We Know
Hold Onto Me
The Three Miss Allens

The Last Of The Bonegilla Girls

Victoria Purman

FICTION
HQ

First Published 2018
Third Australian Paperback Edition 2019
ISBN 978 1 489 29331 2

THE LAST OF THE BONEGILLA GIRLS
© 2018 by Victoria Purman
Australian Copyright 2018
New Zealand Copyright 2018

This is a work of fiction. Names, characters, places, and incidents are either the product of the author's imagination or are used fictitiously, and any resemblance to actual persons, living or dead, business establishments, events, or locales is entirely coincidental.

Published by
HQ Fiction
An imprint of Harlequin Enterprises (Australia) Pty Ltd.
Level 13, 201 Elizabeth St
SYDNEY NSW 2000
AUSTRALIA

A catalogue record for this book is available from the National Library of Australia
www.librariesaustralia.nla.gov.au

Printed and bound in Australia by McPherson's Printing Group

In memory of my grandparents
Stefan Scheirich (1913-1990) and
Maria Scheirich (nee Szimon; 1912-1990)
and for their children, grandchildren and
great-grandchildren.

Pictured at Bonegilla, 1954.

Chapter One

9 April, 1954

Sixteen-year-old Elizabeta Schmidt blinked open her sleepy eyes. *The camp.* The words were being murmured from one family to another on the rust-red train. Like a Chinese whisper, they had spread from carriage to carriage, seat after seat, over hats and scarved heads and little children's curls, in hushed and tired voices, like a wave. Their journey was almost over.

Six weeks earlier the Schmidt family had left their home in Hessental to take the train to Bremerhaven on Germany's North Sea coast, and begun their journey on the *Fairsea* around Europe to Malta, then Port Said in Egypt, and to Melbourne via Perth. After a rough voyage over the Great Australian Bight, during which Elizabeta's mother had been sick every day, they'd berthed at Port Melbourne and then crossed a wharf and climbed aboard the train with many carriages. It was almost midnight now, and Elizabeta was tired and anxious, having had only snatches of sleep on the journey. What would they find when the train finally stopped? The leather seats were a small comfort. She and her family had been forced onto all kinds of trains before with nothing so luxurious; they had had no windows and only wooden planks to sit on. Elizabeta didn't mind this Australian train at all.

She pulled her brand-new winter coat tighter around her and lifted the collar to cover her ears. The sobbing from behind her had begun an hour before and the woman hadn't stopped. Elizabeta didn't recognise the words, but thought it might be Russian perhaps, or Ukrainian. Elizabeta had been surrounded by languages her whole life. She still remembered a few words in Hungarian, was fluent in German, and had picked up some English in the classes provided on the *Fairsea* on the voyage over and from lessons from her father. She recognised the harshness of Polish with all its *zeds* and *jheds*; the passionate roar of Italian and the musicality of Greek, in which everything seemed to end in *ki*. People had picked up languages like scraps of food, anything to help survive the war.

The train slowed and lurched and then pulled up with a brake squeal like fingernails on a blackboard, and the woman behind Elizabeta began howling in earnest now.

Someone whispered in German. No matter where they came from, everyone understood some German. '*Sie war in den Lagern. Sie mag es nicht, Züge. Sie verstehen.*'

She was in the camps. She doesn't like trains. You understand.

There were murmurs and nods of agreement all around.

The rattle of the train stilled and Elizabeta stared out the window into the black nothingness. There wasn't a star in the sky. Dim lights brightened an uncovered platform on its own in the empty dark, but there were no buildings to be seen. There was a strange whistling in the dark, a rustle of leaves, perhaps, in the distance. The sobbing woman howled again, which set off a couple of tired children who began to squawk. Slowly, everyone around her stood, collected their belongings and bags, reached for the hands of children, and moved down the carriage towards the open doors. Elizabeta stayed close to her parents, Jozef and Berta, and when her mother asked her to make sure she held her little sister's hand, Elizabeta clasped Luisa's fingers in hers. Her nine-year-old sister looked up at her, her hair coming loose from her thin plaits.

'*Wir sind hier, Luisa*,' Elizabeta said.

Luisa nodded, her eyes wide and frightened. They shuffled to the end of the carriage and stepped off the train onto the platform. Dirt crunched underfoot. Moths danced and crashed into the lights hanging overhead. This wasn't even a station, Elizabeta realised. It was more like a siding in the middle of a field.

The unexpected chill hit Elizabeta and iced her throat. Her father had told her, promised her, that Australia would be sunny and warm all the time. 'It's always summer somewhere in Australia,' he'd said. This was not what she'd been promised. Luisa gripped her hand tighter and snuggled in close, her little body pressed up against Elizabeta's. Ahead of them, their parents were waiting. Their father, wiry and tense, his short hair covered by a peaked cap, was stern and watchful. Their mother, a bag of bones under her thick coat, was sad-eyed and alert. They looked back to their daughters and beckoned them with an urgent wave. Elizabeta quickened her step and tugged Luisa with her, past a man in a uniform handing out something official to each person.

'Elizabeta, Luisa. *Komm.*' Her mother slipped a cord with a name tag attached around Elizabeta's neck, over her layers of clothes and winter coat. Elizabeta felt the string, rough under her fingertips. She wished it were pearls instead. She'd coveted her mother's pearls, the tiny pale orbs on a delicate strand that sat right on her collarbone, so special they had only come out for church on Sundays. But they were back in Germany with a woman from the village, sold off with the new bedroom furniture and the dinner set and the few books and trinkets they'd had. They needed money for their new life in Australia, not pearls, Elizabeta's father had said when he'd sold them.

Berta slipped a name tag around Luisa's head. She looked down at her daughter. Luisa's bottom lip wobbled and her lips were pulled together to cover her chattering teeth.

'*Ihr zeit bald ins bett,*' Berta said, pinching her cheek as if to warm her. '*Schön warm.*' You'll be in bed soon. Nice and warm.

Elizabeta was too old for that loving touch from her mother. She looked up to the black sky. There wasn't even a moon. All she could see was a bench and the word *Bonegilla*, white letters on a black sign that seemed to float in midair. She desperately wanted to be in bed too, nice and warm. She gripped Luisa's hand, and together her family followed the crowd as people shuffled along in their winter coats, their hats, their new suits, their European shoes, along the siding and down a ramp to a dirt road, where a row of chugging pale blue buses stood in formation to take them all to their temporary home in Australia.

Had she slept on the bus? She wasn't sure when the bus pulled up at the camp a few minutes later. The passengers were guided off the buses and shepherded in the dark towards a large and squat reception hall. Inside Elizabeta squinted. The lights were bright after the pitch darkness of the night. Shoes clicked on the wooden floorboards and people found seats in the rows of camp chairs facing the front of the hall. Luisa climbed into her father's lap and laid her head on his shoulder. Next to him, Elizabeta shivered. Her breath was making clouds even though they were inside. She looked around at the sea of faces. She recognised people from the *Fairsea*. There were mothers and fathers who had befriended her parents. Young children she'd last seen playing table tennis on the boat, happily chasing after the flying white ball. Young women her own age who she'd exchanged shy smiles with in one of the boat's dining rooms. She remembered laughing with them as their wayward plates and cups seemed to have become possessed, sliding from side to side across the dining table when the ship listed in rough weather across the Great Australian Bight. She recognised in their expressions what was in her heart: hope, but fear too. Like her, they'd left everything and everyone they'd known and taken a leap of faith, a journey into the unknown. She wondered if this new place felt like limbo to the other girls too.

Suddenly the crowd hushed. People craned their necks and looked forwards. Elizabeta lifted herself out of the canvas chair to see above the heads in front. A man in a grey suit and a dark blue tie stood at the front of the hall on a stage with a microphone on a stand. In his hand he held some sheets of paper and he was saying something in English. Elizabeta tried very hard to concentrate on his words, but she was tired and disoriented and everything echoed in the cold hall. She tugged on her father's coat. He knew some English, absorbed while working at an American army base in Germany in the years after the war. He'd been teaching Elizabeta ever since they'd got their papers to come to Australia

'*Was sagt er, Vati?*' What's he saying, Dad?

Her father listened and then whispered to Elizabeta in German, 'He says welcome. He's talking about what we're allowed to do and not do. Where the showers and toilets are. There is hot water. There is food in the mess if we are hungry.'

Elizabeta felt too tired to eat. Luisa was asleep in her father's arms and Elizabeta listened as he continued to translate. 'And now he's saying that we are all new Australians now and that we must learn English as soon as we can. Bonegilla is about the future, not the past.'

'New Australians,' Elizabeta whispered slowly. Bonegilla. *Bon – a – gilla*. Elizabeta said the name over and over in her head. It sounded Italian but they were somewhere in the middle of Australia. How could that be?

There was applause and everyone stood. Jozef held onto Luisa, and Berta moved closer to stroke her youngest daughter's hair.

'Ve is new Australians,' Jozef announced in English, and Berta shooshed her husband with an exhausted smile.

She had been seasick almost the entire voyage from Bremerhaven. It had been Elizabeta's job to mind Luisa while their mother stayed in her cabin, her stomach roiling, unable to keep any food down. She was bone thin and her skin was grey. Maybe now they were here in Australia her mother's spirits would lift. She might find solid ground on which to plant her feet, on which to feel safe and to be well enough to love her children again. It was the pearls, Elizabeta knew. If only her mother had been able to keep her pearls, she wouldn't be so sad.

There was more shuffling, but now it was across the camp into the cold and mysterious night, as they followed directions to the accommodation block to which they'd been assigned, ticked off on a list on a clipboard. Elizabeta saw a red door. Her father stepped up the small stairs and pushed it open. He smoothed his calloused hand down the wall inside and flicked on the overhead light. Berta gasped and for a moment stood staring. From behind, Elizabeta looked past her. It was small.

'*Komm herein,*' Jozef urged and Berta took the three steps and was inside, Elizabeta and Luisa close behind her, clutching a fold in her coat.

It was called a hut but it wasn't separate. It was one of a number of compartments in a long dormitory. Elizabeta counted three doors and three windows in this building alone.

'*Mein Gott,*' Berta murmured.

There wasn't much inside the tiny space. Four narrow beds with metal legs on a linoleum floor. Each had a grey-and-white striped mattress on it, barely thicker than a folded blanket. On each bed were five blankets, neatly folded white sheets, a pillow and towels. Next to the towels were four silver trays with melamine dinnerware stacked in a pile. There was two of everything on each tray: cups and saucers, plates, soup bowls, knives, forks and spoons. There was a small wooden table in the room, upon which was a pale yellow packet of something that looked like medicine, two canvas folding chairs, a jug, a basin, a brush, a broom, a bucket, a shovel and a rake. Elizabeta looked up to the bright bulb hanging in the centre of the ceiling and blinked. There were two huge moths dancing in the light. They were so big she thought they were birds come to sleep in their room.

It was no warmer inside the hut than out. Elizabeta's breath clouded. Jozef examined the tools while Berta quickly made up the beds and the girls slipped between the sheets, still wearing all their clothes. She covered them with all five of their thin grey blankets.

'*Gute Nacht, Elizabeta,*' Jozef whispered as he leaned down and kissed his daughter's cheek.

'*Du auch, Vati.*' She watched the moths flit as her parents made up their beds before finally turning out the lights.

Elizabeta lay in the dark and the cold, too nervous to sleep. As her father gently snored, her mother breathed quietly and Luisa kicked her legs about in her sleep, her mind raced. It was cold, the sheets and blankets scratched against her legs and she fought against the tangle of her coat and her clothes underneath. What would she find tomorrow? What would this Bonegilla be like in the light of day?

Back in Germany, when her parents had been approved for migration and received their immigration papers from the Australian government, Elizabeta had told her teacher that her family was leaving for Australia. He'd walked to the bookcase and pulled down an atlas, flipping pages under his chalky fingers.

'It's the other side of the world,' he'd told the class.

She would miss her friends, she knew, but for a long time, Elizabeta had wanted to be far, far away from Germany, and the other side of the world seemed like just the right place to be, far away from everything.

Most of all, she wanted a safe place and a fresh start, far from their memories and their history, a place where they might one day, finally, belong. It didn't seem like much to ask. As she grew warmer under the blankets, the soft breathing of her family was a lullaby as she fell into her first sleep on Australian soil.

Chapter Two

A thump, thump, thump on the roof woke Luisa first.

'*Mutti. Vati*,' she cried out, half asleep. '*Was ist das?*'

Elizabeta had heard those noises too. She lifted her head from the hard pillow and looked around the bare hut. It was still cold and her breath made smoke in the air above her face. A pale light leached in through the mist their condensed breath had made on the hut's single window. She was still wearing all her clothes from the day before but one sock was missing. Her toes rubbed against the scratchy sheets.

'Shoosh, Luisa,' she whispered. A few steps away, their parents were two unmoving shapes under their blankets.

'I'm scared,' Luisa sniffled.

'It's only a bird,' Elizabeta whispered sleepily. She yawned and pulled the blankets up to her chin. 'It's a mother bird looking for food for her babies.' She was still so tired. She didn't want to move from the warm cocoon her body had made, despite the cold in the room. Her eyes drifted closed.

There were two light footsteps on the wooden floor. Elizabeta pulled back her blankets and Luisa slipped in next to her big sister.

'There are birds here in Australia?' she whispered.

'Oh yes,' Elizabeta said quietly. 'And kangaroos. They bounce down the streets here, yes? They hop on their two big feet and they have a very strong tail. You can climb on their back for a ride, like you can on a camel or an elephant.'

'Kangaroo,' Luisa said out loud and began to giggle.

'And my teacher told me we will see natives wearing grass skirts, too. And that there will be beaches and swimming and big, blue skies full of sunshine.'

Elizabeta slipped an arm around her sister and they lay quietly, listening for more of the mysterious sounds, waiting for their parents to wake up. Luisa's breath was hot on her neck and Elizabeta pulled her close.

There should have been another sister in between them, bridging the seven-year gap in their ages, but Angela hadn't survived two months. Elizabeta didn't know how she'd died. One day she was there and the next day she was gone, and then they were in church and she was buried in the cemetery alongside it. She still didn't know how to ask to her mother what had happened. There had been so much suffering in those years that she wondered whether they had simply run out of ways to talk about loss, about war and displacement and a dead baby. There had been a decade of grief circling around their lives like a crow.

Almost three years after the baby died, when the war was over, after they'd been deported from Hungary and were living in Germany, Luisa was born. She had immediately made everyone so happy. Elizabeta had loved her from the moment she'd first held her. Her arrival had created a fresh start for the family. Jozef had work, and so did Berta, and there was food on the table and enough money left for little things. A string of pearls for Berta for her birthday. A new pipe for Jozef and a leather pouch for his tobacco. New shoes for Elizabeta and a new blanket for Luisa. A brand-new set of aluminium pots and pans for Berta's kitchen.

They had lived a simple and quiet life until the day, a year ago, when Jozef had arrived home brandishing a pamphlet, *Gluck in der neuen Heimat*. Happiness in your new homeland. They had been looking for happiness in a new homeland and hadn't found it yet. Germany had never felt like home to them. That night, her parents had had serious discussions around the kitchen table. Elizabeta found the pamphlet on the kitchen table the next morning and had pored over it, reading all about the Australian way of life. Her parents had continued talking into the night on many nights that next week. Finally they decided to apply to migrate to Australia. Elizabeta hadn't wanted to go. She liked going to school and she liked her friends. There was even a boy in her class, Aleksander, who smiled at her and walked her home two times a week. Her life was just beginning and her parents had decided to wrench her from it, and she had cried when they'd left their village and got on the train and cried when they'd walked onto the *Fairsea* at Bremerhaven, all their worldly belongings in four suitcases and a trunk. They'd left behind most everything—but the brand-new pots and pans came with them across the other side of the world.

Once they were on the boat, Elizabeta made the decision to stop crying about having to leave. It had only made her parents upset, particularly her mother. Elizabeta was old enough by then to understand and remember what they had been through already. Her father said they were going to Australia for a better life, and she had decided to believe him. After all that had happened, perhaps it would be best to leave everything behind and not look back. It would be nice to finally belong somewhere, to know there was somewhere in the world that wanted her family.

Elizabeta had never felt the tug of loyalty to any country. She'd never truly imagined she belonged anywhere. In Hungary, where she and her parents had been born, they were treated like Germans, with suspicion. When her family had been deported to Germany, real Germans looked down on them as refugees. But they had German names and spoke German, didn't they? She was still as confused as ever by it. When she'd asked her father about it once, he'd told her that when the war was over, important politicians carved up countries and decided what to do with German-speaking people like them from countries that didn't want them any more.

'They think we are Nazis because we speak German,' he'd said. 'That's why we were put on those cattle trains in Budapest by the soldiers. That's why we are in Germany.'

But all that was past now. Today was to be her first Australian morning.

She wondered, as she curled up on a thin mattress on a camp bed in a small room in an ex-army hut, swathed in blankets and warmed by her sister's breath, what Australia would feel like when she opened the door and saw the big blue sky full of sunshine for the first time.

By the time the Schmidts left their hut for the walk to the mess hall, Elizabeta felt as if she hadn't eaten in a week. There had been sandwiches on the train the day before, on the journey from Port Melbourne, but she'd shivered them away all night in the cold hut. She was impatient for her family to gather up their trays and plates and bowls and spoons and cups and walk across Bonegilla for breakfast.

Their shoes crunched on the frosty grass as they walked. The sky was a pale blue and as she followed her parents and kept an eye on Luisa, it struck Elizabeta that for the first time in six weeks the air wasn't filled with the smell of salt and the sound of waves. She took in a deep breath. Bonegilla smelled like something new, like fresh air and open fields, and the spindly trees dotted here and there, with almost-white trunks and leaves long and thin and grey-green, had a scent like peppermint. And there were birds, black-and-white birds, in the branches of the tree, singing, as if they were calling out hello to everyone below.

There was a low hum from the conversations happening all around them as people walked to breakfast. They had to stop and wait as a truck rumbled past on the road, black smoke spewing from its exhaust. There was a picture of a ram with curling horns sticking out of its woolly coat and letters and words painted on the side in English. Elizabeta tried to spell them out, but her reading was still too slow and it went by too fast.

The camp was big. In the dark of the night before, there had been dim street lights and a chill wind blowing in from somewhere cold. This morning, she couldn't seem to see the end of it, no matter where she looked. The camp was filled with accommodation huts like theirs, neat row after row of pale green corrugated iron buildings with the same red doors. In the distance, there was a collection of bigger buildings and one in particular seemed to be the centre of people's comings and goings. The mess.

And there weren't only buildings but people, coming out of every building and walking along every road and in every direction. The camp had come to life while she was waking up. Two women walked by, laughing, their hair wrapped in coloured scarves knotted at the back of their necks, with fabric bags over their shoulders, stuffed to the brim with clothes, the sleeves spilling out as if there were arms inside trying to crawl out. A group of young men jogged past, dark-haired and wiry, wearing T-shirts and canvas shoes, bouncing a ball, speaking Greek. Three young women walked by arm in arm, smiling.

Elizabeta took it all in, dawdling behind her parents. When they called out her name, she scurried after them and when they reached the front door of the mess hall, they waited politely at the end of the queue.

Chapter Three

'More of them arrived last night. Another trainload of dagoes.'

Sixteen-year-old Frances Burley looked up from her boiled egg and the toast soldiers her mother still insisted on giving her. Her brother, Tom, took advantage of the distraction his purposely provocative statement had created in his sister, and leaned over his bowl of porridge to steal one of her rectangles of toast.

'Tom!' she exclaimed with a huff of indignation. She reached across the table to slap the back of his hand. He pulled it out of harm's way and grinned.

'Thomas Walter Burley.' Mavis Burley sighed and shook her head. She was at the kitchen sink. She opened a cupboard door below, reached for the Rinso and lightly sprinkled flakes from the box into the running water. 'Leave your sister alone. And don't use that word.'

'What word?'

'You know perfectly well what I mean,' Mavis said.

'You mean dagoes?'

'You're awful,' Frances said through gritted teeth as she shook an avalanche of salt onto her boiled egg.

Tom grinned at his sister and chewed teasingly before washing the toast down with a mouthful of milky tea. 'I didn't make it up. That's what people call them. Dagoes. Reffos. DPs. Wogs. Balts.'

Mavis turned from the sink, her lips pinched together. 'I'm so delighted your father and I are spending all that money boarding you in Melbourne while you're studying at university. It seems to have broadened your outlook in a way we could never have imagined. I would appreciate if you left that talk behind when you are up here at Bonegilla.'

'They're just words, Mum. I don't mean anything by them, honestly. Lots of chaps are saying it. I'm just having a bit of fun.'

'May I remind you that your father is in charge of this place? He would be horrified to hear you talk about people that way. Have a think on that, young man.'

Tom kept his smirk firmly in place but lowered his eyes to his porridge. Frances could see he was chastened, although he wouldn't admit it in a million years.

She turned to her mother, taking the opportunity to show her mother how well read and worldly she really was. 'I wonder which countries today's new Australians are from, Mum?'

Mavis turned off the tap over the sink, wiped her wet hands on the floral full-length apron she was wearing and came to the table. 'They disembarked the *Fairsea* down in Melbourne yesterday so I expect they're from all the usual places in Europe.' Her mother smiled at her. 'You're going to name them all again, aren't you, Frances?'

The family's atlas was permanently open on the small wooden desk next to the bed in Frances's room, and she loved to study the yellow, green and ivory countries marked out on the map of Europe. Since her father had become director of Bonegilla five years before, Frances's world had opened and bloomed. Living at Bonegilla was like being dropped right in the middle of a history and geography lesson and Frances had soaked up everything. She'd even learned to say some words in the languages spoken at the vast camp.

'Well, as a matter of fact, I am.'

'Here we go,' Tom sighed and rolled his eyes. It was a game they'd played ever since they'd come to Bonegilla and Frances loved the well-worn routine between the two of them. She and Tom both loved making their mother laugh.

She ignored her brother and counted off the countries on her hand, the index finger of her left hand pressing down on the fingers of her right, pinky to thumb and then beginning again. 'We've had Italians. Greeks. Poles. Hungarians. Germans. White Russians. Lithuanians.'

'There's no such place as Lithuania,' Tom teased.

'Of course there is.' Frances continued. 'Yugoslavians. Bulgarians. Romanians. And ...' she said with mock seriousness, '... Czechoslovakians!'

'Don't forget the Transylvanians.' With his index fingers he tugged at the corner of his mouth to expose his teeth and he rolled his eyes back up into his head. '*I vant to suck your blood.*'

Frances let herself enjoy the joke once more. With three years between them, they were unlikely ever to be real friends, but Tom always liked to make her laugh and she liked that he still tried.

'Tom.' Mavis smiled and shook her head at her children. Frances was aware that it wouldn't be long before she too would finish high school and leave Bonegilla, as her brothers Tom and Donald had done before her. This might be one of the last chances the three of them would have to sit together and make each other laugh. She was growing up too, no matter how hard her mother found that idea, and life would soon take her away from her parents and her brothers and this place she'd called home for the past five years.

She slapped her forehead. She'd forgotten the last line of the performance. 'Oh, no. I forgot the Latvians.'

Mavis tugged at one of Frances's long, brown plaits. 'God forbid we forget the Latvians.'

'What must it be like to travel all the way across the world and end up in Australia?' Frances had begun to think about the world differently in the past little while. The countries she had just reeled off were more than places on the map to her now. They were possibilities. Exotic destinations filled with languages and culture and people so different to her.

'I'm sure they are all very happy to be away from Europe,' Mavis said. 'The war made things dreadfully hard for so many people and some places still aren't the same as they were before. Many of the people who come here have never been able to go back to the homes they once had.' She stood, picked up her children's breakfast plates and placed them on the long metal sink under the window. It was open this morning, despite the chill autumn breeze, and the cafe curtains fluttered. Winter was well on its way in this part of the world, eight miles from Albury, on the southern banks of the Murray River. 'I'm sure people are very happy to be in Australia, to make a new home for themselves, to put all the sadness behind them and start afresh.'

'They'd better not be commies,' Tom said. 'Look at this. "Australian Reds to be accused of aiding spies". It's all about the royal commission on Russian spying. That Petrov chap, he's Russian. There'd better not be any of his fellow travellers on that train today.'

Frances and Mavis looked at the newspaper article from the front page of *The Age* newspaper that Tom was poking with a stiffened index finger. A photo of a crowd outside the High Court building in Sydney was prominent, showing a high iron gate with spikes atop it, and a group of police officers standing around, one with his hands clasped authoritatively behind his back.

'Tom, dear, I think you'll find that all those being investigated are Australians.'

'Really? We've got our own commies?'

Mavis tweaked her son's ear. 'Apparently we do. I'm sure your father can tell you all about it if you ask him.'

'Where is Dad, anyway?' Frances asked. He usually ate breakfast with the family, and had made a point of it when one or both of the boys were up to stay.

'He's in his office preparing things for our latest arrivals.' Mavis turned to glare at her son. 'And I can guarantee that your father has never used any of the words you did earlier, Thomas Burley.'

'Yes, Mum.' Tom sighed and folded the newspaper. He rested his chin in his palm and looked sulky.

'Do you think they're all happy to be coming to Australia?' Frances asked. 'Do you think they're sad to leave behind their families and friends?'

'It must be a terribly hard thing to pack up all your children and take a boat to the other side of the world, to leave the rest of your family.'

'I left my friends when we moved here from Canberra. That was hard.'

Mavis smoothed her daughter's hair. 'Yes. It was. But you're only a train journey away. Do you think you would last six weeks on a boat? Tom felt queasy fishing on the river.'

Mavis winked at Frances and they laughed at Tom's expense.

'Oh, very funny,' he said.

'I'm sure everyone who comes here is exceedingly happy with what they find. It may be a bit of a shock arriving in an old army camp in this little town, but it's not a prison, remember? People are free to come and go. They're only with us until they find work, perhaps on the Snowy Mountains Scheme, or in New South Wales, or Perth or South Australia. They're not afraid of hard work, your father always says.'

Frances was a witness to the fact that there were always people arriving and departing. Sometimes Bonegilla felt like an enormous transit point, like limbo, a place to shuffle and organise people between their old lives and their new.

Tom folded the newspaper and leapt up from his seat. 'Thanks for breakfast, Mum.' He pushed his chair in slowly, having previously been warned about scratching the newly laid geometric-patterned linoleum, and then walked through to the living room, whistling. Soon, the low tones of an ABC announcer mumbled through to the kitchen.

Frances helped her mother by clearing the table. Mavis washed the dishes, dipping her hands and the plates and cups in and out of the sudsy water, in a rhythm Frances found comforting. She liked this small house at the camp. When soldiers were trained and stationed there during the war, one of the important army people had lived there, but Bonegilla hadn't been home to troops since 1947. Australia hadn't needed so many soldiers since then; soldiers like her Uncle Bert, her mother's brother, who'd been killed in Darwin in 1943. He'd been in the navy, serving on a ship anchored in Darwin Harbour. Her mother had never said it out loud, but Frances knew her mother was glad there were no Japanese coming into Bonegilla. Many Australians still couldn't forget the war and Mavis couldn't forget what had happened to her own brother. She'd heard her mother say it once to her father, late one night when she'd slipped out of bed to go to the toilet and she'd overheard her parents talking in the kitchen. She'd stopped and listened to their conversation even when she knew she shouldn't have. It had been the anniversary of Uncle Bert's death, that day, and she remembered because her mother had called her own parents in Melbourne and she'd cried on the phone and then gone to lie down on her bed, the door firmly closed, the blinds drawn all day.

Frances didn't remember Uncle Bert. She'd been five years old when he'd been killed, but she felt like she knew him. He was a ghost in her mother's family, a reminder to them that the war had been so close.

Frances enjoyed the companionable silence as they washed and wiped the dishes. As she stacked the clean china plates in the dresser, her mother made herself a cup of tea, and sat at the table, reading the newspaper. Frances excused herself and went to her room to study her atlas.

To Frances, her home felt as if it was the centre of the world. When the trains arrived during the day, Frances loved watching the new Australians step off the bus and land in a whirl of activity, clutching their suitcases, wearing their winter coats even on the warmest of days. Trucks came and went, delivering food to the mess huts so the staff could feed the thousands of people living there. Her father once told her that Flemington Reynolds, the local abattoir, delivered two hundred sheep a day.

'Imagine that, Frances,' he'd said. 'An entire flock of sheep!' And there was bread and milk and vegetables and fruit delivered every day, too, and firewood and sometimes ice cream and pineapples. Frances loved the freedom of wandering the vast grounds of Bonegilla, all three hundred and twenty acres of it, so her father liked to tell her, past the Greek church and the Roman Catholic one; the cinema; the halls where people met for social functions; the police station and the hospital. She would make her way through the rows of timber-framed corrugated-iron army huts, listening, watching and hearing things unlike anything she'd heard in her own family. Around every corner there was a drama unfolding, or so it seemed to her. Loud and impassioned arguments in foreign languages. Whispered conversations between men and women. Disputes over space on the washing line and the toilet queue. Laughter and tears, in both adults and children. Frances had spent the past five years at Bonegilla listening and had learned to say some phrases in all these exotic languages:

Guten morgen. Auf wiedersehn.

Ciao. Comme va?
Yas sas. Efharisto.

And there were a hundred variations of what sounded to her like *hello*, just with new and different accents.

When the new Australians at the camp called out to her with a wave and a smile, she listened hard and repeated the words back to them. They mostly laughed and waved again, before turning to whoever they were with and continuing their animated conversation with a nod and a wink in her direction. She'd caught couples kissing more times than she had fingers and toes. She'd spotted Italians by the clotheslines, hidden between flapping white sheets, crouched around an illegal kerosene primus, a frypan balanced on top, cooking something. She'd heard fights between adults that had sounded rage-filled; crying children and sobbing women and shouting men. And she'd heard lullabies through the open windows of the huts in every language she could imagine.

With an index finger, Frances traced the borders that snaked across the map of Europe in her atlas. There were new borders now. She'd learned at school that some people's home countries had been swallowed up by the Soviet Union and didn't exist the way they had before the war. That's why so many people needed somewhere new to live.

There were young people everywhere and she was fascinated by them. Everywhere she went there were little ones playing hopscotch or marbles; teenagers twirling a skipping rope in the air or walking in twos and threes, arm in arm, laughing and chattering in their own languages. Australia only wanted young and fit people to come and live here, because there simply weren't enough Australians in the whole country to do all the jobs that needed doing if the country was to grow, to do the work in factories and on the Snowy Mountains hydro-electric scheme. Tom said it was about Australia needing extra people to fight the Japs in case there was another war.

No one wanted another war.

There were lots of young men at the camp and Frances found herself paying close attention to them in particular. With an energy and enthusiasm she was always surprised by, they seemed to be into everything. There were regular soccer games and a fierce basketball competition. On warm days, the young men walked over to Lake Hume and swam and laughed and dunked each other in the shallows. They were always on the move, from the mess hall to the cinema, on the bus to Albury, as if they were intent on discovering everything in this new country. While some of the parents seemed sour, unhappy, displaced, the young men and women seemed happy, released, free.

She was watching a new country unfurl like a flag.

There was no place Frances would rather be.

She checked her watch. It was time to help her mother prepare dinner. They were to have roast chicken, a rare treat because Tom was home for a week, with baked potatoes, peas, carrots and gravy. With Tom home, today was going to be a special occasion.

Frances pushed back her chair and left the atlas open on her desk. The countries of Europe stared back at her, and she smiled. She was determined to leave Australia one day to visit each one.

Chapter Four

'More people came yesterday. From the *Fairsea*. And you know what more people at Bonegilla means? More waiting for breakfast.'

Vasiliki Mitropoulos, her mother Dimitria, and her two younger sisters, Eleni and Constantina, were seated at a table in the mess. It was always noisy at mealtimes, and voices and the clutter of cutlery and crockery echoed around the room. Eleni and Constantina were devouring their porridge. Dimitria half-heartedly nursed a warm cup of instant coffee. Vasiliki spooned crunchy and bright yellow corn flakes into her mouth, milk dripping from her overloaded spoon back into her bowl.

Vasiliki had never tasted corn flakes in Greece.

She missed her family's small village in the Peloponnese Islands. She missed the Greek sunshine and aqua blue sea, even in the cooler months, the whitewashed buildings and

goats and *Yiayia* and *Papou* in the house next door and her
cousins and their cousins all in the same village. But things
hadn't been the same since the war. Everyone said that. One
of her uncles, too involved in politics for his family's liking,
was the first to leave. He'd hopped on a boat to Athens and
then got on another boat to Melbourne, and that had planted
the seed among the families in the village. Her grandparents
had cried when her family had left Greece. Her *papou* in his
fisherman's cap and her *yiayia* all in black, still mourning for
an older sister who had died six months before. The goodbyes
were hard. She and her family had gone house to house in
the village to say goodbye to everyone. Vasiliki didn't know
if she'd ever see her grandparents again. Or her best friends,
Athena and Agape, who waved her off, crying. Their families
had stayed behind, not crazy enough to go. Or at least that's
what Vasiliki's grandmother had said.

There had been angry words when they left the village.

'What's left for you here?' Dimitria had asked her own
brother that last day, before they'd boarded the boat to Athens. 'First the big war then our own war. Like one wasn't
enough. The Germans or the Communists. Take your pick.
No thank you. I choose kangaroos.'

When they'd got on the boat at Piraeus outside Athens,
strangers lined the dock, calling out good wishes and bless-
ings for the voyage to people they didn't even know.

'See?' her mother had said. 'Some people are happy for
us.'

It seemed to Vasiliki that her mother was happier here at
Bonegilla than she had been in Greece for the longest time.
Even though her husband was already away in Melbourne
working, Dimitria was settled at Bonegilla. She teased

Vasiliki about boys and tickled the tummies of her younger daughters to make them giggle. At night, in their hut, she sang songs from home until her daughters fell asleep. And when she heard a bouzouki, she looked like the happiest woman in the world. There was a ragtag band of musicians in the camp who sometimes played on Saturday nights in the hall near the mess. A Yugoslav drummer. A Lithuanian guitarist. A Greek called Andreadis on his bouzouki and an Italian on the accordion. They sounded so funny, this United Nations of musicians, that they made not only Dimitria but all the adults laugh and dance on Saturday nights at Bonegilla, twirling and shuffling around the dance floor. And when the musicians let Andreadis let fly on his bouzouki and he began the familiar strains of a *rembetika* favourite, every Greek in the place cried out and leapt to their feet and, if Vasiliki closed her eyes, she could smell ouzo, and lamb roasting on a spit, could almost see her *yiayia* and *papou*, her uncles and her aunties and her cousins, dancing in a circle, their arms on each other's shoulders, their feet flying, their handkerchiefs twirling.

Vasiliki loved watching the dancing through the windows of the Bonegilla hall. She didn't want to go inside— her mother would most likely make her dance with that horrible Nikolas Longinidis—so she made sure her younger sisters were asleep before walking across the camp to watch through the windows. She loved the smoking and the twirling skirts, so elegant. Her mother was an excellent dancer and had lots of partners.

'He's looking at you again.' Dimitria sipped her coffee but her eyes darted.

Vasiliki dropped her eyes to her corn flakes. 'He is not.'

'Yes, he is. And why shouldn't he be looking at you? You're a beautiful girl. You're sixteen. He is Greek. You can get married to him.'

'*Mama*,' Vasiliki hissed under her breath.

'He's handsome.'

'He's not handsome. And even if he was, I don't want to marry him.' She didn't want to marry anyone, especially not Nikolas Longinidis. He looked at her breasts all the time and stood too close to her when he talked to her. He had a knack of finding her in the playground, where she would take her sisters in the afternoons. While they played on the swings and laughed and called to each other, he would sneak up behind her and pinch her bottom and ask her if she wanted to go to the movies or take the bus into Albury for a milkshake. He never seemed to want to take no for an answer but that didn't stop her from saying no, over and over.

'Oh, come on, Vasiliki. All his family are back in Greece. Take pity on him. He's here all by himself. An orphan.' Dimitria lifted a hand and waved at someone across the room. 'It's only natural that he wants a Greek wife.'

Vasiliki lifted her chin. 'I heard he has a fiancée back in the village who's waiting for him to send for her. A *nyfe*.'

Dimitria waved a hand dismissively. 'You think he'll wait that long? He's here in this camp with all these girls. He'll find a Greek girl here in Australia and then break the heart of that girl back in the village. You wait and see. If you're not going to marry Longinidis, who else is there? Look around, Vasiliki. Make sure you find a nice Greek boy to marry you. I don't want you with one of those Polish. Or Russians. And don't you ever think of going near a German.'

Vasiliki changed the subject. 'Has *Baba* found us a house in Melbourne yet?'

'Not yet, but he will soon. All these new people in Australia and nowhere for us to live but here. It will be soon, I promise. He's working very hard in that cafe.'

It had been six months since Vasiliki's father had left for work in the cafe owned by his brother, Theodorous. Spiros was proud that there had been no railways or factory work for him, that he hadn't had to rely on the government to find him a job. But housing had been harder to find and he was sharing a house with four other men while he looked for a place to rent for his wife and daughters.

Vasiliki wasn't fussed about 'soon'. They wouldn't be at Bonegilla forever, but she was in no hurry to leave just yet. She had grown to like life at the camp. There were things to do every day. She had even made a best friend, a girl who wasn't Greek. She'd met Iliana on the boat coming to Australia and in the six months they'd been at Bonegilla they'd spent time together every day. They went to different churches—Vasiliki was Orthodox and Iliana was Catholic—but that didn't matter to them. Vasiliki could have Greek friends any day but she liked having an Italian friend. She also liked the escape from her younger sisters and her mother's teasing, and she decided that it was a good thing to finally have a friend who wasn't your cousin. The two girls walked every day, in the high heat of summer over Christmas and New Year, and now in the cool of the April mornings that raised goosebumps on their bare legs. They practised their English as they walked. At first it was *porridge, breakfast, lunch, dinner, toast, shower, mess hall, hello, goodbye, boat, camp.* They hadn't needed words to marvel at the kangaroos in the paddocks at twilight or the *ook-ook-ook-ook-ahk-ahk-ahk-ahk* sound of the funny birds in the trees or the oranges that arrived on trucks freshly picked from orchards in Victoria. Now, after six months, they had learned *employment office, factory, work, domestic, home, marriage, husband.*

They looked after their little brothers and sisters while their parents were doing official things—when Iliana's father was at a job interview or at the Social Security office; or their mothers were in the communal laundry doing the family's washing by hand in the frigid water. The girls wrote letters to their friends and relatives back in Greece and Italy, posting them at the post office at the camp, and sometimes went to the cinema or to the shop to buy lollies. There was table tennis and three meals a day and ice cream, and there had been fresh peaches when they were in season. When it had been warmer, they'd swum in Lake Hume and laid out in the sun browning their skin.

Vasiliki wanted breakfast to be over with so she could find Iliana.

Iliana Agnoli was her treasured first Australian friend.

Chapter Five

They had barely set foot out of their hut to walk to breakfast when Iliana's father began joking about the food again.

'What day is it? You see, I can't even keep track. It's this place. There are no Mondays or Fridays or Saturdays or Sundays. There is just day after day of nothing.' He closed the door of their hut and jumped from the top step onto the cement path below. He spun around and held his arms out wide, as if he'd just performed a circus trick. Iliana's little brothers laughed and he swept them up, one in each arm, and kept walking.

'Stop complaining like an old man. It's Monday, Giuseppe,' his wife, Agata, called out, a wry smile on her tanned face. She held her tray and Giuseppe's, one underneath the other, their plates and cups and cutlery piled on top and clattering as she walked. 'And Monday means the boys will go to the school after breakfast and learn more English. Those teachers are helping them learn how to be Australian.'

Giuseppe turned back to her. 'How to be *Australian*? Never. They will always be Italian. And we must always speak Italian to them. Always. They can't forget our language. Our culture. Our food.'

Agata chuckled. 'No chance of that when you're shouting at the top of your lungs all the time.'

Giuseppe laughed and his two sons giggled along with him. Iliana loved the sound of it, her father's deep booming happiness. She loved that no matter where they had been on this journey to a new life, leaving the village, at the port in Naples, on the boat for the slow journey to Australia, he'd made his children laugh every day. He'd made the entire upheaval an adventure for all of them.

He gently lowered his sons, Stefano and Giovani, to the ground and ruffled their hair. They skipped off ahead, and Giuseppe turned and walked backwards as he spoke. '*Cibo*. The food. So it's Monday. Let me remember. Monday is "porridge".' He said the word in English and it made Iliana laugh.

'"Bread with jam",' Iliana added.

'And "lamb's fry and gravy".' His face contorted. '*Disgustoso*.'

Agata laughed. 'You can complain all you like, but I'm happy. I don't have to cook. All I have to do is walk over to the mess with my tray and my plates and the food is there. *Pronto*.'

'You call that food? No, no. There is no decent pasta. The tomato sauce is too sweet. And that bread! It's nothing. It's like fluff. And is it too much to ask for tomatoes? When we leave here, when we get a house of our own, we will have a huge garden. We will grow our own vegetables and fruit and olives, just like home.'

'I'll be too busy looking after the bambinos. You can look after the garden,' Agata told him.

'With pleasure.'

The morning was chilly and Iliana leaned down to rub at her bare legs. Her woollen skirt and ankle socks left her calves exposed and they prickled in the cold. As they walked across camp to the mess, Iliana tried to distract herself by thinking of food from home: her *nonna's* freshly made pasta, juicy tomatoes from their garden and chewy pane di casa. There was nothing like that here at Bonegilla. She hadn't seen olive oil since they'd arrived. Everything was cooked in dripping and there was so much meat it sometimes gave her a stomach ache.

When her father and the other Italians weren't talking about the food at Bonegilla, they were talking about jobs. When they had work, they would be able to take their families and leave the camp for good. Where were the jobs? How many men were needed? When would the jobs start? Why weren't there more jobs? They had been promised work when they came to Australia. That's why the Agnoli family had got on the boat in the first place. Her father had seen a sign in the barber-shop window in the village that had said, "Male emigrants required to work in Australia". It had been hard waiting. Where would they go when her father finally got a job? The Italians had many valuable skills in a country short of labour: they were carpenters, builders, painters, concreters, stonemasons, architects and engineers. There was talk around the camp that jobs were coming up on the railways in the desert, in factories in Melbourne and fruit picking in South Australia's Riverland. Every day, Iliana's father went to the camp's Employment Office for news. Some days there were jobs, other days there weren't. And, with accommodation scarce, there were more choices for single men than there were for men with families. Iliana didn't like the idea of going to the desert. It sounded like a place that would be filled with wild animals like lions and tigers. Did Australia even have tigers? She didn't know. It wasn't until they'd arrived in Australia that she even knew Australia had deserts. In her mind, she had pictured it as a tropical island, like Hawaii. The only deserts she'd ever heard about were in Abyssinia, where Italian troops had been sent to fight for Mussolini.

With no work to occupy people, there was plenty of time to think about the food. A few times, Giuseppe had joined with some of the other Italian men and headed out into the paddocks surrounding the camp, hunting. They'd dug up rabbit holes and killed the animals with sticks. Someone had a *furnello*—a small gas ring—and the meat would be fried with chopped onions and devoured as if it were the most succulent steak. No one was allowed to cook in their own huts—the staff had warned them they might burn down—so these secret meals were like picnics.

It wasn't just her father. Italians had been complaining about the food for years. There had even been food riots back in 1952. The gossip among the Italians they knew was that the cousin of Giuseppe's neighbour from the village had been involved, and that he and his friends had stormed to the director chanting, *Is this the kind of food you expect us to eat?* Six hundred of them, or at least that was the story she'd heard, had held up plates of overcooked spaghetti, floating in a grey-coloured sauce. They had tossed that pasta to the ground right in front of the director's house.

Things had improved a little after the riots when Italians began to be employed in the kitchens, but the food was never quite like it was back home. Complaining had become a sport, something to do to fill in the long days and weeks. Iliana had decided that she liked the strange and exotic food. She loved toast with marmalade for breakfast. There were peanut paste sandwiches at afternoon tea on bread so white and soft that it was like eating a cloud. She loved to drink crunchy Milo in cold milk. She had eaten fresh peaches and pineapples—real ones, not from the tin—and hot milk and bread with jam any time she wanted it. There were bowls of oranges on the tables in the mess and sometimes she took one back to hide under her pillow. One day, a truck had driven into the camp loaded with apples fresh from an orchard and they were the sweetest and crispiest things Iliana had ever tasted.

At the mess hall, a stream of people was going in the front door and a line of people walked past them from the back of the mess; they had washed their dishes in the long trough at the rear of the building and were making their way to take their dishes back to their huts. People were calling out in different languages, looking for laughing, escaping children. There were so many sounds for so early in the morning.

Her little brothers looked up at Iliana and called out in singsong voices, 'Breakfast.'

'Yes. Breakfast,' she replied. Months of English lessons at the Bonegilla school had given the boys a distinct advantage over the rest of the family. She often heard them chatting away to children in their class, every one from a different country, already so fluent in English. *Prenotazione.* Breakfast. Iliana was getting better at making that leap in her head, to think in Italian and then in English.

As she followed her parents and brothers inside, they spooned up food onto their dishes at the bain-marie, and then found seats at a Formica-topped table.

When they left Bonegilla, when they had a house of their own, she wanted to cook with her mother again, the traditional foods of Puglia: orecchiette pasta and taralli biscuits and zeppoli pastries. That's what Italian girls did. That's what she wanted to do in this new country. Be a good Italian girl.

Her *nonna*. Would she ever taste her *nonna's* cooking again? Her eyes were wet now and she wiped them hurriedly, not wanting anyone to see that she was upset. Would she ever see her *nonna* again? *Nonna*, who'd lived through so much herself, who'd lost so much, had now lost her daughter and her grandchildren to a strange new country so far away she couldn't even take in the distance.

Iliana's good mood had disappeared as quickly as the steam from her bowl. A wave of homesickness swept over her. She pushed her bowl into the middle of the table.

She wasn't hungry anymore.

After breakfast, it was Iliana's duty to walk Stefano and Giovani to the classroom at the camp. Her big brother, Massimo, had waved at his family before heading off with his friends to play soccer, as the Australians called it. *Il calcio.* He'd joined the Bonegilla United soccer team and spent most of this time with his teammates, practising, or taking long walks around the local hills and to Lake Hume. He had a freedom that Iliana didn't. She was expected to be with her mother and help look after her two younger brothers. At sixteen she was already too old for school and anyway, they probably wouldn't be in the camp very much longer. She knew that her father would find a job soon.

There must be lots of jobs for hardworking men like her father.

Australia was a big place. Iliana wondered how many Italys would fit into Australia if you cut them out on paper and put them together like a jigsaw puzzle.

Chapter Six

Frances Burley rose early the next Sunday. The day held the promise of warming sun, with clearing cloud and a forecast that predicted no rain at all. She slipped on her woollen skirt and a pale yellow cardigan her mother had knitted for her, which was her favourite, buckled her shoes and tried to tamp down her excitement at having the day to herself. After breakfast she dutifully helped her mother prepare their Sunday roast by peeling the potatoes which would soften and golden in the fat of the lamb; she peeled carrots and prepared Brussels sprouts, which she hated but ate anyway, and set the table ready for lunch at one o'clock. She never complained about helping her mother. If she didn't do it, no one else would. Even when Tom was up from Melbourne, it was never deemed a boy's duty to help in the kitchen.

'Nicely done, Frances,' her mother told her as she looked over the table setting. 'You'll make someone a fine wife one day.' Frances wasn't sure she really ever wanted to be anyone's wife but she liked seeing her mother so pleased. The Royal Doulton china sparkled. Frances had made sure to polish the silverware as well, and it caught the light and gleamed. She had placed a crystal glass at her mother's setting, ready for a sherry after their meal. 'I wish your father were here. He loves roast lamb.'

'How long will he be gone this time?'

'A few days. But we'll be fine without him. We always are.'

Frances hoped to be like her mother when she grew up. Mavis Burley was always immaculately dressed, especially for Sunday dinner. Her slim-fitting tweed skirt was topped off with a pale green knitted twin-set that pulled in at her waist, and her everyday pearls sat neatly on her collarbone. She never left the house without a slash of Coty's lipstick and a powdered face, and her hair was always set and hairsprayed into place. Frances assumed her mother was trying to set an example for all the new Australians, to represent how an Australian woman should dress and comport herself. They needed someone to look up to. Most of them looked quite raggedy, but Frances supposed they didn't have much choice, having had to pack up their lives into trunks and battered suitcases. Even if they'd had fancy clothes and shoes before, they'd probably had to leave them all behind. She thought it highly unlikely that they'd even had fancy clothes and shoes at all. If they did, why would they come to Australia for a better life when life seemed to be rather good already?

'Thank you, Mum. Can I go now?'

Her mother laughed as she walked from the dining room back to the kitchen. 'You know the rules. Don't get dirty and don't get lost. And be back in time for lunch.'

'How can I get lost? I know every tree. Every hut. The post office, the cinema, the mess halls in every accommodation block, the stores and even the hospital.'

Her mother stopped and looked back at her daughter. Frances could see her smile falter. 'You're quite the adventurer, aren't you?'

'Just like Amelia Earhart,' Frances declared.

'Exactly *not* like her, if you please. Be careful.'

'Of course I will.' She went to her mother and gave her a quick hug.

'Be back by half past twelve, please. You'll need to freshen up before we eat.'

Frances shivered with excitement as she walked out the front door and into the world of Bonegilla. She turned her face to the weak warmth of the sun and strode. The weekends were her chance to explore the camp and she relished this time to roam. During the week, she was on the bus to school in Albury with the other children of staff who worked and lived at the camp, and felt she missed out on so many of the comings and goings. On Saturdays and Sundays, she would walk as much of the three hundred and twenty acres of the camp as she could, soaking up everything she saw. There were always new people unsure of where they were, and camp residents who were saying their final goodbyes to the place before they boarded the bus to the Bonegilla rail siding to begin their new lives in Australia.

The staff knew Frances, and would call out hello to her if they saw her. She never felt scared among thousands of strangers. When it was bustling with people, sometimes eight thousand of them at once, it felt to Frances like a huge holiday camp or a seaside town in summer without

the sea but with Lake Hume instead. Staff and residents
even grew to know each other, especially those migrants
who found work at the camp and stayed. The previous summer, there had been a wedding reception at the Hume Club
at the camp. One of the teachers married a Yugoslavian
man who was working as a translator in the Employment
Office. Frances had been allowed to go to the wedding in
the Catholic chapel at the camp. The teacher's dress was
so beautiful and the Yugoslavian man was so proud of his
brand-new Australian suit.

People didn't spend much time in their huts but wandered, played, lived in the open spaces between the huts and
around the buildings. They were so exotic looking: the dark
complexions and black hair of the Greeks and Italians, the
Slavs with their blond hair and the Dutch girls whose hair
was like daffodils. But making friends hadn't been as easy as
Frances had anticipated. She would have dearly loved to have
made friends with some of the girls but hadn't seemed to find
the right way to do that. Firstly, language was a problem. Not
many people spoke more than a few words of English, and
there were so many other languages in the camp that Frances
didn't know where to start. Although they seemed friendly
enough, she found that people tended to stick together. The
Italians with the Italians. The Germans with the Germans.
The Dutch with the Dutch, and the Latvians with the Latvians. Bonegilla was so temporary that perhaps it was easier
that way. Frances had tried to appear friendly, but perhaps
she'd inadvertently given off airs and graces, some idea that
she was better than them. Perhaps that's what stuck to you
when you were the daughter of the camp's director.

The new Australians never knew exactly how long they
were going to be at Bonegilla. As soon as the men were

assigned work, they would be off, leaving Bonegilla for good. To South Australia, to Quorn and Peterborough to work on the railways; to the Riverland to pick fruit. To Melbourne to work in factories and in government utilities; and to Cooma to work on the Snowy Mountains Scheme. Some were destined for Queensland and the cane fields. Australia seemed to be teeming with jobs begging for people to fill them. When her father left his copy of the newspaper at home, Frances would flick right past the women's pages until she found the classifieds. There was work everywhere, column after column of positions detailed in tiny type. Labourers. Farm workers. Factory workers.

Bonegilla was temporary for everyone but her.

Just as her mother did, Frances felt obliged to play her part in welcoming all of these people to Australia but she wasn't quite sure how to do it. They had been through so much, had so many experiences. She and her family had lived in Canberra before moving to Bonegilla. That was the whole of her life experience. In her wildest imaginings, she couldn't imagine what it must have been like to leave everything behind and take a ship across the world to a strange place. So many Australians had done it in the reverse direction during the war, but she'd been too young to understand what that meant, really. Their neighbours in Canberra, the Millers, had lost a son in New Guinea and her parents had gone to the funeral; and her cousin Marjorie was a nurse who'd sailed off to Malaya. She'd married a soldier and came home and was now the mother of two little girls. Frances thought all those who'd gone to war, and consequently all those who were still leaving Europe because of it, were so brave and adventurous. She longed to be brave and adventurous herself.

The radio brought that world into her house. Not just news, but Nat King Cole and Frank Sinatra and Doris Day and Rosemary Clooney. There seemed to be, to Frances at least, a whole world out there that was so much more exciting than Australia, than Albury, than Bonegilla.

Inside the camp, there was life every day. There were people, families, loud and happy voices, cooking smells, card playing, the sounds of a violin or a piano accordion in the air. When the sun was out, families poured out of their huts and set up in the lanes between the rows of buildings. Camp chairs around a table created a perfect spot for cards or the bowling game the Italian men liked to play with great whoops of excitement or groans of dismay.

Frances made her usual start to her walk around the camp, past the hospital, in and out of the rows of huts, soaking in the voices and the laughter and the happy sounds of families. Sometimes she veered off course, if there were things to see, and other times she walked away from the sadness she saw and heard. More than once she'd heard sobbing as she'd walked by the accommodation huts—adults sobbing, not the plaintive cry of young children—and when Frances had told her mother about it, Mavis had patted her daughter's hand and sighed, 'They miss home, I expect.'

Frances was on her usual route north to the oval. It was the weekend, so she knew there would most likely be a fiercely competitive soccer game underway. When she reached the clearing, she wasn't disappointed. A cheering crowd had gathered on the sidelines and the sun shone down on the olive-skinned players. Half were wearing guernseys and the other half were stripped topless, and they took it in turns to enthusiastically chase the ball through the long grass, passing it with their feet, snaking in between the other players.

It was fast; the players were quick on their feet, moving so rapidly she had trouble seeing the ball at times as it shot out from someone's foot, bounced off another player's head and, much to everyone's amusement, got lost in the long grass on the sidelines. Frances moved forward into the crowd of people, following the ball as one of the players kicked it so hard it flew through the air and landed way past the temporary goal posts. A roar went up from one section of the crowd, Italians by the look of them. The ball bounced off into a copse of gum trees and one of the players bolted after it.

Someone moved next to Frances and she stepped sideways to make room. It was a girl, about her age, the same height, with black hair cut short. Gold earrings glistened in her ears, the European kind Frances coveted. No one in Australia had pierced ears, her mother had told her, except for certain kinds of women. Sometimes she snuck into her parents' room to quietly open her mother's jewellery box on the dresser, to touch her diamante necklaces and drape them around her neck. Once she clasped a sparkling pair of earrings to her earlobes, dazzled by how long they were, but her play-acting had only lasted a minute. They pinched something dreadful.

The girl smiled back at Frances. 'Hello,' she said.

'Hello,' Frances replied. 'They are good players.' Then she felt slightly ridiculous. She wished there was a way to tell just by looking at someone if they spoke or understood English.

To Frances's relief, the girl smiled back. 'Good. Yes.' Then she pointed to one of the young men running towards goal, dribbling the ball flamboyantly with his fast-moving feet. 'My brother.' She splayed a hand to her chest. 'Massimo.'

'Oh, he's your brother,' Frances repeated slowly.

There was a shout from the players and they quickly turned their attention to the young man out on the pitch. Massimo. He was lithe and tanned, wearing shorts, knee-high socks with stripes and a long-sleeved guernsey with thick black and white vertical stripes. He had control of the ball, and was sprinting fast, urging it down one end of the playing field, no one fast enough to catch up with him, and then he smoothly kicked the life out of the ball and it soared between the upright posts for another goal.

The girl raised her arms up in the air and whooped, '*Tre*, Massimo!' She turned to Frances, holding up three fingers. 'Three goals.'

'Three goals. Goodness, he is a very good player.' Frances was barely able to keep her eyes from him, as he ran back to his team members, his arms in the air, laughing with delight, his white teeth gleaming against his skin.

'What's your name?' Frances asked.

'Me?' The girl pointed to herself. 'Iliana.'

'I'm Frances.'

Iliana laughed. 'Italian? Francesca.'

'I like that so much better than Frances,' she muttered to herself.

Iliana looked confused. 'I not understand.'

Frances waved her words away with a smile.

'This my friend, Vasiliki.'

A girl, about the same age, wearing a floral dress and a green cardigan, emerged from next to Iliana. Her hair was thick and almost black and hung in two thick plaits. She was little, a good head shorter than Frances.

'Hello.' Frances was too scared to say the girl's name. It seemed very complicated.

'Hello,' the girl said and slipped an arm through Iliana's, leaning close and bumping her friend's arm.

Frances pointed at the players. 'Soccer.'

'*Il calcio.*' Iliana kicked her foot forwards then repeated. 'Soccer.'

'*Il calcio*,' Frances repeated, thinking hard to lock it away in her head. She might need this phrase when she travelled to Italy, one day.

The three girls shyly smiled at each other and Frances turned back to watch the game. One player in particular. Massimo had called out to another player who kicked the ball to him, and then he grinned, as if he loved being in command of the ball and having all eyes on him. He tapped the ball forwards with his right foot, then flicked it to the side, teasing the opposition player who was approaching him, and then he pulled his leg back and swung. The ball soared into the air and Frances turned excitedly to Iliana.

She heard screams and shouts and then someone clutched at her arm and the next thing she knew she was flat on her back on the long grass and her head was pounding, and a crowd of people were gazing down at her with shocked expressions and mouths agape.

There was a loud, fast garble of words she didn't understand.

'*Lei sta bene?*'

'*Der Ball schlug sie auf den Kopf!*'

'*Snel een dokter.*'

'*E morta. E morta!*'

'She is not dead.' Someone was pressing a palm to her forehead. Frances shivered but the hand was warm and strong against her skin. She blinked her eyes open and the light stung. The crowd of strange faces all around her, looking down on her in horror, sucked all the air out of her lungs and all the light from the sky. She felt sick. When she moved to get up, a firm pair of hands on her shoulders pressed her back down to the damp grass

'The ball. It hit her.'

She tried to focus. It was Iliana's brother. The fast runner. The goal kicker. He was leaning over her, saying something fast and direct to one of his teammates and the young man turned his back to them, shoved his way through the crowd and took off.

'You okay?' he asked her, gazing into her eyes.

'Frances,' she blurted.

Then Iliana was there, pushing in next to her brother. '*Lei e Frances.*'

'Frances,' he repeated. *Massimo,* she remembered now. And the memory caused a throbbing in her head that beat against her temples and she closed her eyes to shut it down. And it seemed like only a moment later that another person was pushing through the crowd and she thought someone might have rushed to get her father and she didn't want to get anyone in trouble because it was just an accident, but it was a man, saying *doctor.* And he held her upturned wrist and then pulled her eyelids wide open and stared into her eyes and that hurt. Then there were more words she didn't understand and a moment later she was being lifted, hands under her arms and on her legs and she was carried slowly and carefully to the hospital.

And all she could think about as she closed her eyes, trying to squeeze away the headache, was that she would be put in one of the baby cages in the children's ward. She hoped Massimo would squeeze his hand through the gap and hold hers.

Chapter Seven

'Frances is going to be just fine, Mrs Burley.'

Dr Jenkins from the Bonegilla hospital lay a soothing hand on Mavis's shoulder. She was standing at the end of Frances's hospital bed, dabbing at her red eyes with a dainty embroidered handkerchief, trying not to look at her daughter. The tanned and dark-haired soccer players and the blond Dutch doctor had carried Frances to the hospital across the camp and one of the nurses had been swiftly despatched to fetch Mrs Burley from the director's house. It wasn't far and Mavis was there almost before Frances was tucked up in bed in the adult ward with a cold compress on her forehead.

'She's a sturdy girl,' Dr Jenkins said. 'The ground probably did more damage to her head than the soccer ball.' He chuckled, slipping a hand into one of the pockets on his white coat. With the other, he rubbed his chin. 'Those Europeans do like the round ball, don't they?' He shrugged.

'Don't understand it myself. Cricket's my game. That's what I call sport. Very much looking forward to the Ashes this summer. The Poms are coming, you know, and I'm a member at the MCG. Best five days of the year.'

Mrs Burley's frustrated question pulled him out of his obsessional reverie. 'But what about concussion, Dr Jenkins? I'm sure that Dutchman doctor said something about Frances possibly losing consciousness for a moment.'

He sighed, lowering his voice. 'Those chaps aren't real doctors, not now they're here in Australia. Who knows what their training was like back in the old country? The war and so on. In my medical opinion, he may have got a little bit ahead of himself. Frances looks fine, Mrs Burley. Perhaps I'll prescribe a couple of Disprin just in case and I'm sure that after Frances has a little kip, she'll be right as rain.'

'Are you dizzy?' Mavis peered at Frances.

'It's just a bit of a headache. I'm sure I can come home. Truly.'

'Perhaps the nurses could keep an eye on her for tonight?' Mavis asked Dr Jenkins. 'Mr Burley is in Canberra for a few days for meetings with the department and I would feel so much better if I knew she was being looked after by you and the nurses, Dr Jenkins. Just in case that headache becomes something worse.'

Frances waited, her gaze moving between doctor and mother.

'It's just a precaution, Frances,' her mother told her with a reassuring smile.

Dr Jenkins patted Mavis on the arm and nodded wisely, his glasses slipping down his rather large nose.

'It's easily done, Mrs Burley. Leave Frances with us and we'll keep an eye on her tonight. Don't you worry about a thing.'

Mavis leaned over and kissed her daughter on the forehead, a soft press of her lips to Frances's hairline. It was reassuring, as was the scent of her favourite perfume. Frances couldn't ignore the realisation that something had changed. Her mother wasn't fussing over her as if she was a child. Despite her throbbing head, Frances felt a swell of pride at being treated like a young woman for perhaps the first time ever.

'You rest up now, sweetheart.' Mavis stroked her daughter's hair. 'You be sure to tell Dr Jenkins if anything changes.'

'Yes, Mum. I'm sorry I'll miss your roast lamb. It's my favourite.'

Mavis winked. 'I'll save you a plate for tomorrow's dinner. I'll have to keep Tom away from it first.'

Frances found a smile and held it, even though it made the pounding in her head worse. 'That sounds delicious.'

The next morning, Frances woke to the sounds of voices and squeaky footsteps on the linoleum and the clatter of crockery on trays in the hospital ward. The pale early-morning autumn light was barely strong enough to lighten the room and lights flared overhead. The ward was alive with people and patients getting out of bed, and bedpans being replaced and the shuffle of slippers. The long ward had rows of beds on each side, perhaps fifty Frances guessed, and each seemed to be filled. Around her, she heard all the languages she was used to in the camp, but there was also crying and sniffling and, in the distance, a man was moaning and screaming. The shooshing of a woman's voice seemed to have no effect.

Frances wondered which of the ghosts the wailing belonged to.

Bonegilla was full of people, but it was full of ghosts, too.

She had seen them, even though her parents probably thought she was too young to understand. The ghosts were people who seemed to be only half alive. There was a man whom she had never heard speak and had never seen smile, who walked around Bonegilla, taking the same route over and over as he wore a path in the grass along the fencelines, his head bowed, his hands clasped behind his back. His baggy trousers were held up with a piece of rope knotted at his waist. He muttered to himself incessantly, whispering. He was the saddest man Frances had ever seen. She had never felt threatened by him, the man she believed was a Pole, because he seemed to exist in another place entirely. He physically had migrated to Australia but his mind was somewhere else, still in the middle of something clearly ter-rifying. She asked her father once what had happened to him in the war.

'Hitler, Frances. That's what happened to him, to many of them. Poor old chap.'

The hospital's breakfast trolley had rolled up at the end of Frances's hospital bed.

'Good morning, Miss Frances.' A nurse in a crisp white uniform smiled at her. Her dark curls, held back with bobby pins, made her white cap seem even whiter.

'Good morning.' Frances lifted her head, taking a moment to determine if it still throbbed. It didn't, but she still felt thick-headed. She had slept fitfully, her night-time hours filled with dreams of dark-haired soccer players.

'Here's some breakfast for you. Toast. A little on the cool side, I'm afraid. Marmalade on the side. Corn flakes and a hot Milo.' The nurse manoeuvred the bed table close as

Frances sat up. She plumped two pillows and positioned them behind her patient. Frances regarded her meal. She loved corn flakes. Her mother didn't allow them in the house. Mavis Burley still firmly believed that porridge was a healthy and filling start to the day for growing boys and girls. Porridge with salt scattered on top. Frances felt secretly thrilled to be having such a treat.

'Thank you,' she said.

'So, I've been told I have to take very special care of you. Are you feeling better this morning, Miss Burley?'

Frances was sure her blush could be seen right across the camp. 'I'm feeling very much better, thank you.'

Frances glanced at her name badge. Nurse King fussed over the sheets, which didn't need any attention, and gave her patient a warm smile. She didn't seem much older than Frances herself. Nineteen or twenty perhaps?

'I hear you were clocked on the head by a soccer ball.'

Frances stared down at her toast. 'Yes,' she said softly, feeling the humiliation once again at the memory of what she had been doing in the moments before that. Everyone around her had lifted their arms to protect their heads. She'd been much too distracted.

'How frightful.' Nurse King sat on the edge of the bed. 'Oh, there's no need to blush, Frances.' She leaned down and began to whisper. 'Those new Australians boys are very handsome, don't you think? It's totally understandable that a girl could be distracted by one of them. Especially when they get hot and take off their shirts.' Nurse King grinned wickedly. Frances let herself enjoy the conversation. Perhaps if she'd had sisters she might have had someone to share her embarrassing feelings with. There were some girls at the local school who were quite nice, but she didn't have a best-friend sort of friend. Frances relaxed into the pillow at her back and sighed.

'They certainly are smashingly good at soccer. And they play such a lot of it.' Nurse King sighed and hopped off the bed. 'I suggest next time you're watching a match, you pay ever so slightly more attention to the ball instead of the players?'

'I'd better, hadn't I?' Frances let out a little laugh.

'Listen here.' She leaned in and grinned. 'We gals are only young once and everyone's entitled to take in the scenery, don't you think? You eat up now. I'll ask Dr Jenkins to come and have a look at you and I expect he'll ring your mother to come and fetch you. It's been a pleasure having you here, young Frances.'

As Nurse King moved on to the next patient, her friendly voice trilling in the distance, Frances poured milk over her corn flakes and scooped them up hungrily. Once she was finished, she pushed her bowl aside, smeared her toast with butter and marmalade from the little white china bowl on her tray and tried to ignore the ghost wailing in the distance.

Once she'd eaten, she found she was feeling much better and, just as Nurse King had predicted, when Dr Jenkins visited her bedside he agreed Frances could go home. It wasn't her mother who came to fetch her half an hour later, but her brother, Tom. She wished he'd already gone back to Melbourne. They slowly walked the short distance from the hospital to their house, Tom cracking jokes about a huge lump on her head that only he could see, and when they got there, her mother was waiting with a cup of warm milk and a very relieved smile. Her mother fussed over her, tucking her up with a blanket on the floral linen sofa in the living room. Mavis had thoughtfully placed two books on the table next to Frances: *Five Go Off To Camp* and *The Magic Faraway Tree*. Frances may have been too old for Enid Blyton, but there was something comforting about having her favourites at hand.

'So poor little Frankie got bonked on the head, did she?'

Tom had returned from the kitchen clutching a handful of ginger nut biscuits he'd scooped up from the biscuit barrel on the kitchen sideboard. He bit into one as he flopped on their father's armchair, draping one leg over the wide and flat arm rest. The fabric of his trousers waved as he jiggled his leg and grinned at her.

Frances narrowed her eyes. 'Stop calling me Frankie. You know I hate it. It makes me sound like a boy. And a child.'

'Frankie, Frankie, Frankie.' Tom laughed and his deep voice echoed in the room. 'You're my little sister, Frankie, and I get to call you whatever I want.'

Sometimes Frances longed to be anything but plain old Frances Burley of Bonegilla. She wanted to be someone else far more exciting. Perhaps she might be Francesca Somebody of Rome one day. Or a glamorous princess like Grace Kelly. Or a queen like Elizabeth. She reached for *Five Go Off To Camp* and flipped it open to a random page. It didn't deter Tom.

'Here's what I want to know, Frankie.' He took a bite of a ginger nut and spoke through the crumbs. 'What were you doing at the oval anyway? You don't play soccer. I think you were having a good old butcher's hook at the soccer players, weren't you?'

Why, oh why, couldn't she have had a sister? Frances lifted the Enid Blyton so it covered her face and blocked out her brother's. 'You're awful and I'm not listening to you any longer.'

'Frankie likes the dagoes, Frankie likes the dagoes.' Tom leapt up from his chair and dashed over to Frances, tugging at her legs, trying to tickle the soles of her feet.

She tried to hate it but she couldn't because it was Tom and she did love him, deep down. She kicked him playfully and he groaned when she made contact with a forearm.

'Ow!'

A loud knock distracted him. Tom stopped rubbing his arm and turned to the door. Frances took advantage of the diversion to kick him harder in the shin.

'Ow. That's it, Frankie, you're going to cop it now.'

'Stop it, Tom!' Frances laughed, as he gripped a hand around her ankle.

'Don't like the tickling?' he teased. 'How about this?' He leaned in close and blew out a big breath in Frances's ear and her giggles turned into a howl of protest, which drew their mother from the kitchen.

'For goodness sake, Tom.' Mavis stood in the living-room doorway, her hands at her hips. 'Leave your sister alone. She's been in hospital. She had a concussion!'

'That explains everything.' Tom winked.

Mavis waited, looking from her daughter to her son. 'Is anyone going to answer that door then?'

Tom pulled back and stood. With his back to their mother, he poked his tongue out at Frances. She reciprocated as soon as Mavis returned to the kitchen and her favourite radio program, *When a Girl Marries*. Tom pulled the door open and a cold rush of air whooshed into the living room. Frances put her book down on her lap and pulled her blanket back up to her chin.

Tom cleared his throat, as if he was about to make a big announcement. 'Hello there.' His tone was one Frances didn't recognise. Deep, serious, formal.

Frances looked up. Tom was no longer slouching. With a quick hand, he smoothed down the hair she'd been ruffling just moments before.

Frances heard the shuffle of footsteps on the other side of the door.

'Hallo. Frances. We come to …'

Then there was a sigh and a word in a voice she didn't recognise.

'Her head.'

Iliana? Was it the Italian girl from the soccer? Massimo's sister?

'Righto. Yes. Come in then.' Tom held open the wooden screen door and Iliana entered the living room, her face transforming from shy to smiling when she saw Frances reclining on the upholstered sofa. Close behind her was the short Greek girl, and another girl, slightly taller with lovely auburn hair and the palest of skin, with faint freckles dotted across her fine nose. They stood in silence, taking in every detail of the living room, from the floral curtains to the radiogram across one corner; from the glass lightshade to the rug under the coffee table. Frances knew this room alone was twice as big as the huts they were living in and felt a twinge of embarrassment about the difference in their fortunes.

'Hello, Iliana,' Frances said. 'How lovely to see you.'

Iliana crossed the room and presented Frances with a small bunch of flowers, gum leaves with a few daisy blossoms, tied together with a length of brown string. She opened her mouth to speak, hesitated, and then continued. 'Get well soon.'

'Why, thank you. That's very kind.'

The Greek girl smiled at her. She was slim, and her black hair was fashioned into two long plaits that hung forwards over her chest, the ends curled up into frizzy black pom poms. Dark eyebrows, deep brown eyes and full lips created a mysterious and exotic look.

Iliana pulled the girl forwards. 'She is Vasiliki.'

'Yes, of course,' Frances said. She tried to remember how to say it: *Vas-i-leekie.*

Vasiliki narrowed her eyes, concentrating. 'Get … well … soon.'

Iliana and Vasiliki exchanged glances and giggled and then the girl standing behind them came forwards. Up close, her freckles were darker and her eyes were a piercing blue. 'I am Elizabeta,' she said, her voice soft. 'They have me because they can not speak English so good. It is not good you are hit on the …' She patted her own head. '*Kopf.*'

'Head.' Frances smiled and absentmindedly copied the gesture. 'My head.'

'*Ja*, the head. It is now good?'

'Yes, much better. Thank you.'

Iliana tugged on Elizabeta's dark brown hand-knitted cardigan and spoke to her in a language Frances knew was German.

Elizabeta nodded. 'Also, Iliana says her brother is very sorry he kicked the ball on you.'

'Oh.' Heat flamed Frances's cheeks. Her lungs felt tight. Her heart began to beat faster and she felt it behind her eyes, too. The *thump thump thump* of this new connection between her heart and her head. Perhaps her mother was right and she had been concussed after all. Did she need another Disprin? She made a fuss of rearranging her blanket. 'Tell him he needn't worry.'

Elizabeta's brow furrowed. 'He needs to worry?'

Frances gasped. 'Oh no. He should not worry.'

'Ah, good.'

The four girls smiled at each other in turn.

'We go,' Iliana finally announced. 'Get well soon.'

Vasiliki fell in behind her and Elizabeta nodded before breaking into a smile. 'Goodbye,' she said.

Frances had an idea. '*Auf Wiedersehen.*'

A look of surprise and delight shone in Elizabeta's eyes. '*Auf Wiedersehen*, Frances.'

'*Ciao,*' said Iliana. 'That is goodbye.'

'In Italian. I know,' Frances added. '*Ciao.*'

'*Yia sas,*' said Vasiliki.

Frances lowered her eyes for a moment. She would need to practise that one. She waved at Vasiliki, who waved back.

The three visitors looked to Tom, who still stood at the front door, staring. Frances wasn't alone in realising he hadn't said a word the whole time. Of course. She had forgotten to do the introductions.

'This is my brother, Tom.'

The three young women exchanged glances and giggled, before turning to the door and departing.

'Cheerio,' he finally managed to say as they left. Tom closed the door before moving to the window. He parted the lace curtain and stared out into the front yard and across the camp.

'Cheerio,' he muttered under his breath. 'You idiot.'

'What are you looking at?'

Tom jumped back, looking sternly at his sister. 'How do you know those Bonegilla girls?'

'Why?'

'Just tell me, Frances.'

'I don't know why you're so big brotherly all of a sudden. They seem perfectly nice to me. Look. They brought me flowers.' Frances sniffed the leaves. Eucalyptus.

'Who are they exactly?'

'Why do you want to know? You think they might be communists or something?'

'Oh, don't be ridiculous.'

She sighed. There was no mystery she should be ashamed of. 'I was talking to the Italian one, Iliana, just before I got hit by the football yesterday.'

'It's a soccer ball.'

'The soccer ball then, Mr Know It All. Her brother was one of the players who carried me to the hospital.' Frances wished she could remember more about that part of the previous day's adventure but, sadly, those details had been lost in the fog of her headache. Instead, she'd had to imagine Massimo's arms around her. Every time she did, she felt her cheeks burn.

'At least they've got some sense about them,' Tom huffed as he watched the three girls walk away.

'And as for the other two girls, they are Elizabeta and Vaski ... Veshta ... oh goodness, I can't remember her name, the other one.'

Tom let the curtain fall back into place. He walked to the corner of the room where the big radiogram sat, and fiddled with the dial, flipping between stations. There was Bing Crosby crooning one minute and then the serious tones of an announcer the next. He couldn't seem to settle on either so found some more music, classical this time, and then the room was filled with laughing voices, deep baritones and trilling female laughs. Then with a quick turn to the left, the radio was off and Tom was stalking across the room.

'Vasiliki,' he said. 'It's Greek, you dolt.'

Chapter Eight

Elizabeta, Iliana and Vasiliki reached the end of the path from Frances's house to the road and stopped.

Elizabeta looked to her left and then her right. 'I walk here,' she said pointing ahead, but was then suddenly not so sure. She'd only been at Bonegilla a week and it was such a vast place she wasn't certain she wouldn't get lost on the way back to the family's hut. She remembered that if she found the mess, she knew her way from there.

Iliana pointed in the opposite direction. 'Thank you,' she said, smiling. '*Vielen Dank.*'

'English is good,' Elizabeta said with a shake of her head. 'Not German.'

She didn't want to feel German, not here, when so many around her had been victims of the Germans, just as her family had. But she'd already heard it spoken as a common second or third language by people from all over

Europe. They'd survived occupation by learning some of the language of their oppressors. It had certainly helped this morning when Iliana and Vasiliki had found her at the playground. She'd taken Luisa there after breakfast to give her mother some time alone. She had seemed sad again and not in the mood for Luisa's inquisitive questions. Not long after Elizabeta had given Luisa one hundred pushes on the swing, Iliana had arrived with her two young brothers. There had been a tussle with another boy over taking turns and Elizabeta had intervened. Iliana had been thankful and when she had heard Elizabeta speaking English to the interlopers, she had asked for her help. In German, she explained what had happened at the soccer game the day before and that her family wanted to say sorry, but her English wasn't good enough. She'd tugged on Elizabeta's sleeve, urging her to help.

'*Bitte? Bitte?*' Please, please.

No one wanted to get in trouble with the director of Bonegilla. It would seem ungrateful when they had been welcomed with open arms, provided with somewhere to live, food to eat, and the promise of jobs one day soon. She was glad she'd agreed because she had been able to see inside an Australian house. It had many rooms, with a radio and a carpet rug and armchairs with soft fabric. And it was warm, so warm. Perhaps Elizabeta's family would find a house like that one day.

It must almost be time for lunch at the mess. Her father would be wondering where she was.

'I go. Goodbye,' Elizabeta said.

'Goodbye.' Iliana tugged on Vasiliki's arm but Vasiliki seemed rooted to the spot, staring back at the director's house. Elizabeta looked too and the curtain in the window moved, as if someone was setting it back in place.

'Goodbye, Elizabeta,' Vasiliki said, and the two girls walked off, arm in arm. There was a skip in Vasiliki's step that Iliana tried to match.

Elizabeta dawdled back to the family's hut. There was so much on her mind that she needed the aloneness of her walk to process it all. She walked along the roadway, stepping aside to let a rumbling truck pass her by, on its side the words *Holdenson and Neilson*. She wondered what was being delivered today.

As she walked, Elizabeta pulled the sides of her cardigan closer, and crossed her arms over her chest. The day before the sun had been shining but today, above Bonegilla, the vast sky was cloud-filled and a wind was blowing down from the mountain ranges to the south. There were goosebumps on her bare legs. Her father had told her those mountains in the distance would have snow on them in the winter, and she'd asked him if they were like the Bavarian Alps. He'd laughed.

'They are not so big. They're not the same.' He was right. Nothing about Australia was the same as the places she'd lived in. Not the size of the mountains, not the weather, not the trees or the birds. There was a smell at Bonegilla that was foreign: mutton mixed with the fresh breezes that blew off Lake Hume and the mountains and the scent from the leaves on the trees. When they'd woken up on their first morning at Bonegilla, her mother had looked across the paddocks and the cows grazing in the distance and asked, 'Are we in Texas?'

Elizabeta had the chance to be someone now, someone who belonged to the place in which she lived. How long would it take to feel Australian, she wondered. And what did that really mean? To feel Australian? She was physically in Australia, that was clear, but Bonegilla still felt like somewhere else, somewhere in between her old life and her new one. Learning more English would help, of course, because it was important to be fluent enough to hold a conversation with another person and understand what they were saying in return. She would need that if she were to get a job in a shop. She tried and tried to practise, but because she was already sixteen years old and therefore too old for school at Bonegilla, she had to work hard to think in English and use the words she knew and sometimes the effort became too wearisome and she turned off, letting the words flow over her head like gobbledygook.

Perhaps the Australian girl Frances might help her. She seemed friendly and nice. Maybe it would help if she was able to make friends with a real Australian, to practise the Australian ways of speaking and thinking. Because she needed to help her family make a home here. Somewhere her mother could be happy, where she wouldn't have to remember forced labour camps and cattle trains and schools that were closed and constant hunger and old shoes and her mother looking like a walking skeleton and soup made from flour and water and selling her clothes for food. The memories were still close, even though the war had been over for almost a decade.

All that was in the past now.

They were in Australia now.

But Elizabeta had brought the memories with her too. Of the time her father had been arrested by the Hungarian authorities and sent to a labour camp, forced to work breaking rocks in a quarry. He'd been a weaver before that, making beautiful fabrics and hand sewing white tablecloths with decorative red thread in swirling patterns. She thought of when she and her mother had been interned in a different labour camp in the days before being herded onto a train and deported to Germany. Did her mother still live that agony, of being separated from her husband, of being alone with her child, the indignity and uncertainty and sheer terror of it?

They hadn't known where they were going when they were put on that train. It had seemed a miracle when Elizabeta's father had jumped on board. A kind Hungarian guard at his internment camp looked the other way when her father implored him to let him go to his wife and child.

Elizabeta shivered and she knew it wasn't from the Bonegilla cold.

There were so many just-in-time stories from the war.

Elizabeta tried not to remember her life before the *Fairsea*, before she'd packed her suitcase with her best things and the few mementoes she had: a Bible with an ivory cover she'd been given for her Holy Communion; a small wooden box; her new brown shoes; some dresses and a thick woollen skirt and jumpers. It seemed that she had already lived a hundred lifetimes. And that was too many for someone who was just sixteen.

Her parents told her she should feel special because they had all been chosen by the Australian government to work in the jobs that would help build Australia. If Elizabeta's parents, at forty years of age, had been brave enough to leave all they knew behind for a better life for themselves and their children, then she could be brave too.

Elizabeta had crossed the camp while she'd been thinking about her new life and her old, and finally turned a corner at the end of the building that included her family's hut. There was a loud voice she recognised. She stilled. Something shrunk inside her, gripped at her stomach until it pinched and she wrapped her arms around herself. She automatically glanced left and right to see if anyone was nearby, listening, judging. The walls were so thin between the huts that their neighbours would know what was going on, even if they didn't understand the language. She scurried to the front door, reached for the door handle, but stopped. She let go. She sat on the steps instead, covering her cold legs with her thick woollen skirt, and listened.

'We have to get out of here. For God's sake, can't they get you a job already?'

Her mother's voice was brittle and fierce. Her father's soothing response was unintelligible; he had reverted to Hungarian. The little of it Elizabeta had learned as a very young child had been lost after they'd moved to Germany and she'd enrolled in a German school. Her parents knew both languages and had realised it was better not to speak German at Bonegilla if they wanted some semblance of privacy in their conversation. Too many people understood it.

Elizabeta's chin dropped to her chest. She let her thoughts drift. She didn't want to hear her mother this way. She didn't want to hear that her dream of a new and happier life in Australia might not be real. That it might disappear on a freight train into nothingness. The quieter her parents' voices became, the more concerned Elizabeta grew. Secrets were whispered that way, in the dark, around corners, in hushed voices. Her parents had many secrets.

The door opened and Elizabeta's father stepped out, stumbling over her. He stepped down on to the path below and she tumbled sideways onto the grass, her knee scraping on the step. Her father was quickly at her side, speaking softly to her in German. 'I'm sorry, Elizabeta. Are you all right?' His hand was on her shoulder, firm, reassuring.

'I'm okay, *Vati*.' He reached out a hand to her and she held it, pulling herself up to stand.

He glanced to the door. Someone pushed it from inside and it slammed shut. 'Your *Mutti* is upset. Luisa is playing with the Walkenhorst children. Perhaps you should go for a walk. Leave her alone for a little while longer.'

He turned, strode into the distance, his stocky arms swinging fiercely as he turned a corner after a row of huts and disappeared.

Elizabeta obeyed her father. As she walked in the opposite direction, one step for each of her mother's wrenching sobs, her vision blurred with tears.

'You going to the mess for lunch?'

Massimo stopped, smiled, and ruffled his sister's hair. '*Si*. Where have you been this morning?'

Everywhere, Iliana wanted to say. The playground with Vasiliki and the German girl Elizabeta. The director's house to see Frances. And now, on her way back to her family, she'd run into her brother as he was returning to their hut too. He always seemed to be on the move, like an engine that couldn't turn itself off.

He jogged at a walking pace and she fell into a stroll alongside him. 'You should be thanking me for what I've done for you this morning.'

'What did you do?'

Iliana lifted a finger to scold him. 'I went to see the girl you almost killed with your stupid soccer ball.'

Massimo stopped jogging. Iliana noted the sudden attentiveness on her older brother's face.

'Is she okay?'

'Oh, she was barely alive,' Iliana said, narrowing her eyes. 'She has a lump this big—' she held her hands up to her own head and made the shape of a bowler hat above her hair '— on her forehead. As big as *la anguria*.' A watermelon.

Massimo tugged sharply at her arm. 'You're joking with me.'

Iliana pulled herself free, laughed and ran ahead, snaking her way through the crowds of people emerging from their huts.

'Come back!' He caught up with her with no effort at all. 'Tell me that's not true.'

'It's true. She was in hospital.'

He huffed. 'I know that. I carried her there myself.'

Iliana laughed. 'All by yourself? With those big strong muscles of yours? I think you had some help.'

'Tell me, Iliana. Is she okay?'

She'd never seen Massimo so earnest. 'I am teasing you, brother. She looked healthy. But she was laying down. We gave her some flowers. We found a German girl, Elizabeta, to come with us, to translate. I wish my English was better.'

'A German girl?' Massimo stopped.

'Yes. Well, she speaks German at least. I didn't ask her where she was born.'

Massimo harrumphed.

'We needed someone to translate. Her English is better than mine,' Iliana explained.

'Probably better than mine, too,' Massimo lamented.

'What do you expect? All you do is play soccer with other Italians.'

He laughed. 'There are Greeks, too. And Yugoslavs.'

Iliana tutted. 'The Australian girl, Frances. She was nice. I would like to make friends with her.'

Massimo turned, looking across to the other side of the camp. 'There is no point in making friends here, Iliana.'

'Why not?'

He slipped an arm around her shoulder. 'You cried for two weeks on the boat because you had to say goodbye to your friends back in the village. Wait until we settle somewhere, and we meet some other Italian families. You can make friends with their daughters. I couldn't stand to hear you crying like a baby for another two weeks.'

'I'm not a baby.' She elbowed Massimo in the ribs.

'You'll always be my baby sister. Always.'

She didn't mind always being Massimo's baby sister, but Iliana thought she should be allowed to make friends with whoever she liked, no matter where they came from.

Chapter Nine

Frances had a new mission: not only was she going to become real friends with Elizabeta, Iliana and Vasiliki, but she was going to become their English teacher.

She had convinced herself that they would surely all become friends if only they were able to understand one another better. Part of her motivation was selfish, she had to admit. She wanted to be able to laugh and to crack silly jokes and make friends, to ask them about their lives before Bonegilla. But she also truly did want to live up to her responsibilities as the daughter of the camp director, and she hoped to impress her father by helping the three girls adapt to their new country. She was sixteen already and she could represent her family, in a way that would make both her parents proud of the young woman she was becoming. And anyway, she was lonely at home. Tom had returned to university in Melbourne and despite his teasing, she missed him. Whatever she could do to hasten her friends' language skills would set them in good stead for their futures when they left, she was certain of it.

Her mother seemed as excited about the idea as Frances was.

'How marvellous,' Mavis had said. 'Some of the young people are just lovely. So long as this tutoring doesn't interfere with your school work.'

'It won't, Mum. We'll do lessons every day after dinner. I've asked and it's fine if we go to the mess hall in the accommodation block where the girls live. They've checked with their parents and they all think it's a terrific idea for them to learn English better.'

'It's a good thing if someone in the family can speak the language,' Mavis told her daughter. 'Life will be so much easier for them when they assimilate.'

The next day, after Frances had stepped off the school bus and walked across Bonegilla to the house, she'd gone into her room to put her school case next to her desk and found a pile of books on the watermelon pink chenille bedspread in her bedroom. There were four copies each of Blackie's Easy to Read Book *Three Bad Pups*, with three naughty but very sweet dogs on the cover playing next to a tin of black paint. *Enid Blyton's Bright Story Book* featured a dog pulling a cart rather like a draught horse, and there were copies of *I Can Read English*, a booklet featuring a man lying on the cover reading. Frances picked up the Enid Blyton and skimmed the stories inside. She nodded, excited about having these tools of instruction. Stories like *Forgetful Fanny*, *The Little Brown Bear* and *The Little Girl Who Was Shy* would be just the ticket.

Elizabeta reached over the atlas and the map of Africa and pointed to the top of the continent. The four friends were crowded around the open book, sitting at a table in the mess. At the next table, six young boys were hovering over a Ludo game, squabbling over whose turn it was to roll the dice. On the other side, a group of young girls were drawing pictures on butcher's paper with coloured pencils.

'This is Egypt.' Elizabeta pointed it out on the map.

'That's where the pyramids are,' Frances noted.

'On the boat to Australia, we stopped there. A man … he wants to give money to my father for me,' Elizabeta told them, her expression serious.

Frances was flabbergasted. She leaned across the table. 'You mean like … a slave?'

'For his wife.' Elizabeta answered. 'My father said no.'

'Thank goodness for that. Wife,' Frances said. 'In German that is *Frau*?'

Elizabeta nodded. '*Sehr gut.*'

Iliana leaned in. '*La moglie.*'

Vasiliki added, '*Gynaika.*'

'I don't want to be a wife,' Elizabeta said quietly.

'I not marry Nikolas Longinidis,' Vasiliki declared. 'My mother says I marry him.'

Iliana didn't lift her eyes from the atlas.

For the past month, the girls had met and practised their English every day after Frances got home on the bus from school in Albury. Frances was very pleased at their progress. Elizabeta, of course, had started with a distinct advantage, already knowing more English than Iliana and Vasiliki; she quickly picked up new phrases and her vocabulary grew.

Iliana and Vasiliki proved to be fast learners as well, although Vasiliki struggled with reading in a strange new alphabet.

The friends took turns turning the pages and finding their countries. Iliana showed them where in Italy she had come from—at the top of the heel of the shoe—and Vasiliki found her Greek island. Frances had been surprised when Elizabeta had shown her two countries—Hungary and Germany.

As the girls turned the pages, Frances's mind wandered. *Wife. Frau. La moglie. Gynaika.* The words repeated over and over in her head. Could it be true that Vasiliki's mother was trying to marry her off to a man called Nikolas something or other? How could that be? She was only sixteen? Is that what was done in Greece? Frances didn't know what the future would hold for her. Would she finish school and be a wife and mother, just like her own mother had done? How could she possibly see the rest of the world if that was her future, to be married with children? Not that she wanted to get married but she supposed that's what girls did and if she had to, perhaps if she was very lucky she would find a husband with a similarly adventurous spirit, someone who would be willing to jump on a ship and see the world with her.

There was so much to do before she settled down with a family. There was school, of course, and then Frances would need some kind of job to save up money for her world adventures. Perhaps she could be a teacher? She liked teaching her friends, had felt so rewarded when they learned something and put it into practice. Teaching was a good job for a woman, she knew, except that she would have to give it up when she got married. *If* she married. Perhaps she could apply herself more diligently to the typing and shorthand classes at school and take up in a job in a government department? Her father was an important person in the government. He must know somebody who might need a secretary.

Her brother Tom was studying at university to be a lawyer. He'd always been the smartest of all the Burley siblings, at least that's what her parents said. He was the one who'd sparred with his father over dinner, talking about politics and trade and the formation of the North Atlantic Treaty Organisation or anything else he'd read in the newspaper. Frances always sat quietly during those conversations, trying to learn as much as she could. Everyone basked in Tom's glory in the Burley family. It was a measure of pride for them all that Tom was so clever. Their older brother, Donald, hadn't had such ambition. He worked as a clerk in a shipping office at Port Melbourne. He had a steady girl, Betty, who lived in Fitzroy, and worked on the switchboard at the same company. They were lovely together, the kind of people who were happy with their lot, who didn't want too much more out of life than a decent job, a good meal on the table of an evening, and going to the Brunswick Street Oval on Saturday afternoons to watch their beloved Roys play. Donald loved her so much he'd even switched allegiance from Collingwood. They hadn't talked of marriage yet but Frances expected it would happen soon. She quite liked the idea of being Aunt Frances one day.

Logically, that seemed like the life she would also have, but it wasn't the life Frances wanted for herself. She was doing well at school—very well actually—except for shorthand and typing. Perhaps she could study at university like

Tom. Or she could learn foreign languages—like French or Spanish—and become an ambassador or a diplomat.

Perhaps she could learn Italian. It seemed such a passionate and romantic language.

If she could speak Italian, she might be able to talk to Massimo. What if she were to marry him and have lots of beautiful half-Italian babies? Her pulse spiked at the thought. She hadn't forgotten his words of comfort, his arms around her, his strength as he'd carried her to the camp's hospital. She was being ridiculous. Marry an Italian? And a Catholic? She knew right off the bat what her grandparents would think. Their only granddaughter having Catholic babies? It was unthinkable. But that didn't mean she hadn't dreamt about him.

Frances's cheeks burnt and she pressed her fingers to her face to cool them. There was no good to come from thinking about him that way. He was Iliana's brother, for goodness sake. And anyway, Iliana and her family would leave Bonegilla soon for who knew where.

She pulled herself back to reality, to the Bonegilla mess and her friends. The girls had stopped chatting and were looking at Frances. She'd completely forgotten what they had been talking about.

'Bread with jam?' Iliana passed a plate to Frances, on which were slices of fresh white bread with butter and thick strawberry jam.

'Thank you,' she said to Iliana, before devouring a piece with a huge bite.

'You are welcome,' Iliana replied slowly which earned her a round of applause from her friends. She beamed.

Frances tried to concentrate once again on the lessons she was supposed to be giving. 'Why don't we try this one tonight?' She reached for the booklet she had brought with her. It was something new, something to stretch the girls. *I Can Read English* had been prepared by the Commonwealth Office of Education for the Department of Immigration. It sounded very important and Frances was nervous about her ability to teach what was inside it. But she would try as they were definitely ready to move on from Enid Blyton.

'Here girls. Let's have a look at this.' She opened the front page of the little booklet. There were lots of chapters about the goings on of the Miller family.

She began. '"In the kitchen, Mrs Miller says, Now dinner is finished, help me wash the dishes would you please, George? Mr Miller says, Look, Mary! I work in the mill all day and I work very hard."'

When she looked up from the page there were three blank faces staring at her. 'Oh, that's not much use, is it? Wait a moment. I'll find another page.' She flipped to Chapter 17: 'Mr Miller Reads the Paper'. This was better. It would be much more useful for the girls to be able to read the paper, to help their parents find jobs in the classifieds section, to find a house to rent or to see which pictures were screening at the cinema.

'Ah, here we go.' Frances began to read slowly. '"After dinner at night Mr Miller sits down. He asks Katherine: Where is the newspaper? Katherine goes to her mother, who is washing the dishes. Where is the newspaper, Mum? she asks. It's in the living room on the chair. Katherine goes to the living room and gets the paper. She gives it to her father, who is sitting in an armchair."'

'What is armchair?' Iliana asked.

'It's a chair with big arms,' Frances replied before realising how ridiculous that sounded. She laughed at herself. 'It is a chair with a big space for arms to rest on.' She mimed the armrests, flattening her palms and holding them horizontal on either side of her body.

Vasiliki looked confused. 'Newspaper is important in a family?'

Frances nodded. 'It's where work is. Houses to live in. Films. Sales in shops.'

Elizabeta said something to Iliana and Vasiliki in German and they nodded in recognition and delight.

Frances closed *I Can Read English*. She decided that Mr Miller and his newspaper adventures were not going to teach the girls anything useful. She had a better idea.

'I think we should have an outing,' she announced. 'Girls like shopping, don't they?'

'We go shopping?' Elizabeta asked. 'On the bus? To Albury?' Frances was pleased to see some happiness in Elizabeta's eyes.

The enthusiasm was bright in Iliana's and Vasiliki's faces and they nodded in delight.

Frances clapped her hands together. 'And I know just the place to take you!'

Chapter Ten

Abikhair's Emporium sat grandly on the corner of Olive and Swift Streets and it was Frances's favourite place in all of Albury. The building was two storeys tall with a veranda all around to shield customers from the harsh sun and winter rains. There were columns on the top, like parapets, that reached into the sky, and Frances had always imagined the building to be a little like a castle. An Australian-style castle, at least. There were three different entrances—a main one, and separate doors for men and women. The last thing women shopping for girdles wanted to see was a man wandering through looking for the menswear section to buy some new farm boots, her mother said. A trip to Abikhair's with her mother was always such a special morning for her, and she hoped some of the magic would rub off on Vasiliki, Iliana and Elizabeta. She had decided to make an excursion of it. That's the way it always was with her mother, even if they were simply shopping for new socks, or some wool that Mavis would transform into a new cardigan for winter.

The girls had caught the bus from Bonegilla and hopped off on Hume Street. A short walk later, they stepped across the mosaic-tiled steps from the footpath through the women's entrance and Frances savoured her friends' reactions as they looked around, taking in every detail of the extravaganza. Dark wooden counters and floor-to-ceiling shelves covered the walls, densely packed with cardboard boxes. There were exhibits on every surface and advertising posters and racks created colourful and mysterious displays.

'Oh,' said Vasiliki. Elizabeta and Iliana held hands and gasped.

There was everything from delicate white gloves to sturdy black rubber boots for farmers; sun hats to pull-me-in girdles. There were tins of tooth powder and spotted swimming costumes and hair pins, and long johns for men to endure the winter. In the haberdashery section, bolts of cloth were stacked in piles, and ribbons and lace dangled from huge spools, in every colour of the rainbow. They giggled at the mannequins wearing girdles and garter belts.

Frances led them from counter to counter, getting them to repeat the names of the items. Gloves. Hat. Stockings. Bra. Shoes. Socks. Trousers. Lingerie. Wool. Apron. Handkerchief. Pyjamas.

Each word sounded more and more ridiculous as the girls repeated them and laughed quietly behind their hands. Frances had been tasked with purchasing a bottle of Californian Poppy for her father, so the girls made their way through the store to the mens' section and she quickly made her purchases. Iliana had bought a linen handkerchief, Vasiliki a new hairbrush and Elizabeta a scarf for her mother.

Afterwards, they passed by the Riverina Cafe for a chocolate malt milkshake and sauntered back to the bus stop, happy, laughing, excited.

'Did you like the shop?' Frances asked.

'Yes,' said Vasiliki. 'Very good. Girdles.' She posed as one of the shop mannequins, sucking in her cheeks, creating a vacant, cross-eyed stare. They all burst into laughter.

'My mother?' Iliana said. 'No girdle.'

'Good for her,' Frances added. 'Honestly, they look so uncomfortable. I don't know how you're expected to breath or ride a bike or run or anything wearing one of those.'

When she frowned, the others seemed to understand. Elizabeta began speaking German to Iliana and Vasiliki and Frances didn't mind. She liked the way Elizabeta went slowly with them, having patience with the fact they were trying to keep up in one of the two new languages they were learning. Frances enjoyed their chatter and looked ahead to the bus stop, wondering if they'd have to wait long.

Something caught her eye. Three young men, perhaps Tom's age, had crossed the street and were approaching. As they got closer, Frances recognised them from Albury High School, from the grade above her. She wondered if they were going to warn her the bus was running late. But no. With a second glance, she could see by the lope of their stride, by the set of their shoulders, that they had some intent. Caution prickled the hair on her arms.

'Oy,' one called, his expression harsh. 'You girls from Bonegilla?'

Her friends were suddenly quiet. Frances glanced up and down the street but there were only a few people about and they were minding their own business. She opened her mouth to speak but no words came out. She clutched her brown paper package of Californian Poppy to her chest. The girls slipped in behind her.

The young men circled her and her friends, who had pulled into a tight little circle, looking inward.

'Check out the reffos, Dave.' The tallest one, his face sweet as an angel's, looked Frances up and down, scowling, making a point to linger on her breasts.

'They're not reffos,' Dave answered. 'They're dagoes, Billy. Look at this one.' His mate, shorter, stockier, with a barrel chest, reached across and tugged on one of Vasiliki's pigtails. 'Where'd the frizzy hair come from, love? Africa? And what about this Ginger Mick, hey?'

Frances flung an arm out to her side. She couldn't feel scared. Her heart began to beat hard and fast and the anger swelled in her head, creating a buzzing in her ears. She could not let her friends be spoken to in this way. She was showing them all about life in Australia after all, and the Australia she knew was kind.

'Stop.' One word, it was all she could manage to splutter.

'Ooh,' the one called Dave said, with a high-pitched retort intended to mock her.

Behind her, she heard Elizabeta whispering to Iliana and Vasiliki.

Dave and Billy and the other one, who was staring Iliana directly in the face, his mouth pulled tight, his face inches from hers, bum fluff under his chin, stood up to their full heights, emboldened by intimidating four young women simply standing at a bus stop on a cool May Saturday in Albury.

Billy lunged to the side. Frances startled. 'Speak bloody English, will ya? You're in Australia now.' They began to circle the girls, looking them over from their shoes to the tops of their heads.

'Or better still, hop back on the *Fairsea* and go back to where you came from.'

Billy piped up. 'And while you're at it, tell your dads and your brothers to stop taking all the jobs that belong to real Australians.'

Frances's anger was red hot now, so much so that she was barely aware that she'd flicked a foot out in front of her, just in time for the ringleader Dave to trip and stumble and then sprawl on to the footpath. She could hear his swearing and the guttural growls of his two henchmen rising in their throats. In that instant, she was glad she'd grown up with two older brothers.

She stepped out in front of Elizabeta, Iliana and Vasiliki, holding her arms out to keep them behind her, to protect them.

'Get lost,' she shouted. 'Yes, we're all from Bonegilla. What do you say to that?'

'You speak English?' Billy screwed up his face and stared at her.

'Yes, I bloody well do. And I know that you are Dorothy Smith's older brother and if you don't leave us alone I'm going to make sure your mother and father know about this, you hear?' Then she turned to Dave, who was still half prostrate on the ground, cupping the back of his head, shocked to find there was blood in his fingers.

'You'll bloody well pay for this,' he spat.

Frances took a step towards him, her hands on her hips, and then stood over him. 'Oh, will I? I think your father might be interested in what I've got to say. I see his trucks at Bonegilla three times every week. Who on earth would eat all those potatoes and eggs if everyone from Bonegilla went "back to where they came from", huh?'

Dave slowly got to his feet. Behind her, Elizabeta, Iliana and Vasiliki hadn't said a word. But Frances could feel their strength. There was a strong hand on her left shoulder. Another on her right. And a hand splayed on her back.

'You're crazy,' Dave muttered as he backed away slowly, stumbling. 'You slag.'

'Why don't you rack off?' Frances shouted. 'And take these two drongos with you.'

Billy sneered and spat on the footpath at her feet. They then turned to lope off down the street, their backs straighter, their sneers still set in their faces.

'Wogs.'

'Dagoes.'

'Reffos.'

Their taunts echoed long after they had turned a corner and disappeared.

The hands on her shoulders and her back became a hug. Frances turned into the embrace of her friends and tried to catch her breath.

'Thank you,' they said in turn. She could feel them shaking, scared, quivering.

'What is a drongo?' Elizabeta asked.

They hadn't noticed the bus had arrived at the stop until the driver blasted its horn.

Chapter Eleven

It had been Tom's idea that he and Frances should go to the Saturday-night dance for the camp residents at Tudor Hall. He'd returned the day before from Melbourne to stay for a week with his family at Bonegilla. When he'd suggested it, Frances had been quite taken aback by the idea, puzzled as to why he was suddenly being so charitable towards the new Australians. And as to why he would include her in his plans.

Over their Friday-night staple of shepherd's pie with peas and extra mashed potatoes, Tom broached the topic in front of their father, who had returned from Canberra just that day.

'I think it would be a grand idea, don't you, Dad? I think Frances is old enough now to go to a dance.'

Frances caught his eye. He winked, out of sight of both their parents.

'After all, I'll be back in Melbourne again next week, and studying, so this might be my only chance to chaperone her.' Under the table, he nudged Frances's foot with his and cocked his head at her while their father was passing their mother the peas. He was looking for back-up.

'I think that's a marvellous idea,' Frances said.

'What do you think, Mavis?' Reginald Burley sipped from his glass of water and considered his children's plan.

Mavis set her cutlery on her china plate and set her hands in her lap. 'It might be a good idea, Reg. It would be nice for the children to have a night out, don't you agree?'

Frances looked between her mother and father. 'I really would like to go. I've never been to a dance before. Well, with you and Mum at the Hume Services Club, but never on my own, as a young woman.' Frances feared she was babbling and tried another tack. 'And wouldn't it be nice for the new Australians to know that the director's children were going? It would lend an air of importance to the occasion, don't you think?'

'You do talk about the importance of showing that everyone should leave their past grievances behind them, Reg,' Mavis said. 'That we should all learn to live together in this new Australia?'

'I've said it before, haven't I, Mavis? Sometimes I feel that I'm not only the administrator at Bonegilla, but financial controller, counsellor, negotiator and Dag Hammarskjöld all at once.'

Frances wondered if it was a shock for the new Australians to land at Bonegilla and see a man there as tall as her father. At six foot four, lean and athletic still, he'd been a handy club cricketer in his earlier days. He towered over most of the migrants.

'Dag Hammarskjöld,' Tom repeated and snickered.

'The head of the United Nations deserves your respect, Tom.' Reg's words were stern but there was a glint in his eye.

'Sorry, Dad. I just think of a sheep's dag every time I hear his name.'

Reginald exchanged glances with his wife and tried not to smile. 'Not that we've had problems here between people, except for those Italians and all their complaining about the food.' He chuckled. 'But there's nothing wrong with a reminder every now and then. We're all learning new things from these people, including a lot of new and interesting names we have to get our tongues around. I'm doing my best. I suggest you do too, son.'

'You should listen to the Mayor of Bonegilla,' Mavis said with a proud smile.

'Mayor Burley.' Tom laughed.

'That's what people call your father, you know.'

'Then that makes me the mayor's son.'

'And me the mayor's daughter.' Frances laughed.

Reg looked at his family over the gold wire rims of his glasses. 'My job is to make sure there's no more welcoming place in the world than Bonegilla for Europe's dispossessed and stateless.'

'How lucky they are to come here and be fed, housed, and encouraged until they find work,' Mavis said. 'The air is fresh. Their accommodation is comfortable. They can come and go whenever they please.'

'I heard some of them walk into Albury,' Frances said. 'That's eleven miles, isn't it, Dad?'

'But there's a bus to Albury,' Mavis said, puzzled.

'They're very active, these new Australians, especially the young men,' Reg added. 'And the accommodation and the food is improving all the time. Remember when the pine-apples arrived last summer?'

'They were so sweet,' Mavis sighed at the memory. 'Utterly delicious.'

'Direct from Queensland,' Reg confirmed. 'It really is very important that they learn to eat the kind of food we do, to really help them fit in to Australia.'

Frances nodded in agreement. 'They are very lucky indeed to be here, aren't they, Dad?'

'They are, Frances. This is the best of safe havens for them,' Reg said. 'You know, I was talking to an Italian chap the other day. Shocking story. When the Nazis arrived, everyone fled up into the hills and when they dared go back, six months later, their whole village had been burnt to the ground.'

Frances couldn't believe her ears. A whole village burnt to the ground?

'Poor bloody dagoes,' Tom said.

Reg took off his glasses, put them slowly on the table next to his plate, and turned his full attention to this son. 'I will not have that word used in this house.'

Tom looked down at his dinner. He half-heartedly scooped up some peas on his fork. 'I do apologise. It's just that the fellows down in Melbourne at university say it all the time and—'

'That's never an excuse.'

'No, it isn't. I am sorry.'

'Perhaps,' Frances piped up, sensing the conversation had been derailed, and with it her own chance of going to the dance. 'If Tom were to spend a little more time in the company of the Bonegilla residents, seeing for himself their music and culture, what close and loving families they are, he might grow to understand how offensive that expression is to them.'

Tom chewed his peas and tried not to grin at his sister's ingenuity.

Reg and Mavis exchanged glances.

'That's rather a sensible idea, Frances,' her father said. 'Good girl.'

'Frances has made friends with some of the girls, Reg. There's an Italian lass and a Greek girl.' Mavis forked up some mashed potatoes and ate them elegantly.

'Vasiliki's the Greek one,' Frances said, glancing at Tom. It didn't escape her attention that he was blushing beetroot red.

'And Elizabeta. She's German.'

Her parents exchanged the slightest of glances.

'She's lovely, really. I'm sure they're all going, too. I really would love to go.'

Frances kicked Tom under the table. She'd rescued him so the least he could do was back her up.

'Ow.'

Frances widened her eyes at her brother.

'I'll look after her, I promise. You've been away, Dad, and you and Mum deserve some peace and quiet.'

'I must say, I would be very happy not to have to go to Canberra quite so often.' Reg reached to his left and covered Mavis's hand with his. At that moment, seeing her parents share such a rare and intimate gesture, Frances realised for the first time what they had given up for her father to be director of the camp. They shared their home with up to eight thousand other people at a time.

'Would you like to go to the dance, Frances?'

'I would. And I promise to keep an eye on Tom, too, so he doesn't get into any trouble.'

Tom rolled his eyes and Reg and Mavis laughed.

Reg smiled. 'You may go. As long as you both remember who you are and who you are representing.'

'Thank you, Dad,' Tom said.

'Thank you, Mum,' Frances added. And while she helped her mother clear the table and wash the dishes after dinner, Frances's head spun like a whirling dervish.

Frances only had two dresses which were the slightest bit suitable for a dance at Bonegilla and she had chosen the yellow one. It was pale, the kind of yellow found on the palest of budgerigars. It had a scooped neck and short sleeves, and was nipped in at the waist before flaring out with a skirt that hit her knees. Underneath, a permanently pleated petticoat swished too. A small white bow accentuated her waist and the yellow cardigan knitted by her mother matched her dress almost perfectly.

She'd never been to a dance without her parents. She suddenly felt grown up. A young woman. Anything might happen tonight. She hoped it would.

Frances twirled on the rug in her bedroom, flaring out her skirt, and as she spun she watched the colour and movement in the round mirror on her dressing table. This was the most grown-up outfit she had. With a shiver of excitement, she tugged on a pair of white socks, turning them down so they sat at her ankle, then slipped her feet into a pair of white shoes, with a flat heel and a point at her toes. She had combed her hair up and away from her forehead, careful not to tease it too much, and a white headband—as well as a generous burst of Gossamer hairspray—would keep everything else in place.

There was a knock at her door. 'Frances?'

She checked her reflection in the mirror. 'Come in, Mum.'

Mavis opened the door, took two steps into Frances's room and stopped. She breathed deep and her eyes became wet with tears. 'Oh, Frances.'

'Is it all right?' Frances nervously smoothed down her skirt, pressing it against her thighs, as much to soak up the sweat on her palms as anything else.

'You look just lovely. And your hair? Swept away from your face like that? It's so pretty.'

Frances's hand flew to her head. 'I saw it in the *Women's Weekly* and thought I'd see if I could do it myself.'

Mavis stepped forwards. In one hand, she held a bottle of Arpege. She lifted it to Frances's neck, squeezed the mesh atomizer attached to the nozzle and spritzed. Frances inhaled the scent, so familiar to her.

'And here.' Mavis held out her other hand and unwrapped her fingers from her palm. Her pearls. Her mother's perfume and now this.

'Really?' she asked.

'Yes, really. Turn around and hold up your hair.'

Mavis slipped the pearls around her daughter's neck. They were warm from her mother's hand. Frances felt the little tug against her throat as Mavis pressed the clasp together. Her hand fluttered to her throat, and she caressed the strand, feeling the warm orbs under her fingers. In her mirror, suddenly there was a young woman looking back at her.

Reg and Mavis waved off their children from the front door. Even though she had one of her big brothers by her side,

Frances felt a new sense of freedom. As they walked, she swung her little white handbag back and forth, and looked up to the clear night sky.

Tom moved his face near hers and sniffed dramatically. 'You smell strange.'

'It's perfume,' she replied, pushing his shoulder.

'Are you old enough to wear that stuff?'

Frances scoffed. 'I am sixteen, you know.'

Tom skipped ahead on the roadway and swung his leg, kicking a stone into the dark distance. It pinged on the roadway. 'You seemed awfully keen to come with me tonight.'

'Why wouldn't I be? My friends will be there. I expect that if we lived in the city there would be dances all the time. I'm rather jealous of you being in Melbourne. You're probably out every weekend. Dancing and drinking. And smoking.' Frances threw him a knowing look. She had smelled it on his clothes when he'd arrived on the train from Melbourne.

Tom adjusted his tie and then slipped his hands into the pockets of his black suit. 'It's not quite as glamorous as you think, you know. I do actually have to study. Universities don't let you get away with skiving off.'

'But surely there must be some time to have some fun. Perhaps meet a girl or two?'

Tom threw her a look. She was fishing for information and he wasn't biting. 'You know, Frankie, I don't think you've been the same since you got that whack on the head with the soccer ball. You're still a bit ... well, a bit dozey. Perhaps you did get some brain damage after all.'

Frances sighed. 'I can't wait until you go back to Melbourne. Here I was beginning to get a bit sentimental about you going back. Now I remember how annoying you really are.'

Tudor Hall was up ahead. A crowd of men was gathered off to one side, smoking. White puffs clouded around their heads, illuminated by a light fixed to the outside of the building. Young women were milling about the door, glancing over to the smokers. Frances tried to breathe. Would he be here tonight?

'Shall we?' Tom waved a hand forwards and bowed to his sister. She nodded at him. 'Manners, Tom? I see you have learnt something at university after all.'

When she walked ahead of him, he made sure to reach for her arm and give it a little pinch.

Chapter Twelve

Across the camp in her family's hut, Vasiliki smoothed down the pleats of her floral dress and tried to see her reflection in the small mirror hanging on a hook on the wall. It had cracked on the way to Australia, a lightning bolt down its centre as if it had been stepped on with a stiletto heel, and the effect was that there were two Vasilikis staring back at her. She had learned to adapt. She moved to one side, patted down half her hair, then took a step to the right and did the other side. Her plaits had been unravelled and she wore her hair in a long ponytail over her left shoulder, a fringe feathering her forehead. She pulled her lips together tightly, then pinched each cheek between her thumb and forefinger, just as she'd seen her mother do, and waited for a blush to appear on her olive skin.

She was excited about the dance tonight. It was all she and Iliana had been able to talk about for a week. Who knew when this chance would come again? Who knew when they would be leaving Bonegilla and where they would go?

'What do you think?' Vasiliki tugged at one of her gold earrings and turned to her mother.

Dimitria was lying back on one of the camp beds and as she moved to prop her head on her hand, the bed squeaked. 'You look beautiful—you take after me,' she said, and her laughter filled the room. Her mother was right. Vasiliki had her height, or lack of it, her heavy eyebrows and dark eyes and her full lips. She couldn't claim to have her mother's skin—every Greek had olive skin—but she hoped she had her mother's laugh. It was light and fun and happy.

'What about Dad?'

Dimitria sat up. 'Ah, your father. With no sons, he is blessed to have three daughters who look just like his beautiful wife.'

Vasiliki laughed too and her two younger sisters, Eleni and Constantina, sitting on the floor with their backs propped against their mother's bed, giggled behind their hands. Three girls. One father already gone to work in Melbourne. One older sister to mother the two younger ones. This was her family.

'Well.' She spun around and her skirt twirled up a little. She watched the flowers on the fabric blur. Nervously, she patted down her ponytail. Vasiliki had also inherited her mother's hair. Wiry and thick, uncontrollable. 'I should go. Iliana will be waiting for me at the hall.'

'You look so pretty, Vasiliki,' Eleni said with a little-girl sigh.

'Are you going to kiss a boy?' Constantina asked and then the two young girls laughed.

Dimitria raised her eyebrows and clicked her tongue. 'Shoosh, you two cheeky ones. Now, listen here, my grown-up daughter. You stay with your friend, that Italian girl, and watch out. Especially with those Latvians. They're way too handsome. All that blond hair.'

'*Mama*,' Vasiliki sighed, turning back to the mirror. She needn't have tried to manufacture a blush in her cheeks. They were burning now.

'And if you see Nikolas Longinidis, you dance with him. Or some of his friends. Find out if they have family in Melbourne, where your father is.'

Vasiliki got the message loud and clear. A Greek boy. A good Greek boy.

'There's no point in falling in love at Bonegilla, Vasiliki. Those boys will be going one way and we will be going another. Wait until we get to where we're going. Then you can find a good Greek husband.'

'Yes, Mum.' Vasiliki forced a smile and sighed, took the six steps to the bed and leaned down to kiss her mother on both cheeks. She patted each of her sisters on the head and then stepped out into the evening. Full of an excitement she couldn't name in English—or in Greek—she walked the path between the huts, past row after row of pale green wooden buildings, past the toilet block and the laundry, pale hanging lights leaching into the darkness of the night, to the light shining in the distance in the hall next to the mess hall.

The music pulsed in the distance and, when she was close enough, she walked past the men smoking outside, and stopped to peer through the steamy windows. Inside, there were colourful shapes, people milling about, laughing, happy. The music couldn't be contained by the thin walls and it drew her inside, into the crowd of people and the music and the laughter, and something shimmered inside her at the freedom of this moment.

The room was big but the ceiling was low, with dark wooden beams that crossed from one wall to the other. On one wall, there were big painted pictures of kings and queens, in petticoats and puffy velvet sleeves and long hair in ringlets and sashes across their breasts. Red, white and blue decorations were strung underneath the portraits and at the top of the hall, behind the stage filled with musicians, was a portrait of a young lady with a crown on her head. That was the queen. Vasiliki knew that much. She turned to the front of the hall where the band was playing from a low stage. On the dance floor, couples were arm in arm, and the throb of the music seemed to echo in her chest. She couldn't help a foot from tapping in time to the song.

She loved to dance. She'd grown up with it. With almost any excuse—and sometimes none—people in her village back in Greece would dance. If there was food and retsina and then music, the men would roll up their sleeves and link together, arm to shoulder to arm, and begin to dance to the bouzouki. And then everyone else would join in, from the oldest *yiayias* and *papous* to their grandchildren learning the steps for the first time.

She closed her eyes to hold the memories close. She missed the blue sky and the blue ocean and the heat and white-washed buildings and goats and her *yiayia*'s soup and olives and the fig tree next to her family's house. Her grandparents were still in the village, and there were aunties and uncles and cousins, too. They had all waved goodbye when Vasiliki and her family had left the village.

A hand on her shoulder. It was Iliana. They smiled at each other and linked arms, then moved to the edge of the dance floor so they could more closely watch the couples in their new suits and their best shoes, shuffling as the band played music from every nation represented at the camp.

'There's Elizabeta,' Iliana said. She was on the other side of the dance floor, watching the couples, too. Her head moved in time with the music and there was even a smile in her eyes. Vasiliki hadn't seen her smile much lately. Some people weren't happy to have left home and come to Australia. She couldn't be sure if Elizabeta's family was happy to be here in Australia or not.

In the minute between one song ending and the next beginning, Vasiliki reached for Iliana's hand and tugged her across the dance floor.

'Hello,' she said and the two girls hugged their friend.

And then there was a shouted hello and Frances was there too. 'Good evening,' she said, looking at Elizabeta, Iliana and Vasiliki in turn. 'You all look beautiful.'

'*Sehr schön*,' Elizabeta said.

'*Bellissimo*,' Iliana added.

Frances beamed. 'I love your dress, Vasiliki.'

'Thank you,' Vasiliki said.

'I didn't realise you all had such nice clothes to wear. I thought you might not have …' Frances waved a hand. 'Oh, never mind.'

Elizabeta leaned in close. 'We bring our good clothes from Germany.'

'Yes, I can see.'

The four girls shared warm smiles. Vasiliki didn't know what else to say. She wished her mind worked faster in

English. She had an idea. She pointed at the dance floor, wiggled her hips, then turned a questioning gaze to Frances.

Frances laughed. 'Dancing. Do you remember the word from our lessons?'

'Dancing,' Vasiliki repeated.

'Yes!' Frances smiled. She turned her attention to Iliana. 'Will you dance if a boy asks you?'

Iliana shook her head fiercely. 'No.' She crossed her arms and blushed and moved ever so slightly in behind Vasiliki.

The song ended and enthusiastic applause filled the hall. Another song began and it sounded something like the can-can. Vasiliki looked to the stage. A Yugoslav sat behind the drums and an Italian strummed a guitar. The trumpeter with fat cheeks was Dutch, the pianist with quick fingers a German. The four girls listened for what must have been half an hour. There were folk songs, waltzes and even something that tried to sound like a Greek song. Vasiliki admired the effort, but it wasn't the same without a bouzouki. Andreadis was in the Riverland now and had taken his instrument with him when he'd left. At the end of a song, the Dutch trumpeter held a note so long that Vasiliki held her breath until it ended and she felt such a tightness in her lungs, she could barely breathe. People around her whooped and clapped.

And before she could recover, someone was standing before her with his hand out in invitation.

'Vasiliki.' He said her name like an Australian but she didn't care.

It was Frances's brother. He was so tall she had to crane her neck back. He wore a black suit, with a silver tie around his neck in a slim knot and there were white triangles poking out of the breast pocket of his jacket. His light brown hair was smoothed in a quiff with some kind of lotion. His smile was generous and wide.

For a moment she forgot her own name in any language. 'Vasiliki. Yes.' She glanced at her friends, standing in a line. Elizabeta and Iliana were wide-eyed. Frances was holding in a smile.

'Tom.' He took a step closer to her to be heard above the music. And then he leaned in and said some other words in her ear but Vasiliki only recognised one of them: dance. And when he smiled and lifted his hand out to her again, she put hers in his, and he guided her to the dance floor.

Elizabeta stood with Frances and Iliana, swaying from side to side with the music. The dance floor had quickly filled with people, stepping and twirling, happiness in every step. The girls watched Tom dance with Vasiliki, his hesitant waltzing feet the cause of much laughter.

'His dancing is not good,' Elizabeta noted.

'No,' Frances laughed. 'On the cricket pitch, he can play. On the dance floor? He has two left feet. And I expect he's terribly nervous.'

Elizabeta frowned. 'What is that?'

'Nervous? Oh, it's being a little scared.'

Elizabeta stored that word away in her head. It was what her mother was most of the time. In English, a little scared. *Aufgeregt*.

'I'm rather thirsty. Would anyone like a drink?' Frances asked. 'There's a table by the door with drinks and some food.'

'Yes. Thank you,' Elizabeta said. 'I like a drink.'

Iliana nodded politely.

'I'll be right back.' Frances moved off and then looked back, pointed to her brother and giggled.

'*Guten Abend, Fräulein. Möchten Sie tanzen?*'

Someone moved in beside Elizabeta, in the space left by Frances's departure. She turned to the man's voice. So formal. So properly German. He was older than she was but not as old as her parents. His blond hair was cut short over his ears, with a long sweep at the front. A neat grey suit hung from his slim frame. He smelled of aftershave and cigarette smoke.

Did she want to dance with this stranger? She felt skittish at the thought. She had come to the dance tonight to watch, not to be watched. What would her mother and father say? She knew. They would want her to be polite to a man who was older, to a German. To show her good manners. Before she could answer, he spoke again.

'Ach,' he closed his eyes in a kind of reverie as the musicians began a new song. '"*An der schönen blauen Donau*". *Sehr schön.*'

He stepped out in front of Elizabeta and held out an upturned hand.

She swallowed her nerves, put hers in his, and let herself be led to the middle of the dance floor. When they stopped, the man placed one hand at the small of her back before holding the other in the air. Elizabeta rested her fingers on his warm palm and he led her into the dance, guiding her gently, in and out of the other couples, deftly weaving around them. Elizabeta had never been asked to dance by someone who wasn't her father. Her cheeks were hot and she hoped no one could see the blush. She was too nervous to look directly at him, for fear that he might notice her pink cheeks. The man was very good dancer. He twirled her in time with the beat of the music, so light-footed and practiced that she let herself be led effortlessly around the dance floor, keeping her gaze to her left as they spun and turned. There was no conversation and she didn't know what she would say if he attempted it.

When the song ended, the man lifted his hand from her back and let go of her hand. He stepped back and bowed, and then led her to the side of the hall where other guests were standing in a line, their backs against the wood panelling, watching the dancing. Elizabeta craned her neck, searching for Frances and Iliana and Vasiliki, but she couldn't see them.

'*Danke schön*,' he said. He brushed his hands down the lapels of his suit jacket as if dust had settled there during the dance.

'*Bitte schön*.' Elizabeta fidgeted her fingers together. She had thanked him too but something was wrong. Her mouth felt dry. She wanted a drink of water but didn't want to tell him in case he decided to fetch one for her. If he did, she might be expected to wait for him to return, to begin some kind of conversation, to thank him. She didn't want to stand with him. She wanted to go back to her friends. Where were Frances, Iliana and Vasiliki?

'Tell me your name, *Fräulein*.'

So many men had asked for her name in her short life that it didn't occur to her not to tell him. 'Schmidt. Elizabeta.'

'You're here with your family, yes?'

She nodded, dropping her eyes to the parquetry floor. It zigged and zagged in a perpendicular pattern, like arrows pointing in opposite directions.

'Where are you from in Germany?'

'Hessental.'

'How long have you been here at Bonegilla? Does your father have work yet?'

'No.'

'And your mother? She is here with you too?'

As Elizabeta's unease had bubbled up inside her, so had her courage. She finally lifted her eyes from the parquetry and turned to face her inquisitor. She stiffened her spine, lifted her eyes and looked into his face for the first time.

The jolt of recognition almost blinded her.

Chapter Thirteen

Frances stood at the refreshments table at the front of the hall surveying the offerings. There were silver platters filled with cheese sandwiches cut into small triangles, and a variety of cakes cut into slices, with pale yellow butter thickly lathered on top, like slices of cheese. Jugs of water were half-empty and being replenished by staff, and newly opened bottles of lemonade sat beside towers of paper cups. It would be lemonade for her and Elizabeta, she decided. She was never allowed it at home and Frances felt tonight was worth celebrating. She may not have been asked to dance by a handsome stranger, but she was at a dance without her parents and she felt completely grown up tonight. As she poured two cups full, she wondered where Tom and Vasiliki were. She had lots to tease Tom about when they got home later that night. His silly expression as he'd tried to learn the steps of the waltz. The way he'd looked at Vasiliki and the way she'd looked at him, just like Richard Burton had looked at Jean Simmons in *The Robe*. Or Audrey Hepburn and Gregory Peck in *Roman Holiday*. Frances had loved that movie. She'd seen it at the camp's cinema three times over the last school holidays.

'*Buona sera.*'

All at once, every part of her seemed to have come alive, from the roots of her hair to her toes. She knew that voice.

'Hello there,' she said.

In her dreams, Massimo was always wearing his sports top, the one with the black and white stripes. Tonight, he was wearing a suit, a white shirt and a thin black tie. His dark hair was slicked back in the continental style and his smile was as wide as Lake Hume. Against his olive skin, his teeth were as white as summer clouds.

Frances tried to match his effortless smile but nerves took hold. She was suddenly self-conscious, her tongue thick and her head light. She wasn't used to talking to young men who weren't her brothers. She talked to boys in school, of course, but they didn't count. They weren't Massimo and they weren't looking at her like he was Gregory Peck and she was Audrey Hepburn. She glanced down at the table and reached for one of the lemonade bottles.

'No, no.' Massimo moved quickly. He reached for the cups of lemonade and gave her one.

'Thank you,' Frances said. She was glad the music was so loud or he would have heard the embarrassing girlish squeak in her voice.

'Lemonade,' he said.

'Yes,' she smiled. 'This is for my friend. Elizabeta. I think she still might be dancing. But I can't see her out there. There are so many people.' And then, to stop herself babbling, she quickly downed her lemonade in one gulp and set the cup back on the table.

'Frances.' He took a step closer towards her and leaned in close to be heard above the music. Had his lips brushed her hair on purpose? Everything inside her seemed to tighten.

'Your head,' Massimo asked. 'Is okay?'

'Yes,' she managed.

'I am sorry.'

Before she could find any words to answer him, he'd reached for her free hand and raised it to his lips. His warm breath on the back of her hand tickled, his lips on her knuckles were soft. His eyes lifted from her fingers to meet hers. She stared straight back at him.

'Francesca.'

'Massimo,' she whispered.

He hadn't let go of her hand and somehow, without him even asking, she let herself be led to the dance floor. Then, his hand was at her waist, pressing into the small of her back. Her hand was on his shoulder, and as they made their way around the dance floor, stepping in time to the music from the band, swaying when the next song was slow, she felt his muscles bunch and tighten. When the music demanded it, he pulled her close, and when his body pressed against hers, she rested her cheek against his chest and she felt his heart beat, so fast, as if it was about to burst from his chest.

When the second song ended, he led her back to the food table. He dipped his head and smiled, and then he was gone. As he disappeared into the crowd, music continued to play in Frances's head, spinning, whirling, and her heart had struck up a new tune, one she'd never heard before.

Someone bumped her. It was Elizabeta, reaching for the bottle of lemonade. She hurriedly poured some into a cup, spilling it over the tablecloth in her haste.

Frances turned to her. 'Oh, Elizabeta. I'd poured one for you. Where have you been?'

Elizabeta didn't answer. She was breathing hard and fast. Her face had drained of colour and she seemed not to be able to speak in any language.

Frances reached for Elizabeta's trembling hand. 'Goodness, Elizabeta. Are you all right?'

No answer. Her whole body shook.

'Did something happen?'

Elizabeta stared into the distance, glassy-eyed.

'Whatever is the matter, Elizabeta?'

'I go to my family,' Elizabeta stammered. She tore her hand away and ran.

Chapter Fourteen

The next Tuesday, three days after the dance at Tudor Hall, Elizabeta was finally alone with her mother. Luisa was at school, her father at the Employment Office.

It was a cool autumn morning despite the clear skies and sunshine. She'd taken her coat from the nail behind the front door and slipped it over her skirt and jumper to warm her on the steps of the hut. Her mother sat in a deck chair on the flattened grass in the alley between the rows of huts, her arms crossed, one thin leg draped over the other. For the past hour, she'd been moving her camp chair a foot at a time as the sun moved over Bonegilla, trying to find warmth in the shaft of weak autumn sunlight. Berta was watching the new family in the hut opposite. The Latvians had arrived the day before. There were always new neighbours at Bonegilla. A young child, perhaps only one year old, was taking wobbly steps on the grass, falling over and getting back up again with a push of his chubby little hands, much to the delight of his mother who was hovering nearby. He was a lucky little boy, Elizabeta thought. He was learning to walk in a new country. He was growing into a person in a new country. He would have no memory of the past, or even of being here at Bonegilla. His first birds would be magpies. His first sky would be this big wide blue Australian one. He would grow up fresh and new, without even an accent. No one would ever mistake him for a reffo or a dago or a wop.

As Berta watched the little Latvian boy, she began to hum. *The Blue Danube*. Her foot began to tap in the air to the invisible rhythm, every note matching the little boy's step.

It was the song that did it, that made Elizabeta tell her mother. Her secret had become so big that it was filling her up, pushing on her from the inside, choking her like a growth. She had tried to swallow it down during the past three days but it lived and breathed inside her, growing bigger and bolder and stronger. She'd tried so hard not to think about the waltzing German, about what she'd remembered. She didn't want the news to hurt her mother. Because this would. This would up-end the fragile equilibrium her parents seemed to have found since they'd arrived in Australia, a place far away from the memories that could haunt them.

'*Mutti*?' Elizabeta heard the word squeeze out into the cool air from a throat so tight she could barely swallow.

'*Ja*?'

'At the dance, last Saturday. I danced with a man.'

'The dance?' her mother asked, distracted. She was staring at the little boy.

Elizabeta continued. 'The dance in the hall. The band played *The Blue Danube* and everyone was waltzing.'

'That sounds nice.' Berta chewed on a fingernail. She barely had any left as it was.

'*Mutti* … there was a man at the dance who was asking about you. And *Vati*.'

Berta didn't answer.

Elizabeta wanted to shake her. *Listen to what I have to tell you.* 'The man. I danced with him, before I …' She struggled to find the words. 'This man. At the dance. He was asking questions. He's German.'

'There are lots of Germans here at Bonegilla. Why is that important to tell me?'

The little boy toddled and fell again.

'Yes. I know.'

'Do we know him?' Berta asked. They'd met so many people in so many places over the years: in Hungary, in Germany, on the boat all the way across the world, and now in the thousands of people who flowed through the camp. So many faces. It was hard to remember them, or their names or their families.

But his was a face Elizabeta would never forget.

'He wanted to know if *Vati* has work yet. He asked how long we've been here at Bonegilla.'

'And you said he asked you to dance?' Berta stopped looking at the little boy. She finally turned her face to look at her daughter.

Elizabeta nodded. 'Yes. I didn't mean to. I wouldn't have if I'd known it was him.'

Berta leaned forwards, almost folding her thin body in half over her legs. She looked from side to side to see if there were eyes and ears nearby, then whispered. 'Who is he, Elizabeta?'

'This man ...' Elizabeta waited, knowing the weight of the words. 'He has a scar.' She lifted the index finger of her right hand to her face. She dragged it in a jagged line through her right eyebrow, across her eyelid and in a forty-five degree angle across her cheekbone.

Her mother stood quickly. The magazine she'd had in her lap fell in a flutter to the grass. The front cover was bent in half. Elizabeta could only see half of the lady with the glittering crown on her head. Her mother took a quick step towards her, lifted a hand high and slapped Elizabeta across the face where she'd just traced her finger. The shock stole her breath. Her face stung as if she herself had been slashed with a kitchen knife almost ten years before in Hungary.

'Go. Now. Get Luisa from school.'

Elizabeta held in a sob.

'Go.' Berta reached for her arm and her fingers gripped tight and hard. 'And do not tell a soul. Not even your father.'

When Elizabeta returned with Luisa, having had to tug her away from the activities and her friends she loved so much, they could hear the arguing three huts away. She slowed her pace, kept her grip tight on Luisa's hand, and when they realised what was going on behind the rust-red door, they decided to wait outside. The Latvian woman from across the alley, who had earlier shared a friendly smile with them, lowered her eyes and closed her door firmly, as if anger and hurt were catching and she didn't want them slinking inside her home.

Elizabeta and Luisa sat on the wooden steps, pressed together against the cold. The sun was hidden now behind huge grey clouds that had blown in from the south, and a cold wind blew off the mountains.

'I'm cold. I want to go inside. Why can't we go inside?'

Elizabeta slipped an arm around her sister's shoulders and pulled her in close. 'In a minute.'

The voices inside were loud and angry and the fighting was in Hungarian again, so fast that Elizabeta couldn't make out any of the few words she still remembered, but she knew in her heart it was about getting out of Bonegilla, leaving this place as soon as they could. Would it make a difference if she could understand her parents' weapons of argument?

There were many things she wished she didn't know. But some memories you could never leave behind.

The next morning the family walked together to the mess. Her parents had been curt with each other since they'd got up from their thin mattresses and squeaking beds. Elizabeta had barely slept, on edge about another fight; kept awake by the ache in her cheek where her mother had slapped her. It still hurt to touch and the cool of the sheets in the frigid night air hadn't been much relief. No one had spoken a word as they'd rugged up in their squeaky beds the night before, shivering in the cold. The row had exhausted her parents. After dinner, there had been no energy to sing a nursery rhyme to Luisa, who had sobbed under the blankets until she exhausted herself into sleep. And today, as they trudged across the camp, her father's mouth was pulled tight and the dark shadows under her mother's eyes were like storm clouds about to burst. Words had been exchanged between her parents that she didn't understand and emotions were on show that she couldn't name.

Luisa was irritable and refused to hold Elizabeta's hand as they walked to breakfast, but Elizabeta insisted. Her sister had a habit of running off, hiding between the rows of huts, finding other children to play with and not coming back for hours. Elizabeta had found her up a gum tree once, wedged between the trunk and a spindly bough, half hidden by thin silvery grey leaves.

'Come down,' Elizabeta had called. 'It's not safe up there.'

'I'm climbing the tree,' Luisa had called back. 'I want to get to the top.'

'You're a monkey,' Elizabeta had said, shielding her eyes from the sun, smiling at her sister's exuberant delight.

'I'm not a monkey. I'm a koala.'

Elizabeta didn't want any such fuss this morning. She wasn't in the mood to chase her little sister or rescue her from tall trees. When they reached the queue at the door to the mess, the smell of coffee in the air, Berta's eyes darted around the grounds, scanning the crowd, searching every face. Elizabeta knew with a sinking heart who she was fearful of seeing.

Her father slipped an arm around her mother's shoulders and drew her in close. 'We won't be here much longer,' he reassured her for the hundredth time. 'I will get work soon. I'll go and see the employment agents again after breakfast.'

Berta's face didn't register that she'd heard a word. She had stopped walking. Her eyes were fixed on a spot in the distance, and Elizabeta knew. Had her mother's fear summoned him somehow? The man from the dance was walking towards them, his food tray in his hands.

And her blood turned to ice.

The man stopped and looked too, taking in each member of the family, then he jerked around and walked off in the direction from which he'd come.

Berta shot a searching glance at her oldest daughter. A flash of understanding was there in her bleak eyes and Elizabeta knew. The secret they had kept for almost ten years was in the air between them, crackling like a lightning strike. All these years later, thousands of miles away, they were both back in that cottage in Hungary.

The queue moved and without another word they went inside for breakfast but her mother didn't touch a bite. Her plate sat in front of her, filled with porridge she didn't eat as Luisa chatted away with their father. He offered her spoonfuls of corn flakes from his bowl and she opened her mouth wide to him like a baby bird.

Two days later, on Friday afternoon, Jozef came back to the hut from a meeting with the employment agent with a beaming smile on his face. There was sheen of sweat on his forehead and he was puffing. Elizabeta was sure he'd sprinted the whole way back.

'Berta,' he called from the doorway. 'I have work. It's over,' he'd announced with a slap on his thigh as he bounded up into the hut.

Elizabeta was on the steps watching Luisa playing with her marbles in the grass below. Berta had been sweeping the hut and at the news she dropped the broom and it thudded on the floor. 'We're leaving Bonegilla?'

'There's a job in a factory. In Adelaide. They showed me on the map. Adelaide!' He swept Berta up into his arms and she wrapped her arms around her husband. They laughed together and then Berta's laughter became sobbing and Jozef made soothing sounds as he tried to calm her.

'I can't believe it,' she cried. 'When do we go? Tomorrow?'

'I leave on Monday,' Jozef said.

Berta pushed herself out of his arms. '*You* leave on Monday?'

'I am going ahead. You and the girls will have to wait here.'

Elizabeta spun around to watch her parents. They couldn't go, too? Her heart sank. They were going to be one of those families, like Vasiliki's and hundreds of others. Their fathers were gone and they were stuck here at Bonegilla. They were going to be the half a family left here at the camp.

'Wait here without you?' Berta slammed a palm against her chest and stumbled, and Jozef led her backwards to sit on the bed.

'There is only single men's housing near the factory. I don't like it either but this is our chance, Berta. I know how much you want to leave, to start our new life with the girls. If this is what we must do, then it's what we must do.'

Berta was so pale Elizabeta thought she might faint.

'You would take this job and leave your family here?'

'It won't be long. We knew this when we signed the papers to come to Australia. I have to work for two years and then we are free to go wherever we please.'

Elizabeta felt like a witness to something profound and important between her parents. When her mother began gnawing on a torn fingernail, Elizabeta felt fresh anxiety knot in her stomach. How would she look after her mother? Her father knew how to soothe her. She couldn't do it. What would she do when her mother was upset? How would she make things better for her? And how would she protect her from the German?

'Where is this Adelaide?' Berta demanded. 'I've never heard of the place.'

'It's not far, I promise. As soon as I can find a house to rent, you and the girls can come. All will be good from now on, Berta.'

Elizabeta turned away and buried her head in her hands. She couldn't watch. There was the squeaking of the metal-framed bed, then soft sobbing and her father's voice, quiet and soothing.

'The children,' Berta said in between tears. 'You can't leave us here. We must go, too.'

'A house, keep thinking about that. Three bedrooms. One each for Elizabeta and Luisa. And no more food from the mess hall. A kitchen of your own. You'll be able to cook sauerkraut and spätzle and you can make your own sausages again. No more mutton, yes? Won't that be a good thing for us?'

Berta's sobbing continued unabated.

Elizabeta dropped her head to her knees. After a little while, there were footsteps behind her and then her father was crouching in the doorway.

'Luisa,' he said. 'Come over here to me.'

Luisa picked her marbles from the grass and ran to her father's side. He slipped an arm around her and gave Elizabeta a knowing look.

'I have news, Luisa. The government has found me a job and I'm going to go and work and find a new place for us to live.'

'Will there be school where we are going?' Luisa asked.

'Of course. A very big school with lots of other children for you to play with. We can get a dog for you, if you promise to look after it.'

'A dog, *Vati*? I promise I'll look after it.'

'And there is a beach. You can swim every day!'

Luisa's chin dropped. 'But I don't know how to swim.'

'I can teach you. I can swim. I used to swim in the lakes back in Germany. It's easy.' He ruffled her hair lovingly.

Elizabeta reached for her father's hand. 'Will we be able to come to Adelaide very soon?'

A flash of seriousness darkened her father's expression but he blinked it away. 'As soon as I find a home for us to live in, you will come on the train, *ja*? But until then, you will look after your mother.'

'I will,' Elizabeta promised, and she meant it, but a fear settled in her stomach. She wanted to cry but couldn't let her father see her tears.

Jozef slipped his arms around his daughters and kissed the tops of their heads. 'You are good girls. And now I must go and sign some papers.' He jumped to the ground, and strolled off down the alley between the two huts, turning right in the distance and out of their sight. For the first time in a long time, the girls heard their father whistle.

So, their time at Bonegilla was soon to end. Elizabeta looked down the alley towards the laundry and the toilet block, watching the comings and goings of other residents. How would she remember this place when they were gone? Would she recall the smell of mutton wafting from the mess hall or the scent of the gum trees in the mornings? Would it be the friendships she had made or her mother's sadness? The freedom of being a young woman here or the memories that had been packed up in her suitcase with her clothes?

Bonegilla was filled with sparkling, pretty faces and those wearing the marks of too much suffering. What they shared was a kind of limbo, stuck between the old world and the new, between everything they had known and a wide brown land full of mystery and names they couldn't pronounce and people who would tell them to speak bloody English. Bonegilla was temporary, not the real beginning of their lives in Australia.

Elizabeta would have to ask Frances to look up this place called Adelaide on her book of maps. Perhaps it wasn't that far away. She might be able to come back to Bonegilla on the weekends to see Frances and Iliana and Vasiliki.

But they would be gone one day, too, and probably soon.

In Elizabeta's life, saying goodbye had been a rare thing. People had been snatched out of it without her even knowing. When they'd lived in Hungary, their neighbours the Hermanns had been escorted from their home by soldiers and sent away. No farewells. And a few days later, when her father was taken, there had been no chance to say goodbye either before he was sent to a labour camp, crushing rocks for the Russians. The Blumenthals, who were the bakers in their village, had disappeared in November 1944. They'd lost touch with so many people. Her uncles and aunts, her grandmothers. Most people Elizabeta knew were already ghosts.

Luisa opened Elizabeta's hand and dropped her marbles in her palm. Blue, green, red, clinking against each other like drinking glasses. *Prost.*

'Are you happy, Elizabeta, that *Vati* is going to find us a house to live in?'

'Yes. I am happy,' she replied. It was important to sound happy, perhaps even more important than actually being happy. 'I want to have a room to myself and a bed that I don't have to share with you. I won't have to listen to your coughing. Or the way you snore all night like a goat.'

'That's not me,' Luisa giggled. 'That's *Vati* snoring.'

Elizabeta found a smile for her sister, to reassure her. It was important now that she look after her mother and her sister. Until they left Bonegilla, the weight of that heavy burden fell entirely on her shoulders.

On Monday, Berta, Elizabeta and Luisa stood by the front boom gate of Bonegilla and said goodbye to Jozef. The girls hung back while there were quiet words between husband and wife. Other people were saying goodbye, too. Some families, but mostly men on their own, were going to Cooma, Melbourne, Barmera, Sydney, Townsville. Some of them hadn't stopped moving for years and now they were on the move again. No one looked particularly happy about leaving Bonegilla, which Elizabeta could understand. One woman, a mother with four children crowding around her, wailed as her husband stepped onto the bus.

There were other children saying goodbye to their fathers, with loud sobs, clutching legs and arms and bodies, whatever their little arms could reach. Elizabeta couldn't cry. She was sixteen after all. Jozef let go of his wife's hand and held his daughters in a hug that Elizabeta hoped would never end.

'You be good girls for your mother.'

'Yes, *Vati*,' Luisa said, a hitch in her voice.

'We will,' Elizabeta assured him.

'Will you write me a letter when you get to Adelaide?' Luisa asked. She had to raise her little voice above the chugging of the pale blue bus that was waiting to ferry people to the Bonegilla rail siding.

'Of course I will. Lots of letters.'

Luisa beamed. 'I will read them every night.'

'Good girl,' Jozef said.

After one last kiss for his wife, he stepped up onto the bus. The doors closed, and smoke belched as the chugging of the engine grew louder. When the driver manoeuvred through the main gate and out onto the road to Australia, Elizabeta watched her father go and didn't say another word.

That night, Berta sobbed herself to sleep.

Chapter Fifteen

Berta stayed in bed for two days after Jozef left for Adelaide.

She had refused to eat, so Elizabeta had taken Luisa to the mess and walked her to school in the mornings during that next week. It was a Bonegilla rule that no one was allowed to take food from the mess back to their huts, but Elizabeta had slipped an orange into her coat pocket and left it on the table. She kept everything clean, sweeping out the grit of dirt they all carried in on their shoes, and wiped the window in fierce circles until it sparkled. She made the beds every day and tidied, but it was such a small hut that those chores took less than ten minutes.

Elizabeta needed an excuse to get away, to make sure she didn't get sucked into her mother's grief. She collected up clothes that needed washing and walked past building after building towards the laundry at the end of their alley. She passed a group of Italian men playing a bowling game and four women sitting around a small table playing cards. Two olive-skinned women walked by carrying brown paper parcels tied with string saying the words 'post office' in English, and laughing at the sound of it. Ahead, a brown-haired man sat in a chair, and a darker-haired man with very hairy arms stood behind him, wielding a comb and scissors. He combed and snipped, combed and snipped, and as he worked, little pieces of hair caught in the breeze and fell to the grass. The man in the chair held a mirror in his hand and watched and there was a queue of men waiting their turn.

A shriek up ahead had everyone turning. Then another, then another. At the women's ablutions block, people fled like bees from a newly opened hive. A panic of people rushed through the doorway, little girls and women and mothers with toddlers hoisted off the ground in shaky arms and they spread in all directions.

'Snake!' someone yelled.

Everyone knew 'snake'.

Elizabeta reached the laundry block and went in. She shivered. It was colder inside than it was outdoors. Two long metal sinks were positioned on either side of an exposed pipe with taps every few feet. Two Dutch women were talking animatedly and jostling with a Pole for space in front of a tap, none of them willing to make way for each other. Elizabeta was in no great rush to go back to the hut, so she waited, watching the women working at the flat troughs, their sleeves pushed up to their elbows, pressing their palms into their sudsy clothes, rubbing and twisting and rinsing under the frigid drizzling water. A space became free and

Elizabeta took out each item, singlets, socks, underwear, and turned on the tap. Her fingers stiffened in the cold water. As she scrubbed, the suds making her fingers slippery, she wondered if her father's job at the factory in Adelaide would pay enough money so they could buy the thing called a washing machine. She'd heard some German women in the mess the day before talking about them. It was a metal machine that did all the hard work. Perhaps when they settled in Adelaide her father would buy her mother a washing machine. And a new radio too, and beds that didn't squeak and a fireplace to keep them warm and windows that didn't let the draught in. And another pair of shoes. And a new dress. And a string of pearls. Perhaps those things would make her mother happy again.

Elizabeta scrubbed and squeezed and thought of Frances and Vasiliki and Iliana. She had been so busy with her mother and looking after Luisa that she hadn't seen them for most of the week. She missed them. Their laughter, the new English words she might learn from Frances, the funny way Vasiliki joked and Iliana's shy smile. But she had other responsibilities now. She had her mother and her sister to look after. She had promised her father that she would. Her distance from her friends made it easier not to think about her father leaving, her mother's sickness, the dancing German, and leaving Bonegilla.

Elizabeta hauled the wet clothes to the washing line and fastened them with wooden pegs. She wasn't sure how long it would all take for them to dry in this weather, but at the moment, she had all the time in the world to wait.

The next day, once breakfast was finished and Luisa was in school, Elizabeta walked the camp until she found Vasiliki and Iliana.

The early-morning clouds had cleared and the sun was out, weak but warm, and the girls were sitting near a gum tree by the oval where the young men played soccer, but there was no game that day. In the distance, the big sky was a pale autumn blue and the mountains were dark purple and gun-metal grey. The magpies trilled in the straggly trees and a couple landed on the grass. As Elizabeta approached, they stared back at her. She was fascinated by the black-and-white birds, their long beaks and their calls.

'Hello,' she called and Vasiliki and Iliana waved back.

Elizabeta sat down next to her friends. She looked up at the sound of squawking. A flock of white birds with yellow heads flew over. She made a mental note to ask Frances what they were called.

'A sunny day,' Vasiliki said.

'Yes,' Elizabeta replied.

'Your father is gone?' Vasiliki asked. Her English had improved so much since Frances had begun lessons with them that she was now translating at the camp's post office and at the shop for her parents.

'Yes. He goes to Adelaide.'

Iliana and Vasiliki exchanged glances. 'Where is Adelaide?'

Elizabeta shrugged. 'I don't know.'

'My father says we go to a house soon in Melbourne.'

'We will go soon, also,' Elizabeta told them. 'When my father, he finds a house. It can take a long time.'

Vasiliki looked down at the grass, pressing her fingers to blade after blade and plucking them from the ground.

Iliana wiped her eyes. '*Papà*. Work in New South Wales. One week.' She held an index finger in the air. 'One week. We go on train.'

They sat in silence for a long time.

When the bell rang out across the camp to signal lunch, they went wearily back to their family's huts to get their plates and knives and forks and spoons and cups, promising to tell Frances their news when she got home from school.

When Elizabeta returned from lunch, after a melancholy half hour with her friends, her mother was out of bed, but Luisa was in it in her place.

'What is wrong?' she asked, crossing the hut and kneeling down at her sister's side. Luisa was stripped down to a singlet and her underpants, and was tugging at her blankets, kicking them off with her bare feet, exposing her skinny, pale body. Her head tossed and damp little ringlets had formed in her hair from the sweat on her face. Her pillow was damp.

Berta stood in the corner of the hut, her arms wrapped around her thin frame. 'A teacher brought her home from school.' Her mother may have been out of bed, but she was still speaking and moving in slow motion. 'She is so hot.'

Elizabeta pressed her palm to her sister's forehead.

'Luisa,' Elizabeta asked her sister. 'What did the teacher say when she brought you to the hut?'

'Where's *Vati*?' Luisa moaned and then she coughed weakly. She began to whimper and rub her eyes.

Elizabeta looked to her mother for some guidance, for some hint that she was going to take charge, to be strong. But there was nothing.

They sat with Luisa for a long while, willing her to sleep, but she was too restless, too unsettled, her coughs hacking and rasping. Elizabeta got to her feet. 'I will get some water.' She took two cups from one of the silver trays sitting on the small table and quickly walked to the ablutions block. She was almost running. When she twisted the tap on, she filled the cups, quickly drained one herself, and then filled it again. She took a moment to take a breath, to find her strength, to think about the English words for what Luisa was suffering: hot, sick. To pray to God that her mother might find the strength to help.

Each step back to the hut jolted the bones in her body. Her head was throbbing, her heart racing, as she walked back down the alley, trying not to spill the water. When she reached the hut, Vasiliki, Iliana and Frances were waiting for her.

Frances stepped forwards. 'Hello, Elizabeta. Vasiliki and Iliana have told me about your father.' She looked as if she might burst into tears but Elizabeta didn't have time for anyone else's fears.

'Yes. He is gone …' Elizabeta stumbled for the words but didn't stop walking. 'My sister.' Her friends turned their heads to the red door at the sound of coughing and then wailing.

'She's sick? What's the matter with her?' Frances went to Elizabeta, touched her arm in a gesture of comfort.

'She is very hot. She cries.'

Frances tightened her grip on her friend's arm. 'I will get someone to come and see her. You wait here. Iliana and Vasiliki,' she said, pointing to the hut and shaking her head. 'Do not go in.'

Then she turned and ran, her thick woollen skirt flapping around her knees like a tangled kite as she disappeared around a corner.

Chapter Sixteen

It all happened so fast.

Within half an hour, Luisa was in a bed in the isolation ward at the Bonegilla children's hospital. The urgency of her daughter's condition had snapped Berta out of her sadness and torpor, and she and Elizabeta had raced across the camp. They sat on a hard wooden bench in the corridor outside the ward, staring at the white walls. Berta was praying, mumbling quietly to herself. Elizabeta prayed too, crossing herself over and over. Please God let Luisa be all right.

The ward doors opened and closed quickly behind a man in a white coat and glasses and another man wearing a grey uniform, not a white coat.

'Mrs Schmidt,' the doctor began.

'Yes?' Berta stood on shaky legs. Elizabeta jumped to her feet, trying to clear her head so she could concentrate on the English words the doctor would say.

'Tell her what I'm saying, Klaus.'

'Yes, doctor.' The man stepped forwards. He was neat and slight. '*Frau* Schmidt,' he started in German. 'My name is Klaus Bauer. I was a doctor in Stuttgart. I will translate for you what Dr Jenkins says.'

Berta and Elizabeta studied Dr Jenkins's face but listened intently to Klaus.

'Let me ask. Your husband is still here at Bonegilla?'

'He has gone to Adelaide,' Berta snapped. 'My daughters and I are here alone.'

Dr Jenkins began to talk but all Elizabeta could hear was Klaus's cultured voice, his perfect German. 'Your daughter is very sick.' He paused. '*Die Masern.*'

Measles. Elizabeta knew the word. She clutched her mother's arm and searched her face. Berta was white now, her lips pulled thin, her hollowed cheeks shadowed. They knew all about diseases and sickness. There had not only been hunger and starvation in Europe during the war, but there had been typhus, tuberculosis, dysentery, meningitis, pneumonia. And measles. Berta began peppering Klaus with questions.

He answered them all, patiently waiting while Dr Jenkins explained the answers, and then adding his own thoughts to the translations. 'She is in good hands. Dr Jenkins and the nurses will give her some medicine and soon she will be well again. You'll see.'

'I must see my Luisa.' Berta reached for Klaus's sleeve. 'Please?'

'I have her doll.' Elizabeta pulled it from her coat pocket and showed Klaus and the doctor. It was made from a wooden peg, with a pink, orange and brown floral dress

Elizabeta had sewn herself, with a snip of lace like a shawl around its neck. Elizabeta had drawn on a face: two round eyes and a crooked red smile.

When Dr Jenkins shook his head, Elizabeta put it back in her pocket. He said some more to Klaus, but Elizabeta was too upset to concentrate on them and then she and her mother watched him walk away down the corridor, his lace-up shoes clicking on the linoleum.

'The doctor says the best thing you can do is go back to your hut and get some sleep,' Klaus said, his voice low, a polite attempt at reassurance. 'When little Luisa is no longer infectious, you will be allowed to see her. It's for the best, for you and for all the other children at the camp. There's one other case so it seems like we might have put a lid on it. No one wants it spreading.'

'No,' Berta said quickly. 'No one wants more sick children.'

Klaus stepped forwards. He put a hand on Berta's shoulder. 'It's not like back home, *Frau* Schmidt.'

'I will come tomorrow,' she told Klaus, nodding. 'I will see my daughter tomorrow.'

'That is a good idea. I'm very sorry your daughter is ill.'

'*Vielen dank*,' Berta said and reached out her hand to take his. They nodded to each other and only then did Berta step back and breathe. Elizabeta's shoulders dropped. She was relieved to see some of the tension in her mother's face was gone.

'*Komm, Mutti.*' Elizabeta took her mother's hand. They walked in silence back to their hut. Elizabeta took the long way, past the post office and the canteen, past some of the other accommodation blocks, past Tudor Hall and the lawns where children were playing soccer, because after that they would go back to their hut and stay there until the morning, with the walls closing in and creaking in the night.

The next morning, Berta and Elizabeta ate a quick breakfast in the mess before returning to the hospital. They'd had a fitful night. Elizabeta had listened to the possums on the roof for what seemed like hours and when her mother wasn't mumbling prayers under her breath she was outside in the cold, smoking a cigarette. When the sun came up, Elizabeta had worked hard to convince her mother to eat something and had finally won the battle. Her mother had been slim for as long as Elizabeta could remember, but she seemed not to have gained back any of the weight she'd lost after her long bout of seasickness on the voyage over. She'd become even thinner at Bonegilla; her skin sallow, her collar bones as sharp as knives under the collar of her dresses.

'I'm sure Luisa will be better today.'

They were walking purposefully, Elizabeta's quick steps barely enough to keep pace with her mother. They walked up the alley nearest their hut, past the women's ablutions block, heading towards the mess and then north to the hospital, when her mother stopped suddenly.

Elizabeta almost tumbled into the back of her. '*Mutti?*'

Berta didn't answer. She was still as a post.

'*Mutti?* What is wrong?' Up ahead, there was a queue leading into the mess.

He was standing alone at the back of the line, the German, his tray in one hand and a cigarette in the other. He drew in and then exhaled, the red tip of his cigarette lifting and lowering.

Berta spat something under her breath.

The man dropped his cigarette and ground it into the dirt with the sole of his shoe.

'Don't say anything,' Berta warned her daughter in a tight hiss. '*Sagt nichts*.'

They had to pass the mess to get to the hospital and as they neared, the man looked up.

'*Guten morgen, Frau Schmidt*.' The German smiled. In the light of day, Elizabeta thought how ordinary he seemed. Medium height, slim, his hair short at the sides and the front slicked back. He was slight, inconsequential, ordinary. His cheeks pulled in, making hollows, and his scar was jagged, as if it had healed badly. He wore tweed trousers and a brown jumper. As brown as dirt.

Elizabeta was so close to her mother she could feel her chest rising and falling with words unsaid.

'Who would have thought. To come all this way from Europe and see someone from home. How are you finding Bonegilla? Is the accommodation to your liking?'

Elizabeta was frightened. She knew her mother's strength, knew that once she'd been a fighter, but she hadn't seen that spark since they'd come to Bonegilla. It was as if her courage had fallen overboard into the ocean somewhere on the way to Australia.

'And *Fräulein* Elizabeta. It's nice to see you again.' He came closer, an arm's length away. 'She's quite the dancer, your daughter. She moves quickly. Very light on her feet.'

Elizabeta's heart thumped and a chill shook her from the inside. The morning sun was on their backs but it was as if they were standing in the snow-filled streets of Hungary with the wet seeping into the newspaper-lined soles of their worn-out shoes.

Berta raised her chin, took in a deep breath. She reached her arm out to the side to shepherd her daughter behind her. 'Get out of my way.' Her voice was broken glass.

The man leaned in close. 'The war was a long time ago, yes? We are not the same people we were. Are we?'

Her mother leaned in to the man's face. So close, their noses almost touched.

'*Sie sind der Teufel.*' You are the devil.

'Not a devil. Just a soldier. Like millions of others, who were doing their sacred duty for the Fatherland.'

Berta spat at his feet. 'I will tell the police you are here.'

The man laughed at her.

'And why would anyone believe your stories, old woman? There were lots of soldiers in Hungary. Germans. Hungarians. Russians. It could have been anyone.'

'You forget something. I know who gave you that scar on your face.'

The man narrowed his eyes. 'Look here, *Frau* Schmidt. I'm here for a new life, too. This is my chance to start again. To forget. My homeland has gone, too.' Then he shot a quick hand out and wrapped his fingers around Berta's wrist, jerking her forwards. 'If you tell anyone, I will come after her. Do you understand?'

He quickly looked from side to side, as if he was checking for spying eyes. Satisfied there were none, he felt free to sneer at Berta and stalk away. Elizabeta watched him go. She had been right. It had been him. They'd come all this way to the other side of the world but the ghosts from the past were walking alongside them at Bonegilla, eating alongside them in the mess, breathing the same clean Australian air. Where was her father? What should she do now? She was too scared to move, too frightened to comfort her mother. She slipped her hand inside her coat pocket and clutched Luisa's wooden peg doll.

'That man … that piece of shit.' Berta's breath exploded from her mouth and she wrapped her arms around her daughter, holding her while she shook and cried.

'*Mutti*,' Elizabeta sobbed into the lapels of her mother's scratchy woollen coat. 'I remember everything.'

'I'm sorry you remember. I'm so sorry you remember. We came here to forget. We came here to forget everything.'

Elizabeta pushed out of her mother's embrace and searched her expression. She hadn't always been scared and anxious. Once she'd been strong. Once she'd been a fighter.

'You cut his face with the kitchen knife,' Elizabeta whispered.

Her mother took a shuddering breath. Her voice was nothing more than a whisper. 'Yes, I did.'

Chapter Seventeen

That night, as Elizabeta lay in her squeaky bed in their hut at Bonegilla, the scratchy grey blankets pulled up to her chin, she tried not to remember.

But some memories you can never leave behind.

That day, almost ten years ago, there had only been the two of them, Elizabeta and her mother. There had been no Luisa back then; she was yet to be born. And tonight, in their small hut, so cold their toes turned blue despite the layers, there was once again only the two of them. As Elizabeta squeezed her eyes shut to keep the memories away, she could hear Berta praying quietly in her bed, fighting sleep. They had gone to the hospital that morning, after they'd seen the German by the mess, but they were turned away by nurses in white caps and crisp dresses who tut-tutted and shooed them out of the ward. They hadn't seen Klaus, so there was no one to explain to them in words they could understand how Luisa was faring. Elizabeta knew her sister would be so scared to be there by herself, with only a few words of English, perhaps even those forgotten in her delirium. She held Luisa's little doll, clutched tight in her hand as she shivered under the blankets and remembered.

She remembered there was snow.

It had been winter in their small village in Hungary, two miles from the nearest town where there had been a grocer and a butcher and a baker and her school. It was not much more than a collection of small cottages on a strip of fertile farming land set at the intersection of two dirt roads. It must have been sometime between November and February, when the ground was white and the trees were bare. Had they had Christmas yet? Elizabeta couldn't place whether it had been before or after. Her memories were photographs, not moving pictures; so much of it lost, or so she'd thought, so much of it pushed back into the place in her mind where she had hoped it would remain trapped forever.

She had been almost seven years old; old enough to remember but still too young to understand. By then, her father was in a forced labour camp, having been arrested by the Hungarian Nazis. There was just Elizabeta and her mother. That day, she had been next door at the Hermann's. Her mother and her best friend Greta's mother worked in a weaving factory making woollen and linen cloth, the machines loud and repetitive and grinding in their heads all day, and Greta's grandmother was tasked with their care. Schools were closed because of the war, and with snow three feet deep it was too cold to play outside for long. Elizabeta had loved her days with Greta. Every night she went to bed wishing that Greta was her sister. Her friend was pretty and kind and wore her fine brown hair in two plaits that hung almost to her waist. They found lots of things to occupy them during the dim days of that winter. They sewed little dolls out of bits of string and fabric. Greta's grandmother had taught them how to crochet by pulling apart worn jumpers and re-using the wool. They read books and played marbles and kugels by the fire. They'd talked often about what they would do when the winter was over, when the snow turned to sludge and became puddles and streams and the blossoms budded and bloomed. Despite what she'd seen, Elizabeta longed to go back into the forest, to roam among the towering fir trees, to inhale the scent of them and the fresh air and the smell of wild flowers, to search for wild mushrooms. Her father had shown her exactly where to look: under the tallest trees pines, nestled in the damp undergrowth of the fern fronds. The previous spring, Elizabeta and Greta had picked dozens and dozens and her basket had been so full that her mother had made mushroom soup and even though they hadn't had sour cream, they had sprinkled wild dill on it and it had been delicious.

On that day, the day it happened, she and Greta had been sitting together on the rug on the floor, reading the school books they'd managed to keep, practising their words and eating stale rye bread with a smear of lard and paprika that Greta's *Oma* had made for them. The paprika on top of the white lard looked like orange snow.

When the big clock in the kitchen announced it was five o'clock, it had been time for Elizabeta to go home. She made sure to finish her piece of bread first. She hated the crusts, so thick and hard that they hurt her teeth to chew them, but she knew there would only be flour soup for dinner. Hard crusts were better than flour soup.

Elizabeta had waved goodbye to Greta, called out, '*Bis morgen*'—see you tomorrow—and stepped outside into the snow. There had been a fierce wind disrupting the snow from its drifts and it swirled around her feet like fog. She had quickly turned her head left and right so she could search both ways up and down the street, ever vigilant for Russians. Her mother and Greta's grandmother—all the women of their village—knew to be scared of them. Some women in the village had been desperate for the Russians to invade, figuring nothing could be worse than the Hungarian Nazis or the German Nazis. But now they were more scared of the Russians than the dark. The Russians hadn't needed the cover of darkness to hide their crimes. They would come at any time of the day or night. The women in their village knew the stories, had warned every young girl, 'The Russians will take you away to peel potatoes. They always need young girls to peel potatoes'.

They had very quickly learned that girls weren't taken away to peel potatoes. Those taken away by soldiers would return as shadows. One girl, three houses down, had jumped from the roof of her family's house. Another girl in their village had hung herself in a barn, and had been discovered by her mother, dangling lifeless in between two milking cows.

'Women and girls aren't safe,' Berta had said, scolding Greta's grandmother when the old woman scoffed at the stories. It was the only power women had, to warn others, to spread the word, to convince mothers to hide their daughters in cellars or attics until the soldiers were too drunk to do anything but sleep. 'Don't go out on the street. Warn your girls. And those women who are happy the Nazis are gone and that the Russians have come? Crazy. The Germans. The

Russians. The Hungarians who've locked up my husband. They're all as bad as each other.'

Elizabeta had never told her mother or anyone, but she'd seen for herself what the Russians had done. Before the winter and the snow, she and Greta had walked into the forest looking for flowers. They'd been chattering away, counting trees and looking for birds, when they'd heard shouts from nearby and then *pop pop pop* echoing through the forest. It seemed to be coming from the river to the east, near where they'd gone fishing with their fathers in the summer, before the soldiers had come and taken their fathers away. The girls had crept cautiously, trying not to make any sounds, until they found a spot where they were able to look through the trees and into the light and see the river below, flowing fast and clear until there were more shots and then the river ran red. The Russians had lined a group of German soldiers on the ground by the riverbank and shot them, *pop pop pop*, one by one, and the dead Germans tumbled down into the water below. *Pop pop pop* then *splash splash splash*. The water had become swirls of grey and red like bobbing apples.

Her feet suddenly hadn't worked, and she wasn't able to make a sound with her mouth. She and Greta had made themselves as small as they could and hidden until there was no more shooting, and then they had stealthily crept back to the path that led them into the light and home. She and Greta had kept their secret.

On the doorstep of Greta's house, Elizabeta had checked four times and when she had been certain there were no Russians, she ran the twenty steps to the front door of her family's cottage. With two rooms and a thatched roof, it was small, but it would be warm inside if her mother had already lit the fire. She had rapped her knuckles on the front door waiting for her mother to unlatch the lock and let her in, but with her knock, the door had eased open.

'*Mutti?*'

The house was quiet. A bag of flour lay on the table in the middle of the kitchen, opened, a scattering of white around it. A slotted metal spoon and a sharp knife lay on a worn wooden cutting board. A cast-iron pot of water sat on the wood stove, boiling over, the water hissing and spitting on the heat of the plate.

'*Mutti?* Where are you?' Elizabeta crept around the table. She heard a muffled noise from her parents' bedroom and stopped.

Her chest pounded with excitement. Was her father home? Had the soldiers let him go? She'd skipped to the door to her parents' bedroom. '*Vati?*'

She put her hand up to the wooden door. Light came through the splits in the timber.

'No, Elizabeta,' her mother cried. 'Don't come in. Go to the kitchen.'

There was something angry in her mother's voice and Elizabeta did as she was told. She had walked back to the kitchen and, using a cloth to wrap around her hands as she'd seen her mother do, she lifted the pot from the fire. Then she sat at the table and waited. She traced shapes in the flour dust. A cat. A wild flower. A fluffy cloud.

It had seemed like a long time before Elizabeta heard the bedroom door creaking open. She looked up. Her mother walked towards her, but the figure behind her wasn't her father.

This man was wearing a uniform, grey trousers and a jacket with a dark green collar. On each shoulder there were epaulets with silver buttons. There was a black cross sewn in white on the left breast pocket and a silver eagle on the right. He was buttoning his jacket, but his trousers were still tucked inside his jackboots. The man had a gun in a holster at his hip. He looked around the room and his eyes fixed on Elizabeta sitting at the table.

'*Deine Tochter?*' Your daughter?

Her mother didn't say a word in reply. There was blood on her bottom lip. One eye was turning purple. Her thick woollen dress was ripped down the front and her skin was pale where it was exposed. Her head was still wrapped in a woollen scarf. She seemed to stumble towards Elizabeta. '*Sagt nichts,*' she whispered when she leaned down to kiss the top of her daughter's head. Don't say anything. 'I'll make soup in a minute.'

Then she raised her voice, half turned back to the soldier. 'You came here for food. I don't have anything but flour. And one potato.'

He stormed across the room. 'Give it to me.' The potato was sitting half-peeled on the wooden cutting board on the table and he lunged for it. Elizabeta remembered the muddy strips in a spiral next to it, her mother's brown fingerprints on the pale flesh.

He shoved it against his teeth, biting a huge chunk and chewing fiercely. He was a wild animal eating the carcass of another, spittle flying as he used his other hand to tuck in his shirt. That's why he didn't see Elizabeta's mother grab the knife from the cutting board; didn't see her spin around and lunge at him, so fast he only had time to lift his hand with the potato and not his gun, trying to shield his face, his palm out, his elbow out, but Elizabeta's mother's arm was high and she slashed downwards with the knife, along his face, and the potato dropped to the dirt floor.

When he screamed, Elizabeta froze, then something inside her stomach began to make her whole body tremble.

The soldier slammed both hands to his face and she saw a trickle of blood dribble onto the flour on the table, all over her cloud. She hadn't dared move. She'd practised becoming invisible that time in the forest and she did it then.

Her mother held the knife in the air, her panicked breathing fast and loud.

The soldier lifted his hands from his face. Blood had dribbled down his wrists into the cuffs of his dirty grey uniform. His breath was fast, shallow, rasping.

'*Die Huren ist vurückt,*' he'd snarled. The whore is crazy.

'And if you don't get out, I will use this again.' Berta was primed, ready to lunge at the soldier again, waving the bloodied knife from side to side as if she were smearing icing on a cake. 'Get out! I will tell the Russians. They like killing German soldiers. Or I'll tell the Germans. I know what they think of deserters. They'll find you!' Her shriek reached right inside Elizabeta's body and squeezed her bones.

The man stood dazed, unmoving. Berta jumped forwards and lunged at him again and he stumbled backwards to the door. Berta opened it with her one free hand and kicked him out. When the door was slammed and bolted, she dropped the knife to the stone floor with a thud.

Elizabeta was still invisible but she saw the blood on her mother's hand, and then more blood. A bright red trail trickled down her legs, to the inside of her ankle, catching and staining in her baggy grey socks.

Elizabeta looked at her mother. Berta looked at her daughter. A lifetime passed between them in that moment.

There was movement at the window. Elizabeta slipped silently from her chair and hid under the table. The soldier was coming back to kill them. She knew it. She'd seen his gun. She knew what guns could do. She covered her ears with her hands and squeezed her eyes shut. She tried to pray but had forgotten the words. She had forgotten all her words in the dark behind her closed eyes. Where was her father?

There was a *tap tap tap* at the window.

Berta jumped. 'Veronika,' she whispered. Greta's grandmother.

From under the table, still as the dead, barely breathing, Elizabeta watched her mother's shoes shuffle across the floor, her socks red with her blood. A hand picked up the knife and there were footsteps and a clatter in the sink.

'Elizabeta,' she whispered. 'You can come out. It's *Frau* Hermann. Can you open the door?' Her mother's voice shook, broke.

Elizabeta slid out from under the table and scurried to the door. When she unbolted the door, *Frau* Hermann swept in with a cold gust of wind and a flurry of snow at her back. Berta lunged at the door and slammed it shut.

'I heard screaming. What is going on?' She looked Berta over. Her ripped dress. The blood.

'The Russians?' *Frau* Hermann gathered her apron in her hands and kneaded the worn fabric.

'A German,' Berta stammered.

Elizabeta pressed her back to the cold stone wall by the front door. *Frau* Hermann went to the pot on the stove, took a piece of cloth hanging on a hook by the steamed-up window, and dipped it in the water. She squeezed it out on the floor and went to Berta, dabbing the blood from her hand. From her face. She gently patted her bruised and swelling eye.

'Oh no, oh no.' *Frau* Hermann knelt down and wiped the blood from Berta's foot and swept upwards to her knee. A fresh flow trickled down in another rivulet. 'What did he do to you?'

Frau Hermann turned to Elizabeta, her voice catching, crying, tears in her eyes now. 'Go be with Greta. Go now.'

She wasn't invisible any longer. She didn't want to be sent away from her mother. Her mother was all she had and there was blood on her body and she might be dying and *I can't be next door playing with Greta when my mother is dying.* 'I don't want to go.'

'Go,' Berta said. 'I will come and get you soon.'

Elizabeta's memory was confused about the time after that. She remembered that she had spent the night at the Hermann's, snuggled up tight with Greta to ward off both the cold and the soldier. But the days and months after that were a blur. The war ended, but things hadn't gone back to the way they were before. Soldiers had taken the Hermanns away in a truck and soon after, Elizabeta and her mother were interned and then sent to Germany on the train just as Jozef had found them.

'The Americans and Russians and the English have decided,' Jozef had told Berta. 'I heard it in the camp. All the *Volksdeutsche* are being deported from Hungary. Some to Russia. We're going to Germany.'

'But we were born here. My parents and yours, too,' Berta had answered.

Almost ten years later, a world away, Elizabeta saw it all again. *Frau* Hermann and her stale rye bread smeared with lard and snowed with paprika. Greta with her books and her pretty hair. Maybe Greta was in America, eating those things called hot dogs and listening to Frank Sinatra records. Wherever she was, Elizabeta hoped it was somewhere warmer than Bonegilla. California would be warmer. She'd seen photos in magazines of young people on long wooden boards standing on the waves at the beach. She hoped Greta was as far away as she was from home. From everything they'd seen.

Elizabeta turned on her side and listened to possums leaping across the tin roof of their hut. In the thin moonlight through the window, her breath made a cloud. She crossed her fingers for luck and wished her little sister was having happy dreams.

She tried to sleep but couldn't. There was much to forget about the war. Elizabeta would need a whole lifetime to forget what she'd seen.

Chapter Eighteen

When Berta and Elizabeta arrived at the hospital the next morning, directly after a quick breakfast, Klaus, the German porter, was in the hallway of the isolation ward. When he saw them, he sloshed his mop into the metal bucket and came quietly to them in the hallway. His eyes were sad. Elizabeta clutched her mother's hand but Berta shook her off as if she was swatting a fly.

'My Luisa? What is it?'

Klaus dipped his chin. His voice was quiet and low as he spoke German to them. 'I'm sorry to tell you, *Frau* Schmidt, that your daughter is very sick. She has pneumonia.'

Klaus caught Berta in his arms before she hit the floor. He called something out loud and then there were nurses and doctors running from every direction. They lifted Berta onto a bed with wheels and pushed her into a small room. There was a chair and Elizabeta was pressed into it and

given a cup of warm milk with Milo, and she watched and
tried to listen as Klaus stood by the end of her mother's bed,
watching her and discussing something with the doctor and
the nurse in the white cap. Elizabeta was too confused to
translate the words in her head but she understood they had
decided that Berta was in no state to take in any more bad
news, no matter the language in which it was delivered. She
was given something to calm her and Elizabeta watched
while her mother fought sleep and then finally succumbed
to it.

When her mother's breathing steadied, Elizabeta lay her
arms on the crisp white sheets and buried her head against
her mother's thin body. Where had her mother's strength
gone? Elizabeta didn't know what to do now. She had been
witness to her mother's suffering before but this time seemed
different. That strength had drained from her over the years,
like grains of sand through a clenched fist. Elizabeta saw
her again in her mind's eye, waving the kitchen knife at
the German, wild, her eyes flared, her words spat out of her
mouth like shards of glass. Bit by bit, that fierceness had disappeared, one day at a time, one year at a time. Perhaps from
now on she would be like this, asleep and small, pressed
into a bed between the white sheets. Maybe her mother had
already used up her lifetime's worth of courage and perse-
verance. What would Elizabeta do if her mother had nothing left now?

Elizabeta wished for home, but where was home now?
Here at Bonegilla? With her father in the place called
Adelaide?

A hand pressed gently on her shoulder. Elizabeta looked
up. Frances was holding a small bunch of flowers.

'Hello.' Frances paused, wiped a tear from her cheek with her free hand. 'Here.' She presented the bunch. 'They're for you and your mother.'

Elizabeta took them wordlessly, and pressed the blooms and the gum leaves to her nose, searching for the scent of fir trees and wild mushrooms.

'I'm very sorry to hear about your sister,' Frances said.

Elizabeta watched as tears welled in her friend's brown eyes.

'The doctors and nurses here are very good and they will be doing all they can for her.'

'Yes.' Elizabeta concentrated on the English words but she didn't need to translate the expression of sympathy on Frances's face. Her bottom lip quivered.

'I was here myself, remember?'

Elizabeta made a fist and knocked her forehead. 'Your head,' Elizabeta said. 'It was hurt.'

'Yes.'

The click of a woman's heels on the shiny linoleum echoed and they looked up. Mavis Burley walked towards them.

'Mum,' Frances said. 'This is my friend, Elizabeta Schmidt.'

'Hello, Elizabeta.' Frances's mother touched her shoulder too, patted it three times. Then she turned to her daughter. 'Frances, bring Elizabeta. We'll take her home and give her some lunch.'

Elizabeta felt the tug of Frances's hand and they didn't let go of each other until they'd crossed the camp and reached the director's house.

That evening, just as people from the camp were heading to the mess, the task fell to Mavis to tell Elizabeta that her sister was dead.

They'd just had a light supper of tomato soup and toast and were still sitting at the table in the kitchen when the phone rang in the hallway. Mrs Burley had excused herself and answered the call. Frances heard a gasp.

'The poor family,' her mother whispered, but Frances could still hear every word through the thin walls. 'What's to be done? Yes, of course I'll tell her but I don't know if she'll understand much of anything. She's barely said a word all day. I'll do my best.' Frances heard the Bakelite click of the phone being returned to its cradle.

A moment later, Mavis returned to the kitchen. She smoothed down her tweed skirt with jittery hands and then cleared her throat. Her pearls sat neatly at her neckline, just above the collar of her pale green twin-set. Frances searched her mother's face for a clue about what had just happened.

'Elizabeth, I have something to tell you.' Mavis pulled out her chair and slowly sat down.

'Her name is Elizabeta, Mum, not Elizabeth,' Frances said.

Mavis glanced at her daughter and nodded. 'My apologies, Elizabeta. That was Frances's father on the phone.' She sighed and turned to her daughter. 'Can she understand me, Frances? Does she speak much English?'

'A little,' Elizabeta said. Frances reached for her hand and covered it with her own. Elizabeta's fingers were stiff and cold.

'Your sister ...' Mavis linked her fingers together in a steeple under her chin. 'Dear girl. I'm very sorry to tell you that your sister has passed away.'

Elizabeta glanced at Frances, her face pale. 'I'm sorry. What is "passed away"? Is she leaving *das Krankenhaus*? The hospital?'

'Oh dear.' Mavis shuddered.

'Oh, Elizabeta.' Frances felt a pit open in her stomach and her head spun as everything inside her body plummeted into it.

'She has died, Elizabeta.' Mavis lifted her chin and her eyes glanced to the ceiling. Frances could tell she was trying not to cry, but Frances couldn't control her own sobbing. It filled the kitchen and echoed back at her.

'She has died?' Elizabeta repeated.

'Yes. She was so very sick from the measles.'

'Oh.' Elizabeta sat in almost total stillness.

'You do understand, Elizabeta?' Frances asked gently, trying so desperately to stop crying. How dare she when her friend was dry-eyed and calm? When she was so stoic in the face of such heartbreaking news?

Elizabeta nodded. 'I understand. My mother. I must go to her.'

Mavis filled Elizabeta's water glass. Elizabeta drank it down in one gulp.

'Your mother is still in hospital,' Mavis said slowly and deliberately. 'The doctors are looking after her. They have given her some medicine so she will sleep.'

Elizabeta stood abruptly, pushing the chair back with a scrape on the linoleum. 'Please. I go to my mother. My father. I must tell him.'

Mavis nodded. 'Mr Burley is doing all her can to get word to your father. We know where he is working in South Australia. Someone will tell him.'

'Thank you,' Elizabeta said.

Mavis stood and Frances followed. 'We're so very sorry. You and your mother and father will be in our prayers tonight and forever.' She walked around the table and put an arm around Elizabeta's shoulders, pulling her in close. 'The doctors think it's best if you wait until tomorrow to see your mother. It's been decided you will stay here with us tonight, in our home. We will look after you, dear.'

Frances held Elizabeta's hand. 'Come with me. You will sleep here tonight. I'll show you your bed.'

There wasn't a funeral. At least not one that Elizabeta and her mother were invited to. Luisa was laid to rest two days later in the Albury Cemetery, in the Roman Catholic section, near the graves of the twenty-one children who were buried there in 1949 and 1950 after they died of malnutrition soon after arriving at Bonegilla.

Plans had been put in place, Frances told Elizabeta. Mr Burley had arranged for her mother and father to talk to each other on the telephone and then Mr Burley arranged for the Schmidts to be reunited as soon as possible. In a week, they were to go to Adelaide.

'On compassionate grounds,' Frances explained. 'My father says that people in the immigration department are very sorry about what has happened. We will get you to your father as soon as we can. You need to be together at a time like this.'

Her mother had buried two daughters and she wasn't yet forty years old. One in Hungary, a place that was never really home for them, and the other here in Australia, which wasn't home yet either. Luisa would remain in Albury, sheltered by the long spindly arms of the gum trees in the cemetery, serenaded by songs every day from the magpies, and warmed by the brown earth. Her sweet little sister, who loved nothing more than her mother and father, her sister, school and climbing trees, would be always have a home here on the Murray.

Chapter Nineteen

In the week after Luisa's burial, Elizabeta found offerings on the doorstep of their hut every day. A bunch of silver gum leaves tied with a string. A handwritten note. Oranges. Three tins of peaches. A bag of sweets. Elizabeta had arranged everything on the small table in their hut, alongside Luisa's peg doll and a painting she'd made at the Bonegilla school.

Her mother didn't leave the hut except when she was called for meetings with one of the camp staff; the Austrian man, who spoke German, Italian, French and Spanish, had been charged with arranging things for their departure. The doctor at the hospital had given Berta some medicine to help her sleep and she was often in bed.

Elizabeta had kept herself busy. She packed up Luisa's few clothes and took them in a bundle to the schoolroom, where the young Australian schoolteacher had taken them in her arms with teary eyes. Surely another child could use her almost-new winter coat with the tan buttons, and her black shoes, even though there were scuff marks on the toes. Elizabeta kept Luisa's peg doll and stored it and her hair clips in a wooden box that she had carried with her all the way across the world from her other life.

Her friends Iliana and Vasiliki and Frances came by every day, bringing an orange or an apple for Elizabeta's mother, and some cold milk and Milo for their friend. Five days after Luisa was buried, Elizabeta allowed herself to be coaxed out for a walk. She had news to tell them.

'We will walk. It is a sunny day.' Iliana held Vasiliki's hand tightly. Vasiliki reached for Elizabeta's hand and then Frances's and the four girls walked together, linked to each other, and took in every sight there was to see. Elizabeta simply nodded. She didn't want to talk—it took too much effort and she had spent most of the energy she had taking care of her mother. And anyway, she didn't want to have to think hard about the words she wanted to say, but wanted to take in everything about this place so she could remember it as the last place she had had a little sister.

Bonegilla felt like a big paddock in the middle of nowhere, a town plonked in an empty country. This would always be her first memory of Australia. She took in the grey hills in the distance, the apple-green paddocks with lazy cows grazing, the pale blue sky above with wisps of cloud strung out like spun sugar. Then she closed her eyes and tried to imprint those memories there instead of the ones she had brought with her on the boat. There was the tree Luisa had loved to climb, a lonely presence in the grassed area near the mess. The ablutions block, which had scared Luisa so when she'd told her about the snake. The mess in which she'd first tasted corn flakes. The school Luisa had loved so much.

Their meandering walk led them to the weir. They clambered over a small embankment and once they made it to the top, they took in the view across the blue-grey water.

'I swim in the water,' Iliana said. 'In summer.'

'We have lakes in Germany,' Elizabeta answered. 'But I cannot swim.'

Vasiliki mimed swimming, bringing her hands together in front of her chest, pushing them outwards, and sweeping them around in a half circle. 'Swimming. The sea.'

Iliana laughed. 'Fish.' She rubbed her stomach and grinned.

It was quiet. There was no breeze to speak of and the only sounds were the gentle lapping water at the edges of the weir and the birds flying overhead, the strange *caw caws* that were just a little bit familiar to Elizabeta now. The girls walked to a fallen gum tree and sat on it so they could remove their shoes and socks. They ran to the water's edge, dancing across twigs and dried leaves and stones, and dipped their feet into the frigid water.

Iliana gasped and laughed and Vasiliki bent down and flicked an arc of water into the air. Frances squealed and Elizabeta watched from the water's edge. She would never have a sister again but she had friends. She had these three girls. They had not left her alone in her grief, but had come to her every day with what little they had. Iliana and Vasiliki knew what it was like to have left everyone they knew to come to a strange, unknowable place, and they wouldn't let her feel adrift and alone. And Frances? Elizabeta knew she had a big heart. She had room enough in there for three girls so different from herself, from parts of the world she had only ever seen on a map.

Elizabeta turned back and sat on the fallen tree. Before long, Frances was on one side of her, Iliana and Vasiliki on the other. They were laughing and shivering.

Elizabeta breathed deep. 'On Sunday, I go to Adelaide.'

The laughing ceased.

'Oh, no.' Frances was the first one to speak. 'To be with your father?'

Elizabeta nodded. 'My mother is very sad when he is not here. We must be all together.'

'That is good,' Vasiliki nodded. 'A family must be together.'

'I don't know where I go to.' Iliana's bottom lip began to quiver and Vasiliki threw an arm around her and pulled her close.

Frances leapt to her feet, picking her way on her toes through the stones, and stood in front of her three friends. They looked up at her as if she was their teacher. 'We will always be friends,' she announced. 'From Bonegilla to wherever we go. Do you understand? Friends?' She linked her two pinkies together and pulled. They remained firmly held.

'*Freunden*,' Elizabeta explained.

'*Amici*,' said Iliana.

Vasiliki thought on it. '*Kalliteri fillie.*'

'Friends.' Frances nodded. 'The Bonegilla girls. Friends forever.'

On Sunday, Frances, Iliana and Vasiliki walked to Elizabeta's hut to say goodbye. They'd found a trolley on which they loaded Elizabeta and Berta's luggage, and they took turns in pushing it to Bonegilla's front gate where the chugging blue bus was waiting.

'You will write to us,' Frances said. It wasn't a question.

Elizabeta nodded. 'Yes, of course.' She thrust an envelope towards Frances. 'You will read it?' she asked.

Frances opened the flap and slipped out a form. Iliana and Vasiliki were by her side and together they stared at the words.

'It says you're going to a Department of Immigration holding camp at Woodside. That's in South Australia. Near Adelaide, I think.' Frances tried to keep a brave face as she slipped the notification back inside the envelope and passed it back to Elizabeta. 'I'm sure it won't be long until you can be with your father. Now I'll know where to send my letters. You're off to South Australia on a new adventure.'

'Yes,' Elizabeta said, but she didn't smile.

'I'll still be here at Bonegilla,' Frances said. 'I will think of you every day.'

'I will think of you every day also,' Iliana said.

'I too.' Vasiliki sighed.

'Elizabeta,' Berta called. '*Komm. Wier gehen.*'

Frances had promised herself she wouldn't cry but her promise was of no use in that moment. Elizabeta and her mother were leaving behind something more precious than anything she could name. They would only have the memory of Luisa to take with them. She suddenly stepped forwards and reached for Elizabeta's hand. She leaned close. 'I will put flowers on Luisa's grave, I promise.'

Elizabeta nodded quickly and cast her eyes to the ground. 'Thank you. And goodbye,' she whispered.

The four girls became a huddle as they threw their arms around each other and held on. Then Elizabeta wriggled herself free and stepped up onto the bus. Frances watched through the windows as Elizabeta walked down the aisle and settled in a window seat near the back. Berta sat next to her and Elizabeta lifted a hand to wave.

'*Ciao*,' Iliana called out. '*Ciao!*' She linked an arm into Vasiliki's.

Vasiliki waved and waved, and her hand became a blur of motion in the crisp air.

Frances watched as the bus moved off. The boom gate lifted and it only took a moment for Elizabeta and her mother to disappear out of sight.

Chapter Twenty

1956

'Hello!'

Vasiliki Mitropoulos raised her arm high as she called out over the noise of Flinders Street Station on the bustling corner of Flinders and Swanston Streets in Melbourne. It was a sea of people, of hats and well-tailored suits and men in overalls and flat caps and women wearing gloves and children in school uniforms. This was the beating heart of the city; where trains disgorged passengers from all over the suburbs only to be filled again in minutes by people on their journeys out of the city. Diagonally across from the station, the twin spires of St Paul's Cathedral reached for the sky. A block away the muddy Yarra flowed on its journey to Port Phillip Bay.

The whole world passed you by if you stood at the corner of Flinders and Swanston Streets. And this was her world now. Vasiliki was part of Melbourne's life and energy and meeting *him* here only made that feeling more profound.

The green trams swept up Flinders Street and Vasiliki lifted her gaze. She could only laugh now at her confusion the first time he'd said 'Meet me under the clocks'.

She'd blamed her English at first, even after nearly three years of living in Australia. But the more English she knew, she more she realised that some Australian expressions still made no sense at all. Standing there on the corner, looking up at the copper dome, tinged green in the sunlight, the clock tower, the archway and the clocks that indicated the times of departure for all the suburban lines, Vasiliki once again practised saying the destinations: Box Hill, Mordialloc, Williamstown, Oakleigh, Brighton Beach and Essendon. Oakleigh was her train. She knew that route off by heart.

They had taken to meeting under the clocks on Saturdays after her shift at work had ended. It felt so romantic to her that she didn't care if they weren't the only ones in Melbourne who met there. The clocks was their place, their time together, their secret. It seemed like a dream to Vasiliki to have a boyfriend. And an Australian boyfriend—one she'd chosen for herself, not any old boy from the village her parents had arranged for her to marry, as if they'd never left Greece and the rules of that old life still applied.

Her life had changed completely since she and her family had left Bonegilla two years earlier. Sometimes she looked at her life and decided she was Elizabeth Taylor in a Hollywood movie. He'd taken her to the pictures to see *The Last Time I Saw Paris* and Vasiliki had instantly fallen in love with the actress. At home that night, she'd posed in front of the rusty mirror in the bathroom, looking back over her left shoulder, staring at her reflection, pouting her lips. There was definitely a resemblance. She'd been inspired to cut her long hair short and had begun to wear it the same way, short and full, swept back from her forehead with a curl. Lots of girls wanted to be Grace Kelly but Vasiliki knew that wasn't realistic for a Greek girl.

She felt like a young woman in love. He was coming. Her palms grew clammy inside her gloves. She hoped her red lipstick was still unsmudged. She hoped he thought she looked beautiful.

And then he was right there in front of her, grinning, and Vasiliki felt a glow deep inside her, as if someone had lit a fire in her chest.

'Vasiliki.' He stopped short before he came too close. He tipped his brown hat to her.

'Hello,' she said again, looking down at her shoes and then up to his happy caramel-brown eyes. She fought the insatiable urge to grab his lapels, stand on her tiptoes and kiss him on the lips. But she knew not to. Girls shouldn't be seen kissing their boyfriends in public. She had learned those rules already, had absorbed them from magazines and the other girls working in the cafe and the customers she served every day. There was the added complication of having to be careful in case they were seen by someone either of them knew. Someone who might know her parents. Just in case that happened, they had been rehearsing their story for months and months.

'This is someone I met at Bonegilla, where my father is the director. She is my sister Frances's friend,' Tom planned to say if he were ever called on to explain.

'I know him from Bonegilla. My friend's brother,' Vasiliki had practised.

He stood before her now, tall, smiling, so handsome. 'You made it,' he said, almost sighing.

'Yes, I am here.' Why was it suddenly so hard to breathe?

'Was it busy at the milk bar today?'

Vasiliki laughed. 'It's always busy.'

They were secret lovers making small talk in the middle of a crowded street and every time they met, Vasiliki heard Doris Day's 'Secret Love' in her head. It had played on 3AK late one night and she had known in that moment that it was her song. Their song. Vasiliki wasn't supposed to be with an Australian boy, and especially not with someone who wasn't Orthodox, she knew that. It was her obligation to honour her parents' wishes but she had met all the young Greek men at their church, had been paraded before them like a mannequin, but none of them made her feel the way Tom did with just a smile. She had managed to convince her parents to keep searching on her behalf for just the right Greek man, and her father had taken on the challenge with renewed vigour. Her mother continued to buy and store things Vasiliki would need in her new home: new sheets, lace tablecloths, crystal sherry glasses, pots and pans, a dinner set. They were stacked in her wardrobe and she had learned to shut the door quickly so she wouldn't have to think about who they were for.

She knew she would have to respect her parents' wishes but she had bought herself some more time. And they were all in a new country now. She wasn't brave enough to raise it with her parents, but she wished so hard for herself that different rules might apply.

'You look very pretty.' Tom took in her pale pink dress, belted at the waist and full in the skirt. It was new, something she'd picked out just for today. She wore a matching cardigan slung over her shoulders, and a clutch purse was tucked under an arm.

'Thank you.' She wanted to take his hand in public but stopped. 'You are very handsome, too.'

Tom laughed. 'That's a new word for you. Handsome.'

'Yes. I learn that a boy is not pretty. A boy is handsome.'

'And a girl is perfect.'

My, how she loved Tom Burley more and more every day.

Working in the milk bar had been like studying an intensive English lesson every day. Serving customers was excellent practice and her work friends had been kind and considerate too. She was smart and all those lessons with Frances at Bonegilla had given her an excellent grounding. When she had begun working at the Majestic, her father and his brother, Uncle Theodorous, had wanted her in the kitchen, not out the front waiting on customers. The told her it was better for business if they found pretty British-Australian girls to wait on customers out front. They wanted to create a successful business, her uncle said, which they wouldn't be able to do if customers thought it was a Greek cafe.

'The Australians like it better when they can understand the waitress,' her father had insisted.

'Well, how am I ever supposed to get better at English if I don't talk to the Australians?' she'd argued back.

'Ach,' he'd said, finally relenting. His acquiescence was an admission of how much he now relied on his daughter. Since they'd moved to Melbourne and rented a house in

Oakleigh, one street away from her uncle, she'd become a conduit to a new country for both her parents. They still struggled with English, and anything more than hello, thank you and goodbye was still beyond them. She understood how hard it had been for them, already in their forties and having to learn new words. They had the Orthodox Church, the business and their growing children. Two of her father's cousins had come to Australia in the past year, as well as her mother's sister and her family, which meant learning English became even less important. Melbourne wasn't called Greece's third biggest city for nothing. Vasiliki tried to encourage her parents to learn English, but it had been easier to become their translator and assistant, especially when it came to the doctor or the chemist or any part of government and its paperwork. It gave her a measure of power in her relationship with her parents and even her uncle. She thought back to the English lessons at Bonegilla: Frances and those silly children's books and all the hours spent in the mess with Iliana and Elizabeta. She realised now that Frances had given her much more than a vocabulary. She'd been patient and kind. She hadn't judged her, hadn't assumed that her lack of English meant she was stupid. She had become her friend. She had much to thank Frances Burley for. There was no doubt about that.

So, with her father's grudging permission and her uncle's wary approval, Vasiliki had begun work as a waitress at the Majestic Milk Bar in Bourke Street. She worked harder than everyone else to prove to her father and her uncle that she could be as good as the British-Australian girls. She had memorised the staff rules that everyone had to abide by while on duty. Her uncle Theodorous was very strict about his list:

- Always wear a clean uniform with a smart apron and a cap.
- Be civil to customers; always try to understand what they want and serve them to their satisfaction.
- Don't stand and talk to customers at the counter.
- Don't shout to other staff.
- Don't pass any remarks against customers or laugh at them as they may get offended.
- Be obedient and do as you're told. (Vasiliki didn't believe she would have any trouble with that one— she was a Greek daughter, after all.)
- Don't be cheeky.
- No chewing gum while on duty.
- Don't fix your hair or face in the shop.
- Don't loaf with your work.

Vasiliki had quickly become the perfect employee. She smiled, she took orders, she delivered food to customers, she refrained from being cheeky and she always looked perfect. She was grateful to the Majestic for giving her such an introduction to Australian working life. And she would always be grateful that it had been the place of her lucky reunion with Tom Burley.

It had been a busy lunchtime and Vasiliki's new white shoes had given her a blister on her heel, which ached and stung the longer she was on her feet. Uncle Theodorous had insisted that the waitresses wear white shoes and this new pair was driving Vasiliki crazy.

'They match your uniforms,' he'd told her. 'A white dress, a white cap. It looks clean.'

'I look like a nurse,' Vasiliki had pointed out with a teasing smile. 'Maybe I'll give the customers some medicine as well as a milkshake.'

The waitresses' uniforms were white short-sleeved dresses with a buttoned belt around the waist. Vasiliki had to admit that it was easy to keep them clean with a soak in Velvet flakes overnight, to take care of the inevitable coffee, tea and tomato sauce stains that often decorated her by the end of the day.

On that particular day, she'd been trying not to think about her blister, but as the hours passed it rubbed and annoyed her more and more. She had slipped out the back to the small staff room, found a chair to sit on, and pushed down her stockings. She covered the throbbing bubble of skin with an adhesive bandage, thinking that the sooner this day ended the better. When she walked back out to the front counter, hobbling a little, Tom Burley had just walked in through the door. He'd taken off his hat and was smoothing down his hair as he looked around.

She recognised him instantly. He looked older, it was true, but he was still the kind of handsome that had made her blush back at Bonegilla. In that instant, she remembered every moment of the night they'd danced at the Tudor Hall, before he'd had to go back to university. She and her mother and her two younger sisters had left Bonegilla before he came back again. She hadn't seen Tom since they'd danced that night. She shook her head to get rid of the pounding in her ears. It was her heartbeat, fast and strong.

Tom had found himself a stool at the counter and was studying the menu with great concentration.

'How's that foot?' Shirley, another waitress and her friend, peered down at Vasiliki's white shoes.

'It is okay. I have a bandage on there.'

'Why don't you go out the back and take a load off, pet? I'll cover you for ten minutes.' Shirley winked. 'Don't tell your uncle, and we've got a deal.'

Vasiliki grabbed Shirley's arm as she passed. 'No, it is all right. I will take this one.' She glanced quickly in Tom's direction.

Her friend looked back over her shoulder, then raised a saucy eyebrow. 'Ooh, the handsome one, you mean?'

Vasiliki's cheeks heated. 'He is … an old friend.'

'If you say so.' Shirley giggled. 'Though judging by the look on your face, pet, you want him to be a new one as well.'

Vasiliki wiped her sweating palms down the front of her uniform. She took a deep breath and walked to the front of the counter, where she stopped and pulled her notepad and pencil from the large pocket on the front of her dress.

She thought hard to make it sound just right. 'What can I help you with today, sir?'

She held her breath. It was definitely Tom Burley. Not a teenager now but a grown-up man in a three-piece suit and a tie. His white shirt looked crisp and he looked important.

He looked up at her. His face lit up. It was a long moment before he spoke. 'Bonegilla,' he said, his voice warm with delight.

'Yes.' She'd smiled, secretly thrilled that he'd remembered her after all this time. 'Hello.'

'Vasiliki.' He said it properly, almost the way it was pronounced in Greek.

And right there, right then, she wanted to prove to him how much she had grown and changed. How Australian she was now. 'Tom Burley,' she replied, slowly, deliberately. 'It's been a long time. How are you today?'

'Well, I'm just fine, thank you very much.' He grinned. 'I had no idea that you were in Melbourne.'

'Yes. My family went from Bonegilla … two years ago. We live in Oakleigh,' she said as she glanced around the milk bar. 'This is the business of my father and my uncle. I work here.'

Tom glanced up at her cap and looked her up and down. There was a hint of colour in his cheeks. 'The uniform is a dead giveaway.'

English was a crazy language. She shook her head. 'What is that? A dead giveaway?'

'It means you are wearing the uniform of people who work here. It was a clue. So I imagine you work here, too.'

Another Australian expression she had to store away and learn. A dead giveaway. She must ask Shirley about it after work.

Tom looked around, taking in the rounded counter, the gleaming silver milkshake cups stacked on the bench along the wall. Above them were signs advertising Peach Melbas and Crushed Lemon Sodas for three shillings each.

'What will you have today?' Vasiliki asked, her pencil poised over her notebook.

'Well, let's see.' Tom lifted the menu and studied it. 'It all looks rather tempting but I think I'll have this sundae here. The Passionfruit Special.'

Vasiliki wrote it down in Greek. 'And something to eat?'

'I think I might like an egg sandwich. Thank you very much, Vasiliki.'

'You are welcome. It won't be long.'

Tom stared at her, as if he was only imagining she was there. He let out a little chuckle. 'I can't believe you've been in Melbourne all this time and I didn't know. I've walked past the milk bar a hundred times and never come in.'

Vasiliki tore off the page from her notepad. 'This must be your lucky day, Mr Tom Burley.'

He took in every detail of her face before settling on her mouth. 'You're deadset right about that.'

Tom came back for lunch every day for a month. Each day he waited at the end of the counter until Vasiliki was free to serve him and they would surreptitiously have a little chat while she took his order. Vasiliki thought he must have spent his whole salary on passionfruit sundaes and egg sandwiches, for he had made a habit of ordering the same thing every day.

At the end of the fourth week, Tom worked up the courage to ask Vasiliki to the pictures. *Love Is A Many-Splendored Thing* with William Holden and Jennifer Jones was playing at the Hoyts Regent. She was so happy, she had said yes before she'd even thought through how she would lie to her parents about it.

After their first date, they spent every Saturday night together. In secret. Shirley had agreed to cover for her, promising to do anything to secure the course of true love between a young man and a young woman.

'And if he's got a friend, make sure to invite me on a double date,' she'd said. Vasiliki didn't know what this double date was but she'd smiled and nodded, which seemed to make Shirley happy.

Vasiliki had told her parents she was having a coffee and dessert after work with Shirley and a few girlfriends, and Shirley had helped her out by leaving at the same time. It was a small lie and a social concession she was able to nego- tiate because she worked almost every day. She wasn't afraid of hard work—she had learned that from her parents—and was pleased to be able to hand over most of her wage to them, for household expenses and for the house they were aiming to buy. Her father worked at the milk bar every day of the week, from early morning until late, and her mother cleaned houses during the day and then came into the milk bar when it was closed to push a mop around the premises and keep it sparkling. And on top of that, her mother ran the house and cared for Vasiliki and her two brothers. On the weekends, she cooked meals for people at church. Vasi- liki figured that her parents hadn't had a day off in two years.

She was very careful with her own money, holding back just enough to buy herself something special every now and then, a pretty new dress or perhaps some lipstick and a new scarf. When they went out on a date, Tom paid for every- thing. He was a good, kind man. He'd finished his univer- sity study the year before and was working in a small legal firm in the city. Vasiliki thought how lucky he was not to have to work on Saturdays or Sundays.

Tom looked up at the clocks above Flinders Street Station.

'The night is young,' he said. 'And I've an idea, Vasiliki.' His brown-eyed gaze drifted back to her, hesitating on her eyes before drifting down to her Elizabeth Taylor–red lips. 'Why don't we catch the tram down to St Kilda and have a bite to eat in Acland Street?'

'Yes. I like that,' she said. Tom held out an arm to indicate she should walk with him, and they ambled slowly towards the tram stop.

'Tom,' Vasiliki said. They stopped and waited for the traffic lights to change. 'There is something I ask you.'

'What's that?' he asked breezily.

'From today, you must call me "Vicki".'

Tom looked perplexed. 'Why on earth would you want me to do that?'

She shrugged, clutched the handle of her handbag with both hands and swung it from side to side. 'The girls at the milk bar. They help me with my English. They are very nice. They say that Vasiliki is too hard. They call me Vicki now. I like it.'

'But that's not your real name.'

The lights turned red, the cars stopped and they stepped off the footpath onto the street. 'Tom is not your name,' she answered, indignant. 'You are Thomas but we say Tom. It's the same.'

He chuckled, bumped an arm against her shoulder. 'I can't believe your parents will think of it that way.'

She so wanted to be brave in front of Tom. She so wanted him to think that she was free to make these decisions for herself. That there might be a future for them if they were both willing to fight for it. 'They always want me to be Greek. They will always call me Vasiliki. But I live in Australia now.'

How could Tom ever understand what she meant, this desire to fit in, to be something she was not. She knew a new name wouldn't stop people staring at her hair, which became frizzy when it rained, or her olive skin, and her dark eyes and her thick eyebrows. But she could hope, couldn't she? She had been trying so hard to be like the British-Australian girls she worked with in the milk bar. They had so many freedoms compared with her. Their families didn't seem to care who they dated, or so it seemed to Vasiliki. Perhaps if she were more Australian, she might be the kind of girl that an Australian boy might fall in love with. An Australian boy like Tom. If she were more like an Australian girl, he would propose to her on one knee right in front of the clocks and no one would laugh or stare but applaud instead, and they would get married and live in a nice house and have children called Susan and David and she would be a good mother. Tom had a good job and she could be a good wife. She could cook and clean and would learn to prepare the kind of food Australian people liked: chops and mashed potato and corned beef. Perhaps one day, if she were Australian enough, Tom would introduce her to his parents.

Would she ever live in a world where she could introduce Tom to hers?

That was too much to think about. Their relationship was still a secret to everyone, even Frances. That had been the hardest thing. It felt like a betrayal of her dear friend, but Tom had insisted.

'Frances will tell someone, Vasiliki. She'll write to Iliana or Elizabeta, I know it. You all write letters to each other all the time with news and snippets of what you're up to. Frances has told me about the photos. She won't be able to help herself. You know how girls like to gossip. She'll let the cat out of the bag, I know she will. And then my mother and father will find out and it will become difficult to explain. You can't tell her.'

Let the cat out of the bag. In Greek, people said it was to be bursting with a secret. *Skao to mistiko*. She didn't want to burst her secret about Tom. She wanted to hold it—and him—in her hand and her heart and treasure every moment they had together. Once the secret was out in the open, it would have to end. If Tom knew it, he had never admitted it to her, and she had never spoken the truth of her reality to him.

The tram rocked from side to side all the way to St Kilda. The boy she loved was smiling at her. Vasiliki didn't care what they ate for dinner. She was with Tom. Nothing else mattered.

Chapter Twenty-one

One week and one day after she'd had dinner with Tom on Acland Street in St Kilda wearing her new dress and her new red lipstick, which they'd managed to smudge walking on the beach when the sun had set, it drizzled all the way to church on a cold April Sunday.

Vasiliki collapsed her umbrella, shrugged off her coat and followed her parents inside. She kissed the icons, lit a candle for her grandparents back in the village, listened to Father Spiros, took communion and did not think about anything or anyone but Tom the entire time. Her Tom, her beloved Tom, who couldn't seem to let go of her hand at Flinders Street Station when she had to get on the Oakleigh train. Her Tom, who had waited on the platform and waved as the carriages had pulled away.

She had opened her heart to Tom and she wanted to hold him there forever.

When the service ended, her mother took her arm and led her outside to the bottom of the steps, where her father was talking animatedly to her uncle Theodorous and another man, a stranger to her.

As she and her mother approached, her father turned to her with a proud expression and a puffed-up chest. 'Ah, Vasiliki.' He reached out for her and she went to him. She felt his protective hand in the space between her shoulderblades.

'This man is Stelios Papadopoulos,' he announced. 'Stelios, this is my first daughter, Vasiliki.'

The man Stelios stepped forwards and held out his hand politely. Vasiliki was wearing white gloves and was glad of them because she didn't want to feel another man's skin on her fingertips. Tom was still there, would always be there.

'Hello. I am pleased to meet you,' she said, in English, on purpose. Her mother jabbed her in the side with an elbow.

'Stelios is the brother of your uncle Theodorous's best friend,' her father told her, lifting his chin. 'He knows the family from back in the village. He has been in America working in a cafe with his cousins, in ... where is it?'

'Maryland. Delaware,' Stelios replied.

'Maryland, Delaware,' her mother repeated.

'Hello, Vasiliki,' Stelios said in English. She studied his face. He looked Greek and sounded Greek. If he'd been in America, shouldn't he sound like William Holden or Cary Grant?

'Delaware. Yes,' her father said. 'He will come and work in the milk bar.'

'Oh,' Vasiliki said.

'Vasiliki works there too,' her father announced. 'She is a waitress. She serves the customers. She is as good as any of those Australian girls.'

'I hear it's a good business,' Stelios said, his attention on Vasiliki and not on her father, who had taken a step back, no doubt to observe them better.

Vasiliki sized him up. He was only slightly taller than she was, with a pleasant enough face and a strong chin. In the middle of it was a dimple. He seemed friendly. It would be good to have someone else in the milk bar to help her father and her uncle. They worked too hard as it was, and maybe soon they would hire someone else to give her mother a break from the seven days a week she too was doing.

'It's a busy place,' Vasiliki said. 'Lots of customers. Australian people like the sandwiches and cups of tea.'

Stelios smiled. 'The Americans too, but they drink coffee, not so much tea.'

Vasiliki gave him a little smile. She'd served enough milky tea to last her a lifetime.

Her father brought his hands together in a loud clap. 'Vasiliki, you like him. That is good. It has all been arranged by our two families.'

Vasiliki's head jerked to her father. Her mother's grip became tighter on her arm. The more Vasiliki shivered the stronger her mother's hold became.

And before her father even said the words, she knew. This man, Stelios, was her future. She had been living an Australian dream for almost three years but now she was Greek again and even more importantly, a Greek daughter with obligations to her family and her parents and everyone in this church and the whole community and, come to think of it, every single relative back in Greece, too.

Her mother was whispering something in her ear. 'He is a good man, Vasiliki. Handsome.'

Tom is a good man, too. And he's handsome and he loves me. She could never tell them. Not now. Their shame would be her shame, too.

Her father pumped Stelios's hand. 'You will marry Vasiliki. Good. This is very good.'

Stelios smiled at her father and then glanced at her. She tried to make sense of his face but he was becoming smaller and smaller. Then her father shrunk too and she no longer felt her mother's fingers on her arm, digging in, pinning her to the spot. Her mother knew. Her mother knew that her daughter was fighting the instinct to run.

She saw this strange man and her family as if through the end of a long camera lens. They were from somewhere else, from another place and another time. The words they were saying were jumbled and muffled and all she could hear was the beat of her pulse in her ears like a crashing, rhythmic cymbal.

She was being traded like a goat. All this time in Australia had changed nothing. What had she expected? She may as well have been back in the village before the war instead of here in Melbourne in 1956.

What young man new to Australia could resist an offer like that? Here is a job for you, young man, if you marry my daughter.

'Stelios is coming to our house for lunch today,' her father announced. There was pride and happiness in his voice at the match he and his brother had made. 'You will have the chance to talk more together. Now, we will go.'

Vasiliki felt dizzy and sick. She was to marry this man and had no power to disobey her father about it. All she could do was say, 'Yes, *Baba*,' but something inside her was trying to rebel. It tasted bitter in her throat and it pounded in her chest but she swallowed it down, buried it deep in the pit of her stomach.

Her father slipped an arm around Stelios's shoulder and the two men walked ahead with Uncle Theodorous. The men had made a deal.

How she could she argue after all the sacrifices her parents had made for her? They had left their families and friends back in Greece and now, in Australia, they had worked hard from almost the moment they had arrived. They lived in a house with a toilet inside and running water and enough rooms for Vasiliki to have her own. They had a car and good jobs and money in the bank. Vasiliki was grateful for all of it. She was grateful to her family and would honour them. She knew in that moment that her hopes of being with Tom, living a completely different life, had been a cruel trick she had played on herself. A life with Tom would never have been possible. Her family would never have allowed it, nor would his. She would never be able to show her face in this church or any other if she married someone who wasn't Greek Orthodox. She could never have the blessing of her family for her marriage if she wed someone they didn't approve of. And she would need their blessing to be truly happy. She would always need her family around her, would always need to be part of her culture and her community, especially in a new country.

In her heart of hearts, she knew. Tom was not Greek and that was it.

Her mother slipped an arm through Vasiliki's. She was jolted back into the moment, the cold wind at the back of her neck and the pressure of her mother's arm on hers.

'Isn't he handsome?' her mother whispered. 'And he's been in America. His English is very good. He's very prosperous. Your father and your uncle think that one day he can buy the milk bar. You will have a good future with him, Vasiliki. And such beautiful children.'

The words fell automatically from her lips. 'Yes, *Mamou*.'

Her mother kissed her cheek. 'It will be a good marriage. You'll see.'

It didn't escape Vasiliki's attention that Stelios was given the seat at the head of the table for lunch. The small green laminate table in the middle of the kitchen was simple, but the food Vasiliki's mother had prepared was anything but. As Vasiliki helped her mother, pulling dishes from the oven, taking salad from the fridge, setting plates and serving spoons for their guest, she slipped back into her old world. Her parents' world. Each day, she lived in Australia, talking to and serving Australians, laughing at the jokes she was beginning to understand. Each Saturday night, she was the girl with the Australian boyfriend, sitting at the pictures, free.

But at home, and each evening, she was tugged backwards. There were no ham sandwiches at this table or steak and eggs or fish and chips. At her family's table, there was lamb baked with garlic and oregano. Cabbage rolls stuffed with rice. Spinach and beans drizzled with olive oil and lemon juice. Olives. Fetta cheese in chunky cubes. Yoghurt. Pastries brittle and sweet and filled with crushed nuts or custard so creamy it coated your tongue when you ate it.

Vasiliki sat down at the table and ate politely, listening to her father ask Stelios about America and the cafes there.

This man was to be her husband, the handsome man with the dimple. It wasn't his fault that she looked at him and felt nothing. He was polite with her parents. When he'd arrived, he'd brought her a bunch of flowers and some chocolates that he'd handed over complete with a compliment to her mother about her clean home. He spent lunch shooting her surreptitious glances across the table, as if he was trying to figure out if she was beautiful or not.

Tom always made her feel beautiful.

Vasiliki was only able to raise a polite smile when Stelios left. It was arranged. She would see him at church the next Sunday and he would come every Sunday for lunch until they were married in six weeks.

A June wedding to a man who wasn't Tom Burley.

A good girl would never go against her family. A girl who did would bring shame on them. She knew that in the deepest marrow of her bones. Her family would win.

Chapter Twenty-two

The next week passed in a blur for Vasiliki. She went to work and put on her best smile for her customers. Her feet ached the same after being on them all day. Her back continued to twinge when she lifted stacks of dishes to put away on the high shelves behind the counter. Shirley tried to make her laugh and her uncle Theodorous kept a close eye on his waitresses from the kitchen.

But nothing else was the same. There was a clock ticking for Vasiliki and she felt each minute contract and shrink until it felt as if her life was about to disappear.

On Monday she slipped out the back when she saw Tom push through the front doors. She simply couldn't take his order today. It would be a sandwich and Passionfruit Special, the same as every other day. It would be too sad to pretend his world hadn't changed too.

Vasiliki sat on a bread crate in the storeroom at the back of the milk bar and stared at her fingernails. She kept them short and neat, scrupulously clean for her customers just as her uncle had demanded. Once she was married and not working anymore, she could let them get as long as she liked. Perhaps she would even paint them red.

The door opened. It was Shirley, curious.

'What's got your goat?' She sidled up alongside her friend, bumping Vasiliki's shoulder with her hip. 'You all right, Vicki?'

Vasiliki looked up at her friend. 'I get married,' she said quietly. Shirley became fuzzy and Vasiliki wiped her eyes.

Shirley didn't say anything for a moment. Then she kneeled down to look Vasiliki in the eye. 'They don't look like tears of unbridled joy, pet.'

'What does that mean? I don't understand.'

Shirley laid a comforting hand on Vasiliki's knee. 'What that means is … you don't look all that happy about it.'

'My family found this man. Stelios Papadopoulos. He is coming to work here in the milk bar. We are marriage in June.'

Shirley huffed. 'Crikey, you don't wait, do you? You bloody Greeks. All this arranged marriage nonsense. You're in Australia now. You and your family and all the other bloody Greeks have to learn to do things the Australian way. Look at me. I can marry whoever I damn well please.' Shirley thought on it a moment. 'Well, as long as he's not a Catholic. Or a dago.' She rolled her eyes. 'Fathers, hey? I reckon they're all the same, no matter where they bloody well come from.' She leaned closer, lowered her voice. 'You don't want to marry this bloke, do you?'

Could she put it in words that Shirley would understand? 'It is the Greek way. I must honour my family.'

'What does your mum say, hey? Surely she'd want you to marry someone who floats your boat. For love, I mean.'

'She didn't know my father when they married. She says I will love this man.'

Shirley sighed sympathetically. 'But not like you love your Tom, hey pet?'

Vasiliki covered her quivering lips with a hand.

'Don't worry, Vicki. You stay here. I'll go and tell your Tom that you've gone home with a mighty headache. Maybe you'll feel up to seeing him tomorrow.'

It was a full five days before Vasiliki was able to even think about seeing Tom. He had come in at his usual time, just after midday, and taken up his regular spot at the end of a row of hungry customers waiting on their black vinyl upholstered swivel stools at the counter.

She picked up a menu and walked to him. He was leaning over the counter, clasping his hands together, his shoulders hunched. When she was closer, she could see his lovely face was drawn and his caramel eyes were pale and unsmiling. The moment he noticed her approaching he got to his feet.

'Vasiliki. Where on earth have you been? I haven't seen you all week. I've been worried sick. Are you all right? Is everything okay?' He leaned over the counter, struggling to keep his voice low.

'I am good. What can I get you today?' She struggled to keep her eyes on her notepad, so she focussed on her lead pencil poised over the white of the paper.

'You can get me an explanation, that's what.' She looked at him. He wasn't angry. He was sad and his eyes glistened. She had spent all week trying to think about how to tell him. He was owed an explanation at the very least. She stared at her notepad, her pencil poised above it, as if their conversation was about lunch.

'Saturday. The clocks,' she whispered. 'Can we meet there?'

He leaned in. 'Of course we can. What's the matter, Vasiliki?'

'Can you get a car to drive?'

His brow furrowed. 'A car?'

'Yes. We need to drive somewhere.' She scribbled nonsense on the page.

'You know I don't have a car. What's this all about?'

She glanced around quickly, looking for the prying eyes of her father or Uncle Theodorous. 'Please, Tom.'

He thought on it. 'I can perhaps borrow my friend Nigel's.'

'Pick me up on the corner of Little Bourke Street. I will wait there.'

'All right,' Tom finally answered.

Vasiliki nodded. She couldn't meet his eyes. Tom tossed his hat on his head and abruptly left. His spot was soon filled with another customer who'd been waiting in the queue at the end of the counter.

She forced a smile and concentrated on her accent. 'Good afternoon. What can I get for you today?'

Tom pushed through the front door of the milk bar then stopped and turned and looked back at her through the gleaming front window. Something inside her pulled itself closed.

She wasn't Elizabeth Taylor. Her Hollywood dream of a marriage to Tom was over.

The next evening, Tom picked up Vasiliki in Little Bourke Street, as arranged, and they drove down to St Kilda. They motored past Luna Park, ignoring the temptation to walk through Mr Moon's mouth and see the amusements. Vasiliki had heard about the Ghost Train and had always been too scared of it to go in and ride it. Tom continued towards Brighton, and where there was a quiet spot by a park, Vasiliki asked him to pull over.

He did as she asked and turned off the engine of his friend Nigel's Ford.

It was quiet, exactly how she wanted it to be. The street-lights were dim and the streets were empty of people and if she closed her eyes a little it was just her and Tom and no one else in the entire world.

Tom had been quiet, nervous, not saying anything during their drive but now, in the cold quiet of the car, the words burst out of him. He turned to her, resting his arm behind her on the bench seat. 'Now will you tell me what's been going on, Vasiliki? You've had me damn well worried. All this cloak and dagger stuff about tonight.'

Vasiliki didn't know what he meant by coats and daggers but she was too sick with nerves to ask for an explanation of yet another strange expression. She didn't want to feel stupid tonight, any more than she did already. Her fingers twisted the handle of her black velvet handbag. 'There is something to tell you.'

Tom stiffened. 'Oh, heavens, Vasiliki. You didn't spill the beans to Frances, did you?'

'No, no. I do not tell Frances.' There was so much to say and it was important, now more than ever, to find the right words, the words that wouldn't hurt Tom or shock him. 'My family have a man I must marry.'

The silence felt long and empty. Vasiliki's breath clouded in the cold air.

'What on earth are you talking about?'

She breathed deep. 'It is a man. He is Greek.'

Tom stared past the dash and through the front window into the dark distance. 'Hold on just a minute. Are you telling me you have another boyfriend?'

'No, it's not like that.' She put a hand on his thigh, felt the muscles tense under her touch. 'Last weekend, Sunday. At church. My father told me this man is the one I will marry. Only one week, Tom. I don't know him.'

'Is this one of those … proxy marriages?'

'I must do what my family wants me to do.'

'But this is Australia, not Greece.'

'But I am Greek. My family is Greek.'

Tom took his arm from the back of the seat and began to fidget, his leg dancing up and down under her hand. 'You can't be auctioned off to some bloke you've never met just because he's Greek. What do these things matter these days? It's 1956. Things are different now, Vasiliki. Your family can't do this to you. You've got to tell them you can't marry him.'

'I cannot say no to my family.'

'You bloody well can say no.' He twisted towards her, gripped her fingers in his. 'I'll come with you to talk to your parents. I'll tell them they can't do this.'

'No, Tom, no.' Vasiliki turned away to the window.

'I've been so stupid too. Thinking this is something we should hide. Why don't we run away to Sydney? I'm sure I could get work up there. There must be hundreds of jobs for a junior lawyer. You could come and …' He turned to her, cupping her cheeks with his hands and looking lovingly into her eyes. 'We can get married, Vasiliki. No family. Just you and me. We can make a life together.'

Vasiliki squeezed her eyes closed. Tom would never understand the bonds of her family, of honour and tradition. She could no more go against the wishes of her mother and father than she could fly to the moon. And it seemed he couldn't either. They had both been big on words and promises but neither of them were brave enough to break the rules.

'No.' It was all she could say.

He took his hands away. There was silence in the car. A man in a flat cap rode past on an old bicycle, so slowly Vasiliki wondered how he hadn't fallen over already, his shoulders dipping from side to side with every revolution of the pedals. She didn't know what else to say to help Tom understand.

He slammed his hand on the steering wheel and grunted. 'This is all my fault. I should never have asked you to hide what we have. I was only thinking of me and what my father would say. For all his talk at Bonegilla, I didn't think … damn it, Vasiliki. I should have been brave and told them. Especially Frances. I should be the one to marry you. I should have been the one to ask you, hang the consequences. I love you, Vasiliki.'

She hadn't heard the words from him before but she heard the truth in them. 'And I love you, Tom.'

He let out a laugh, but it was angry. 'I've loved you since the first time I met you, at Bonegilla, when Frances came home from hospital, after she was stupid enough to get hit on the head during that soccer game. You and your girl-friends came with flowers.'

'Yes. I remember.' Vasiliki's eyes filled with tears. Tom passed her the handkerchief from the pocket inside his suit. She looked down at it. The initials *T.B.* were embroidered in one corner in navy.

'Your parents, just off the boat. They were never going to accept a chap like me, were they?'

'You are not Greek. And your parents, they would not like a Greek girl.'

Tom shook his head. 'They don't even want me to marry a Catholic. That's been obvious since I can remember. But if it didn't matter, if your family didn't matter and mine didn't either, would you have said yes, Vasiliki?'

She turned to him, reached for the lapels of his suit jacket and pulled him closer. This was to be the last time she would ever see Tom Burley and she needed every detail. The night, the quiet, the warm vinyl of the car seats, the smell of Bryl-creem in his hair, the coarse weave of his suit. The feel of his lips on hers and the strength in the arms that were now crushing her, pulling her in so tight she felt his heart pound-ing in time with hers.

And then kissing wasn't enough. Vasiliki pulled back from him. Their hot breath had fogged the car windows, as if they were together in a cloud. There was one more thing she wanted from Tom before they said goodbye. There was one thing she wanted to share with someone she loved. She knew the words in English but was too shy to say them, so she reached for the hem of her skirt, gathered the fabric of her petticoat and pulled both of them up. She slipped her hands underneath and lifted her bottom, tugging off her rayon panties. She dropped them by her shoes and searched his face.

Tom was speechless. His fingers swept up her bare thigh and then inched higher, and she threw her head back, pressing it on the back of the bench seat while his fingers explored her.

'Please, Tom,' she said. 'One time.' She clambered over the front seat into the back and Tom followed, whispering in her ear how much he loved her while they made love for the first and last time.

On 16 June, 1956, Vasiliki married Stelios Papadopoulos at the Greek Orthodox church in East Melbourne. As was the tradition, the only one to speak during the entire ceremony was the priest. The lace on Vasiliki's beautiful A-line wedding gown that her parents had bought from Myer in Bourke Street scratched at her the whole day. Her family and all their friends, old ones from the village and new ones from Australia, came. Vasiliki was allowed to invite one friend, and it was Shirley from the Majestic. She didn't want the Bonegilla girls there. She didn't want them to see the wedding for the lie it was, and the idea of sharing the day with Frances—Tom's sister—would have been too much to bear. She distracted herself with thoughts of the wedding gifts: dinnerware and silverware and linen tablecloths and sheets for the bed. Dishes and crystal glasses and an elaborate punch bowl decorated with large purple flowers. Wedding gifts for a wedding she hadn't wanted.

Weeks later, she finally summoned the courage to write to Frances and Iliana and Elizabeta, sharing the news that she was Vicki Papadopoulos now. She had slipped in each envelope a photo of her in her scratchy wedding dress with her arm slipped in Stelios's elbow. It was easier than having them there in person to see her marry a man she didn't love.

She and Steve—for Stelios had decided to simplify his name too—moved into a house next door to her parents in Oakleigh. That had been the biggest surprise of all. She hadn't known until the day of the wedding that they had bought it for her, but by then she was immune to being shocked about the decisions they made for their daughter's life. This was her future. Her parents had chosen her friends, her husband, her house and even her wedding dress. She was a piece they moved around from place to place on a chess board. They had created a new life for her in Australia but it was a closed circle: her husband, her home, her parents, the milk bar.

But there was one thing Vasiliki had created for herself.

When she walked down the aisle, she was already pregnant.

She would never have the life she wanted for herself, but she would forever have a part of Tom with her.

Chapter Twenty-three

Elizabeta sat on the edge of her bed, rubbing her aching feet, from ball to heel and back.

The ten-minute walk home from the train station always irritated her already sore feet and the second she arrived home she would slip off her shoes. She would never complain to her parents about her sore feet when her father worked so hard, so this ten minutes in her room after work, alone, was the time in which she rested, cleared her head of the demands of her boss and her customers and thought about dinner. She knew her mother would be waiting for her in the kitchen, for that little extra help, so she slid her feet into a pair of soft slippers and went out to say hello.

'What can I do, *Mutti*?' Elizabeta kissed her mother's cheek and then reached for the apron hanging on a hook on the door leading to the laundry.

'Salad,' her mother said. Elizabeta slipped the apron over her neck and then took the lettuce from the fridge, and the salt and pepper and vinegar from the cupboard. They finished preparing the meal together. Peeling potatoes. Making salad. Chopping cabbage. Elizabeta and her father worked and Elizabeta and her mother kept their home. That was the routine they had settled into in their new house in Clark Street in Woodville, a dozen stops on the train from the city where Elizabeta worked.

It was only half an hour before Elizabeta set a bowl of steaming spätzle on the small dining table that sat in the middle of the kitchen.

'How was your work at the cafe today?' Jozef asked. He was wearing a clean shirt and trousers, and his hair was wet and slicked back as if he'd smoothed Brylcreem through it. He smelled of Old Spice and soap; of a familiar evening routine that Elizabeta cherished. He always showered when he got home from the factory to wash away the grease and the dirt from his hands.

'It was very busy,' Elizabeta replied. She sat down opposite her father, her mother in between them at the end of the table, and passed her father the serving spoon.

Under the table, Elizabeta kicked off a slipper and rubbed her stockinged feet, the arch of her left on the sole of her right, and then reversed. 'One man came in today and ate four pieces of Pflaumenstreusel.'

'What did he want with four pieces?' Jozef asked, his eyebrows jumping up into the creases in his tanned forehead.

'It's very delicious,' Elizabeta replied. 'He ordered one piece, sat down at the counter and ate it in four bites.

And then he said it was better than his own mother in Dusseldorf used to make. So he had three more!'

Elizabeta looked to her mother at the head of the table. Berta looked up with a forced smile, as if she knew what was expected of her and she was doing her best to oblige. Had she seen her mother happy since Bonegilla? Elizabeta's heart shrank at the realisation that she hadn't. Places you can leave, but memories come too, no matter where you go.

'Four pieces.' Jozef howled with laughter as he loaded his plate. He picked up a spoon—he always ate with a dessert spoon and a fork—and scooped up the slippery noodles. His spoon was US military issue, souvenired from the post-war years in Germany when he'd worked on a base. The handle was oval shaped at the end with an oval cut out of it. Just below the cut-out was stamped *U.S.* When soldiers went home to the States after their tours of duty, they dumped everything. Elizabeta's father had been too used to having nothing to let such useful things go to waste. It had no value to anyone but it was so special to him that he'd insisted it come to Australia in the wooden chest with their rest of their most valued possessions. A Bible. A set of almost brand-new saucepans. Some photos from their time in Germany. Their best clothes.

They sat in silence for the rest of their meal, Elizabeta slowly chewing on her chop bone. Perhaps it was because Berta never seemed to have much to say and Elizabeta talked all day to her work colleagues or her customers, because Jozef was after relief from the grinding noise of the factory, that this silence was a reprieve for all of them. Elizabeta always thought of Luisa during those quiet meal times, wondering what she might look like now, two years older, if she had lived. Would she would have enjoyed going to the local school, just a short walking distance away? Would she have liked having her own bedroom with a view over the back yard? Would her parents have bought her the dog she had so desperately wanted?

Elizabeta missed brushing Luisa's hair and forming it into long, perfect plaits, so thin at the end there was not more than a few thin strands, and then looping them up and fastening them. 'Circles,' Luisa had called it. She'd always wanted her plaits in circles. Elizabeta missed her funny laugh and the way she tried to skip along, getting it wrong, losing her rhythm, stopping and starting again with great concentration. Luisa would always be happy and young in Elizabeta's memory. Always perfect. She chose not to remember her sister as sick, moaning, incoherent, pale. Elizabeta had developed a strength for blocking out those memories, the kind that tore at her, and those of her sister were among the most haunting.

It was a huge house for three people. Elizabeta still couldn't fathom how much bigger it was than their Bonegilla hut, or the second one at the Woodside holding camp in the Adelaide Hills. They'd lived there a month before they'd found a suitable rental home. The sandstone bungalow had three bedrooms, a living room, a bathroom with a bath, and a kitchen with enough room for the table in the middle. The toilet was outside by the side fence and Elizabeta was still scared of the spiders with the long fine legs that inhabited it. There was a twin cement laundry tub in an asbestos room set off the back veranda. They had a wringer washing machine with rollers and it squeezed and creased their clothes into thick pancakes. The large backyard was a square of lawn and a Hills Hoist and vegetables: capsicums, chillies and potatoes. An old lemon tree gave them abundant fruit and a peach tree by the back fence yielded the sweetest peaches. Her father had built a chicken coop with scrap wood he'd got from the factory and second-hand sheets of galvanised iron. The chickens scratched around the backyard, eating the kitchen scraps, and laying more eggs than Berta would ever need for the cakes and noodles she made.

Elizabeta had a comfortable bed, with bedsprings that didn't squeak, and a dark-stained wooden wardrobe with a hat drawer and more than enough space to hang her clothes. There was a dresser with two small drawers and two big ones underneath with a large framed mirror attached to it, on which she'd set out her special things. The wooden box from Germany with Luisa's peg doll inside it. A matching hairbrush and comb she had bought with her first pay. A two-inch square photo of Luisa's grave in Albury in a small silver frame, a bouquet of flowers on it, which Frances had sent to Elizabeta. Her mother hadn't wanted it on the mantelpiece in the living room.

Her father pushed his plate into the centre of the table. '*Schmeckt gut*, Berta.' He rubbed his stomach and pushed back his chair. He didn't have to tell his wife and his daughter that he was going into the garden. They knew his routine by now. While they washed the dishes and cleaned up, he watered the vegetable garden, tugged at some weeds, smoked a cigarette or two and then came back inside to listen to the radio for a little while before going to bed.

It was a small, quiet life they lived. They had no other family in Australia. There were no aunts or uncles for Elizabeta, or cousins. They hadn't made friends with any neighbours. The family on one side had made an art form of dashing away when Elizabeta or her mother and father were in the front yard. She was sure the young man who lived in the house across the road caught the same train as she did into the city every day, but he'd not once said hello or even smiled.

'Some people just don't like new Australians,' her father had told her. Elizabeta knew that to be true. She saw it in the suspicious looks of strangers when she spoke German to her parents when they were out. It seemed to her that Bonegilla had given her the wrong idea about Australia. People from all those different countries had come here for a new life. They'd all come in their different boats but were all in the same boat at the camp. They'd seen up close what could divide people and turn them against each other and they didn't want that here. They had travelled halfway across the world to get away from that. But Australians were suspicious. How lucky they'd been to be so far from the war. How could Elizabeta make them understand that all her family wanted, all the other people from Bonegilla wanted, was the chance to work and live and be free.

Elizabeta cleared the table, gathered the plates and cutlery and stacked them on the side of the kitchen sink.

'Go and listen to the radio, *Mutti*,' she said and Berta obeyed. A moment later, the sound of strings and a crooner filled the living room. Elizabeta lost herself in the suds as the sink filled. Her neighbours might be unfriendly, but there was one place she felt a part of the country in which they had chosen to live. And it was at work.

It was what Australians called a continental cafe, the kind that served real coffee from ground beans and always had an array of European cakes on display. The Kirschners had been in Australia for twenty years, refugees from another time, and liked employing staff who could speak German. Elizabeta worked Mondays to Saturdays, and on Sundays there was church with her parents. They dressed up for church, more for an outing and a routine than out of belief, her father in the one charcoal grey suit he had brought with him in the trunk from Germany, her mother in a lovely floral dress she'd had for years, with white gloves on her small hands and a hat on her dark brown curls. It was Berta's only excursion during the week. Now that they were settled, she didn't much like to leave the house. Elizabeta wondered if she was scared of seeing the German man again. Elizabeta tried not to think about him, about where he had gone for work and where he was living now. She hoped he was far away. Perhaps in Queensland or Perth.

After dinner, when the dishes were put away and the table wiped clean, Elizabeta found the present she had brought home for her mother and went into the living room to give it to her. Berta was listening to *Blue Hills* but Elizabeta knew she wouldn't understand much of it. Her English was still sparse and what little Elizabeta had tried to teach her was only enough to say hello. It was the sound of the voices she must have found comforting.

'*Mutti?*'

Berta looked up and put her knitting in her lap. '*Ja?*'

'Here. I found this today for you.' Elizabeta handed her mother a slim brown paper bag. Berta pulled a magazine from inside it and smiled. It was quick, but it was a smile, and Elizabeta hung on to it.

'*Heimat Romans*,' Elizabeta said, encouraging her mother to open the cover. 'I know how you like them.' They looked at the cover, with its distinctive red border and a handsome couple kissing within its frame. Elizabeta had discovered the magazine while browsing in a newsagent in Regent Arcade one lunchtime. The magazines were filled with love stories, all in German. Her mother had read every copy Elizabeta had brought home and there was now a pile stacked in the corner of the living room by the radio, so high it toppled over one day when Elizabeta was sweeping around the edges of the rug.

Berta reached for her daughter's hand and kissed the back of it. 'I'll read it tomorrow. Thank you, Elizabeta.'

If her mother didn't want to engage in the world, Elizabeta had taken it upon herself to bring the world to her mother. One romance at a time.

Berta was anxious about it but Elizabeta was excited.

After more than two years in Australia, Elizabeta's parents had finally made some new friends and now they were coming for lunch—the Mullers would be the first guests they'd ever had at their home in Woodville. Jozef had swept the path in the backyard and weeded his vegetable garden. Berta and Elizabeta had spent all of Saturday morning mopping and polishing the floors, shining every surface and picking flowers from the garden to set in little green vases on the mantelpiece in the living room and on the telephone desk in the hallway.

They prepared sauerbraten, stuffed capsicums filled with minced beef and rice, and potato salad. Because the winter sun was shining, they had set up a picnic table in the backyard.

The Mullers had recently arrived in Adelaide. They were German and had also spent time at Bonegilla after they'd arrived in Australia on the boat a couple of months earlier. After meeting at church, Elizabeta's father and *Herr* Muller had become fast friends. Suddenly, there were plans for lunch the next Sunday after church.

'His wife is Carolina and they have two children. Nikolas is twenty-two and there is a little girl, Angelika.'

And when Elizabeta opened the front door to them, the scent of sausage took her back to their house in Germany. Herr Muller was a butcher and he had brought along a gift basket of smallgoods—bratwurst and weisswurst and mettwurst he'd smoked himself in his new Australian backyard.

Berta gasped when she'd spotted the succulent sausages. '*Herr* Muller. This is too kind.'

He smiled and nodded proudly. His cheeks were puffed and red, his smile friendly. 'Just like home, hey?'

'There is nothing like this in Adelaide,' Berta said. And she smiled and Elizabeta held on to that small moment of her mother's happiness before welcoming the Mullers into their home.

After lunch, Elizabeta's father gave *Herr* Muller a walking tour of his vegetable garden, and even dug up some potatoes for the Mullers to take home. Her mother and *Frau* Muller sat at the picnic table, chatting quietly, watching. Elizabeta didn't want to put a name to what she was feeling, seeing her mother look so at peace. Perhaps that was all she needed, to find a friend. Someone who reminded her of home, someone with whom she could speak in a language that was easy, that didn't require effort and confusion and a gnawing feeling of incompetence. Someone who spoke the language of her dreams.

Elizabeta watched as the two women spoke. She had stretched out a blanket on the square of green lawn, neatly trimmed by her father that morning. Nikolas was at her side. Through lunch, she had noticed him looking at her, and she'd looked away, feeling the heat in her cheeks. She had been looked at before by men. At the cafe, on the train, on the street. He seemed different to those men.

'Your sister is …' Elizabeta searched for the word. '*Ein Affe*. What is that in English?'

'A monkey.' Nikolas sipped from his glass of beer, laughing into the foam. He had short brown hair and a barrel chest. His English was as good as hers and she had started their conversation in English to impress him.

'A monkey,' Elizabeta repeated. 'Yes. She is a monkey.'

'I think she is trying to see Germany. Angelika thinks that perhaps if she can climb high enough in the sky, she will see home.'

What was home now, Elizabeta wondered? What was that? What would it feel like to live in a place that was yours, where the streets were familiar, where there were friends and family, in which you understood people's jokes and everything that was said on the radio between the songs? What would it feel like to have the language effortlessly inside your head mirrored by the language you heard on the streets and in the shops? Australia didn't feel like home yet to Elizabeta. But where was this place of her heart? It wasn't back in Europe, either. But here? She still didn't feel settled in or part of anything.

She still felt like a stranger in Australia.

Elizabeta glanced up to Angelika in the limbs of the tree. She was Luisa's age, and the realisation of how alike they were created a wave of fresh memories and grief in Elizabeta. The sadness came at the strangest times. Sometimes when she was serving a customer, she would see a small child standing by her mother. A little girl's smile would make her scared all over again and she would hold it in tight until she was at home that night and sob into her pillow.

'*Pass auf,* Angelika,' Nikolas called out to warn his sister. She waved to her brother and poked out her tongue.

'Why is your sister trying to see Germany? Doesn't she like Australia?' Elizabeta lay back on the rug, her face up to the pale sun.

Nikolas leaned in closer to her and spoke quietly. 'She had a dog in Germany. When we got the papers to say we would come to Australia, we had to give it to the Dorfmanns next door. He was Oskar. She loved him very much.'

Elizabeta held her breath. Luisa had so wanted a dog. Now, when the dog next door barked, she and her parents pretended not to hear it.

Elizabeta and Nikolas watched Angelika. She jumped onto the grass, tumbling happily and then sprang to her feet, running her fingers across the long branches of the willow, as if they were the strings of a harp. Their fathers had finished their tour of the vegetable garden and had walked over to their wives, joining them at the table, and were now drinking beer and talking.

'Elizabeta,' Nikolas said.

'Yes?' She looked over at him.

'Perhaps you would like to go to a dance next weekend?'

'Me? A dance?'

'Yes, you. A dance. I am very good.' He laughed and it warmed her from the inside. 'Would you like to go and dance with me?'

This was the first time Elizabeta had ever been asked to go to a dance. It would be the first time she had danced since Bonegilla. She swallowed the memory, pushing it back deep down where it lived like an ogre.

'Yes. I would like it.'

Chapter Twenty-four

'Why hello, Frances. This is a lovely surprise. You're calling and it's only Thursday.'

Frances Burley stood in the busy hallway of her student digs. The shared phone sat on a small desk and she pressed the black Bakelite handset hard against her ear. 'So tell me, Mum, how's everything at Bonegilla?'

'You know the routine here. People come and go. Your father is in Canberra this week, so I'm all by myself. It's not the same here without you, you know.'

They had developed a routine since Frances had begun studying at Sydney Teachers College: she would call every Sunday night and the conversation would include the inevitable questions about the food ('Are you eating enough?'), her studies ('You're not finding the subjects too hard?') and whether they needed to put any extra money in her account. She was proud of the fact that she had never overspent her allowance. Eighteen-year-old Frances Burley was too careful to ever be so careless.

It was the kind of chitchat with her parents that Frances had missed terribly since she'd moved away from them. She was in her second year of teachers' college and she was living in the student digs with loads of boarders from the bush who only went home in the holidays and spent most of their time having too much fun or, like her, missing home too much. Her life was very different now than it had been at Bonegilla. There were no exotic languages spoken and no cultural differences to learn more about. It was just as well she hadn't lugged her atlas all the way to Sydney for she didn't need to consult it to find out where her fellow students were from. They were from Tamworth and Coonabarabran and Orange and Wagga Wagga, not Greece or Italy or Germany or Poland or Lithuania.

When she had announced to her parents that she had decided to become a teacher, they weren't surprised by her choice, although her mother had tried to convince her to specialise in home economics rather than languages.

'Languages? Everyone coming here will need to learn English, darling, not French and Italian. Yet every girl needs to know how to cook. You'll have a good job until you get married if you can teach home economics.'

Some of her fellow students at the teachers' college shared the same view, although they made their opinions known in a less sophisticated way.

'What's the point, Frances?' one young man had memorably pointed out to her. Thommo was from Bathurst and had never met anyone who wasn't born in New South Wales. 'All the reffos and the wogs should learn to speak English.

That's how they'll get on in Australia. Why should we learn to speak their lingo?'

No one—not even her mother—seemed to understand that learning a language meant so much more than being able to ask what was on a restaurant menu for lunch. If she could speak the words of other cultures, she would have a window into those worlds, those exotic and foreign places she'd studied in her atlas since she was a child. She'd had a taste of the world at Bonegilla and it had lit a fire in her to one day see it all for herself. She imagined herself staring up at the Eiffel Tower and into the blue summer skies over Paris. Touching the stone of the arched entrances to the Colosseum in Rome. Hearing Big Ben sound and touring the Tower of London.

'How's the weather in Sydney, Frances?'

'It's been warm and sunny today, Mum. Just lovely.' Frances hadn't called her mother to talk about the weather, though. She had disrupted their routine because there was some news she had to share with her parents but she wasn't sure how to broach it. 'Mum. The reason I'm calling on a Thursday is that there's something I need to tell you. It's about Tom.'

'What's the latest with that brother of yours?' Frances heard the smile in her mother's voice.

'A letter came from him today. Someone had slipped it under my door and I found it when I got back from lectures.'

Her mother harrumphed. 'A letter? Well, you're lucky indeed. It's been months since he's written to your father and me. Come to think of it, perhaps even longer than that.'

Frances sighed. Damn her brother for giving her the responsibility of breaking the news. 'Mum, it seems that Tom is off to London.'

There was silence from Bonegilla. 'I beg your pardon?'

'I'm a little flummoxed, too. He wrote that he's booked his passage with P&O and he leaves in two weeks.'

'Two weeks? He hasn't breathed a word to me. Or your father. What on earth is all this about?'

'I don't really know.' Frances felt a responsibility to lighten the mood. She tried to sound jolly. 'Just think. In eight weeks he'll be in London. Perhaps he can pop in to Buckingham Palace and have a cup of tea with the Queen and Prince Phillip.'

Her mother huffed indignantly. 'What else did he tell you about this plan? He has his career to think about. He's in a good firm. He has the brains and the drive to go places if he puts his mind to it. Your father thinks he might even make the Supreme Court one day.'

'He didn't tell me much of anything else. I must admit to not having heard from him lately.'

'Nor I. Oh, goodness me. I'll have to call your father. Will you ring on Sunday?'

'Of course I will, Mum.'

'We'll talk then. Bye, darling.'

Frances hung up the handset and trudged back to her room, flopping down on her familiar watermelon chenille bedspread and staring at the ceiling. She felt more than a pang of envy at Tom's adventure. She turned over and cupped her chin in her hands. It wouldn't be long now, she reminded herself, and she too could have her own. Once she was qualified as a teacher and was able to save up enough money, she would begin her own adventure. With Tom in London, she would have somewhere to stay at least. That thought cheered her. And from there? Paris and Rome, just as she'd promised herself. And perhaps Morocco and Egypt, too.

It wouldn't be long now.

A month later, in early July, Frances received another letter from Melbourne. Vasiliki had written with news of her marriage and details of her new address. Once she'd recovered from the shock of her friend being married at such a young age, Frances meticulously recorded Vasiliki's new details in the notebook she'd carried with her since Bonegilla. She noted that all that had changed about Vasiliki's address in Oakleigh was the street number. She had written down every detail of her friends' whereabouts, from immigration hostels to rental homes to homes of their own. There were workplaces and now, the first marriage. It was a big country and it would be easy to lose people if one didn't take care not to.

There was a photo and as Frances studied it, bringing it closer to her eyes to make out the detail of Vasiliki's wedding dress, she tried to tamp down the little pang of hurt at not having been invited. The only wedding she had ever been to was her cousin Betty's and she'd been eight years old and had been asked to be a flower girl. Betty's husband had been sent home from the war after being injured in Singapore and they'd married as soon as he'd been released from hospital. Perhaps the Greeks only invited other Greeks to their weddings. Maybe that was their tradition.

And wasn't eighteen too young to be married, anyway? Was that a Greek tradition too? She and the Bonegilla girls had talked once about weddings when they were together at the camp, but they'd brushed it off. Vasiliki had been adamant that she didn't want to get married yet, hadn't she? Frances thought on that for a moment. One of the other teaching students in her French class, a girl from Bourke, had left after only six months and gone home to Manildra to marry a farmer. She was just eighteen as well. Maybe it wasn't just the Greeks after all. She couldn't imagine that for herself, walking down an aisle on her father's arm wearing a big white dress and then having a husband and children to look after. Perhaps if these girls were older, twenty-one maybe, it would be more understandable. That was a much more sensible age to marry, Frances thought.

She grabbed her pillow and covered her face.

Oh, what did she know about boys and men, about marriage, anyway?

She screamed silently into the linen, pressing her face more deeply into the pillow to muffle the sound.

Why, oh why, was she still in love with Massimo?

She screamed into the pillow for him and at the ridiculous longing she'd carried since Bonegilla. When Iliana and her family had left, at such short notice that it seemed to happen in a day, she'd cried for her friend, to be sure, but she'd also wept for him. Standing at the front gate of the camp, Frances had watched the Agnoli family climb onto the bus. Giuseppe, Agata, the young boys Stefano and Giovani. Iliana had held back and clutched Frances as she'd said goodbye, crying as she'd accepted Frances's gift of one of the books they'd used for their English lessons before running to the bus in tears. Massimo had been the last to board. He had come to her to shake her hand and he'd held it longer, tighter than Frances had expected. She had never wanted him to let go. Then he'd slipped a hand into his pocket and pressed something into her hand. It was a coin, with Italian words on it. Then he'd turned and was gone too. She'd clutched it in her palm until she'd gone to bed that night, willing the warmth from his hand to remain enclosed in her fist.

The coin was in her jewellery box sitting on the chest of drawers in her room at the college. When she finally made it to Rome, that was one coin she would never throw in the Trevi Fountain. In all the letters she had written, she had never asked Iliana about Massimo, and Iliana had offered no news of him in her replies.

He was her secret.

She was eighteen and had never even been kissed, for goodness sake. Thommo from Bathurst had tried once at a mixer but she'd pushed him away and called him a yob.

She put the pillow back in its place and flipped to Iliana's page in her Bonegilla notebook. She was still in Cooma with her family. Her father and Massimo were working on the Snowy Mountains Scheme. At least she knew where he was.

She would write to Vasiliki to congratulate her and thank her for the photo and then she would write to Iliana and Elizabeta and tell them how happy she was for Vasiliki. It had always been her responsibility to bring the Bonegilla girls together and she wouldn't let a marriage get in the way of that now.

Chapter Twenty-five

1957

'What took you so long, Iliana? I send you out for flour and rice and it takes two hours?'

Agata Agnoli stood at the wood stove, waiting for a pot of water to boil. Her face was flushed from the heat of the fire, the sleeves of her dress were pushed up to her elbows, and there was a smudge of flour on her cheek. Iliana looked to the table, still dusted with flour, and saw the rows of orecchiette her mother had just rolled sitting like tiny puffy clouds.

'*Mamma*, why didn't you wait for me? I said I would help you when I got back.' Iliana crossed the room to put the paper bag of groceries on the sink. She quickly reached for her apron and slipped it over her head.

'What were you doing all this time in the shops, huh?'

Iliana avoided her mother's gaze. She opened a cupboard door and took out a dinner plate, then scooped some of the little pasta ears onto it, before handing it to her mother. Agata slid them into the boiling water.

'I forgot what time it was. The rain stopped and I went for a walk.' That was half the truth. Being sent on an errand into the main street of Cooma had given Iliana the chance for some privacy and time to herself. The small house was barely big enough for a family of six and since she stayed at home helping her mother, she never seemed to be able to leave it. Her two little brothers, Stefano and Giovani, went to school each day. Her father, Giuseppe, and her big brother, Massimo, had jobs on the Snowy Mountains Scheme and they left every day too. Most of the time, it was just Iliana and her mother and while she loved her mother, sometimes she loved her solitude too.

While the pasta cooked, Iliana thought back to the dress she'd seen in Woolworths. She loved that shop. She hadn't even cared that she had to scurry past the Australian Hotel next door and listen to the wolf whistles of the men on the footpath. She loved many things about Cooma that were so different from Italy. The saddler, the laundromat, the florist, the Hain's department store and the wide main street with Holdens and Austins parked at angles on both sides. She had picked up a copy of the *Women's Weekly* at the newsagents for nine pence, which she would flick through in more detail in the evening when her brothers were in bed and the day's chores were complete. She loved looking at the photographs of the young Queen Elizabeth and was able to understand some of what was written in the stories in the magazine. It was hard to come by things written in Italian so she practised and practised and she had convinced her father that listening to *When a Girl Marries* on the radio would help her with her English.

The dress. Oh, the dress. She had thought about it all the way home. It was simple, in a floral fabric of pink and purple swirls, with three-quarter length sleeves and a boat neck. Its cinched-in waist would easily fit Iliana's slim frame and the flared skirt folded in ruffles to the knee. She coveted that dress. She had compared it with her plain brown house dress that she was wearing under her second-hand coat and felt plain. She had no need for a dress that pretty because there was nowhere to wear it in Cooma. It wasn't that she wanted to still be living at home with her family. She would like a husband, but she wasn't likely to find one while she stayed at home with her mother all day, cooking and cleaning like she was already a wife.

Agata spooned the cooked pasta from the boiling water into a dish. 'Where is your father and your brother?' She glanced up at the clock on the wall by the kitchen table. 'They are never this late.' She *tsk tsk*ed. 'If they are drinking beer at the pub instead of being home here with the family…' Agata said *pub* in English, almost spat the word out, and made sure to cross herself three times.

'I'm sure they are not drinking beer, *Mamma*.'

It wasn't drinking beer that her mother was worried about. The pubs and clubs were a big distraction for men in the town who worked hard underground in difficult and dirty jobs all week, and then liked to let off some steam. One of the other Italian ladies in Cooma, Francesca Milese, who cleaned at one of the town's motels, told Agata and Iliana after church one Sunday that women arrived every Friday on buses from somewhere called Kings Cross.

'*Puttana*,' she had whispered fiercely before crossing herself. 'You should see the hair teased up to here and the make-up. They say they are *dancers*.'

'*Prostituta?*' her mother had queried.

Signora Milese had nodded and pinched her eyes closed, as if merely saying the word would send her straight to hell. 'The men here earn too much money. They spend it on women instead of saving it up for the future.'

Iliana had asked Massimo once if he'd ever been to see the dancers. He'd glared at her and told her it was none of her business.

'This food will go cold,' Agata complained as she shifted the pot to the other side of the stove where it was cooler.

'*Papà* and Massimo should be here soon, *Mamma*. Here, let me take that.' Iliana took the dish and set it in the middle of the table. She covered it with folded tea towels to keep the pasta warm and then quickly set the table for six.

'Stefano! Giovani!' she called. 'Dinner is on the table.' There were quick stomping footsteps up the hallway and her younger brothers slammed into their seats.

'No, no. You two,' Iliana said, pinching their ears. 'Wash your hands before dinner.'

The boys were used to taking orders from their older sister but made a point of rolling their eyes at each other before racing to the bathroom, chattering in English. Iliana envied them their friendship and their easy way with a new language. They were doing well at Cooma Public School and had found playmates from a dozen different nationalities. She wished she had such chances to practise her English.

The front door opened and closed and there were heavy boots on the floorboards. Her mother lifted her chin and smiled. 'About time they are home.' Iliana took a whole loaf of bread to the table and sliced it, passing pieces to her little brothers, who began to wolf it down hungrily.

Massimo came straight to the kitchen. The work on the scheme, tunnelling through solid granite rock, was wet, noisy and smelly, and he still wore the dust and grime of his day underground. He stood in the doorway, his heavy coat over one arm.

'*Ciao, Mamma,*' he said. 'Sorry for being late.'

'Clean up,' Agata replied. 'Then come and sit down.'

There was something in his voice that made Iliana look over at him. Tears pooled in his dark eyes, streaking the dirt on his face. She dropped the bread knife with a clatter on the table.

'What's happened?' she gasped. 'Is it *Papà*?'

He held up a hand to calm her. 'No, he is here.'

'Then what?' Agata demanded.

Massimo breathed deep. 'Someone died in the tunnels today.'

Agata crossed herself three times and began to pray. Massimo walked across the room to his mother and rested a hand on her shoulder. He wouldn't kiss her until he was washed up. 'It was Angelo Zocchi, *Mamma*. There was a rock fall up ahead in the tunnel. The ambulance came but it was too late. *Papà* saw it.'

'Oh, my Giuseppe.'

Iliana's legs had turned to rubber. She pulled out a chair and fell backwards into it.

'*Papà* wasn't hurt. He is all right. But Angelo was a friend. We have worked with him for more than a year. He died for nothing.' Massimo's voice broke and he wiped his tears away with a shirtsleeve. 'Something has to change. They throw us in the tunnels and don't care if we die. Workers are being killed to make a dam for farmers, did you know that? Italians. Greeks. Poles. Norwegians. Croatians. Yugoslavs. People came here to make a better life for their families, not to be killed working all day and night.'

Agata began to cry. Her little brothers watched their older brother, their mouths agape.

'Massimo.' Iliana pushed back her chair and went to her brother, throwing her arms around him. She didn't care that he was filthy. She felt the tension in his shoulders, the bristling of his body when she tried to comfort him. But she wouldn't let go.

'I'm going to talk to the union,' he said. 'We can't stand for this. Angelo has a wife and five children. Five! How long before this happens to someone else? What if that was *Papà* or me?'

'Massimo,' Agata cried. 'Don't you dare say such a thing.' She crossed herself again.

'Being silent won't save men's lives, *Mamma*.'

'Please don't make trouble,' she urged through her tears. 'You don't want to lose this job. Or make problems for your father.'

Massimo eased out of Iliana's hold and went to his mother, clasped her shoulders. 'I won't make trouble.' He kissed her on the forehead.

'I will go and speak with your father. Iliana, you and the boys eat.'

Iliana suddenly wasn't hungry. 'So many children,' she said softly. She passed her little brothers another slice of bread then looked up at Massimo.

'Tomorrow, there will be a collection for Angelo's family,' he said gruffly. 'Imagine it, Iliana. A new country. Five *bambinos*. You don't even know English and your husband is dead.'

Tears clouded her vision. She reached for Massimo's hand and squeezed it. 'You will tell me what I can do to help and I will do it.'

That evening, Iliana sat in the living room on her own. Her parents had gone to bed early. The boys were in bed and Massimo had left the house shortly after dinner. She had a cup of hot milk, a blanket on her knees to warm her as the fire settled and glowed, and a stack of letters. They had been delivered to her father at work and he'd brought them home that night but in the commotion of the news about Angelo Zocchi's death, they'd been forgotten until now.

Four were from Italy, including one from her father's uncle, Mauricio. Her father had been writing to his uncle, urging him to give permission for his four young sons to come to Australia. Four single men, with no wives and children to think of, and with trade skills, were a valuable commodity in a labour force still facing shortages after the war. Many Italians came to Australia to join their families and sometimes Iliana wondered if everyone in Italy hadn't packed up and taken the journey to Australia on the *Fairsea* for a better life in Australia.

She set that letter aside for her father. There was a letter from her aunt Antonietta, her mother's sister, which she knew would make her mother cry when she read it. They had been in Australia for three years now and Agata still cried every day for her own mother and her sisters. Iliana had heard her sometimes. Agata would walk down to the back of the garden, sit on the stump of a dead apple tree, smoke a cigarette and sob. Coming to Australia had been a different adventure for her parents, she realised. They had abandoned everything and everyone they loved in their quest to find a new and better life for their own family.

There were two more letters from Italy, which she shuffled into a separate pile for her parents and then her heart leapt when she saw her own name on three separate envelopes.

She had letters from Vasiliki, Frances and Elizabeta.

She hadn't seen her Bonegilla friends since she'd left the camp in 1954, two months after Elizabeta had left with her mother to go to Adelaide. When Giuseppe and Massimo had got the word they had secured jobs on the Snowy Mountains Scheme, they too had packed up their meagre belongings and taken the train away from Bonegilla to begin their journey to Cooma. Vasiliki and Frances had waved her away, and Frances had given her a farewell gift: a copy of an Enid Blyton book she had used to teach the girls English. It was still on Iliana's bedside table and she sometimes read the stories out loud for fun to her little brothers, but they had so often corrected her English and laughed at the way she said the words that she had stopped. She remembered the last time she had seen Frances. She had come to Bonegilla's main gate to say goodbye and had cried and cried when they had climbed onto the blue bus to take them to the Bonegilla rail siding. She remembered that Massimo had said goodbye to Frances too, which she thought was a nice thing, that he was thanking Frances for everything she'd done for his sister. Iliana asked him later, when they were on the train, if he'd apologised one last time to Frances for putting her in hospital after hitting her on the head with that stupid soccer ball.

'*Si*,' he'd muttered and said no more about it.

After they'd left Bonegilla, Frances wrote regularly, telling her all about where she was and what she was doing. She was in touch much more than Elizabeta and Vasiliki but Iliana put that down to the language. Sometimes it was hard to think in other people's words and even harder to remember how to write them. It was Frances who told Iliana that Vasiliki had moved to Melbourne. That's also how she found out that Frances had moved to Sydney to learn to be a teacher.

They were spread all around the country now, the Bonegilla girls, scattered by the mountain winds that had blown through the camp.

Iliana opened Frances's letter first.

Dear Iliana,

I hope you are well up there in the mountains and not getting too cold at this time of year. I hope you have a very warm winter coat! I don't know if Vasiliki has written to you to tell you her news? Or should I say, or write, "Vicki", as she wants to be called now. It has been so long since we have heard from her but she has a good excuse. She has had her baby, a girl they have named Aphrodite. It's the name of the Greek goddess of love and fertility. Isn't that romantic? She writes that she is enjoying being a mother. I, for one, am very happy for her and her husband. I expect that her parents will be very happy to be grandparents.

How is everything with you? I am well, still at teachers' college but will be finishing quite soon and glad to know that I will be able to put everything I've learnt into practice in the classroom with real children.

Please write and tell me your news and please don't worry about your English. I have been learning Italian so please help me practise by writing to me in your language.

I miss you very much and often think of our time together at Bonegilla. My kindest regards to your parents, and your brothers, Massimo, Stefano and Giovani.

Yours sincerely,

Frances

Iliana put the letter on her lap. She was certain she had understood most of what Frances had said. Vasiliki had had a baby? She couldn't remember knowing that she was expecting. The last time she had heard from Vasiliki was that she was newly married. But then, Vasiliki had always struggled more with learning English than she and Elizabeta had. Next, she picked up Vasiliki's letter, ripped the top open and a small black-and-white photo fell onto the blanket on her lap. It was Vasiliki and a baby in a christening photo. She was wearing a formal dress with white gloves and a hat, and high stiletto heels. The baby was almost entirely covered in an elaborate lace dress, which draped almost to Vasiliki's knees.

Iliana peered at the photo, trying to make out her friend's features. Vasiliki had grown up. The photo was small, less than two inches square, which made it hard to see much of the baby's face, if she had much hair, or even if little Aphrodite looked like her mother or her father. There was no letter with it but Iliana didn't mind. The photo was enough. She would put it on her dressing table, this photo of the first Bonegilla baby.

Elizabeta's letter was short and to the point.

Liebe Iliana,

I hope you are good. I am very busy with working in the cafe and helping my mother and father. I am engaged now. His name is Nikolas Muller and he is German. We will not get married for at least one year when we have money in the bank to buy a house. There are Italians here in Adelaide who grow tomatoes. They taste very good. There is one place to eat gelato and it is called Flash Deli in Hindley Street. I think of you when I go there after work on the way to the train station on North Terrace. I would like to go to Sydney on the bus to see Frances very soon. Will you come too?

Elizabeta

Iliana rested her head on the back of the upholstered sofa and stared into the embers of the dwindling fire. So there would soon be another wedding and Elizabeta would become Mrs Muller. That was a reason to be happy, Iliana thought. Such an event would bring some joy to a family that had suffered so much. They had left a daughter behind at Bonegilla, so far away from Adelaide that they couldn't even visit her grave. Perhaps now there would be some happiness in grandchildren, something to lighten the days for Elizabeta and her parents.

It would be another wedding Iliana would not be able to go to. And what of the talk of a bus trip to Sydney to see

Frances? What if Iliana was forced to sit with some of the prostitutes on their way back to Kings Cross? Her parents would never let her go. Perhaps if Massimo went with her they would approve of it. She would have to ask him, once he was past the death of Angelo Zocchi, and then see if they agreed. Would he like a trip to Sydney to see the Harbour Bridge and swim in the ocean at Bondi? She knew her brother. He would not go. He would not leave their father unprotected at work.

She would write to Frances and Vasiliki and Elizabeta on the weekend.

As she drifted off to sleep by the warmth of the fire, her friends' letters in her lap, Iliana dreamt of the perfect dress and the kind of life in which she would wear it.

No one begrudged Angelo Zocchi's widow when she got married the day after her husband's year's mind mass.

She was marrying a Yugoslav, Miroslav, a man who'd worked with her dead husband. He'd paid his respects to her after her husband's death and a love had developed between them. The Yugoslav had been lonely and wanted a wife. The widow needed someone to support her and her five children. The money the workers on the scheme had generously donated to her would only last so long.

The Agnolis attended the wedding, a small affair at a Catholic chapel in Cooma. The bride had worn Iliana's dress, the one she had coveted in Woolworths, but how could Iliana be angry about that? About a widow who wanted to be beautiful on her second wedding day? Afterwards, there was coffee, tea and refreshments at a local hall.

Iliana and her mother and many of the wives of the Snowy workers had baked for days to ensure there was enough for everyone. Some happy news was welcome after the tragedy of Angelo's death and, Iliana thought, only the most pious and pitiless would judge a widow who wanted a husband for herself and, more importantly, a father for her five children.

There were many compliments on the cakes and there was joy all around for the new husband and wife. She tasted her first cup of tea and decided she didn't like it. And, after everything was cleaned away, she walked home with her family to the little wooden home, full of happiness and joy at a new marriage

When they turned the corner into their street, Iliana saw someone by the front door of their house.

It was Frances Burley. She was sitting on her suitcase and when she heard them approaching she looked up.

Her face was streaked with tears.

Chapter Twenty-six

1958

Iliana's mother hurriedly warmed a cup of milk and made a salami sandwich for Frances, who had been ushered quickly through the house and into the kitchen. The room was warm from the fire and the table was crowded. Giovani and Stefano stared at Frances as if she had landed from another planet. Giuseppe sat at the head of the table, his elbows down, his fingers linked, his lips pulled together tightly. Massimo sat at the other end, staring at Frances, as if he was wondering what on earth she was doing here, all the way from Sydney, with a suitcase and tears.

He wasn't the only one.

He'd barely said hello to her and now his gaze alternated between the table in front of him or the clock on the wall above the fridge.

The only sound was the glass rattling in the kitchen window and the roof creaking in the wind. No one spoke as Frances slowly nibbled at her sandwich. She kept her eyes down as she swallowed a mouthful and then seemed to surrender, placing the chunky bread on her plate. Iliana noticed that only the tiniest of bites had been taken out of it. A small half moon. Perhaps Frances didn't like Italian food like salami or crusty pane di casa.

Agata hovered in the kitchen, wiping the sink, folding and unfolding tea towels, fussing with the curtains over the window.

'Your friend is not hungry,' Giuseppe said to Iliana in Italian.

'Perhaps she is tired from the bus trip,' she replied.

'Did you come on the bus?' Stefano asked Frances in English.

'Yes,' Frances answered, her quiet voice almost lost in the room.

'Where did you come from?' Giovani asked, tag-teaming with his brother.

'From Bega.'

'Bega?' Massimo straightened his shoulders and lifted his chin.

'Yes. I am ... I was a teacher there.' Frances lifted a linen napkin and pressed it to her lips. The imprint of her pink lipstick remained there, like fallen petals from a spring rose.

'Yes, your first job with children,' Iliana remembered.

'That's right,' Frances nodded

Then Agata was behind Iliana, pressing against her back and looking over her shoulder at Frances's plate. 'What is wrong with her? Why has she come to see you?'

Iliana was relieved her mother's question was in Italian. She answered the same way. 'I don't know.'

Frances looked up from her plate and smiled sadly at Giuseppe, at Giovani and Stefano and Iliana. She didn't look at Massimo.

Frances pushed back her chair and the scraping of the legs on the wooden floor was loud. She stood. Massimo leapt to his feet.

'Massimo,' Iliana hissed.

'Please, Iliana. I didn't mean to upset your mother. Or your father. This was perhaps not the best idea I've ever had. I'm sorry. I will go.'

Iliana quickly reached for Frances's hand and held it in hers. 'You will not go. It's okay.' She looked back over her shoulder at her mother, started in Italian. '*Mamma*, I'll talk to her, and find out why she's here. But I can't do that with you all here hovering like crows.'

Agata opened her mouth to speak but hesitated.

'Boys,' Giuseppe said. 'Go into the living room and read your books for school. Massimo and I will go for a walk.'

'*Papà*,' Massimo started.

Giuseppe placed his hands on the table and he stood. 'Agata. Come.' He cocked his head and she *tsk tsk*ed loudly but she moved to the door as her husband had directed. 'When you find out what is happening, Iliana, you will come and tell me everything. *Pronto.*'

'*Si, Mamma.*'

Agata closed the kitchen door behind her. Finally Iliana was alone with Frances. Her friend's mousy brown hair was short now, curled in waves and styled like all the movie stars, brushed up and away from her face. But she hadn't put a comb to it since she'd arrived and it was messy and knotted at the back where her head had probably rubbed on the back of the bus seat during the long trip. Her face was pale, her brown eyes dull from her tears, and there was a pale outline of lipstick on her lips.

Where should Iliana begin?

'Thank you for your letters,' Iliana said.

Frances finally smiled and squeezed Iliana's hand in return. 'And thank you for yours. Your English is getting so much better.'

'No, it is not,' Iliana replied, embarrassed.

'It's true.'

'I do not talk to people here in Cooma. My family ... it is all Italian. The boys in school, they speak English. You helped me. At Bonegilla.'

'And I can help you more, if you'd like.'

Iliana wasn't sure how that would work when Frances was back in Bega and Iliana was in Cooma.

'I like to hear what you are doing. All about your life here with your family. Cooma seems lovely.'

'It is cold. Much colder than Bonegilla or even Italy.'

'Bonegilla,' Frances sighed. 'That feels like a million years ago. Many things have changed since then, that's for certain.'

Iliana smiled. 'Vasiliki has her baby.'

'Yes. Aphrodite must be walking by now.'

'Did you see it? Have you been in Melbourne?'

Frances sniffed, looked down at her napkin, folded it into a neat square. 'I was down in Melbourne for my brother's wedding a year ago but I didn't have time to see Vasiliki. Or Vicki, I should say. I can't get used to calling her that.'

'Tom is married?'

'No, my oldest brother, Donald. Tom couldn't make it back from London to be best man, unfortunately. He was preparing for a case.'

'I forget you have two brothers.' Iliana tried to lighten the mood with a laugh. 'Having one big brother is enough trouble. Massimo wants to know everything that I am doing. All the time.' Iliana reflected for a moment that this was something new. He never used to be so protective. There had been a time when he had not paid much attention to his siblings but since Angelo Zocchi's death in the tunnels, he'd become cautious about everything.

'You are all very close. I can see that.'

Iliana laughed. 'Massimo always wants to know. And he must know the news of you, too.'

Frances jerked her head up to meet Iliana's eyes. 'He does?'

'Yes. He remembers you. Your head. He feels sorry.'

Frances gazed dropped to her plate. Iliana couldn't wait any longer. She covered Frances's hand with one of her own again. What could be troubling her, this lucky girl who had been to the important university to learn how to be a teacher? Who was so clever that she taught children how to learn? Who had been so kind when she'd taught them English in the mess?

'Frances,' she asked. 'What is wrong?'

'Oh, Iliana,' Frances whispered. 'Everything is an utter mess.' She pushed her plate away and dropped her head to the table, cradling it in the crook of her elbow. Iliana waited, stroked her friend's arm while her shoulders shook. She wished she had a pot of coffee on the stove so she could offer Frances a cup. She didn't know what else to do but lay a hand on her friend's arm.

'You have come a long way to see me.'

'I need a friend.' Frances's voice was muffled against the sleeve of her cardigan.

'I am your friend,' Iliana said. They held hands tight.

Frances took a deep breath and looked up, shuddering as she tried to stop her sobbing. 'The thing is, Iliana, I'm expecting.'

Iliana tried to remember what that word meant and drew a blank.

'A baby. I'm having a baby.'

It took a moment for Frances's words to sink in. A *bambino?* A baby?

'But you have no husband.'

'That's right. That's why I'm in a mess, Iliana.'

Iliana made the sign of the cross and stared wide-eyed at her friend.

'I didn't know where else to go. I've had to leave my job in Bega, right in the middle of school term. I had to lie to everyone. Those lovely little children. I had to make up a story to explain, to cover up, so I told them my mother was ill and that I had to return to Bonegilla to care for her. But that's all a big lie.'

'*Bella*,' Iliana soothed.

'I can't tell my parents and I can't go back to Bonegilla. I have made a right mess of everything and I have nowhere to go. This is the closest place I could think to come. To you.'

Iliana's head swam with questions. 'The father of your baby? Where is he? Will he get married to you?'

'I had hoped he might … but no. I've been so stupid, Iliana. I'm not a silly girl. I've been to teachers' college, for goodness sake.' The tears streamed down Frances's face and her mouth crumpled.

Iliana didn't know what to think. Frances had committed a sin before God. But wouldn't God want her to help a friend who was alone and frightened?

'You will stay here tonight,' Iliana said. 'Come, I'll show you.'

Later that evening, after minestrone soup and bread had been served for dinner, the table cleared and the dishes washed, Iliana's two younger brothers were sent off to bed. Iliana had tucked Frances up in her own bed, and she'd remained there. When Iliana had checked on her, Frances had been fast asleep.

Iliana's parents joined her in the kitchen. Massimo insisted on being there too. To ease the shock of what she had to ask of them, Iliana had popped the cork on a bottle of home-made red wine, a gift to her father from some other Italians working on the Snowy, and it sat in the middle of the table along with four jam jars. Iliana father poured a slurp in each glass. They each took a sip.

'You have something to tell us,' Giuseppe said. 'About her.'

Her mother leaned forwards. 'What is wrong with that Australian girl?'

Iliana waited a moment until the wine had begun to work its magic on her nerves. Up until this moment, she'd been a child in her family. She'd never made decisions of her own. She had followed the wishes of her father and her mother, had dutifully obeyed them, had cooked and washed and cleaned alongside her mother, because that's what daughters did. She had shed that skin now. Frances's secret had changed her too, because she was going to ask something of her parents that she would never have dared just twenty-four hours ago.

'Her name is Frances. She is the daughter of Mr Burley from Bonegilla, the camp director.'

'*Sì*,' Giuseppe nodded, not oblivious to the fact that they had an important guest in their house. 'She writes the letters to you.'

'Did you know she was coming?' Agata demanded.

'Good question,' Massimo asked. 'What is she doing here in Cooma and why didn't you tell us she was coming?'

Iliana held up a hand to quieten her family. '*Per favore*. I didn't know she was coming until I saw her at the front door today. If you will all listen instead of bombarding me with questions, I will tell you but please let me tell you everything. And you, Massimo. No interrupting.'

He ran a hand through his hair, nodded his head in agreement.

Agata sucked in a deep breath. 'Is she in trouble?'

'Yes, *Mamma*. She is in trouble.' If they agreed to Iliana's plan, they would see it with their own eyes sooner rather than later.

'I knew it.' Agata slammed her palm on the table. 'A young girl with a suitcase and tears. It can only mean one thing. A woman knows.' She crossed herself. Four times.

'What trouble?' Massimo looked confused.

Iliana glared at him. 'What other kind of trouble is there for a young woman with no husband, huh?'

His eyes flashed.

Iliana's mother muttered a prayer.

Iliana looked to her father. He considered his wine. 'She is your friend, this Australian girl from Bonegilla?'

'Yes, *Papà*. Frances was so kind to me. She taught me English every day in the mess. She became my friend and she didn't care that I was Italian. Or Catholic. She stood up for me when I was called dago by some boys in Albury. She is a teacher now. Or, she was a teacher. She has had to leave her job.'

'What about her family?'

'She says she cannot tell her *mamma* and *papà*. She is ashamed.'

The clock above the fridge ticked. Iliana looked over at the bottle of wine and wanted to gulp the whole thing down.

'What are you asking of your family, Iliana?'

Iliana breathed deep. 'I want Frances to be welcome here. Until the baby is born.' It was hard to say but Iliana found her strength. 'I want to be a friend to her.'

Giuseppe thought long and hard. 'Agata?'

Agata chewed her lip. 'But she is not married. What will people say when they find out what she has done?'

Their father reached for his wife's hand. 'After all I've seen and lived through, I'm not going to judge this young girl. I'm not sure what is a sin and what isn't any more.' He turned to Iliana. 'You tell your friend. What is her name?'

'Frances,' Iliana said.

'Francesca,' Giuseppe said with a smile. 'That's a good Italian name. We will not turn her away.'

Iliana had never been prouder of her father.

'But.' And then his face became stern and he lifted a finger to point it in her direction. 'You will never, ever do this to your family.'

Iliana crossed herself. 'No, *Papà*. Never.'

Chapter Twenty-seven

It didn't happen easily or without its hurdles, but over the course of the next few months, Frances was slowly folded into the warm and loving arms of the Agnoli family.

She really had been in a mess when she'd arrived in Cooma. The shame of her pregnancy had been burnt on her skin like scars and she'd felt as if she had nowhere else to turn. Frances hadn't known what to expect when she'd arrived on their doorstep. She'd only been hoping for a short stay, perhaps a few weeks, while she could sensibly get her thinking straight and decide what to do. She had laid everything out to Iliana, reckoning it wasn't possible to be more humiliated than she was. And when the Agnolis had agreed she could stay, she'd been so humbled that she'd taken to Iliana's bed and sobbed herself to sleep.

Iliana had sat by her side until she stopped crying.

'I don't know what to say.'

'You say nothing. All our family is a long way away in Italy,' Iliana had told her. 'My *nonna* and *nonno*. My mother's and father's sisters. Our cousins. Being separated from family is hard. We don't want that for anyone.'

Agata had been cool and distant for many weeks and Frances understood. She'd seen how Iliana's mother had struggled to reconcile the helpful and courteous young woman living in Frances's room with the idea that she had been so careless as to get herself pregnant when she wasn't married. Agata wore a gold cross around her neck and pressed her fingers to it every time Frances entered the room.

She still couldn't tell her own parents that she was pregnant. In a breezy, completely untruthful letter to them not long after she arrived in Cooma, she explained that she'd managed to find a job there. She wrote that she'd wanted to have an adventure and had landed in the mountains. Her parents hadn't detected anything suspicious, at least they hadn't hinted at it in their reply, and sent letters to a post office address she had given them. They hoped she was well, and that she might come back to Bonegilla in the school holidays for a visit.

As her way of saying thanks, Frances had determined to make herself as useful as possible. She had saved a little money while she'd been teaching. She'd had high hopes for the overseas adventure she'd dreamed about since she was a girl that was now not to be, so had something to contribute to Iliana's family in return for having her. It would never be enough to repay everything they were doing for her. Her debt to them was so much bigger than that. She made a point of helping in the kitchen whenever she was allowed. Iliana's mother slowly warmed to her pleas to be taught how to cook real Italian food. She learned how to make pasta from scratch, with nothing but flour and eggs. She baked bread with Iliana. She practised Italian with them even though their dialect was unlike anything she had learned in college, and helped the family with their English. Within a few weeks, she had become an unofficial after-school tutor to Iliana's two younger brothers, and before long they were excelling in all their subjects. He didn't tell her, because he didn't have the words in English, but she knew she had earned Giuseppe's gratitude when Giovani and Stefano had brought glowing reports home from school.

And Massimo?

Frances didn't dare talk to him, no matter how much she longed for a conversation. He had barely said a word to her in all the time she had been living in the Agnoli house, other than hello and goodbye and thank you when she set a plate in front of him for dinner. What must he think of her? She didn't want to know. She couldn't find out for fear it would be crushing. The boy who'd said goodbye to her all those years ago, the boy who'd given her the coin she still treasured, was now a man who couldn't look her in the eye.

The quickest flash of a smile from him over dinner was enough to last her a whole day of his absence. Knowing he was in the house, sleeping in the next room, put her on edge, the pull and push of wanting to see him and at the same time needing to hide her shame. He worked very long hours, both on the Snowy Mountains Scheme and for the Building Workers' Industrial Union. When Iliana had told her about the man who'd died, she understood why. Her affectionate feelings for Massimo had been nothing but a childish fancy and she was far from being a child now. Perhaps that was why she had hung on to the idea. Imagining being with Massimo was so much more preferable to her reality with Gerald.

When she was in bed at night, the house quiet, Iliana breathing softly beside her, she thought back on what had happened. She was a good girl, a sensible young woman. A trained teacher with plans to travel the world and see all the countries she'd studied in her atlas. How had it all gone so wrong?

She had never set out to let things go so far with Gerald. When she had arrived at the small school in Bega for her first teaching position, she'd been bursting with excitement. It was her first job and those early months in the classroom had been exhilarating, exhausting and terrifying all at once. Corralling a classroom full of forty-five eight-year-old children was very different in practice to everything she'd learned at teachers' college about being a high-school languages teacher, but beggars couldn't be choosers and her first job placement by the department was in a primary school. She worked hard, sought out textbooks in the staffroom and asked for advice from the other teachers to try to understand some of the challenges she was facing, none of which was very helpful.

'Don't mind the Atkins boy. He's a little thick in the head. He never follows instructions.'

'That McDonald girl? Oh, she drifts off every now and then. Stares into space. I find a good smack across the head brings her back to the present.'

Frances didn't think smacking a child was ever a good idea, no matter how much her new principal enjoying swinging his cane on the soft palms of boys who'd transgressed the school's rules and his own prejudices. Much to her regret now, she would never get to help little Stephen Atkins or find out how curly-haired Pamela McDonald fared because she'd ruined everything.

She and Gerald had hit it off immediately. They were the two youngest teachers in the staffroom, both in their first teaching positions, so it seemed almost inevitable they would gravitate towards each other. Things became serious quite quickly, but they had to hide their growing relationship from their headmaster, who didn't believe that staff, especially young women, should engage in such extracurricular activities. Frances had come to believe he didn't like the idea of young women teaching at all. The clandestine nature of what she and Gerald were doing was perhaps what had made it more exciting than it might have been if they'd simply gone to the pictures or dances or milk bars like all the other young people in Bega.

They were young and curious and kissing soon became something more.

'I promise I'll pull out just in time,' he'd whispered, late one night in his bedroom in the house he shared with two other young men who worked at one of the local banks. He'd been next to her on his bed, his hand up her skirt and creeping up her thigh. 'I promise I'll be careful, Frances.'

When that time came, he didn't, and she found she hadn't wanted him to.

It had been her first time and it was her biggest mistake.

When she'd missed her period that first month, she had tried not to think about it. Perhaps her cycle had been disrupted by the excitement of her new job and all the anxieties that went along with having moved to a new place. When two months went by and she began to feel sick, not just in the mornings but all day, the feeling she'd had the first time she'd got drunk on gin, she knew. As soon as she could talk to Gerald alone, in the janitor's storeroom at school once everyone else had left for the day, she broke the news to him. He was a decent chap. She liked him very much. Later she could admit to having harboured a faint hope that he might be overjoyed at the news and propose right there on the spot. That way, they could fudge the dates and recover from this mistake together. Such a plan meant she would still have to give up her job as soon as they were married. But at least she would be married.

Her fantasy about what might happen had been fanciful. It turned out she didn't know Gerald at all.

He'd reacted as if she'd struck him on the cheek. 'Well, that's a blow,' he'd blurted. He pulled a pack of cigarettes from the inside pocket of his suit coat, and lit one. He drew in hard and leaned back against a shelf full of rolls of toilet paper. He was smirking to hide his nerves. The light at the end of his cigarette shook harder with every drag he took.

The smoke in the confined space made her stomach roil. 'A blow? Are you saying that me being pregnant is a blow to *you*?'

'Well, yes. It is rather. I don't want to be stuck with a kid. Not at my age. C'mon, Frances. It's not like this …' He waved a hand between them. 'It's not like this was anything special. We were just a bit of fun, weren't we?'

'Oh my goodness,' Frances said faintly. She clutched her stomach, tried to stop the sickness from rising up in her throat.

'Look,' Gerald stammered. 'I don't have any money if that's what you're asking. This is my first job.'

She felt as if he'd slapped her across the face. Her cheeks reddened as if he had.

'This isn't about money.'

'And if you're looking for me to propose …'

She didn't want him to now, not after this, not ever. 'You clearly aren't going to.'

Gerald dropped the cigarette on the cement floor of the storeroom, crushed it under his shoe with a brutal twist. 'Look, Frances. The truth is … I can't propose to you because I'm already jolly well engaged to someone else. In Sydney. She's waiting for me to finish this country stint. Once that's over, we'll be married.'

Frances vomited all over Gerald's shoes and left him to clean it up.

An appointment with Dr Elliot in Bega a few days later had confirmed what Frances already knew. Unfortunately, his youngest daughter Lorraine was one of her students, which meant he'd felt free to stare at her patronisingly and advise her that her only option was to leave the classroom immediately. If she didn't, he would tell her headmaster.

'It is absolutely insupportable that you can be anywhere near my daughter or the other children at the school. You will not go back to the classroom, young …' She knew why he'd stopped mid-rebuke. He'd been about to call her young lady.

The doctor scribbled something on a piece of paper and pushed it across his dark mahogany desk. He couldn't even bring himself to hand it to her. She had tried to make sense of his terrible handwriting, but her shaking fury and the tears that had welled in her eyes had blurred her vision.

'Here's a place I suggest. It's run by the Salvation Army. A home for unwed mothers. Silly girls like you who can't keep their legs closed. I'll make a call and arrange it. You might be surprised to know you're not the first girl from here to get herself in trouble. You will stay there and earn your keep until the child is born and then an adoption will be arranged with a decent Christian family.' He eyed her up and down. 'This is, of course, unless something can be sorted out with the father.' He waited for the killer blow. 'If you know who the father is.'

Frances had walked out of the surgery as if in a trance. She went directly to school, told her headmaster that her mother had taken ill suddenly—a story he was unlikely to doubt given the look of pale-faced shock on her face—and went to her accommodation to pack a suitcase. She wasn't even able to say goodbye to the children from her class. She'd left a note for her housemates, left her share of the next week's rent on the kitchen table, and walked to the bus station where she bought a ticket to Cooma.

But she knew this refuge couldn't last forever. As sure as the moon rose in the evenings, this baby would come. Frances turned onto her back, trying to find a comfortable position beside Iliana in the bed they shared. There had been no other option because there was no spare bed in the small Cooma house with only three bedrooms. Massimo was in the sleepout built at the back and the two young boys shared a single bed, one at each end, kicking each other with glee when they fought.

When the baby kicked and danced, she covered her belly with her hands and felt each movement, committing it to memory. Was it a boy or a girl growing and moving inside her? She might find out that much at least before she gave the baby up for adoption. For that was her only choice. She would give up her baby to a good family and then move on, pretend it had never happened. What life could she give a child? She was an unmarried mother, a sinner, a stupid girl who'd brought shame on herself and her family.

She had been hesitating for months about how to tell her parents. She'd fudged the reasons why she couldn't tell them, about why she couldn't leave Cooma.

I can't leave in the middle of term, she'd written. Then, *I can't leave as Giovani and Stefano need my help.* It amused her to see them speak with her and each other in broad Australian accents and then lapse into Italian to speak with their parents or Iliana or Massimo. It was as easy as breathing for them.

The baby lurched to one side in her stomach and pressed on her bladder. Frances glanced over at Iliana in the darkness, a shaft of pale moonlight from the gap in the curtains creating a sliver of silver on her peaceful, sleeping face. She propped herself up with her hands, swung her legs over the side of the bed and shuffled her feet into her slippers. When she found her breath, she felt for the spare blanket folded at the end of the bed and draped it around her shoulders, covering the thin nightdress she wore.

Quietly, Frances opened the bedroom door, turned right and tiptoed to the back door. Unlocked, it opened with a squeak and she carefully descended the three cement steps and took the path that led to the outside toilet. When she reached the corner of the house, a flickering light caught her attention. It was all she could see as her eyes adjusted to the dark.

'Frances.'

'Massimo,' she said, surprised. Her breath caught somewhere between the baby and her heart. She recognised the smell of his cigarettes. She had smelled it on his clothes for the past six months she'd been living with the Agnolis. His cigarette smoke. The cologne he wore. What he smelled like after a shower. Even the particular pattern of his footsteps, his long loping stride on the wooden floorboards of the house.

The tip of his cigarette flickered up and down as he lifted it to his mouth to take a drag. 'I not scare you?' he said.

The light flicked to the ground and she heard the sound of his shoe grinding in the dirt.

'No. Not at all. What are you doing out here?'

'A cigarette. *Mamma* doesn't like it in the house.'

Frances knew that. She knew all about the way Agata ran the household. What she liked, what she didn't. What she would let her boys get away with and what she would scold them for. The way she poured love into every meal and hated washing their clothes but did it anyway. One day, she would be a mother just like Agata. Just not now, not with this baby. She would never be a mother to this baby.

'You mother likes the smell of fresh flowers,' Frances said. 'And basil from the garden.'

Massimo smiled at her. 'Yes.'

A pain streaked against her back and she let out a groan. He strode to her and as her eyes adjusted to the darkness she could make out his lovely face. His lips pinched, his brown eyes heavy with something she couldn't name. 'You okay? The *bambino*?'

He reached a hand out and moved it towards her but hesitated. His fingers hovered a few inches away from her stomach.

'I'm okay. Nothing is wrong.'

'The baby is coming?' His deep breaths were the only sound she could hear.

Her exhalation was a cloud in the night air. 'No, at least I hope not. Not quite now.'

'That is good. But it must come soon, yes?' His hand disappeared into the pocket of his trousers.

Frances pulled the blanket tighter around her shoulders, the cool air making goosebumps on her skin. 'Soon, yes. About four weeks.'

'And then you will leave Cooma?'

'Yes. I will have the baby and leave Cooma.'

She looked up to the night sky. A few pinpoints of stars twinkled down at them. They were alone in the dark. How many times had she wished for this, to be alone with him? Those dreams had been the only thing keeping her going, the only thing that helped her not think about the pregnancy and her future and her life without this baby she had loved and carried for eight months.

'Frances …' He took a step closer.

She looked up into his brown eyes. 'Yes?'

'Where will you go?'

'I don't know. Back to Sydney perhaps. I'll have to look in the papers and apply for another teaching position somewhere. Perhaps in a place no one knows me. Where I can be a stranger. Somewhere I can start again.'

'Why must you go? You can be a teacher here in Cooma.'

'No … I …' Could she do that? Cooma had been her place of refuge, but staying here? No. Staying would remind her of what she'd done. Cooma would always be the place where she'd hidden from the world, and she needed to leave that shame behind if she was to get on with her life.

When his hands were suddenly on her belly, cradling her baby, caressing her taut skin through her nightdress, she gasped. He hadn't touched her since Bonegilla, since that last day when he'd said goodbye and given her the Italian coin before he'd got on the bus.

'Your baby,' he said, and she could feel his breath on her cheek. 'It is big.'

Her baby was big and it was to come out soon and she was frightened. What did she know about having a baby? A friend of Mrs Agnoli, who was a midwife from Italy, had come to check on Frances every few weeks, but that had been it. She didn't want to see a doctor and have to explain all over again how she was in this predicament. The judgement of that one doctor back in Bega had been enough to last her whole pregnancy.

'The baby is healthy,' Iliana had translated as the midwife had smoothed her warm hands over Frances's belly and listened to the baby's heartbeat. 'And so are you.'

She was frightened of labour and she was frightened about having to give her baby away. She had tried not to think about it these past months because it was a rabbit hole she couldn't fall into, but now the tears welled and drizzled down her cheeks.

'Don't cry, Francesca. Please.'

She hadn't meant to but the tenderness of his gesture, the way he was touching and embracing the shame she was carrying, sent her into the kind of sobbing she had been holding in since she'd discovered she was carrying Gerald's child. Everything leached from her: her shame, her disgust, her fear, her anger, all in great heaving sobs. She had ruined her life and she was paying the cost, but it seemed a dreadful price to pay. When Massimo's arms enveloped her, she cried even more. In that moment, she hated herself. She hated her life. She hated how ashamed she felt. She hated that she had wanted to have sex with Gerald, a man she had liked but not loved, not like this, not like she loved the man who was standing with her in the dark, clutching her, holding her as tight as he could around her swelling secret. And she hated that she loved this man she couldn't have.

Why hadn't she waited for someone like him?

'Francesca,' Massimo murmured into her hair. 'Francesca ...'

And she let him hold her for just a moment. She let the warmth of his body seep into her in the dark of the night, in the private silence of the Agnoli's backyard at midnight.

When she pulled away she didn't look back at him, and when her quick trip to the outside toilet was over, he was gone.

Chapter Twenty-eight

'*Bene.*' Agata smiled at Frances and patted her on the shoulder. Frances knew that was a compliment and she was pleased with herself. She had managed to roll the little orecchiette pasta all by herself. She looked down at the kitchen table, covered with a dusting of flour and her attempts at the little ears, as Iliana had translated, and laughed.

'Not as good as yours, *signora.*' She smiled.

Agata laughed and splayed a hand to her chest. 'Mine very good.'

Iliana laughed along too. 'My mother has been making the orecchiette from six years old. With her *nonna.*'

'Goodness,' Frances said. She arched her back, feeling stiff from bending over the table. Eight months pregnant now, she had to overcompensate and the pose made her back ache even more than it had. She winced, propped a hand on the small of her back and rubbed.

'Sit,' Agata commanded and Frances didn't fight it. Iliana quickly poured her a glass of water. The two women had been fussing over her for months: ensuring she drank a cup of warm milk every night. Seeing that she was never hungry. Refusing to let her do any of the chores now she was getting closer. Giuseppe had even given up his arm-chair in the living room, the one closest to the fire, so she could be warm and comfortable with her legs propped up on the stuffed leather footstool. She had grown to love them as if they were her own family. Once Agata had warmed to her, Frances felt as if she'd found a second mother. Giuseppe seemed too shy to speak to her much, but he fussed over her, too. Giovani and Stefano had been perfect pupils and Iliana, her dear friend, had become her best friend.

Frances learned more from Iliana than she could ever repay. She had given her words in English, whispered and practised at night when they were snuggled between the sheets, but Iliana had given her unconditional love, friend-ship and her own family.

'Dinner tonight will be ...' Iliana held her pinched fingers to her mouth and made a smacking sound.

'*Bellissimmo!*' Frances replied and that made Agata giggle too. *Signora* had been so patient with her. She was a wonder-ful mother. One day, she would make a wonderful grand-mother too.

They turned at the sound of footsteps.

Massimo walked into the kitchen, smelling of soap. She hadn't seen him for a week, since he'd touched her belly and she'd cried in his arms in the dark. Her cheeks flamed with the shame of it, of what he must think of her.

'*Ciao, Mamma*.' He walked to his mother and kissed her cheek.

'What is this?' he asked in English. His question was directed at Frances.

'Your mother has taught me how to make this pasta.'

Massimo stepped closer to the table. He brushed against her shoulder as he leaned over to inspect her work. 'Almost as good as *Mamma's*,' he said and then for just the briefest of moments, his hand was on her shoulder.

She resolved right then to tell the Agnolis she had to leave.

Because if she stayed one more day, she would want to stay forever.

After dinner that night, Frances pleaded tiredness and the need for a rest and left the family in the living room listening to the radio. Slowly, she packed up her things. She didn't have much, really. The clothes she'd arrived in, which hadn't fitted her for months, were already packed away in her suitcase. Mrs Agnoli had sewn her two maternity dresses, which she alternated wearing, so she packed one. There were two pairs of shoes. A book she'd brought with her, some toiletries. The note from Dr Elliot in Bega with the address of the Salvation Army home. A bundle of letters from Elizabeta and Vasiliki and her parents, and wafer-thin aerogrammes from Tom in London. She had been careful not to let too many possessions accumulate around her; she hadn't wanted the Agnoli house to feel like home. And even if she had wanted to buy pretty things, the money she'd had when she'd arrived in Cooma was all but spent, and the humiliation of that burnt almost as deep as her pregnancy.

She was pregnant, and alone, with money enough for a bus ticket back to Bonegilla and not much else.

She lifted her small brown suitcase and set it on the end of her bed. This tiny room had been such a place of freedom and sanctuary for her. How could so plain a room, filled with so few possessions, feel like home? There was a double second-hand mattress on a plain wooden frame, which she and Iliana had been sharing since she'd arrived. Every night they'd played tug of war with the five blankets before laughing and drifting off to sleep. Whenever Frances had apologised for taking up space in Iliana's bed, Iliana had told her that if either Giovani or Stefano had been a girl she would be sharing with a little sister anyway, and that it was much more fun to have a friend to talk to at night as she fell asleep.

Iliana didn't have much but had shared it anyway. A dark dresser with a round mirror and rounded edges on its two drawers was set across one corner. On sunny days, the light from the north-facing windows reflected in the mirror and brightened the room. A plain wardrobe with a few wooden hangers in it to hold their few dresses. There was no need for cocktail dresses in Cooma. A rug cut from a piece of carpet, of swirling floral greens and pinks, covered the floor on one side of the bed. An ornate silver and carved wood crucifix hung on the wall above the bed. Iliana crossed herself in front of it every night before turning out the lights.

Frances would remember this room. Her friend. This family. Their kindness. Their open arms. Their slow acceptance of the wayward Australian girl who had got herself into trouble. When Frances thought of this time of cocooning, of hiding her sin and shame, she would at least have her memories of the Agnolis.

She would find the courage to tell them that the next day she was going back to Bonegilla to tell her mother and father and face the truth.

When she opened the door to the living room, the warmth of the open fire flushed her cheeks. Everyone looked up at her, smiling. She truly loved this family and had grown to feel like a daughter to Giuseppe and Agata; a sister to Iliana and Giovani and Stefano. And Massimo? She couldn't think about what she longed to be to him. How would she ever be able to repay what they had all done for her?

'*Buone notte*,' she managed.

'Come. Sit.' Giuseppe waved at her, gesturing to the chair nearest the fire. They had kept it empty for her. She crossed the room and lowered herself backwards into it. Iliana was on the sofa, flicking through the pages of *Women's Weekly* magazine, and she reached across and patted the back of Frances's hand.

She looked at each member of the loving family who had taken her in and felt a wave of grief about having to leave them. Iliana's father, so kind to her to let her stay. Her mother, who had taught her to cook the most delicious food. The two little brothers who had been the best students she'd ever had. And Iliana. Her dear friend Iliana who had fought for her, felt her baby kick inside her, brought her dry toast when she was feeling so sick she couldn't get out of her bed, and who had loved her like her own sister. The family had welcomed her so lovingly, with so little judgement or censure, considering what she'd done and their own religion and culture. She'd been so lucky to have been welcomed into their family, but she had always dreaded the day when it had to end.

And it seemed today was that day.

This was a familiar scene. Giovani and Stefano were lying on the rug, reading Biggles books. She had introduced them to the adventures of the wartime pilot, and they were devouring *Biggles Gets His Men* and *Biggles, Foreign Legionnaire*. Frank Sinatra's voice was crooning from the radiogram in the corner, and the fire cast a warm glow over the room. Iliana's mother was mending a pair of Giuseppe's trousers and Massimo sat on another armchair opposite her. He was gazing down at his linked fingers. She was glad for the heat of the fire to disguise her blushing cheeks.

He was all she had thought about since that night, in the dark with the stars and his breath on her cheek and his warmth and the safety of being in his arms.

Frances rested against the upholstered plumpness of the chair and arched her back. She closed her eyes, tired from the baby, tired of the lie, tired of keeping secrets. She tried to take in every part of the tableau she had just stepped into. If it was to end, she wanted to remember every detail. The boys' cheeky smiles. Their mother's laugh. Their father's wrinkled forehead. Iliana's silky black hair. The fire crackled and Giovani and Stefano giggled with each other, turning the pages of their books. Frank Sinatra's croon gave way to Doris Day and Frances flickered her eyes open.

'My favourite,' she said to Iliana.

'This song?' Iliana asked.

'Secret Love'. Frances had heard it for the first time back at Bonegilla, when *Calamity Jane* had played at the camp's cinema. Without thinking, she looked at Massimo. He was looking back at her.

It was time.

'I have to tell you all something,' she announced.

Agata and Giuseppe looked to Massimo for the translation. '*Voglio dirti una cosa*,' he said.

'What is it?' Iliana sat up. 'Is the baby coming?'

Frances held up a hand to calm them all down. 'No, it's not that. I have decided that tomorrow I will go back to Bonegilla. To my mother and father. So the baby can be born there.'

'You're going away?' Giovani asked. Stefano looked sad too and it was more than Frances could bear.

'Yes.'

'Tomorrow?' Iliana held a hand to her mouth to stop her lips quivering. 'You did not say anything before?'

Frances linked her fingers under her huge belly, moved in her chair to find a place of comfort. 'I decided today. It's not long now before the baby comes and I should travel now before it will be too late to go.'

Agata began to cry. Giuseppe sighed. They may not have understood every word she'd said but they knew baby and Bonegilla.

Massimo got to his feet. The move caught everyone's attention. He cleared his throat and said something fast and loud in Italian. The rest of the family left the room quickly. When the door to the living room closed, she heard stomping footsteps and the back door slamming.

'Frances.' Massimo was by the fire, close to her.

'What's going on?' she asked. And because they were alone, this was the first time she was able to look at him the way she wanted to, without hiding her interest, without pretending she didn't love him. She gave herself the freedom to take in every detail of his face. Massimo had a hint of his mother in his dark eyes, but he had his father's strong mouth and jawline. His dark hair was curly and thick and pushed back from his forehead. His lips looked soft and his cheeks were shadowed with growth. His olive skin gave him the appearance of a tan, even in mid-winter. She willed herself to remember everything about him.

'Francesca,' he said softly. 'I need to tell you something.'

'Massimo. Before you say anything,' she started, trying to catch her breath. 'There is no possible way I can thank your parents, your family, for letting me stay here with you. I will forever be grateful. Truly.'

He was silent, serious. His eyes darted from her eyes to her mouth and the baby and back. 'You go tomorrow.'

She folded her hands in her lap. 'I must. It's time I told my parents, no matter what it will cost me. You have been very understanding, having me here. I know what you think.'

'What?' His chest expanded and he held his breath.

'It's not enough that through my careless behaviour I have brought shame upon myself, but I never wanted your family to share in it. Your brothers think that I had a husband who died in a car accident. I lied to them in case they said anything at school and in case any parents wondered who the pregnant lady is living in their house. I have had to lie to everyone, except you and Iliana and your parents. And I have been so grateful for that. But now, the lying has to stop. I have to go back to Bonegilla and face my family. I've been too ashamed to do that. They will help me put the baby up for adoption. There are many good families who want babies. My little one won't bear the stigma of what I've done. Of being born to an unmarried mother. He—or she—will be able to start afresh in a new family.'

Massimo's expression was dark and unknowable. She couldn't really be sure how much he understood, but she needed to say it all.

'All this time I have been here, living in your house, under your parents' roof, you have kept your opinions to yourself, about me and what I've done. That must have been very difficult for you.'

He stared at her.

'I want to thank you for that. You can't think less of me that I already think of myself.'

'Frances, you don't understand.'

'I do, I—oh!' She clasped her hands to her stomach.

Massimo knelt by her side. 'Is the baby coming?'

Frances tried to breath. 'The baby just kicked me right here.' She pointed a finger at her rib cage. Massimo splayed a hand on the spot she was rubbing, covering her hand with his, and when he felt the next kick, through her fingers, he looked up at her. Instantly, spontaneously, he began to cry. He grasped her hands in his. 'You should not go. I have not said anything all these months.'

He kissed the back of her hand and held his lips there, warm and soft.

'Massimo?' she murmured. What was he saying?

'I not care if this is another man's baby. It is your baby. You cannot give it to a family. Stay here with me. We make a family.'

He kissed her on the lips this time. It was everything she'd ever imagined a kiss from him would be.

He pulled back.

She could still taste him.

He pulled her hand to his chest and pressed it there. 'Francesca. Will you marry me?'

Chapter Twenty-nine

Elizabeta knew they would come.

After she'd nervously walked down the aisle to marry Nikolas Muller, after the vows and the first wedded kiss and the congratulations from each side of the church as she'd walked back towards the wooden doors and the steps outside, she'd seen them there standing together in the last pew.

Vasiliki, Frances and Iliana.

She'd tugged Nikolas to a stop. 'Nik, they're here.'

He'd slipped an arm around her waist and said in her ear, 'The photographer is waiting.'

But she'd wriggled out of his grasp and run to her friends, the Bonegilla girls. When she held out her arms, all three came to her for a hug.

'You look so beautiful,' Frances exclaimed. 'And your pearls!'

Elizabeta's hand flew to her neck. 'A gift from Nikolas's parents.' The Mullers owned a continental butcher shop

now and were doing well. The pearls were a welcome to
their family and Elizabeta had fastened them that morning
with a knot of guilt in her stomach, not the joy she might
have expected. Her mother had had pearls like this once,
fine and delicate orbs with a silver clasp. They were someone
else's now.

'Your dress. It's lovely,' Iliana said.

Vasiliki held Elizabeta's face between her hands and cried.
'Married life is very good. Welcome to it.'

In a heartbeat, Elizabeta was back at Bonegilla with these
girls. These women, now. 'I must go for the photos,' she said
quickly. 'But I will see you at the reception?'

There were nods all round, and Elizabeta went to pose
outside for the photographer, her mother Berta carefully
fanning out the train of her gown on the steps so it sat just
so, her father taking his own photos on his small camera.

'Elizabeta,' her mother scolded. 'Stand still. For the photos.'

'But my friends are here,' she insisted.

'The photos,' Berta snapped. 'Stand still for the photos.'

Her parents had one photo from their wedding. Elizabeta
knew it because it was the only photo they'd taken with
them when they'd been deported from Hungary. On the
day of their wedding, they'd gone to a photographic studio
and posed. Her father sat in a chair wearing his best suit
and tie, his stiff collars pushing up into the softness of his
chin, his hands forming fists on his knees. Her mother was
standing next to him, a hand on his right shoulder. They
weren't smiling, but perhaps people didn't smile in photos
back then. Her mother wore a pale cotton dress with pin-
tucking in long lines down the front of it, with a lace collar
at her neck. Over the dress, a fine leather pleated apron fell

almost to her ankles. There was a thin gold band on her right ring finger.

Her mother had been determined that Elizabeta would have more wedding photos, so a man had been engaged from one of the studios in Adelaide Arcade.

When he'd finished, their friends rushed forward and flicked their palms upward, showering the newlyweds with rice.

That's what she would remember about that day.

A husband. Photos. Friends. Rice.

'Is that your going-away outfit?' Vasiliki demanded, laughing. She had crossed the small church hall to tug Elizabeta away from Nikolas and his family, and she had all but frogmarched her to the table where Iliana and Frances sat. There was polka music playing from a record, and the trestle table, so carefully covered with a white linen tablecloth, was filled with scattered champagne glasses and ashtrays filled with butts with perfect lipstick impressions on the filters.

'Do you like it?' Elizabeta stood and posed like one of the models she'd seen in *Women's Weekly* magazine: her hands on her hips, one foot out front, her hip cocked. She lifted her chin and looked up at the ceiling.

Iliana clapped her hands together. Vasiliki leaned forward to feel the fabric between her thumb and forefinger. 'Silk,' she said approvingly. Elizabeta had saved up for three months to buy the outfit she'd seen in David Jones in Rundle Street. The skirt was slim cut and the jacket fitted her neatly. She wore pale pink shoes and a handbag to match.

She'd never spent so much on an outfit in her whole life: seventy-two shillings and sixpence. She hadn't dared tell her parents.

'It's beautiful, Elizabeta.' Frances was holding a handkerchief to her eyes and smiling through sad tears. Iliana moved in next to her and slipped an arm around her. It seemed they had become very close from their time together in Cooma, and Elizabeta swallowed down a little tug of envy. She wished Luisa could be here today, of all days. She wished Luisa could be here every day.

'Thank you, Frances. Why didn't you tell me you were all coming to Adelaide? I could have cooked dinner for you at home. We would have had time to catch up with all our news, to hear everything about each other.'

'We like to surprise you,' Vasiliki grinned.

'What about your girls? Who is looking after Aphrodite and Elena?'

'My mother. She will make sure they are not hungry.' She held a hand to her flat stomach. 'And I have something to tell you. I have another baby coming.'

'Congratulations.' Elizabeta hugged her friend. 'You must be very tired with two girls and another baby.'

'I don't work in the cafe anymore,' Vasiliki told them. 'I am too busy at home with the family.'

'I will not go back to work,' Elizabeta said. 'I want a baby too. Very soon.'

Frances leapt up from her chair to hug her. Elizabeta thought that Frances looked so grown up now. She wore a fashionable floral dress with a white cardigan and white shoes and a diamante necklace glistened at her collarbone. It was the only jewellery she wore. Not even a ring.

'I wish you every happiness, Elizabeta. I really do.' They held on for a long moment.

Iliana was next. 'I know you have to go for your honeymoon, but we are so happy for you. My mother and father send their regards.'

Elizabeta found herself smiling. 'What is this? Listen to your English. It is very good now. Have you been taking lessons?'

Iliana smiled down at Frances. 'I have spent a lot of time with a good friend who helped me every … all the time.'

An arm was at the small of Elizabeta's back. She knew the scent of Nikolas's aftershave. He nuzzled her neck and she shivered. She hadn't loved him right away, but she loved him now.

'We must go,' he said over the conversation and the music.

'Wait a moment, Nik,' Elizabeta said hurriedly. 'You must meet my friends. From Bonegilla. Frances. Iliana and Vasiliki.'

Nikolas shook hands with them politely. 'I have heard very much about you. Thank you for coming.'

'We wouldn't have missed it.' Frances smiled.

Nikolas tugged at Elizabeta's hand. She kissed him quickly on the cheek. 'My friends, I have to go. I will write soon, I promise. I will tell you my new address.' She blew them all kisses and the bride let herself be led away into her new married life.

Chapter Thirty

1963

Elizabeta jabbed her husband in the ribs.

'Nikolas,' she whispered in his ear, loud enough to wake him. He didn't stir. She tugged at his earlobe and he sleepily swatted her hand away as if it were a mosquito.

'What is it?' he murmured, his eyes still closed, his morning breath stale.

'Wake up, Nik. It was just on the news. The president. He's been shot.'

His eyes flickered open and he turned towards her. 'Kennedy? Are you sure?'

'Listen.'

Elizabeta reached for the volume knob on the clock radio that sat on the bedhead shelf. She turned up the volume, so quickly at first that the staticky noise blared, but when she stopped shaking she was able to settle it lower. They lay in silence, listening to the announcer's grave tone.

The president had been killed in Dallas.

'He was so young.' Nikolas reached for his wife's hand and held it tight in his strong grip. They listened, still, as the spring sunshine grew brighter outside.

'His poor wife. That Jackie,' Elizabeta whispered. 'Those children.' She turned her face away from Nikolas and stared at the ceiling, the plaster pattern in the middle, its Art Deco swoops and curves, the light hanging from its centre. There were no sharp corners. She wished for a life with no sharp corners. Grief, long buried, swelled up inside her like a rolling wave. John F Kennedy was dead. Another death to remind her of those who were lost. The baby who came after her who had died. Then Luisa. Her beloved Luisa. In the Albury dirt so far away.

And now two more children in the world with no father. The idea made her feel wrenched open. Tears welled and slipped down the sides of her face into the pillow.

'Come, come,' Nikolas chided softly. He turned on his side and slipped an arm over her swollen belly. 'Ssshhh. You'll wake up little Luisa and you need your sleep.'

His hand swooped over her stomach, slipped inside her nightgown and rubbed softly over the taut skin. This one, a sibling for little Luisa, was due in three months. Little Luisa. That's what they had called her since she was born, their curly-haired angel. When she'd first told him, Nikolas had baulked at the name. She had only delivered her an hour before. Nikolas had finally been allowed into her maternity room, after the nurses had cleaned her up and the baby had been whisked away to the nursery. He had stared at his wife, gawping.

'You can't call the baby after your sister, Elizabeta. That's too sad. You'll think about your Luisa every time you look at our baby. That won't be fair to her. Why should she have to grow up knowing she was named after her dead *Tante*?'

'It's for my mother. She lost her Luisa.'

'She won't like it. You'll see.'

Elizabeta had lied. It wasn't for her mother. It was for her. She had needed to hold on to the memory of her sister, which was already fading. She needed something to remind her of her Luisa; of her round cheeks and her hair in two thin plaits down her back and the look of wonder on her face and the little round 'o' her mouth made when she looked into the gum trees at Bonegilla and heard a kookaburra for the first time. Of the feel of her soft little arms and the size of her new shoes, bought especially to come to Australia.

She had her Little Luisa and soon she would have another. She covered Nikolas's hand with hers.

'Not long now,' he said.

The idea came to her in that moment. 'If it's a boy, I would like to call him John.'

Nikolas sighed. 'John. Okay, okay.' He leaned over to kiss her cheek and then he slipped out of bed. He took a fresh white singlet and slipped it over his head. He picked up his shirt from the day before, which he'd laid out on the end of the dresser, and pulled it on, buttoning it quickly. While he sat on the end of the bed and tied his shoelaces, Elizabeta lay still, staring at the ceiling, listening to the radio man talk about the president, the sounds and smells of Nikolas getting ready for work so familiar. He worked at Holden on Port Road, making cars on the production line. It was hard work but it paid well and he liked his workmates. There were so many other new Australians, he liked to tell people, that when he looked around the factory floor it was as if half of Bonegilla had been uprooted to Woodville to make cars.

Footsteps. The bathroom door opening, closing and opening again. Footsteps. The soft hiss and pull of the fridge door. The smell of coffee. The scrape of a butter knife on toast. More footsteps.

Elizabeta hadn't worked at the cafe in Rundle Street since before her daughter was born. And now, while Little Luisa slept and the house was still quiet, Elizabeta stayed in bed. Despite the work of it, she loved being a mother. Little Luisa had brought a new joy to Elizabeta's family. Every day, she walked to her parents' house, just fifteen minutes away on the other side of Port Road, and she and Little Luisa would spend the day with her mother. They would make a coffee before walking to the shops on Woodville Road to pick up a loaf of bread or visit the greengrocer for fruit and vegetables. The man behind the counter, a Greek, always gave Little Luisa a banana. Then, after lunch of rye bread and sliced meats and gherkins, Berta and Elizabeta would make dumplings or strudel—cherry in the summer and cheese the rest of the time, or perhaps bake a *marmerkuchen* or apple cake. It would still be hot when Elizabeta's father drove the car into the driveway, and she would wrap half in a tea towel and slip it into the basket in the bottom of Little Luisa's pram and take some home for Nikolas.

Food had become a great comfort to Berta and she wrapped herself in its nourishment, which was revealed in her plump cheeks and her wide hips. Baking was a routine that helped her mother get through every day, or so it seemed to Elizabeta.

Berta had taken to her granddaughter with such love, such fierce possession, that Elizabeta let herself believe that the birth of Little Luisa had worked. She let herself think that a new life had been able to wash away the grief of a lost one and, on some days, there was no lurking memory of her sister. On other days, grief was like the taste of bile in the back of her throat. Some days, she saw her mother look at her with a sharpness and hardness in her eyes. The question was unspoken but as sharp as a knife's blade: *why do you have your Luisa when I lost mine?*

Perhaps it was not possible to get over the grief of losing a child. It had been six years between Luisa's death and Little Luisa's birth. They had never been back to Bonegilla, to Albury, to visit Luisa's lonely grave. Elizabeta still had the framed photo that Frances had sent her, but it was hidden away in the top drawer of her china cabinet. She could never put it on display. Her mother was at her house too often for it to be safely on the mantelpiece in the living room above the gas heater. Nine years gone, and buried so far away. There was immense pain and loss at that distance, too.

The world was full of the ghosts of dead people, Elizabeta thought.

She turned and levered herself up.

Nikolas came back into the bedroom. He leaned down to kiss her on the top of her head. 'You going to your mum's?'

She nodded, yawning. 'Today we are making spätzle. And there are pork chops in the fridge.'

'My favourite.' He smiled and turned to go. 'Have a good day. Kiss Little Luisa for me.'

'I will,' she said and looked up at her husband's back as he left. Something clicked into place.

The front door opened and closed. The cover of the door chime, a circular sphere on the inside of the wooden door, rattled and echoed. The screw needed tightening. Elizabeta added it to the list in her head of all that needed doing before this baby arrived.

There were tiny little running footsteps in the hallway. *'Mutti! Mutti!'*

She held out her arms and Luisa fell into the space between her knees and her stomach full of baby. She hugged her daughter tight, sniffed her hair—baby shampoo—and let herself have this moment. A moment between mother and daughter that had been taken from her own mother. She would always love and hold her own Little Luisa in honour of all her mother had lost.

'Bist du hungrig? Willst du etwas zu esssen?'

'Ja, Mutti.'

Nikolas didn't like that she spoke to Luisa in German. 'What about when she goes to school?' he'd demanded to know. 'She will already be behind. How can she do well if she doesn't know English like the other Australians, huh?'

She had never argued with Nikolas, but she wanted Luisa to be able to speak with her grandparents, her *Oma* and *Opa*. Berta and Jozef had barely any English and what little they had was almost impossible for Australians to understand. Their accents were thick and they put the words together in a way that made sense in German but seemed to confuse Australians. Not that they tried very hard to understand. Elizabeta heard the whispers when they left shops.

'Why don't they just speak English?' It was usually uttered out loud, as if Elizabeta and her mother were invisible.

'How will they ever get on if they don't,' someone else would reply, tut-tutting.

Little Luisa tugged Elizabeta's hand. '*Frühstück, Mutti.*'

'Okay, okay.' She pretended to let Luisa pull her out of bed and they walked hand in hand to the kitchen. Nikolas's coffee cup was on the sink, next to his plate and knife. She stared at it, trying to make sense of it.

'Your father's shirt smells like another woman's perfume,' she said.

Little Luisa looked at her, puzzled. She didn't understand. Neither did Elizabeta.

Elizabeta had married Nikolas two years after they'd met, in a Catholic ceremony at the church where their fathers had become friends. The new priest, an Irishman, had had trouble pronouncing her name. During the ceremony, he called her 'Elizabeth', like the queen. They had taken a bus to Mount Gambier for their honeymoon: three nights in a new motel, a look at the Blue Lake, and then home. They rented a house between her parents and his in Adelaide's western suburbs. They owned an old Austin, which Nikolas drove to work every day. There was a Hills Hoist in the backyard and a washing machine with rollers on the top that squeezed clothes flat. Elizabeta had a frying pan that plugged into the power point because the oven in the rental house didn't work, and they ate from an old dinner set because the new one they'd received as a wedding present was on permanent display in the china cabinet in the corner of the living room.

They only used the good dinner set at Christmas time and on birthdays when her parents and Nikolas's parents came to dinner. There was a new television in the corner of the living room, on which they watched *The Wonderful World of Disney* on Sunday nights and Bob Dyer's *Pick a Box* each Monday. There were neighbours on each side who didn't speak to them and tut-tutted when she and Nikolas spoke in German. She heard the grey-haired lady at number 87 whisper about the Germans once. There were two voices out by the back fence, near the patch of dug earth in which Nikolas grew potatoes. Elizabeta heard a scraping on the fence, as if a garden implement had gone wild and was trying to escape.

'You're joking.' She heard the *scrape, scrape, scrape* against cement and the wooden slats of the fence.

'I'm not, Beryl. We went to war with the buggers and now they're bloody well living next door.'

Elizabeta had stilled, listening. Would there be any use in explaining the complications of who she was? About what the Nazis had done to her and her family, too?

Elizabeta often thought of the German soldier. She wondered where he was living, if anyone else knew the truth about him. In her mind, he was the man who knocked on the front door selling the Funk and Wagnalls encyclopaedia. He stood next to Nikolas on the assembly line at Holden. He delivered the mail that was slipped through her letterbox first thing every morning. He was the man slicing carcasses into chops and grinding meat into mince at the Continental butcher on Tapleys Hill Road. He was the baker smoothing freshly whipped cream onto Black Forest cakes at the German bakery on Port Road. He could be anywhere. Or nowhere.

Or everywhere.

Elizabeta had never talked of the German soldier again with her mother, not after they'd left Bonegilla. They had tried to bury the memory of him there too. Talking about him meant bringing him back to life and they both wanted him to be dead.

Elizabeta propped her elbow on the kitchen table and rested her chin in her palm. Her legs were spread wide to make room for her bulging stomach, distended, tight, full. Little Luisa sat opposite her, eating her scrambled eggs, her child's fork scratching against the melamine of her plate. She would start kindergarten the next year. How odd. Elizabeta and her family had come all this way to the other side of the world to something in German. Pre-school was kindergarten—children's garden—in South Australia. Or kindy. If a name was long, Australians liked to make it shorter. If it was short, they did the opposite.

She'd bet the lady next door was even suspicious of kindergarten.

The bile rose and she swallowed. Heartburn from the pregnancy had made her life a misery in the past few months.

'That means the baby has lots of hair,' her mother told her. Little Luisa had been born bald and had been like that for twelve months. Now, Berta plaited and pinned and clipped her hair in different ways every day, but never in looped plaits. Never like her own daughter's.

'*Genug?*' Enough?

Little Luisa nodded and slid off her chair. She skipped to her bedroom and returned to the table with her favourite doll. Elizabeta took the plate and fork and slipped them into the hot sudsy water in the sink. The lemon scent of the detergent wafted.

Who is she, this woman who leaves her perfume on my husband's shirt? Who is she, this woman whom I must keep secret too? Naming the wound would not heal it, she knew that. Naming Little Luisa had not stopped the pain they all felt at losing the first Luisa.

Later that night, after Little Luisa had gone to sleep, Elizabeta sat in the living room. Her feet, ankles swollen like freshly cooked dumplings, were propped up on the low laminate coffee table. Nikolas still wasn't home. The thin gold hands of the clock above the mantelpiece told her it was eight o'clock. All the pubs in Adelaide were already closed, the six-o'clock swill long over. It wasn't her business to think about where he was.

In her lap was a stack of recent letters from Iliana, from Frances and from Vasiliki. She had read them all at least twice but needed them now, in the loneliness of Adelaide, so far away from the only friends she had in Australia. She hadn't seen them all together since her wedding, that surprise visit four years before.

There had been so many letters over the years that she had a special place for them all. It was an old suitcase, brown and battered, one clasp having failed years ago, that she had brought with her from Germany. Crammed inside it was almost a decade's worth of correspondence.

There had been times when the letters had become infrequent, and Elizabeta was saddened to think that their friendships had faded and frayed, unable to survive the geographical distance and the burdens and responsibilities of marriage and children. A few years back, letters from

Frances had stopped. Nikolas joked that maybe she'd gone on that adventure to Africa or the South Pole that she'd always talked about. But just as mysteriously as they had stopped, one day there was a letter from Frances in the letterbox. She was in Sydney again and she sent a photo of her standing by the Harbour Bridge, wearing a patterned scarf tied around her head and dark sunglasses, a broad smile on her face. There were photos too of Vasiliki's girls, sitting on the low brick fence of her house in Melbourne, with matching dresses and identical hairstyles. Elizabeta had a photo of Iliana with her brother Massimo making snow angels in the front yard of their house in Cooma. When Elizabeta had told them that Luisa was born, Iliana had sent knitted pale yellow booties; Frances a copy of *Seven Little Australians* by Ethel Turner; Iliana a white rattle with bells inside that chimed as Luisa chewed its hard edges when she was teething.

They were women now. Two of them mothers, two still single women.

Elizabeta pulled Iliana's letter dated two weeks prior out of its thin envelope. There was good news in it and it cheered Elizabeta to read it again. Iliana's father and her older brother Massimo had started their own construction business in Sydney, having finally left Cooma for good. Iliana worked in the company's office and her job was called 'secretary'. Elizabeta remembered the secretary girls walking up and down Rundle Street past the cafe in the mornings, their white gloves neat, their handbags in the crooks of their elbows, giggling at their Australian jokes and stories, as if they owned the place. She liked that Australian expression. People had accused her of walking around Woodville as if she owned the place. She had heard it said often. Did that mean she belonged now in this place of meat and three veg on a plate for dinner and schooners of beer in the front bar for the men and being shunned in the suburbs if you were a woman from somewhere else?

Elizabeta had searched Iliana's letter for clues about a boyfriend or a wedding but there were none this time, nor in any letter in the past. Elizabeta's immediate flash of pity transformed into something else in a blink. Iliana was lucky. She would never have to decide what to do when she smelled another woman's perfume on her husband's shirt. Elizabeta had no friends in Adelaide. The girls she knew from the Rundle Street cafe had drifted away. Nikolas's sister Angelika, who might have been a friend, worked on the production line at the Phillips factory at Hendon making small electrical components with thousands of other women, and had found it easy to make friends. She was always going to the cinema or Glenelg to eat ice cream or to dances on Saturday nights at the Semaphore Palais.

Today, there had been another letter from Vasiliki—Vicki—to add to the collection. Elizabeta still had to remind herself to call her Vicki. She and her husband had four children now, all girls: Aphrodite, Elena, Stavroula and Euphemia. Her husband had a cafe of his own and was working very long hours. Vicki was busy with her girls, two were already in school, and she was excited to share the news that they had a new television set. She expressed her disappointment that *Six O'Clock Rock* with Johnny O'Keefe had ended but was quite enjoying *Bandstand* with Brian Henderson. Elizabeta didn't know who she was talking about. She and Nikolas didn't watch those kind of programs.

A key searched for the lock at the front door. She put down her letters. Nikolas came inside, unsteady on his feet.

'Hello,' he said.

'Hello,' Elizabeta replied.

'Luisa is in bed?' he asked as he ran a hand over his Brylcreemed hair.

'Yes.'

'I will have a shower.'

Elizabeta stared at the clock, tried to hear its ticking. She wished the girls from Bonegilla were in Adelaide with her. She wished she could tell them about the woman with the perfume and her husband, that she could ask them what she should do. She resolved to write her letters tomorrow. After a good night's sleep, she might be of a mind to craft a letter full of happy lies in broken English. She was practised at it. She had been doing it for years, after all.

Chapter Thirty-one

'*Mamma*, how many bridesmaids does she need?'

Iliana folded up the pages of *La Fiamma*, and moved the newspaper to the other end of the kitchen table. Her empty coffee cup stared back at her, the grounds in the bottom probably an omen. She crossed her arms and sat back in her chair. For months now, every conversation in her family had been about the wedding. How many sugared almonds in the bomboniere? What should the bridesmaids wear? How beautiful will her wedding dress be? One flower girl or two? Or three? How soon before they will have children?

Iliana's mother, Agata, turned from the stove, pots and saucepans laid out in front of her like a drum kit. Her tomato sauce-covered spoon waved in the air. 'You don't want to be a bridesmaid?'

'Of course I do. It's just that …'

'Stop with your complaining. You will be her sister-in-law so of course you should be in the wedding. No matter what that mother of hers says.' Agata *tsk*ed and went back to stirring her ragu.

Iliana thought about making another coffee but there was no room on the stove top now her mother had begun the weekend's cooking. Her only choice was to sit at the table and try not to think about exactly how ugly her bridesmaid's dress going to be. The one she was going to wear as fifth bridesmaid for her brother Massimo's wedding to Domenica Marinelli.

Fifth bridesmaid. *Fifth.* The afterthought bridesmaid. The woman the bride had been forced to include to appease her husband's family, something that did not come naturally to Domenica. Iliana knew that much about her. Apart from the matron of honour, who was Domenica's already married sister, there were Domenica's two other sisters, a cousin, her best friend, and her soon-to-be sister-in-law. *Oh, poor Iliana, Massimo's spinster sister.* Iliana had imagined the conversation.

'Put her in the wedding, Domenica.' She was confident Massimo would have stood up for her.

'But she's ugly, Massimo. She won't look good in any dress. I don't want her to ruin my wedding. Or the photos.'

'She's not ugly. She's … interesting. Have some sympathy for my sister. It's as close as she's ever going to get to the real thing.'

No, that's probably not what Massimo would have said. He was the kindest, most loving big brother in the world. But that's how Iliana felt these days. How could she not? She was twenty-five years old and still not married, still living at home with her parents, who were increasingly worried about what was going to become of their only daughter. Iliana was certain they hadn't worried about Massimo the same way, even though he was older than her by two years and was only just now getting married himself. And hadn't he found himself a perfect wife? Domenica was beautiful, slim, younger than Iliana at twenty-three years old, from a prosperous Italian family in Sydney, and she seemed determined to be the perfect Italian wife. To the outside world at least. Domenica batted her heavily mascaraed eyelashes and agreed with everything Massimo said, as if having no opinion of her own was a measure of her own devotion. Iliana loved her big brother, but he wasn't right all the time. She knew that because they worked together in the family business. She kept the books in order, paid accounts including wages, answered the phone, met new clients who were looking to build their first home, and mediated between her father, who still had little English, and the banks and suppliers who spoke no Italian. In fact, she ran the show.

The only thing Iliana could claim was that her family had become what some might call prosperous. Her father's construction business—now Agnoli and Son, for Massimo was officially a partner with his father—had quickly become successful. They'd ridden the housing boom of the early sixties to prosperity.

Massimo had become a partner the day after he'd announced his engagement. He was doing what a son was supposed to do. Iliana had failed in doing what an Italian daughter ought to do.

She knew Domenica would not make him a good wife. She'd known it from the first time they'd met, when Massimo had brought her home for dinner to meet the family.

'This is my sister, Iliana,' Massimo had said, clearing his throat.

Iliana had held out her hand to shake Domenica's, but Domenica had kept her arm resolutely at her side. She'd looked Iliana up and down, glanced at her work outfit and sighed. Iliana believed there was nothing wrong with her jacket and pencil skirt, with a ruffled white shirt underneath. It looked professional and neat. Her hair had been pulled back in a French twist and her make-up was artfully applied. She took great pride in being the professional face—if not the brains—of Agnoli and Son. She had to look respectful and professional.

'You didn't have time to change into something more appropriate to meet your future sister-in-law?' Domenica asked, looking her over.

'I've just got home from work.'

'Work.' Domenica sighed and slipped her arm through Massimo's. She shrugged her shoulders and laid her head to rest on his arm, as if uttering that one word had exhausted her. She gazed up at him lovingly.

Iliana noticed that Massimo wasn't looking at her in quite the same way.

'You poor thing. I can't wait to make a home for Massimo and our children. That will be my blessed work.'

'And we are very much looking forward to that day,' Iliana's mother said, before politely bestowing a kiss on each of Domenica's cheeks.

From that day forward, Iliana wished with all her strength that her brother wasn't marrying Domenica.

Iliana's mother pushed a chopping board in her daughter's direction. 'Here, do the onions.'

'*Si, Mamma.*' Iliana sliced through the ends of the onion and bounced her sharp knife against the wooden board, her eyes watering and stinging, and she wondered how many more years she would have to sit at her family's kitchen table helping her mother cook dinner for the boys.

'It's not long now, the wedding.' Her mother's knife slicked through sticks of celery and peeled bulbs of garlic.

'No, it's not long.'

'She will be a good wife to Massimo.'

Iliana stopped, putting her knife down. 'Really, *Mamma*? How do you know?'

'Ah, don't be ridiculous with such a question.'

'I really want to know. How do you know they'll be happy?' Iliana rested her hand on her mother's, a silent plea for her to stop her work and talk to her daughter.

Agata put her knife down on the chopping board. 'She loves him, can't you see that? She smiles at him. She hangs on to him like she wants to stop him from running away. I know she will make him happy. And that's good, because Massimo …' Agata's voice trailed off. She lifted an arm and wiped her eyes on the sleeve of her dress. 'My Massimo. He has not been happy for a long time. Not since Cooma. Your father and I thought he would never find a wife so we are happy now for him. He is successful. Domenica will make him a good home and give him children. Give us grandchildren. A family needs grandchildren.'

Iliana didn't want to remind her mother that it was Giuseppe who had found Massimo a wife. His business associate only had to mention that he had a beautiful single daughter and the fathers had almost picked out the wedding ring and the reception venue before their children had even met. Iliana couldn't shake the niggling doubt that Massimo had come reluctantly to the idea. If she truly believed her brother loved this girl, she wouldn't have said a word. Once, he had looked at a woman as if he loved her. And that woman was Frances Burley, a long time ago, back in Cooma. She had never asked him about what had happened between them the night before Frances had left, and neither Massimo nor Frances had ever spoken of it. She had come to bed, after, and cried herself to sleep. Massimo didn't even go to the bus station to say goodbye to her.

It hadn't been her business to tell her big brother what to do then, and it wasn't her place to tell him what to do now.

'I think you and *Papà* are looking forward to grandchildren,' Iliana said.

Agata sighed, exasperated. 'Of course we are. Massimo is twenty-seven and you are twenty-five and nothing yet? People look at me in church and I know they think something is wrong with our family.'

Iliana put down her knife. Surely it was only the onions making her cry. '*Mamma*, is there something wrong with me?'

'What are you talking about?'

'No one wants to marry me. I will never find a husband.' It was hard to admit the fear that she would never be loved, that she would never move out of her parents' house, that she would never find someone who wanted to make love to her. Her body had ached for that intimate touch, the touch of a man's lips on hers. An arm around her waist, pressed to the small of her back. And she wanted to have babies, too. As each year passed, Iliana could feel it all slipping through her fingers. Was she soon going to be too old to have children?

Perhaps that was why, in her heart of hearts, she was so envious of Domenica. Domenica who was beautiful and so close to being the perfect Italian wife and mother. Her sister-in-law would have what Iliana desperately wanted: a husband, a home of her own, children. She was twenty-five years old now. An old maid.

'My beautiful daughter. There is one man out there for you. I know it in my bones.' Her mother crossed herself three times, as if invoking God might help speed the process.

'Look at where we are and where we were when we came to Australia nine years ago. Nine years.' Her mother shook her head. 'We have had so much luck. We have a home here in Leichhardt, close to our church. A business that employs not just your father and your brother, but you, too. And if your little brothers were as interested in working as they are in playing that *calcio*, it would have been for them as well. Your father has worked hard to give his family all of this.'

'You've worked hard too, *Mamma*.'

Agata waved her daughter's words away. 'It has all been for our children. For you to have a better life than we did. You will have that life too, Iliana. A family. One day. Be patient.'

Iliana fought a familiar tightness in her chest, a memory, a feeling of old arms around her, of the course black of her clothing. 'I miss *Nonna*.'

After all this time, at the mere mention of her own mother, Agata's lips trembled. 'My *mamma*. I miss her too. She didn't want me to come to Australia with your father, you know. We didn't know anything about Australia. She was scared. I changed my mind. I told your father I didn't want to come. Your father and I had a big fight about it.'

'You did?'

'I didn't want to leave the village. My mother and my *nonna* begged me not to go. But it was what your father wanted. He wanted to provide for his family and there were no jobs in Italy. I gave up my family to come here to Australia, Iliana. That's why, here, in Australia, making another family is important.' Agata stopped, searched her daughter's face. She reached across and cupped her chin. 'But I want you to make the right kind of family. You should wait for a good man.'

'You mean it, *Mamma?*'

'I do. Wait for someone you really love. Massimo? I don't know if he loves Domenica the way she loves him, but he is ready to settle down, to make a home of his own. Thank God for that. But does he love her?' Agata shrugged.

Iliana was so stunned at this honesty from her own mother that she sat, speechless, staring at the face that was so familiar to her. Her mother's brown eyes shone with tears. Her olive skin was wrinkled now, creasing in the corners of her eyes and in the lines above her top lip. Her hair, black with strands of wiry grey, was pulled back in an efficient bun on top of her head. Her narrow shoulders were still so strong, her heart inside her chest bigger than Iliana had ever imagined.

'Iliana, I want you to be married. I want you to know the joy of children and a family of your own. I want to see your grandchildren one day. But I know who really runs the business. I know who is there when Massimo is off playing soccer and your father is at the club. Your father and Massimo have both had their heads turned by a beautiful girl from a good family.' She winked. 'And Massimo will find out soon enough if there is more to her than her long eyelashes.'

Iliana laughed. To hear her own mother say something so subversive was a delight but a shock, too. '*Mamma!*'

Agata waved her hands in the air and grinned through her laughter. 'Wait until she has to put her hands in the sink every night and wash the dishes.'

They continued working in silence, the smell of garlic and onion, basil and tomato sauce comforting and familiar. As she chopped, Iliana thought over what her mother had said. It was true about Massimo. He'd been drifting since they'd been in Cooma. He railed against injustice wherever he saw it, whoever meted it out. When they'd moved to Sydney, he'd found another cause to be angry about. He had met an old man at their church, St Fiacre's, and when Massimo had discovered the man had been interned in Australia during World War Two, he had come home, furious. He'd pounded his fist on the kitchen table during dinner, startling the crockery.

'He's been here since 1928, *Papà*. How could Australia do that to him and all those men?' he'd demanded. 'I know why. They locked us up during the war and then they never trusted us, did they? We are Italians and Catholics and fascists for Mussolini, right? Enemies. And now they want us to be ashamed of what we are. Not me. I am not ashamed to be Italian or Catholic. The Australians ... they want us to come and do all the dirty jobs, to work in the dirt and the heat and the cold, to dig underground for the Snowy, to grow their food and work in their factories. But they don't really want us to be Australians.'

'Massimo,' Giuseppe had urged. 'Calm down.'

Her brother had pulled his lips together and fumed. He'd carried an anger inside him a long, long time.

Iliana lifted her chopping board and swept the chopped onions into a large cast-iron pot her mother had positioned in the middle of the table. She'd brought it with her from Italy in the family's wooden chest.

'I hope Massimo is marrying Domenica because he loves her,' Iliana said. 'I will wear that bridesmaid's dress and I will be happy for my brother.'

'Good. And who knows?' Agata smiled. 'You might meet a nice man at the wedding. You will look *bellissimo* in your bridesmaid's dress.'

'*Signorina.*'

Iliana looked up from her bomboniere on the table in front of her, the torn white mesh and single sugared almond remaining in its folds evidence that she'd eaten the other five already. She wasn't hungry in the slightest, after five courses and three glasses of prosecco, but she was sitting all alone, having completed all her duties as fifth bridesmaid, watching numbers one, two, three and four twirling around the dance floor with their boyfriends or fiancés or complete strangers.

A man was standing next to her. 'Why is the most beautiful girl in the world sitting here all by herself and not dancing, huh?'

He was very handsome. His dark hair was swept back fashionably, his suit modern and slim, but it was his eyes that caught hers. Smiling, sincere, honest.

Iliana straightened her back, smoothed her hands down the apricot shantung of her bridesmaid's dress and looked up at him. All those glasses of prosecco had given her some courage.

'Who are you?' She lifted her chin, daring.

He slipped his hands behind his back, bowed. 'My name is Vincenzo Gonelli. I know your father and your brother. I am a tiler. I worked on a house they built in Haberfield.'

Iliana held a hand out over the arrangement of white roses to shake his. 'Iliana.' His grip was firm.

'I know who you are.' He smiled. He didn't let go of her hand. 'You look very beautiful tonight, *bella*. Would you like to dance?'

Iliana pushed her chair back and stood. 'Yes, I would, Vincenzo Gonelli.'

Their first dance was the beginning of everything.

Chapter Thirty-two

'*Hrónia pollá*, Aphrodite!'

The crowd of people milling in the backyard of Vasiliki and Joe's house in Oakleigh cheered loud enough that the Greek music was drowned out for just a moment. There were so many people that Vasiliki had lost count. Her mother and father, her sisters Eleni and Constantina, their husbands and their children (one daughter, two sons), her husband Steve's family and siblings, the Angelopoulos family, the Koutsameniotis family, the Georganases, three sets of neighbours and people from church. Enough guests to eat all the lamb slowly roasting on the spit by the shed and the trestle tables full of salads and desserts Vasiliki's mother and her friends from church had spent two days making.

But none of it seemed to impress her oldest daughter. Aphrodite threw her arms around her mother and hid her face in her skirt.

'What's the matter, Aphrodite?'

She began to whimper. Vasiliki crouched down, her toes pushing into the fierce point of her stiletto heels, and stroked her daughter's curls away from her face. 'This is your birthday party. You're supposed to have fun today. Six years old, already going to school. Can you imagine that? You're such a big girl already.'

Aphrodite sniffed and tears welled in her huge brown eyes. 'All those people make me scared, Mummy.'

Vasiliki huffed. 'What are you talking about? You know everyone. You've seen them all a hundred times.'

'I don't want a party.' Her little voice quavered. 'I want to go to my room.'

'What is wrong with her?' Vasiliki's mother had rushed over to investigate her granddaughter's wilful behaviour, wiping her hands on the apron tucked around her waist. She lifted Aphrodite's chin and searched her face for some sign of sickness or disease. 'Ach, she won't even give me a kiss hello on each cheek today.' She shook a finger in her granddaughter's face. Her Greek was harsh. 'Aphrodite, don't be a naughty girl. You must be nice.'

Vasiliki turned her daughter away and slipped into the space between them. '*Mamma*. Don't say that.' Vasiliki slipped an arm around Aphrodite. 'Please, give your *yiayia* a kiss.' Aphrodite slowly pressed her lips to her grandmother's cheeks. Dimitria huffed and headed back to the table, which was groaning with food.

Without a word, Vasiliki slipped her hand in Aphrodite's and took her away from the people and the noise. Up the back steps, inside the house, past the laundry and down the hallway to her own room. Her other daughters Elena and

Stavroula were playing happily outside with the Georganas boys and little Euphemia—Effie—was tucked up in a blanket in her pram under the back veranda.

At the door to her room, Aphrodite pulled free, ran across the pink rug and jumped onto her bed. Four of her teddy bears and her favourite rag doll bounced up and tumbled to the floor as if her bed were a trampoline. Aphrodite snuggled up in a foetal position and burrowed into her pillow. Vasiliki's heart ached at the sight. She pulled the pink nylon bedspread from the end of the bed and covered her daughter's legs.

'You have a sleep.' Vasiliki found a spot on the bed by her daughter's side.

'Thank you, Mummy.'

Aphrodite's English was perfect. She barely had an accent when she spoke. She sounded like all the other little Australian girls in her class and Vasiliki was proud of that. She always spoke English to her children. She wanted them to do well at school, and in this life in Australia, and they would only be held back if they couldn't talk to the teacher or their friends. Everything was in English: their school, the radio, the television and, eventually, work. Steve felt the same way and the only Greek spoken in the house was between husband and wife when they didn't want the girls to know what was being discussed: the business. His mother. Her mother.

Vasiliki stroked Aphrodite's hair, hoping it would soothe her daughter, watching as her eyes slowly closed. Soon, her chest was rising and falling in deep breaths. How was it possible that she was so different in personality to her three sisters? Elena and Stavroula were like their father: loud, playful and adventurous. It was too early to know what Effie would be like, but she was already a terrible sleeper, up for hours on end, which made Vasiliki believe she might be cut from the same mould.

Her firstborn was different and Vasiliki held on tight to the reason why. She had never told anyone about Aphrodite's real father. She hadn't needed to explain away her pregnancy. Her arranged marriage to Steve had been quick and, with some fudged dates from the doctor and a slight untruth about the baby being a few weeks early, everyone believed the lie that she had conceived her child on her wedding night.

'How lucky we are!' Her mother had been thrilled that a child was on the way so soon. Vasiliki had smiled and agreed that yes, she was blessed. Blessed to have this piece of Tom Burley with her forever.

For long stretches of time, she would forget all about her secret. She had a busy life—four daughters and Steve's thriving business—and she rarely had time for memories. But every now and then, like today, she allowed herself to think about Tom. As she stared at her daughter, taking in every detail of her perfect, olive-skinned face, her long, long eyelashes and her full lips, Vasiliki let her thoughts return to him and the daughter they shared. If she looked closely, Vasiliki could see him in Aphrodite. Her eyes were different to those of her sisters, a light caramel brown, not the almost-black depths the others shared. Aphrodite's curls were tight ringlets at her neck, while her sisters had straight hair. And she seemed to not like parties, even though today's was in her honour. The first child, the first grandchild, and she wanted to be alone in her room rather than out in the back-yard opening her presents and playing games with the other children.

Vasiliki understood. She knew it was wrong to have favourites, but oh, how she did. Her little Aphrodite would always be her most special child. Her gift from Tom. She relished this time, the simple peace of watching her daughter sleeping, the freedom of being able to look for Tom and seeing him there in her six-year-old's face, for reminders of the love she had felt for her daughter's father. Vasiliki didn't know how it all worked, who or what or how it was decided what a child inherited from a mother and what was passed down from a father. Perhaps wrapped up in that mix were pieces of their grandparents, too. Vasiliki knew she didn't look like her own mother, but put her next to a photo of her own *yiayia* back in Greece and the resemblance was striking. The same eyes, the same chin. Some things did run in families, she knew that to be true. And perhaps they skipped a generation every now and then.

Sometimes, it was only her secret that got her through the days and weeks and months and years. Effie was only six months old; Vasiliki had spent almost seven years pregnant or breastfeeding. She was the kind of tired only mothers knew. And there was Steve the night before, hinting that they should have another baby. He'd come home from work late, as usual, having had to wait until the milk bar closed and then supervise the cleaning up, and he'd stripped off his clothes and snuggled into bed next to her. She'd been asleep for hours by then and roused to his breath smelling like ouzo.

'Vasiliki,' he'd moaned as he'd pressed his erection into her back and sloppily kissed the back of her neck. He wanted sex every day. Every single day.

'Go away. You stink,' she'd said, reaching behind her and slapping him on the thigh.

'My beautiful wife.'

'My drunk husband.'

'C'mon, Vasiliki. We can make a son this time. Don't you think there are too many girls in this family already?'

With a shove from his wife, he'd rolled onto his back. Within half a minute, he'd begun to snore.

She had never once complained about him coming home late like this, for all the extra hours she was alone with the children, for all the time she was alone with herself after they'd reluctantly gone to sleep.

Vasiliki was relieved. She didn't want to have sex with her husband because she didn't want another baby. Four was more than enough. When she'd asked Steve to pull out before, well before, he'd said, 'Yeah, yeah, oh, I will, I will, just a bit more, wait just a minute, I'm about to …'

But he'd done the exact opposite every time.

She was done with babies.

At a Christmas party the year before, some of her Greek friends had been talking about an Australian doctor who was giving medicine to married women so they didn't have to have babies if they didn't want to.

'It's called …' Her friend Athena had glanced around the shed in the family's backyard to make sure none of their husbands or mothers-in-law could hear. 'It's called the Pill.' Elena had six children already: four boys and two girls. Vasiliki could completely understand why she was so interested in this miracle you swallowed to stop more babies.

'The Pill?' Vasiliki said. 'How does it stop the babies?'

'I don't know exactly. But my cousin's friend's neighbour is taking it. She got it from a doctor in Fitzroy.'

'And you have to take this medicine every day?'

'Exactly,' Athena whispered. 'Like Bex.'

Vasiliki didn't know what Steve would think if he found out she was taking a pill like that. She wanted to believe what Athena had said but she was cautious about asking the family doctor about it. He was an old Australian man with grey hair and a stooped back with a surgery in the next suburb. He'd served in the war and had little tolerance for babies or, in fact, any of his patients. She had to walk for forty-five minutes to get there, pushing the pram with two of the girls inside it and the older two walking alongside, which sometimes made her late. Neither the doctor nor the receptionist had any sympathy for a mother juggling four children and they always spoke loudly and slowly to her as if she didn't understand English. She understood every word, especially their complaints under their breaths about these new Australians.

'I do speak English,' she'd wanted to shout at them. 'And stop being so bloody rude.' She liked the word *bloody*.

But she never did shout at strangers that way. She smiled and thanked the doctor profusely when he pronounced her babies well, when he told her they'd been putting on weight and that it was about time the little one was put on the bottle.

'Formula is much better for the baby than breastmilk. You'll know exactly how much the child is consuming,' he'd said, condescending to her over the tops of his silver wire-rimmed glasses. He'd slipped his fountain pen into the top pocket of his white coat and stood up, just like that. The appointment was always over when he decided it was over.

Vasiliki decided she would think about the pills, maybe. She would perhaps look out for advertisements on the television during *Bandstand*, or search the advertisements in the *Women's Weekly*. She liked that magazine very much, when she had a few minutes to sit at the kitchen table with a black coffee and a cigarette, although she sometimes had trouble keeping track of all the English princesses who were getting married.

She was living the life arranged for her by her parents. Her marriage to Steve had been happy on the whole, and she had her obligations to her own mother and now her four daughters. Her role in life was to make a home, cook and clean, raise children and make sure they had the best of everything. She knew in her heart she would never have been able to have this life with Tom. How would he fit in out there in the backyard with all those Greeks?

Over the years, Frances's letters had conveyed snippets of information about him. He was still in London working as a lawyer. There had been no mention of marriage or children, which made her so sad for him. He deserved to be happy. She wanted nothing more for him than that.

She had wrestled for years with the guilt of not telling him about his daughter. How to explain why she had kept it a secret all this time? How could she tell Steve the truth, knowing it would break his heart? And her parents? Some things were better left unsaid. No good would come of telling the truth.

Aphrodite moved in her sleep, murmuring something in her soft little voice. Vasiliki slipped off her stilettos and lay down next to her daughter.

Her heart. Her joy. Her lifelong secret.

Chapter Thirty-three

1964

Someone whispered under their breath. 'Here she comes.'

Frances pulled her quivering lips together and tried not to cry when she turned and saw her beautiful friend Iliana walking up the aisle towards the pulpit. Her wedding dress was so voluptuous that its Chantilly lace skirt, puffed up by voluminous petticoats, and her twenty-foot-long veil brushed against the wooden pews on either side of the aisle of St Fiacre's in Leichhardt. The swish was accompanied by gasps of delight as guests on both sides of the church—her family on the left and his on the right—saw the bride on the arm of her beaming father. Everyone stood. Somewhere, someone was singing *Ava Maria* and Frances found herself holding her breath with the beauty of it. Iliana looked up to the altar, towards her fiancé, Vinnie, and Frances could see her beaming smile. There was a loud sigh and when she glanced across at Vinnie, there were tears rolling down his cheeks.

Frances gripped her bouquet and tried to focus. Don't look at Iliana or you will cry. Don't look at Vinnie again or you will cry.

And in particular, don't you dare look at the best man.

When *Ava Maria* ended, the church organist's rendition of the bridal waltz began and by the time it reached its full crescendo Iliana was at her future husband's side. She looked radiant.

Frances's fellow bridesmaids, all seven of them, stood in silent and identical formation. Their pale blue sleeveless gowns with narrow skirts matched the groomsmens' ties. They held cascading bouquets of white roses and carnations.

It had been a long time since Frances had dressed up—she'd managed to avoid social situations for a long while—and she was wearing more make-up than she had ever worn in her life, including eyeliner expertly applied by Iliana's maid of honour, her sister-in-law Domenica. Her face was stiff and her eyelashes felt as if she'd walked into a spider's web. As well as all the bridesmaids, there was a best man and seven attendants. Frances thought they all looked like Dean Martin. So debonair. So handsome.

And when she let herself take a glance at Massimo, the best man, she thought he was the most handsome of them all. He stared back at her across the altar, his dark eyes questioning and curious, intent on her. When he turned this gaze on her, she still felt like the only woman in the world. Still, after all these years.

She had never got over him.

It had been almost six years since she'd left Cooma. Iliana had written and told her about Massimo's engagement. Frances had bought a bottle of gin and got so terribly drunk she'd had to have the next day off school, pleading a stomach flu. She still felt like crying at the unfairness of it all, of what had happened and why she'd had to say no to him. So she looked away, concentrated on keeping her bouquet straight in her hands. She gripped it so tight her fingers ached. Light beamed down from the stained-glass windows. Massimo was married now. He was happy.

She was so glad of it.

I could never have made him happy, not back then. Not now. Not ever.

She wished Vasiliki and Elizabeta were here, but too many children and not enough money—in Elizabeta's case—meant they hadn't been able to come to Sydney.

The priest cleared his throat and Frances's attention snapped back to the present. '*O, Iliana, prendo te, Vincenzo …*'

'I, Iliana, take you, Vincenzo, as my husband and promise to be faithful to you always, in joy and in pain, in health and in sickness, and to love you and every day honour you, for the rest of my life.'

The groom slipped the ring on the bride's finger and when they kissed, a wave of emotion rose up from the guests and Iliana and Vinnie kissed again, to a loud cheer.

Iliana had chosen the tallest wedding cake Frances had ever seen. Nine tiers high, with bright white icing and a lace pattern that matched her dress, it might be just enough for the two hundred guests at the reception. The huge room at the reception centre was decorated with swathes of fabric draped from the ceiling and small chandeliers. Mirrors reflected the light and flickered like stars on the bridal couple, and rows and rows of tables were full of guests.

Frances sat quietly at the top table during most of the formalities of the reception. She picked at each and every plate put in front of her to be polite, but she wasn't really hungry at all. She had slipped her bomboniere and her place card into her purse as souvenirs of the special day, and had stopped at two glasses of prosecco. Just enough to calm her but not enough to stop her wishing for things she couldn't have. Speeches had been made—in Italian—and when it was time for the bride and groom's first dance, Vinnie swept his wife into his arms and they moved as one around the parquetry dance floor brought in especially for the occasion. The tears in Iliana's eyes were expressions of true joy. Frances spotted Giuseppe and Agata. They were crying and hugging each other. How lucky they were to have two children already married. How lucky Iliana was to have married for love.

Halfway through the bridal waltz, Massimo and Domenica joined the bride and groom, as matron of honour and best man, and slowly, the groomsmen moved behind the bridal table to reach for the hand of their bridesmaid. Frances's dance partner was Claudio. He held out a hand to her and she nodded politely. He was an excellent dancer, but spoke little English, which meant their turn about the floor was polite and almost wordless. There were cheers when the first song ended and Claudio gave Frances a little bow and then disappeared.

She wasn't alone for more than a moment when Massimo was by her side.

'Frances.'

'Hello, Massimo.' That's all she could bear to say. There were no other words for this man, this good man whose heart she had broken when she'd said no to his proposal back in Cooma. And now he was standing right by her, his hand out, wordlessly asking her to dance. How could she take his hand?

But she did. She couldn't stop herself. She allowed him to pull her close, and she came alive when his hand gently caressed the small of her back. She followed his lead, turning, moving, his thighs against hers, surrounded by him. This was easier than talking, easier than explaining all that had happened to her since she'd seen him last.

She lifted her gaze to his face to see what expression was there. Would it be anger or hate or pity? His full lips were parted as if he was about to speak but he said nothing. He just looked at her, his dark eyes full of something she didn't want to see. Something that shouldn't have been there.

'Iliana is such a beautiful bride.' Frances glanced over her shoulder. Iliana and Vinnie had returned to the wedding table and were eating wedding cake. She was spooning huge chunks into Vinnie's mouth and he was laughing hard. She supposed that wasn't the only thing they had a hunger for.

'She is. Beautiful and happy. Vinnie is a very good man.'

'Iliana has written to me about him. She loves him very much. She told me she met him at your wedding.'

Massimo's eyes narrowed. Was she imagining things or had he pulled her in tighter? 'Yes.'

'I'm sorry I haven't had the chance before today to say congratulations to you and your wife.'

'Thank you.' They moved silently around the dance floor to the beat of the music, one step after another, one heartbeat after another, one song ending and another beginning. There seemed to be so much to say but Frances couldn't find a place to start. When Massimo broke the silence, she exhaled with relief.

'Iliana tells me you're teaching here in Sydney now.'

She swallowed. 'Yes, that's right. It's a new primary school in the western suburbs. Australia is having a baby boom, don't you know?'

'I know all about it. We're building the houses they are living in.'

'Your business is doing very well, Iliana tells me. Congratulations.'

He was proud of that, she could hear it in his voice. 'We have worked very hard. My father and Iliana, especially.'

'I'm sure you have worked hard, too.' Under her hand, his shoulders felt strong. 'I hope you are happy being married, Massimo.' Frances had to say it. She had loved him since Bonegilla, but she had rejected him in Cooma. He had wanted to marry her, had wanted to keep the baby and had offered to raise it as his own, but she couldn't have saddled him with another man's child. It wasn't his burden to take on. And she wouldn't have been able to live with the thought that he was doing it out of honour, of obligation, rather than love. That's all she had ever wanted of him. Love, uncomplicated.

Frances breathed deep, willing away the ache inside her chest. 'And how is your son? His name is Giuseppe, isn't it?'

'Yes. He has the name of my father. His *nonno*. He's three months old now.' This made Massimo smile, at last.

Frances leaned up close to his ear. 'I'm sure he looks just like you. Handsome as anything.'

Massimo smiled down at her. 'He's a beautiful little boy.'

Did he know how lucky he was?

Her own baby—not a baby anymore—would be six years old by now. The age of the students in her classroom. Most days Frances wouldn't think about her own son, what kind of toys he might be playing with, what kind of life he had. Until a little boy from her class fell in the playground and scraped his knee, or another needed help with his reader, and then she would think about all the things mothers did for their children: comforted them when they fell, read to them when they wanted a story, hugged them when they needed love.

Frances had returned to Bonegilla the day after Massimo's proposal. She had said her tearful goodbyes to Iliana, Giuseppe and Agata and the young boys at the Cooma bus station. Massimo wasn't there. Agata had pressed a brown paper-wrapped parcel in her hands as she got on the bus. Inside was a knitted blanket. She had covered her knees with it all the way back to Bonegilla.

She hadn't called ahead to tell her parents she was coming home. When she arrived back at Bonegilla late that next night, eight months pregnant and lugging her suitcase, her mother had turned a ghostly shade of grey. She had remained cloistered away until the time came, and her mother had driven her to a hospital in Albury to give birth—having the baby in the Bonegilla hospital was never an option—and the doctor had arranged an adoption with a local couple. They were a good Christian family, he'd reassured her parents, who would welcome Frances's baby into their home with loving arms and open hearts, despite his sin of being born to a single mother.

Hours after giving birth, the shock of it still trembling in every part of her body, Frances had insisted on giving her son a name. 'He deserves that, at least,' she'd told herself. The official paperwork was laid out on the rollaway table in front of her. Her pen hovered over the section marked *Father's Name.* She had been warned not to fill it in, that there was no good to come of roping an innocent man into the scandal and anyway, did she even know who the real father was? She wished she could put Massimo's name there. She wished he was the father of her baby.

But he wasn't. Instead, she gave his name to her son.

In the line where she had to record her baby's birth name, she wrote *Massimo Reginald*, adding Reginald after her father. She hadn't been able to accept Massimo's proposal, but she had paid tribute to his honourable offer in the only way she had known how.

Six years ago still felt like yesterday.

She felt it then, the quivering of those post-birth hours, the trembling inside her chest. The wet pain between her legs, deadened with drugs and thick cloths to catch the bleeding, which went on for weeks. The shame of her baby flared in her cheeks. The shame of wanting Massimo sat like a stone in her gut.

'Frances?'

Massimo's hand pressed ever so slightly more firmly into the small of her back. He guided her around another couple on the dance floor.

'Francesca?' Her real-life Massimo bent down a little to look into her eyes. 'Are you dreaming?'

In her dreams, he called her Francesca. In her dreams they were in Rome, tossing a coin into the Trevi Fountain, making a wish together.

'I'm sorry, I'm ...'

'You are thinking of something.'

'Yes, I am. Just memories from the past, that's all.' And then she couldn't keep it in any longer. 'I still have the coin you gave me at Bonegilla, you know. I've kept it all these years.'

'You have?' He closed his eyes and sighed deeply.

She nodded. Did he understand what that meant? What she couldn't say here in front of his wife and his family and Iliana?

'Oh, Francesca. There is something I need to say—' He suddenly stiffened in her embrace and his grip on her waist and her hand eased. His expression transformed in a blink from warm to stone cold.

'I would like to dance with my husband.' Domenica, elegant, perfectly coiffed, her chin held high and her eyes narrowed, placed a hand on Frances's left shoulder and pushed her back from Massimo. She slipped into the space between them and shot a last condescending look over her shoulder.

'Of course.' Frances stepped back, glanced around. The humiliation burned and burned. She turned, wound her way through the crowd of dancers and the tables full of wedding guests and made her way down the side of the reception hall, to the toilets. She rushed inside the cubicle, fumbled with the bolt lock, sat down on the closed lid and bit down on her fist. Silent tears streaked her cheeks and her head throbbed with an instant headache, one she was familiar with after all these years.

This was her life.

She was twenty-five years old. A spinster teacher with a shameful past. She'd been in love with a Catholic boy for ten years. She was surrounded by people all day: teaching colleagues who admired her; students who hung on her every word; parents who sought her out for her advice at the end of a school day.

But she went to bed every night feeling like the loneliest person in the world.

Chapter Thirty-four

1966

The cherry strudel was still hot from the oven when Elizabeta sliced it, set a piece on a plate, and passed it to her mother. Berta held the plate up high for her inspection. Elizabeta waited for her mother's approval.

She had practised and practised this recipe over the past six months. With Little Luisa in school now, and young Johnny almost three years old, she had time during the day between walking her daughter to school and picking her up to learn more from her mother. John was a placid little boy, nowhere near as boisterous as Little Luisa had been at the same age, so Elizabeta was able to sit him in front of the television to watch *Play School* and some of the other new programs meant for the little ones. He loved the song about the bears and the chairs and would happily sit on the rug in the living room, singing along with the lady and the man talking to him from the screen.

At twenty-eight years old, Elizabeta needed distractions. Little Luisa and Johnny weren't enough. Nikolas was a vague presence in her life and the lives of her children. He worked, he was out at the German Club many nights of the week, and she was at home with her cooking and her memories. For three years now, there had been someone else in his affections. The woman with the perfume was still making her mark on Elizabeta's husband, staking her claim on someone else's life.

Her mother needed her more than ever now, to help her cope with the ghosts in her family. And it wasn't just Luisa.

The ghost was in her mother. It took her over sometimes, sending her to bed for weeks on end, stealing her energy and her smile and her love for her own granddaughter. Perhaps it had been there when her first daughter died, but Elizabeta had been too young to know it then. She had been old enough at Bonegilla to see it come back when the German soldier found them, to understand how it haunted her mother after Luisa died. Elizabeta had begged her mother to see a doctor but Berta had refused.

'What would an Australian doctor know?'

'They have very good doctors here.'

'What do they know about what happened to me? These people who didn't have a war. They didn't have all the things that have killed me from the inside.'

'*Mutti*,' Elizabeta had pleaded. 'You're not yourself. We have a good life here, better than we would have had in Germany, or Hungary, or anywhere. Look at me. I'm married with two grandchildren for you. Aren't you happy about that? Aren't you happy that we're in Australia?'

A look came over Berta that scared Elizabeta.

'Happy? Australia killed Luisa. That's what Australia did to me.' The roar from the back of her mother's throat silenced Elizabeta. The rage in her was frightening. 'And then you dare call your daughter the same. You did that to hurt me, didn't you? Calling your own daughter after my daughter. My Luisa is gone. I don't want your Luisa. Take her away.'

Over the previous few months, Elizabeta had tried to talk to her father about it, cautiously, politely, respectfully, but he had made his own peace with living with the ghost, and careful avoidance was at the heart of it.

So, Elizabeta did what she knew might make her mother happy. She cooked. Every day at her mother's house, Elizabeta asked Berta to teach her the recipes of her mother's life and she cooked while her mother fussed and corrected her from her seat at the kitchen table: stuffed capsicums, strudel, Apfelkuchen and sauerbraten and goulash and jam dumplings and uborkasaláta and cabbage rolls and chicken paprikash and beigli and mushroom soup and cabbage balushka and palacsinta.

She cooked for all those years when there had been stale bread and flour soup and the sniff of a piece of bacon instead of a fat, smoked rasher. Food soothed her mother but it didn't heal her. It rounded her stomach and plumped her chin but no matter how hard Elizabeta tried, it couldn't fill the hole made by her two dead children or the German soldier. The secrets sat inside her like stones.

As each day passed, Elizabeta's children felt more and more Australian. They were slipping away from her. They had lost their German and didn't speak to their *oma* other than to say hello or goodbye and reluctantly bestow a kiss on her cheek. There was a gulf between them and Elizabeta felt tossed in the middle, neither one thing nor another.

She had lived longer in Australia than anywhere but did it feel like home? Where did she truly belong?

For her, there was the tug of loyalty to a place that hadn't wanted her, and it was confusing.

She had assumed it was clear for her children, her little Australians. But she'd been wrong about that too.

It was a Friday and Elizabeta had finished with her mother for the day and had sat Johnny in his pram for the walk to school. It was a warm November day, with north winds blowing in from the deserts up north and rustling the leaves of the bottlebrush trees in the streets.

When Elizabeta reached the school gate, she parked the pram away from the other mothers. A clutch of them looked over at her, and then turned away, continuing their discussions without her. They had never smiled or waved or said hello.

Johnny sat in his pram quietly. In eighteen months he would be going to kindergarten and then a year after that, this school. She wondered if he would make friends with the Australian boys, if the sons of those women who turned their backs on her would not care that Johnny's parents didn't speak English well enough for them, that they were from somewhere else in the world that wasn't Australia.

The bell sounded to signal the end of the day and there was a rush of children to the gate, jostling, laughing, their satchels bouncing against their legs as they came out to meet their parents. Elizabeta waited and waited. Finally, Little

Luisa emerged from the back of the crowd, dawdling, her face downcast, her mouth angry.

Elizabeta didn't want to call out her daughter's name. Her accent was thick and people would stare at her, so she waited until Luisa came to her and Johnny and stood quietly, holding on to the handle of the pram as she'd been taught to do for the walk home.

Elizabeta stroked her daughter's hair, tucked the curly strands that had come out of her long plaits behind her ears.

'Did you have a good day at school, *mein Liebling*?'

Her daughter shook her head and cast her eyes to the ground.

'What happened today?'

Luisa wasn't one to keep secrets from anyone and she quickly blurted out, 'One of the boys in my class, Kevin. He teases me all the time.'

'Ach.' Elizabeta smiled. 'Boys will be boys. Perhaps he likes you and that's why he teases you.'

'But *Mutti*. He calls me a Hitler.'

Elizabeta stilled. 'He did what?'

'He calls me a Hitler and a Nazi. And he points his finger at me and shoots. *Bang bang bang*.'

Elizabeta snatched Luisa's satchel from her little hand and bumpily turned the pram around towards home. Step after step, she got faster. Luisa began to jog along alongside to keep up.

'What is a Hitler, *Mutti*?'

Elizabeta was shaking. 'That boy is stupid. And I say you can tell that to him. I don't care what the teacher says.'

Chapter Thirty-five

1974

The twenty-year Bonegilla reunion was her husband's idea.

In the backyard of their North Shore home, lying languidly on plastic sun loungers, Frances and Andrew watched their girls romping like seal pups in the brand-new above-ground pool, their Christmas present. It had taken days to fill, but the sounds of delight and the squeals of laughter coming from eight-year-old Vanessa and six-year-year-old Lyndall had been worth it.

The humidity stuck to them like fog and Frances was sleepy. She'd had a busy year at school now that she was back full time, and she was relishing the summer break, spending weeks in a bikini and bare feet, eating dinners of cold salads and sliced left-over Christmas ham.

Andrew reached across from his sun lounger and clinked glasses with her. 'Here's cheers, big ears. To our darling girls.'

'To our wonderful girls,' she replied, laying back and closing her eyes to the sun. 'And to my wonderful husband for being brilliant and buying them a pool for Christmas. Which, coincidentally, gives us plenty of time to lie here watching them. I believe I might even finish this book.' Frances lifted her paperback from the grass and opened it to her bookmark.

'You're reading *Jaws?*' Andrew chuckled.

Frances regarded her husband's incredulous expression over the top of her sunglasses. 'Yes. It's very good. Why so surprised?'

'Because it's about shark attacks. And we live in Sydney. With all those miles and miles of beaches.'

'This is light relief after a year teaching nine-year-olds. And anyway, you can't have a go at me. You're reading *The Hobbit*. Again.'

'Every year at Christmas and I'm not apologising for it.' Andrew lifted an arm and rested it casually above his head. He turned towards her. His feet hung over the end of the lounger. Long and lean, he looked like a fast bowler.

'Frances, darling. Have I ever mentioned how much I like being a teacher, specifically because of all these holidays?'

She lifted her eyes from her book. 'I believe it's what first attracted me to you. Such an endearing lack of ambition.'

Andrew grinned widely. He had come into her life at exactly the right moment. Perhaps that's why she'd allowed herself to fall in love with him. She'd met him when she was twenty-six, just a few months after Iliana's wedding back in 1964, when she'd been at her lowest. Andrew was a new teacher in her school, fresh off his country service. He was unlike anyone she'd ever met. He'd arrived in the staff room with skinny trousers and a two-tone knit jumper, his hair sitting at his collar, and he asked out loud, in front of the very straight-laced headmaster, 'How many weeks until school holidays then?'

Ten years later, they were making a comfortable life on Sydney's north shore in a solid family home. They worked at two different schools now, both not that far from where they lived, and life was good, settled and easy. Vanessa played piano and netball and Lyndall tortured her parents with her new recorder. It was a somewhat ordinary existence, but it suited Frances. So many things had happened in her life before she'd turned twenty-five that to be sitting in a sun lounger in the backyard reading a book, with her husband next to her and her girls swimming in the new pool, seemed like all she would ever need. They had dear friends—mostly other teachers—and weekends were filled with barbeques and progressive dinners and sleep-ins.

There was a squeal from the pool and then calls of 'Daddy! Daddy!'

The girls' candy-pink-coloured ball had bounced out of the water onto the lawn. Andrew leapt up, loped across the yard to retrieve it and then walked over to the pool. Vanessa and Lyndall scrambled over to the edge for a hug from their dad. Frances loved watching him with their children. He was a good father. When she was frazzled at the end of the day after hearing 'Mrs Coleman, Mrs Coleman' for what seemed like the hundredth time, he had infinite patience. He bounced into the house, wrestled with his daughters, helped them with their homework and still had enough energy to read them a bedtime story every night. They loved his dramatic readings of Carolyn Keene's *Nancy Drew* series. And the girls loved their father equally as fiercely.

Andrew refilled her glass of Moselle before resuming his position on the sun lounger.

'Oh, I forgot to tell you.' Frances put her book down on her bare thigh. 'A letter came from Adelaide yesterday. From my old friend Elizabeta. It's tragic really. Her father's been diagnosed with cancer.'

'God, that's awful. She's one of your Bonegilla friends, isn't she? The ones you met when the Sar-Major was running the camp?'

Frances *tsked*. 'Don't call my father that. You know how he hates it. And as I've pointed out a million times, he was never in the army. He was a Canberra bureaucrat. A paper pusher.'

'Oh, he loves it. I think it actually broke his heart when they had to leave. How long has he been retired now?'

'Three years, and Mum still goes on about how much she misses it. Dad had to explain that there was little point in having a camp director when migrants aren't staying at the camp any more. It's all gone back to the army now.'

Frances had felt more than a pang of sadness when her mother had called to tell her the news. Bonegilla had meant so much to Frances as a child. It was her playground, her education, the place she'd made friends with Elizabeta and Iliana and Vasiliki, and where she'd fallen in love for the first time. Frances closed her eyes and let her memories take her back to those days. Her little room in the director's house at the camp. Her atlas, full of the promise of places that she'd never visited. The cold. The gum trees. The myriad of languages like the bird calls of a hundred different species chattering all around her. The cinema. Posting letters at the post office to her cousins and her grandparents. She smiled at the memory of mutton cooling in the mess kitchens. It was a wrench to know that she couldn't go back now. But who could revisit those places of childhood and have them remain exactly the same? She had put those childish thoughts away, of travel, of adventure, of the kind of love she might have had with a man she could never marry.

And she tried so hard never to think about the baby she'd given away.

'Frances?'

She turned to her husband. 'Yes?'

'I asked, what kind of cancer is it? Elizabeta's father.'

She laid her book on her stomach. 'Lung. He's not actually that old, you know. Her father must be only about sixty or so. Although, it's funny. When I think back to those days, I thought all the Bonegilla mums and dads were so old. They seemed … worn out, I think. I suppose the war and everything they'd been through took its toll on all of them. They were the same age as my parents back then but they all seemed like grandparents. Sixty.' Frances pulled a face. 'That's not old, is it?'

'Ancient.' Andrew reached under the sun lounge and pulled out a worn leather pouch. He flipped open the top and pinched some dried leaves between his thumb and forefinger.

'Oh, not now, Andrew. The girls are just over there.'

'Loosen up, darling. They're totally distracted.' Andrew expertly rolled a joint, lit it and took a deep drag. He moved to hand it to Frances but she waved it away. 'Not today.' She was feeling too melancholic already.

'So, these friends of yours. It's been ages since you've seen them.'

'I know.'

'Why have you let it go so long?' Andrew's eyes drifted closed. He took slow and deep drags on his joint.

Why had she? It was hard to explain to anyone. Seeing Iliana always reminded her of Cooma and Massimo and that had become more painful as the years passed. And the others? They were so far away. She supposed she could have hopped on a plane to see Vasiliki and Elizabeta, but Vasiliki was so busy with her four daughters and her family and the business. And Elizabeta? She had called her once or twice on the telephone, mindful to keep the call brief because of STD rates, but Elizabeta wasn't very chatty and Frances had felt uncomfortable, as if she was trying to get blood out of a stone in trying to get her to talk. Letters had been easier. A few brief words, an update on what the girls were up to, a photo every now and then. She had decades worth of letters from them all.

Frances looked past the pool and her girls and into the hazy blue summer sky. She reached an arm out to Andrew and he passed her the joint. She took a long drag and passed it back.

It was easier to let the past be the past. Hers was full of too much hurt and fear and shame. She had been desperate to begin again when she'd met Andrew, when they'd embarked on this life together, this ordinary suburban existence. Perhaps that was why she'd fallen in love with him, because he offered her simple and uncomplicated and beautiful ordinariness. When she was a girl, she'd longed for big adventures and grand tours to exotic places all over the world.

Where had she wanted to go? Rome? Paris? Morocco? She'd had that huge atlas, had been obsessed by it. Where was it now? And what use would it be? Boundaries had changed. Countries had disappeared and new ones invented in the years since it had been printed. The past was no longer the past: it had been rewritten, redrawn and recreated.

The wine and the heat and the dope had gone to her head. She shouldn't have taken a drag for she knew what it would bring. Thoughts drifted in and out of her memory; images danced behind her eyelids.

Her baby would be fifteen years old now. That little boy she'd never been able to hold, or see or love, who had been given to that good Christian family, was a teenager. For a flicker of a second, Frances closed her eyes and imagined him in the pool with his sisters. That's what her family should look like but she could never say that out loud, that she was the mother of a son and two daughters. She had been pregnant three times and when she'd told the doctors in the hospital that Vanessa was her first labour, she'd seen the looks of disbelief on their faces, the knowing glances the doctor and the nurses shared. Her body had betrayed her secret. When she'd left that hospital in Albury back in 1958 she had been a good girl and done what everyone had told her to do. To walk away and forget her baby.

'He's someone else's child now,' the matron had told her with a look of disgust she hadn't even tried to conceal. 'It's for the best that you leave here and pretend this never happened. Go and start your life again. Learn the lessons of what you've done to yourself and your family.'

The baby had remained a secret even to her brothers. She had been pregnant in Cooma. Tom had been in London and Donald was in Melbourne. Neither of them had to see her swollen and pregnant. How easy it was for the entire nine months of her pregnancy to be wiped from the family's history. No one ever spoke of it, or even hinted at it, and on the day when it was her baby's birthday, Frances stoically ignored the waves of grief and almost hysterical sense of loss that threatened to overcome her.

She hadn't been back to Bonegilla or Albury since she'd had the baby. At first, she'd been too terrified that she wouldn't have the strength to fight the urge to search every woman's pram, glaring at every child's face, to see if the child was hers. She had been told her baby's adoptive parents farmed a large property in the district. Perhaps her son was a farmer, too. She tried to picture him. A strapping lad wearing farm boots and a checked shirt and a farmer's hat, chewing a piece of hay like Peter Finch in *The Shiralee*. Everything about him was so clear in her imagination until it came to his face. She had never been able to imagine his features. Did he take after his father, Gerald, the man she'd tried to wipe from her memory too? Or was he like her? Brown-haired and brown-eyed, medium height, ordinary.

She'd decided even before she'd met Andrew that if she were to ever marry, she would never tell her husband all the details about her life before him. She had started anew.

The past was the past.

And since her marriage to Andrew, and the arrival of their girls in quick succession, she'd been happy. Andrew was a wonderful man who loved her very much. Their life was settled, easy, loose. Her parents were living in Queanbeyan now, and they made the trip down to see Frances and Andrew and the girls a couple of times a year. At Easter time, Frances and Andrew would pack up their station wagon for the trip to her parents, something they'd dubbed their Coleman Family Road Trips. They had lots of funny little traditions like that, things that make family folklore, which were making new memories for Frances. Happier ones. Andrew had filled her life with love and laughter and joy and spontaneous fun. She felt so lucky to have met him.

'So,' he sighed, dopey from the weed, his voice slow and quiet. 'You haven't seen the Bonegilla girls in years. Why don't you get together, huh? It's twenty years since you all met. Surely that's worth a party, isn't it?'

And Frances hadn't been able to let go of the idea.

Chapter Thirty-six

'I can't go to Sydney.'

Elizabeta spooned fried noodles with cabbage from her electric frypan onto a dinner plate. She passed it to Luisa, who passed it to Johnny, who passed it to Nikolas along the mustard-coloured breakfast bar in their kitchen in their new house in Grange. Two years earlier, they'd managed to save enough money to buy their first home. The beach was only a ten-minute walk away and there were good schools nearby. Construction work had already begun on a brand-new shopping centre, West Lakes Mall, which would be opened later in the year. It had been the talk of the western suburbs for months. It was a good area with lots of parks and playing fields and open skies and fresh air. They had a front yard and a backyard and a chicken coop and some fruit trees and an incinerator by the back fence.

'Of course you should go.' Nikolas nodded as he chewed. 'You should see your friends. How long has it been?'

'A long time.' It had been fifteen years since they'd all been together, when they had turned up unexpectedly at her wedding. Sometimes she wished they had whisked her away instead of watching her marry Nikolas.

'If you're going to Sydney, can I come too?' Little Luisa asked.

Elizabeta joined her family at the breakfast bar, swivelling the orange vinyl bar stool to sit on it. 'And who do you think will look after your father and Johnny if I go to Sydney and you come too?'

'I'm sure they can look after themselves,' Little Luisa huffed. 'It's not like Johnny's a baby anymore. He is ten years old.'

John poked a tongue out at his sister and crossed his eyes.

'Although he sure seems to act like one sometimes.'

'Elizabeta, go,' Nikolas urged. 'It will be nice for you. Luisa knows how to cook a few things. We won't go hungry while you're away.'

'No, I won't go. It's too far away and it will cost too much money.'

Elizabeta didn't want to say any more in front of the children but it was impossible. She knew her own family could fend for themselves if she was away, but how on earth could she leave her parents? Her tone had ended any further discussion and they finished their meals in silence. When the plates were scraped clean, Nikolas moved through to the living room and switched on the television. Little Luisa went to her room and Johnny raced out the back door with his football. Elizabeta collected the dishes, stacked them on the sink and stared out the window to the corrugated iron of the side fence. She'd made a macramé pot hanger the previous summer and had screwed a hook into the gable so a pot filled with fishbone ferns could decorate her view. It needed watering. The edges of its green fronds were crisp and brown. She turned on the water and filled the sink, opened the cupboard below and squirted dishwashing liquid into the water. It foamed and she submerged her hands into the warmth.

This was the only time she had to herself. Time spent with the dishes. She had never gone back to work after the children, and even if she had thought about the idea, once her mother became sick it was out of the question. Her days were filled with getting the children off to school before driving the five miles to her parents' house in Woodville and washing and shopping and cooking and ferrying her father to doctor's appointments at the Queen Elizabeth Hospital and making sure her mother took her medication. Her parents' household would have fallen apart after her father's cancer diagnosis if she hadn't stepped in.

Sometimes, very occasionally, it seemed Elizabeta's mother was trying very hard to be happy. She would knit or sew a dress for Little Luisa. She would speak on the telephone with Nikolas's mother and invite her over for coffee and cake. But in the past year, those times had seemed further and further apart and Elizabeta had stepped in to care for both her parents. During the week it was trips to hospital for treatment, full of waiting and interpreting for them with the medical staff, and to the chemist for medication for both of them. Washing, cooking, cleaning. Paying bills. Trips to the bank. On the weekends, she took them both to church at Henley Beach, and then back to her own house for lunch. It was always roast pork with dumplings and sau-erkraut, which she'd risen at seven o'clock to prepare. After-wards, there was cake and coffee and Nikolas would drive them home. And then Elizabeta would do her own family's washing and ironing and cleaning.

She had to do the work of three sisters. If Luisa were still alive, would her mother be going mad?

The back door slammed and John was back in the kitchen. 'Mum, are there any more noodles?'

Elizabeta nodded to the kitchen sink. 'In the frypan. Help yourself.'

Later that night when they were in bed, Nikolas had taken hold of Elizabeta's hand and kissed her cheek. Inside, she froze at his touch. After all these years, she hadn't been able to forgive him. She knew she should, because she was his wife, but the anger of what he'd done, how he'd betrayed her, burnt still. He had made promises to her that he hadn't kept. He had lain with another woman for four years. She remembered when it stopped. She had collected his clothes from the floor of the bedroom one day after dropping Johnny off at kindergarten and it was gone. She held the clothes to her face and smelled Old Spice and grease. She couldn't name the feeling that made her cry over her husband's dirty clothes. Was it relief that it was over or humiliation that it had gone on for so long? Jackie Kennedy Onassis had ignored it, and that's what Elizabeta had done too. What good would it have done for the children to know? She had to keep up appearances for them, for her parents and his. No matter how much it hurt.

'I'm tired,' she said and turned on her side, away from him, to the moonlight in the window.

He let go of her hand. 'You should go, see the girls. I can look after everything. And as long as you put some dinner in the freezer, we'll be fine. What do the kids like? Fish fingers?'

'No, Nikolas.'

'You have time to think about it, the reunion.' He stroked her arm tenderly. 'Let's see how things go.'

Elizabeta watched the lace curtains billow in the sea breeze coming from the street. The streetlight illuminated their bedroom, streaking light through the venetian blinds, creating lines on the carpet, on the sheets, on their bodies. She knew what he was saying. Her father would probably be dead by then. At the hospital the day before, the doctors had told her he wouldn't survive another four weeks. In her heart, she hadn't needed them to tell her what she could see with her own eyes. Death was already there in his gaunt face and in his breathy wheeze. The cancer had worked voraciously to shrink him.

The next day, after Nikolas had left for the work and the children had scooted onto their bikes to ride to school, in the half-hour before she was due at her parents' house, Elizabeta wrote a quick letter to Frances. She would have to wait and see, she said.

Four weeks later, Elizabeta's father died in hospital in the early hours of the morning. The nurses called her instead of Berta, as they had been instructed to do, and Elizabeta had waited until breakfast time to drive to her mother's place and wake Berta with the news that her husband was gone.

At her father's funeral, her mother turned to Elizabeta during the service. The priest from their local parish was in the middle of his sermon. All around them were the few friends they had made over the years in Adelaide, from church, other new Australians, Nikolas's family and two sets of Australian neighbours from the street. Death, it seemed, was easily understood.

'Your father was the best of men,' Berta said, dabbing her tears with a delicate lace handkerchief as she sobbed.

'He was the best father,' Elizabeta replied. She covered her mother's hand with hers. 'I couldn't have asked for a better one.'

'That's why I could never tell him.'

The mourners stood and began to sing. The old wooden pews creaked as people moved. The organist began to play.

'Tell him what?'

Berta gulped in a deep breath. 'I could never tell him that he wasn't Luisa's father. It would have broken his heart.'

Elizabeta's head snapped to her mother's. 'Who was?'

Her mother's face was white. She looked like one of the ghost people of Bonegilla. 'That bastard German.'

Chapter Thirty-seven

'I'm only driving to the north shore, Vinnie. It's not like it's the other side of the world.'

Iliana's husband leaned down to look into the car. 'Are you sure you fit behind that steering wheel?'

'Just.' Iliana struggled to get her breath. She was eight months pregnant, bloated and, at thirty-five, feeling way too old to be having a baby.

'Get out,' Vinnie suddenly demanded. 'I'll drive you.'

'No you won't.' She pushed down the lock on the door.

He reached through the fully opened window and unlocked it, which made her laugh. 'Vincenzo, I'll be fine. It's just hot and this baby is making me hotter.'

He looked solemn now. 'You'll be careful?'

'You think my brother would let anything happen to me?' She'd made it this far in a pregnancy only once before, and little Anita was inside the house with her *nonna*. Iliana's mother had offered to come over for the afternoon and look after her while Iliana went to the Bonegilla reunion. Vinnie was perfectly capable of looking after their nine-year-old daughter, but it made her mother feel better to help, so she helped.

'Have fun,' Vinnie said. 'It was a good idea of yours to take Massimo. Just in case.'

'He knows Frances from all those years ago at Bonegilla,' she replied. 'He'll have fun, too. He can stand in the back-yard by the barbeque talking to her husband. That's what Australian men do, don't they?'

Vinnie shook his head and chuckled. 'My wife is so funny with the jokes.'

'I promise I will call you if anything happens with the baby. Or Massimo will.'

'He'd better.'

Everyone in the family had been on tenterhooks during this pregnancy. Iliana had had three miscarriages between Anita and this growing bulge and no one wanted her taking any risks. At her last check-up, her doctor had reassured her that everything was fine and that all she needed now was bed rest until the baby was born. Her mother had volunteered to move in to their house to look after her and Anita. Iliana had shooshed her mother's offer away.

Her love, her handsome Vinnie, had given her everything she'd ever wanted. A beautiful house, this new car she was driving, a daughter and now perhaps a son. Her own family's business was prosperous, enough to give her parents and Massimo everything they could want, and she and Vinnie had started their own construction company. The two family businesses collaborated on projects, housing developments and commercial properties. They were a Sydney success story. Who would have thought that twenty years after they'd arrived at Bonegilla with nothing, they would be living such a life?

Iliana pursed her bright red lips and blew her husband a kiss, but that wasn't enough for him. He leaned in through the window and kissed her noisily on her right cheek.

'And if anything happens with the baby, go straight to hospital. Do you hear me?'

Iliana rolled her eyes at her husband and started the engine of her brand-new Holden Statesman. She gave it a rev just to rile him and reversed out of the driveway of their Leichhardt home.

Ten minutes later, she pulled up out the front of a single-fronted 1930s bungalow in Hurlstone Park. She beeped her horn. The front door opened and her big brother stepped over the low front gate and opened the passenger door.

He nodded in her direction. 'Get out. I'll drive.'

'If I get out, I won't get back in. I'll drive.'

Massimo shook his head. 'You are about to have a baby. You can't drive.'

'Well, how do you think I got here then? Get in already.'

'I always drive. A woman's place is the passenger seat. This feels *stupido*.'

'Really? This is the 1970s. Haven't you heard of women's liberation?'

Massimo folded himself into the front passenger seat with a pretend scowl. He had always loved getting a rise out of his only sister and nothing had changed in all these years. As they drove north along New Canterbury Road, Iliana thought how strange it was for the two of them to be alone together. Both had been married for so many years now, and the only times they were together they were surrounded by spouses and children and their parents and friends. She loved her brother more than anything, but she had never warmed to Domenica. She had tried hard over the years. Really tried. Domenica had always been the most Italian of all of them. Nothing was good unless it was Italian. Food, wine, cars, clothes. She acted as if she didn't even want to live in Australia. Iliana had never mentioned a word of any of this to Massimo, but she got the feeling he suffered in silence, too. Domenica had never worked, and her own mother came and cleaned her house and practically raised the children while she was shopping and doing who knew what.

Iliana stopped herself. They were not gracious thoughts. Massimo had married Domenica and that would have always have to be enough for his sister.

'Did you tell them I'm coming, too?' Massimo turned down the car radio, which had been blaring 2SM and 'Evie' by Stevie Wright.

'I haven't said a thing. I thought it would be a big surprise for Frances.'

Massimo thumped a fist against his thigh. 'You mean you haven't told her? It's not right if you haven't told her she'll have another guest. I mean, it is at her house.'

'Ah, Massimo.' Iliana reached across and covered his clenched fist with her hand. 'That's the thing about a surprise. You don't tell people. I thought it would be fun for you too to see her after all this time. You haven't seen her since my wedding. And I'll say you're my bodyguard in case the baby comes, okay?'

Massimo looked ahead. 'You're too close to that car in front of us. Stop going so fast. You're a maniac.'

Iliana checked her rear-view mirror and then glanced at her brother. 'It runs in the family.'

Iliana followed Massimo's directions as he navigated using her UBD from the glove box, all the way across the Harbour Bridge and into Sydney's northern suburbs, until finally they pulled into the driveway of Frances's home. It was a large, long block, on a quiet suburban street, with gum trees filling the front yard, their spindly limbs overhanging the front of the squat brick house. There were two cars in the gravel driveway; a white VW Beetle with rusted scratches in the rounded, sloping boot and, beyond it, a cream-coloured Volvo station wagon.

Massimo dipped his head to look through the front car window. 'This is where Frances lives?'

'Yeah. They bought the house a few years ago. 1970, I think.'

'It's not what I expected.' He turned to her. 'It looks like hippies live here.'

Hippies. What would her brother know of hippies? He'd probably seen a Vietnam war protest on the news once. 'You think anyone else is here yet? Oh, can you bring the Tupperware from the back seat? I bought some cannolis from that new pasticerria on Parramatta Road.' Iliana pulled her keys from the ignition and opened the door. She twisted her body to get out, and Massimo's hand was on her arm.

'Stop. I'll help you.'

'I can do it.' She pushed his hand away from her shoulder, but he was too fast and a moment later was by her side, reaching for her hand, hauling her to her feet.

'You sure you're not having twins?' Massimo smiled.

'Just one baby.' Iliana patted her tummy. 'One big Italian bambino.' She smoothed down her billowing brown, orange and white patterned kaftan. Her flat white sandals peeked out from underneath. It was all she could fit into now, with the baby so close and the humid Sydney heat swelling her feet almost beyond recognition. Massimo closed the door behind her and took the food from the back seat. Their shoes crunched on the gravel driveway that led to the front veranda. It was filled with bikes, roller skates, a deflated netball and an assortment of sneakers and rubber flip-flops. By the door, there was an orange ceramic pot filled with a dead bird's-nest fern. Iliana and Massimo exchanged glances.

'Australians,' he said. Then, 'I look okay?'

'You look gorgeous.' For a forty-year-old, Massimo was still handsome. His high-waisted trousers and clinging body shirt showed that he worked for a living. Iliana wasn't sure his wife Domenica appreciated him. How good a husband he was. How hard he worked and how well he provided for his family. All she seemed to do was complain.

Iliana pressed the doorbell and a moment later the front screen door flung open and a man appeared, wearing nothing but shorts. His hair sat on his shoulders, he was tanned and lean and he looked like he hadn't shaved in weeks. 'Hey, you must be … let me guess … Iliana?'

'Yes.' She held out her hand and he shook it heartily.

'I'm Andrew. Frances's husband. And is this Vinnie?'

Iliana laughed heartily. 'No, Vinnie's at home with our daughter. This is my brother, Massimo.'

'Oh, cool. Nice to meet you, man.' Andrew held out a hand and Massimo shook it cautiously. Iliana could bet

Massimo had never been called 'man' in his whole life. 'Yeah, come on in.'

Iliana and Massimo followed Andrew down the shag-carpeted hallway to the back of the house, where the kitchen was situated on one side of a large family room. The windows across the back room overlooked the backyard.

'Iliana!' Frances tossed a tea towel onto the sink and rounded the breakfast bar to hug her friend. 'It's so wonderful to see you.' She pulled back, smoothed her hands over Iliana's stomach. 'You must be about to burst. How are you feeling?'

Iliana smiled. 'Hot. Sweaty. Huge.'

'When are you due?'

'Two weeks.' Iliana tried not to sound nervous about it.

Frances slapped her hands to her cheeks. 'I can't believe this. I can't believe we live in the same city and yet we've waited so long. There's so much to catch up on, Iliana.'

Massimo stepped up next to her. 'I brought Massimo, just for old time's sake. And so he can take me to hospital in case the baby comes.'

Frances faltered. 'Of course. Welcome. It's so lovely to see you too, Massimo. It's been …'

'A long time,' he said gruffly. 'Here. Some cannoli.' He held the pale yellow Tupperware container out to Frances. She seemed embarrassed to take it and Iliana wondered if she shouldn't have brought any food. Didn't Australians take food when they were visiting someone's house? An Italian would never turn up to a party empty-handed. Why, after twenty years in Australia, did she still not understand things like this?

Frances studied her bare feet. Her toenails were painted blue and the polish was chipped. 'Thank you, that's really nice of you. I don't think I've had a cannoli since …' She looked up. 'Oh well … for ages and ages.' Frances put the container on the burnt orange laminate counter behind her. She tucked her long, straight hair behind her ears and glanced out to the backyard, before looking back at Massimo. 'Now, can I get you two anything to drink? Water? Wine?'

'Water will be fine for me,' Iliana said.

'And for you, Massimo?'

He cleared his throat. 'A beer would be good. Thank you.'

Frances went to the fridge, took a bottle from the door and gave it to Massimo. Then she poured a water for Iliana from a jug filled with ice that sat on the counter.

Frances smiled and cocked her head to the back doors. 'Why don't you head out into the backyard? I'll just finish up here and be out in a sec.'

'Sure. Are you sure you don't need a hand with anything?' Iliana asked.

Frances waved her away. 'Go rest.'

Massimo went first. He held the back door open for his sister and headed over to Andrew and the barbeque. When Iliana looked out into the backyard, she gasped. 'Oh my God.' She crossed herself three times and clutched at the doorframe. Elizabeta and Vasiliki were walking towards her, smiling, laughing, and in that moment Iliana was back at Bonegilla, to a time when they were all young, when life was about to unfurl before them.

She held out her arms to them and they both came to her. They hold onto each other in a long embrace.

'I can't believe it,' Iliana whispered breathlessly. 'You two … Frances didn't tell me anything about you coming. What are you doing here?'

'Surprise!' Vasiliki laughed and squeezed her friend tighter.

'Elizabeta. Your letter. I'm so sorry about your father. God bless him.'

'Thank you. It was quick in the end.'

Iliana made the sign of the cross. 'And your mother? How is she?'

Elizabeta looked downcast. 'Not very good. She has moved in with my family now. She was very lonely without my father.'

'You are a good daughter to her.' Vasiliki leaned up and kissed Elizabeta's cheek. 'Come, let's sit down.'

They walked back across the lawn to a wooden outdoor setting under a huge gum tree.

'Here I am looking like a whale and you two … you are both still so beautiful,' Iliana said. They searched each other's faces across the table. 'Vasiliki, look at you. Hardly a day older than when we first met on the boat coming to Australia.'

'Please,' she laughed, 'No one calls me Vasiliki except my parents. Call me Vicki.'

'Vicki, of course. I know you've told me that a million times but I can't get used to it,' Iliana smiled. 'It's very Australian.' Vasiliki's long and silky hair was tamed into large, bouncing curls. Her purple silk pantsuit with bell sleeves was stunning and her mission brown wedge heels made her seem much taller. There were lines on her face now that she hadn't worn at sixteen, but she was still the Vasiliki she remembered.

'And look at you. I was sure you would have had the baby by now,' Vasiliki said.

Iliana held up a hand and crossed her fingers. 'Two more weeks, with luck. I'm at that stage now where I just want this baby out of me. Phew, I'd forgotten how this feels. I pee eighteen times a night.'

The three women laughed, the sound competing with the call of the birds in the trees above them.

'Remind me how old your girls are now?' Elizabeta asked Vasiliki.

'My girls? All grown up. Aphrodite is eighteen and a hair-dresser. This is her work.' Vasiliki smoothed down her hair. 'I'm trying to keep her away from boys but you know what that's like these days. All this freedom the young girls think they deserve. Elena works in Myer in Bourke Street, in the shoe department.' Vasiliki flicked out a wedged heel to table height. 'There are some perks with that, let me tell you. And Stavroula and Effie are still in school.'

'Four daughters.' Iliana sighed. 'One is a handful.'

'Imagine a houseful! They are all so beautiful and clever. But poor Steve, surrounded by all these women in the house. It drives him so crazy sometimes that he goes off on the weekends to watch the Cannons play, to be with the boys a little bit.'

'What about you, Elizabeta?' Iliana turned. 'What are your kids up to?'

'Well,' Elizabeta began. 'Luisa is fourteen and in high school and could be doing much better if she wasn't listening to the radio and that pop music all the time. Johnny is ten and in grade five and he would rather play football than be doing anything else.'

'He plays soccer?' Iliana asked.

'No. The other football. The Port Adelaide kind.'

Vasiliki chuckled. 'Remember the boys at Bonegilla playing soccer? They were crazy for it.'

Iliana looked over to her brother with Frances's husband at the barbeque. She wondered what he was thinking, if he had forgotten about Frances. In all the years since, he'd never mentioned her name once. 'That was all Massimo would do. All day, play with the Bonegilla United soccer team. Nothing else.'

'And he hit Frances on the head with his kick, remember?'

'I remember,' Elizabeta said, smiling. 'I translated for you.'

'And we took her flowers,' Iliana added. 'Massimo felt so guilty and my father thought we would get kicked out of Bonegilla by the director for hurting his daughter.'

'What are you all laughing at?' They looked up. Frances was crossing the lawn to them. Her long straight hair was parted in the middle and hung down her back. Her flared denims were loose and casual and Iliana noticed that she wasn't wearing a bra under her deep brown halter-neck top. Her breasts bounced with each step. How could any woman go out without a bra, especially after having children? She quite liked her Playtex Cross Your Heart, thank you very much.

Vasiliki urged Frances to the table with a wave. 'We were remembering when you were in hospital back at Bonegilla.'

Frances's mouth opened in surprise. 'I haven't thought about that in years. Lucky there was no harm done, but I remember you came to visit me at home when I got out of hospital. That's how we all met, right? If it wasn't for your brother, Iliana ...' Frances's thoughts trailed off. She held a white plastic tray with three spumante glasses and a refreshed glass of water for Iliana on it. She set it on the table. 'I thought you might like this. This is a celebration indeed and Iliana taught me years ago that spumante is just perfect for celebrating.'

Frances reached for a glass of honey-coloured bubbles and sat down at the table. 'Well, cheers to us.'

The four women clinked their glasses together and took a ceremonial sip.

'*Prost*,' Elizabeta said.

'*Saluti*,' Iliana said.

'*Yamas*,' Vasiliki said with a smiling cheer.

'And ... well, cheers!'

'To the Bonegilla girls!' Elizabeta said. 'My dear friends.'

Another clink of glasses, another sip for them all. Another round of smiles and then silence. The hundreds of letters over the years were one thing, but being with each like this, after so long, was something else entirely. Letters were edited highlights of a life. That's all they'd had from each other in so long, with the sadness and heartbreak skimmed over and the achievements emphasised by repetition and exclamation marks.

Iliana wondered, did they still really know each other at all?

She looked at each of them while they sipped. Frances's casual cool. Vasiliki's preened perfection. Elizabeta's sad dowdiness. They had been friends when they were young, when they were able to celebrate the freedoms of a new life in Australia, thrown together by the circumstance of being at Bonegilla at the same time. They'd supported each other, laughed and learned English together for a few months. And somehow, their friendships had survived all the years since then, even though they were in different states, living very different lives, and came from different backgrounds.

Perhaps that was the measure of true friendship after all. Iliana still felt a deep bond with all these women, something she hadn't felt with anyone but her family.

'I can't believe we've finally done this,' Frances said. 'After twenty years. Look at us.'

The four women smiled and took in the details of each other's faces. There were lines now, faded freckles. There was a pregnant belly and other rounded ones. There was love and heartbreak and experience in their expressions.

Iliana looked over to the barbeque. Massimo and Andrew seemed to be chatting happily. Andrew was flipping sausages and Massimo was drinking his beer, looking more relaxed than she'd expected. Every now and then, he glanced over to the table, his gaze serious. Iliana thought it was so like him to be protective of her.

'How's Massimo and that wife of his?' Vasiliki asked.

'They're okay.' Was her brother happy? Who knew? They would never speak of such things.

'He's gorgeous, your brother.' Vasiliki winked at Iliana and took a gulp of her spumante. 'Look at me, being so cheeky. That's what happens when you leave all your family behind and have a holiday in Sydney with your old friends. Cheers!'

Iliana clinked glasses with Vasiliki and Elizabeta. Frances was staring over her shoulder at her husband.

'Elizabeta,' Vasiliki said suddenly. Her face fell. 'I've just realised. It's twenty years since your sister died, too.'

Chapter Thirty-eight

'Vicki,' Iliana scolded. 'It was so many years ago. Why bring that up now?'

'Because she was there too. Elizabeta. I remember your sister. I remember Luisa with the red hair just like yours. She used to have two long plaits that your mother tied up in loops. And she wore ribbons, too.'

All eyes were on Elizabeta. She was lost in her thoughts for a moment. 'My father used to put his finger in the middle, like he was poking a hole.'

Frances flicked her long hair over her shoulder and leaned forwards. The frayed hems of her flared denims rustled at her bare feet. 'She was such a sweet little girl, Elizabeta. Have you ever been back to Albury to see her grave?'

'No. My mother, she didn't want to go. I still have the photo you sent me, Frances. Of her grave. It's hidden away.' Elizabeta put her glass on the outdoor table. She didn't look at anyone. Her hands were in her lap, her fingers together in a knot.

Frances let out a little gasp. 'No. That's so sad.'

Iliana drained her water in a long gulp. 'It was so many years ago. The past is the past. Sometimes it's best to leave it there.'

Vasiliki reached for Iliana's arm. If only that were true. The past rises up, Vasiliki knew. Just when you think you've forgotten it, the memories surface and float.

The smell of burning sausages and onions wafted over from the barbeque. Elizabeta breathed in deep and straightened her shoulders. 'Just after my father died, my mother told me something about Luisa.'

The three women sat to attention.

'What did she tell you?' Vasiliki asked.

'There was a man at Bonegilla. A German soldier. My mother ...' Elizabeta searched for the words. Tears welled in her eyes and she let them fall without embarrassment. 'This man. He raped my mother during the war. I was there, in our house in Hungary when it happened. He was the father of Luisa.'

'Oh my God,' Iliana gasped.

Elizabeta's words were slow and deliberate. 'I didn't know until my father's funeral. She couldn't tell him while he was still alive. You see, he loved her very much and he perhaps loved Luisa even more. My mother lived with the shame for thirty years and when my father died, she could finally tell someone the truth. I have spent these past weeks trying to understand it.'

Vasiliki took in Elizabeta's expression. It had been twenty years since her sister had died and, in that moment,

Elizabeta's face mirrored the grief of it as fiercely as if it had happened just yesterday. She looked white as a ghost.

'I think there was a curse on her from the beginning. I lost her twice. I know that now. When she died, it was so hard, being in a strange new country, so quickly I didn't even get to say goodbye. And then we left Bonegilla and we left her behind.'

Elizabeta's voice was quiet, but tears streaked her cheeks. Iliana handed her a handkerchief she'd dug from her handbag. She took it with a nod and dabbed at her eyes as if she wanted to soak up the grey shadows under them.

'My mother has been in hospital a few times over the years, to make her better.'

'Oh, dear Elizabeta.' Frances slipped an arm around her friend's shoulders.

'But it doesn't work. She is living with us now.'

'How terrible for your mother,' Iliana said, crossing herself three times. 'And for you. That must be very hard on you, looking after everybody.'

Elizabeta shrugged. 'It's what I must do.'

'*Kefi*,' Vasiliki announced. She lifted her empty glass.

'What's that?' Frances asked.

'In Greek, *kefi* means living right now. In the moment. We are very good at it. There is sadness, yes. We all have broken hearts, no?' A shiver goosebumped her arms even in the warmth of the Sydney heat. 'Let us be happy for one another. For what we have. Right now? I am so happy to see my Bonegilla friends. My first real friends in Australia.'

Frances raised her glass. 'Let's toast the Bonegilla girls.'

Elizabeta managed a sad smile. 'We are not girls any more.'

Iliana patted her kaftaned stomach and grinned. 'I don't know about you all, but I still feel like a girl.'

'To the Bonegilla girls,' Vasiliki shouted.

'To the Bonegilla girls,' they called out together.

Vasiliki looked at her friends and was grateful for each of them. Twenty years spun past her in a blur. Leaving Greece with her family. The voyage halfway across the world. Arriving at Bonegilla. The move to Melbourne and the years she'd worked at the Majestic Milk Bar. Meeting Tom. Marrying Steve. Keeping her secret. Four children. The new business.

Andrew called across the backyard from the barbeque. 'Dinner's nearly done.'

Frances slowly got to her feet. She pushed her hair from her face. 'I'll go and get the salads and plates. You all keep talking.'

'Can I help?' Elizabeta stood.

'No, please. Stay here. I won't be long.' Vasiliki watched Frances walk across the lawn to where her husband and Massimo were at the barbeque. There was some discussion, then Andrew began loading the meat onto a brown platter. Frances flicked her hair and turned to walk into the house. Massimo followed her.

Vasiliki didn't know Iliana's brother at all, really, but something had just passed between the two of them. She saw it, the moment Andrew's back was turned. Frances had cocked her head just slightly towards the house and Massimo moved. Vasiliki looked around. Andrew seemed oblivious. Iliana was deep in conversation with Elizabeta and Frances's daughters were still splashing in the pool.

There was a curiosity she couldn't quell. She picked up her empty glass. 'Anyone for a refill? I think I'll go get a bottle.'

Her wedge heels sank into the long grass as she walked to the kitchen. She stepped inside and looked over to the island bench.

A man turned to her.

Vasiliki dropped her glass.

It was Tom Burley.

Chapter Thirty-nine

Vasiliki couldn't find her breath. It had been sucked from her lungs as if she'd stepped into a vacuum.

'Ta da!' Frances emerged from the hallway. Massimo was behind her, lugging a large suitcase. 'This is my other surprise! He's just landed and come right here from Mascot. Oh gosh, Vasiliki. You've dropped your glass.'

Vasiliki looked at the ground. 'I'm so sorry. I got a shock.'

Tom approached her, looked down at her sandals. Frances and Massimo were next to each other, his hand on her arm holding her back from the splintered shards. They had scattered all over the slate-tiled floor, and the stem lay askew by Frances's bare feet.

Vasiliki couldn't speak. She looked up at Tom, Frances and Massimo. This was too much of a surprise. She wasn't ready for her past to come slamming at her at a million miles an hour.

'Vasiliki. I mean, Vicki,' Frances corrected herself. 'It's okay. Don't worry, really. I'll go fetch a dustpan and broom.'

'Not with bare feet. Stay right there,' Massimo stepped in front of her, holding out an arm to keep her back. 'Where is the broom? I will get it.'

'Don't worry, Massimo. I'm used to tiptoeing around here avoiding every piece of Lego ever made and all those tiny little Barbie shoes.' Frances shrugged. 'Kids, you know.'

Massimo turned to Frances. He slipped one arm under her knees and the other around her waist and lifted her. Vasiliki and Tom exchanged glances and laughed.

'How damn chivalrous of you, Massimo.' Tom raised an eyebrow.

'Now take me to the broom. And let's find a pair of shoes for you. You and your stupid bare feet,' he muttered.

Frances laughed too. She pointed in the air as if she was directing a convoy of tanks. 'Laundry. That way.'

Frances and Massimo disappeared down the hallway. When Vasiliki turned back to Tom, he was watching her.

He held out a hand. Vasiliki shook it. It seemed very formal but it was appropriate. She had to resist the compulsion to throw her arms around him and hold him tight, the way she would have if he was any other long-lost friend. But they weren't friends anymore, no matter what they once had been to each other.

'Well,' he chuckled. 'Wasn't that all rather dramatic.'

She took in the sight of him, older but still the Tom she had known. 'Listen to you. You don't sound like Melbourne anymore. You sound like Prince Charles or something.'

Tom laughed and she recognised it, deep and full of fun, the same sound she'd held in her heart for twenty years.

'And listen to you. You're not the Greek girl I remember. You sound sort of, well, half Australian, half Greek. Is there such a thing?'

'Yes, there is.' That's how she felt these days. Half and half. She'd lived longer in Australia than she had in Greece and, although she was still part of the culture, part of the family, spoke Greek every day, there were things about her life that were distinctly Australian now.

'And you've finally convinced people to call you Vicki, I see.'

Vasiliki laughed. 'I tried for so many years but my family still call me Vasiliki.'

Tom held his arms wide. 'Whatever your name is, you're still as beautiful as ever.'

Her face felt hot. 'Thank you. And you haven't changed either.' Tom was wearing simple navy trousers and a short-sleeved white shirt, as if Carnaby Street and modern London hadn't rubbed off on him at all.

'What are you doing back in Australia? Are you on holidays?'

'No, not holidays unfortunately. I have a legal conference here in Sydney next week, and when I mentioned to Frances that I was coming home, she planned this whole reunion around my trip. She was rather sneaky about the whole damn thing, actually.'

'She didn't say anything about it. About you being back in Australia. Not a word.'

Tom took a step closer, searched her face. 'Do you think you would have come if you'd known?'

How could she know that? Would she have been able to prepare her heart in advance for the pain of seeing him, for the longing that had suddenly emerged about what might have been? Could she have imagined what seeing him would still do to her? Because as she stood in Frances's kitchen, taking in the sight of Frances's respectable-looking brother with his hair cut short, his warm smile still moved her as much as it always had.

And with a jolt that hurt her heart, she saw her daughter in his face. Aphrodite had the Burley eyes, caramel brown, she could see that now that she had the real-life Tom to compare her with. The hair colour, a dark brown rather than the black of her sisters; the pert nose and the thin top lip that her daughter always complained about. If Aphrodite and Tom Burley were ever to meet, they would know with one look. Everyone would know about Vasiliki's lies and the truth she'd hidden from the world.

'Yes, of course I would have come,' she lied. 'It's so good to see you after all these years. You enjoying your married life?'

'Yes, very much. Sally's a lawyer, too. We have a house in Green Park and two corgis.'

'Just like the queen,' Vasiliki said. 'Do you and your wife have any children?'

Tom's eyes dipped to his brogues. 'Rather unfortunate, that. It seems that we can't. But, you know, life is good. We travel. Florence is nice at this time of year and in July we're going to the Greek Islands for a week.'

'You're going to Greece?'

His eyes softened. 'Yes. I've always wanted to go. Everyone is raving about Mykonos.'

Tom couldn't have children. And he was going to Greece. Perhaps, just maybe, he'd never forgotten her either.

'You still in Melbourne then? How are all your daughters?'

Her daughters? *Your daughter.*

She swallowed hard. 'We're still in Oakleigh, living next to my parents. We have two greengrocer's shops now, which are doing well. Our daughters are growing up. Aphr ...'

Say her name. Tell her father her name.

'Aphrodite is eighteen and a hairdresser.'

'Oh, charming. There'll always be work in that sort of job. Everyone's hair grows, doesn't it? Unless of course you're like Frances and Andrew who never seem to cut theirs.' He laughed.

She laughed too.

'And the others?'

'My other three daughters? They're good girls, too.'

Tom cleared his throat and studied his shoes for a long moment. 'You're very lucky indeed, Vasiliki. Very lucky.'

Over the years, she had wondered what she would do if she saw Tom. And each time she thought about that possibility, she'd counted the hearts that would be broken if she told the truth. Tom's. Aphrodite's. Her parents. Steve. Her lovely Steve. How could she live with herself if he found out she'd been lying to him for almost twenty years?

'Vasiliki,' Tom murmured.

'Yes, Tom?'

He stepped closer, spoke more quietly. 'I honestly wish things had been different for us. I look around these days and see the freedoms young people have, especially in London, for goodness sake, and I can't help but think ... well, I can't help but think about what might have been. Between the two of us. The time just wasn't right, was it?'

'No, it wasn't.' Vasiliki put her arms around him and held him. Slowly, his arms went around her too, tight and strong.

She could tell him this secret because this much was true. 'I never, ever stopped thinking about you, I promise.'

'It's just down here on the left.'

Massimo strode down the hallway, Frances still in his arms, and stopped at an open doorway. He glanced inside and met Frances's eyes, a question in his.

'This isn't the laundry. And there are no shoes in here.'

'No.' Frances quickly looked over her shoulder. 'Quick. Go inside.'

Massimo swung her right then left so he didn't knock her legs on the door frame. She reached back for the door handle and pulled it quietly closed. He looked around the room. There was a desk by the window with a sewing machine and a messy pile of clothes next to it. An open sewing box displayed rolls of brightly coloured cotton, scissors, pins and needles; and a dressmaker's dummy was half-undressed, one hard foam breast exposed.

She couldn't take her eyes from his face. 'Please, Massimo. Just a few minutes alone.'

He didn't loosen his hold on her. Her arms around his neck, her fingers clasped together, holding on to him. His face was so close, she could see the shadow of his stubble, the depth of his dark, almost-black eyes, and the small laugh lines by his mouth.

'Frances,' he began, then stopped. He slowly put her down and turned towards the door.

Please don't go. Please don't open the door and leave me. 'I couldn't bear seeing you after all these years and not being alone with you. If only for a few minutes.'

'Francesca.' He stopped. 'All that was so many years ago. You made your choice.' He took a deep breath. 'And then I made mine. There's no point looking back, is there?'

'Yes, there definitely is.'

'You've been drinking,' he said, looking at her mouth.

'Yes. And the spumante has made me brave. I want to tell you something, about what happened between us all those years ago. There are things I understand better now. There are things I didn't know how to say back then. My life was such a mess.' Frances was close now, and she trailed a finger down his forearm, slowly, across the dark hair there, into his hand. She slipped her fingers into his. 'I want you to know that I did love you, you know. Not just at Cooma, but at Bonegilla, too.' Frances shivered, her body tense and on edge.

'At Bonegilla?'

Frances nodded. 'Oh, how could I have not been in love with you? You were as handsome as you are today and my sixteen-year-old heart melted at the sight of you. Do you remember the dance at the Tudor Hall?'

'You were wearing a yellow dress.'

'Yes,' she said. 'I loved you from that day. At Cooma, when you asked me to marry you, I wanted to say yes. So much. But I couldn't. I couldn't tell you then because of my situation, but I can tell you now. It wasn't because I didn't love you.'

His voice was gruff, demanding. 'Then why, Frances?'

There were so many secrets in the thick and humid air that Sydney Saturday afternoon. 'Because I didn't want to keep the baby.'

He pulled back.

She gripped his hand tighter. She couldn't let him walk away now. 'I didn't want to remember anything about the man who was his father. Can you understand that? And I didn't want you to look at the baby and be reminded every day that it wasn't yours. I knew your family by then, Massimo. They were so proud of you, the oldest child and the first son. How would your parents have felt about any marriage between us, knowing that the child you had claimed as your own, their first grandson, at least in everyone else's eyes, wasn't yours?'

He swallowed hard. 'It was a boy?'

'Yes. And you are Catholic and I'm not and it would have been too hard, Massimo.'

'I didn't give a shit about any of that, Francesca. You know I didn't. I meant it when I asked you.' His words were quiet, forceful, full of sadness.

Frances pressed her breasts against his shirt, laid her hands on his shoulders. She was so relieved when he didn't back away this time, when he stayed close, when he lost his breath at the nearness of her. There was a moment of guilty hesitation, and then he slipped a warm hand inside her top, covering her breast, and then his lips were on her neck, pressing there.

She wanted one thing from this man. Another kiss. But not like the chaste one they'd shared when she'd been eight months pregnant with another man's baby. 'Kiss me, Massimo. Please. Just one more time.'

He pulled back, taking her face in his hands. His chest rose and fell and she could feel that he was hard, pressing against her. She needed him, to close the book on the longing she'd had for him all these years. For the memories that wouldn't fade, for the life she sometimes wished she had.

'We can't do this,' he murmured. 'It's not right.'

Frances stood on her toes and put her mouth on his, slowly, hesitantly, tasting him, feeling the soft fullness, the desire for her. She undid his belt.

'I know,' Frances whispered into his lips.

'The snags and patties are done.' Andrew stood at the back door, waving his tongs in the air, beckoning the guests outside. Beside him, Vanessa and Lyndall were finally out of the pool, their hair long wet strings down their backs, towels wrapped around them as tight as pastry on a sausage roll.

'Cheers, Andrew,' Tom called out from the kitchen. 'Just refreshing some drinks here. Can I get you anything?'

'Cheers mate, I'm right.' Andrew looked over to the kitchen. 'Where's Frances?'

Vasiliki held out a hand. 'Don't come in. I dropped a glass and there are bits everywhere.' She exchanged glances with Tom warily. 'Frances is finding a broom to clean it all up.'

'No worries. Tell her the food's on, will you?' Andrew turned and walked out across the yard. 'Who's up for a sausage?'

'Why don't I go and find that broom, hey?' Tom said. 'You should go outside and grab something to eat.'

'I will.'

Before she could move, Frances and Massimo reappeared in the kitchen. Frances took in the scene and slapped a hand to her red cheek. 'Damn it. The broom.'

'I was just on my way to get it,' Tom said. 'In the laundry, did you say?'

Without a word, Massimo walked past Vasiliki to the sliding doors.

Frances and Vasiliki were alone. They searched each other's faces. Vasiliki guessed what had just happened without one word of an admission.

'Frances,' she exclaimed in a fierce whisper. 'How could you?'

'Don't judge me,' Frances said quietly. 'And please, whatever you do, don't say anything to Iliana. Her family have been so good to me.'

'He's married. And so are you.'

'You don't understand, Vicki. You see … I've loved him since Bonegilla.' Frances cast her sad eyes to the ground, tiptoed around the glass in her bare feet and went outside.

A moment later, Tom was back with the broom. 'Be careful there, Vasiliki.'

Vasiliki couldn't take it all in. Her head spun. How had she not known about Iliana's brother and Frances? How could she have done that to her own husband, who was a few feet away in the backyard?

And then the realisation hit.

She was no better. In fact, she and Frances were more alike than either of them knew.

Did anyone know about her and Tom?

She grabbed his arm. 'Tom,' she whispered. 'Did you ever tell Frances?'

He looked stricken. 'Of course not. I didn't ever tell a soul.'

She loosened her grip and from deep within her sobs exploded. She covered her face with her hands and let them wrack her chest.

'Oh, hell. Vasiliki. Don't cry.' Tom stood by her side, holding on to the stupid broom like it was a shield of armour.

In that moment, Vasiliki envied Frances. Her friend was free to do what she pleased. To love who she wanted.

Why couldn't she do the same?

Chapter Forty

The only light in the backyard was the glow cast by a mismatch of candles in the middle of the table. Scattered around it were wine glasses with dregs of red staining their bowls, an empty bottle of vodka that Andrew had retrieved earlier in the evening from the cocktail cabinet in the living room, and a platter with scatterings of chopped cabana sausage, a few pickled onions and cubes of cheese impaled on stray toothpicks, limp parsley sprigs and two lonely devilled eggs.

Andrew was putting Vanessa and Lyndall to bed, and Frances and the rest of the Bonegilla girls were at the table, with Massimo and Tom at either end. The humid evening was filled with half-drunk conversations and promises and the scent of jasmine.

Frances held on to her empty wine glass and listened to the quiet chatter. She felt drunk now, both from the excitement of being with Massimo, and on the reconnection she felt with the part of her life she had long ago swept aside. Being with Massimo, with Elizabeta and Iliana and Vasiliki, had reminded her of the dreams she'd had when she was young. When she'd first met these people, she'd wanted to travel the world, to visit each and every country in alphabetical order, from Albania to Zimbabwe, to see and experience the things she'd had just a taste of at Bonegilla.

Elizabeta smiled at something Massimo said, and Frances was so relieved to see it. Elizabeta looked so much older than her thirty-six years. Her outfit—a floral shirt and crimplene trousers—was sensible and plain. Her hair was pulled back in a simple bun that sat at the top of her collar. It was as if Elizabeta wanted to fade into the background. Frances thought back to Bonegilla to remember how Elizabeta had been. She had always had a sober nature, even when they had fun together, but there had always been something in her, a spark of intellect and curiosity, that revealed her quiet intelligence. Since those first days, grief had swallowed her whole. It had come to Australia with her family, as clearly as the clothes and mementoes they'd packed in their luggage, and it had been a constant companion all the way, on the voyage to Australia on the *Fairsea*, each day at Bonegilla after Luisa died and still, it seemed, in Adelaide.

Someone made a joke. Iliana chuckled and Massimo laughed out loud, blowing the languid smoke from his cigarette into the air above his head.

His imprint was on her skin. She still felt him inside her, so fast and strong. Her lips stung from his kisses. She watched him smoke, and something inside her was reborn. The love she had felt for him, the love that had been so important to her in the lowest moments of her life, bloomed back to life, obliterating every idea about what was right and what was wrong.

Frances had to admit to herself that she had purposely put a distance between herself and Iliana over all these years. It was nothing Iliana had done. It was about Massimo and the other things she hadn't wanted to remember. She had never been able to find the words to explain how giving away her baby had changed her life. Her baby. The son she had never held, never comforted.

How could she describe to anyone the restless aimlessness of her life in the years after? The moving from school to school, the distance she'd put between herself and her students so she didn't feel, didn't wish, didn't grieve. All those plans she had to see the world had been packed away with the memories of her child. She'd lost any spirit of adventure. She hadn't wanted to leave Australia after that. She needed to know that she was walking in the same continent as her son. Tom had asked her to go to London to visit him; had urged her more strongly when he married Sally. But she'd had her own children by then, and didn't want to be parted from them for a night, much less three weeks.

Iliana had understood Frances's desire for secrecy, for privacy, and had never asked about the baby. Frances had tried so hard to put it all behind her, to pack it in a memory box and lay it to rest. She had buried those feelings of shame in the free-spirited demeanour she had so carefully cultivated, but inside she was still the humiliated and shamed young woman who'd been forced to carry the entire burden of a mistake. Iliana could never know that side of her. Iliana looked blissful, and for that Frances was so happy.

How could she not compare her life to her friends'?

Vasiliki was the most glamorous of all of them, the most successful in business and in life, with a loving husband and four daughters. Frances had a collection of all the photos Vasiliki had sent her over the years: first birthdays, first day of school, Greek Easter and Christmas. Happy family gatherings.

How harshly would Vasiliki judge Frances for what she'd seen in the kitchen earlier in the afternoon, for what she'd instantly understood had happened with Massimo? Frances couldn't think about that. Because she had decided, right then, as she looked at Massimo across the table as he smoked and laughed and snuck glances at her, that they would see each other again. Now that she'd had a taste of him, she craved him, she craved who she could be when she was with him. It was like an instant addiction to a drug.

The past wasn't over. Perhaps it would never be over.

Elizabeta yawned. 'I think it's time to go.' She checked her watch. 'Goodness me. It's ten o'clock.'

'I don't know how I've made it up this late.' Iliana blew out a breath. 'Perhaps it was the fun of seeing you all after so many years.'

'Speaking of which,' Frances said into the night air. 'I've got an idea. Why don't we do this again?'

'Another Bonegilla girls reunion?' Vasiliki asked. 'I'm in. But let's do Melbourne next time, huh?'

'And Adelaide after that,' Elizabeta added.

'I assume you mean girls only,' Tom said jealously. 'It seems rather a shame that the chaps have to miss out, doesn't it Massimo?'

Massimo looked at her. She knew what he was thinking. That they wouldn't be waiting years to see each other again. She was surer of that than of anything in her life.

'Sorry,' Vasiliki announced. 'It's Bonegilla girls only.'

Frances pulled herself to her tired feet. 'If we had any wine left I'd suggest we drink on it but we don't. We'll just have to promise.'

And with their goodbye hugs and affectionate kisses, the Bonegilla girls agreed.

Chapter Forty-one

1984

'Stop joking. I don't want to be a grandmother yet.'

'Why not?' Vasiliki refilled Frances's wine glass.

'Because I'm only forty-six, for God's sake.' Frances shuddered at the thought. 'And Vanessa and Lyndall are only eighteen and sixteen. You think I want them having babies now? God no.'

It was a warm sunny day in Melbourne—at least it was for the moment—and Vasiliki and Frances were waiting for Elizabeta and Iliana to arrive for their reunion dinner. The women had kept their promise to meet ten years after the reunion at Frances's in Sydney, and this time it was Vasiliki's turn to host. The Bonegilla girls were coming for the weekend—no husbands and no children—and the venue was one of Melbourne's best Greek restaurants, in Lygon Street. Vasiliki knew the owners through business, and she'd managed to secure a private area on the balcony overlooking the street.

For a public-school teacher from Sydney, Frances felt very spoilt indeed.

She'd never seen a spread like it. Even before they'd been given menus, a huge platter had arrived and it bulged in the middle of the table. It was groaning with wedges of pita bread, dips of all colours, including an intriguing pale pink one, cubes of fetta cheese, vine leaves wrapped into little cigar shapes and meatballs. Frances had never eaten Greek food before and didn't quite know where to start.

'They should be here any minute.' Vasiliki checked her elegant watch. 'They're staying together at a motel just around the corner and they must have decided to walk.'

'Don't worry,' Frances said. 'I'm sure I won't starve while we're waiting.' She studied the platter, trying to decide what she would taste first. It all looked very different to her kitchen staples: roast lamb every Sunday night, spaghetti bolognese, schnitzel, sausages with three veg, and sweet and sour pork—with sauce from a jar. Frances had finally admitted to herself years ago that she simply didn't like cooking. She'd lost all the skills Iliana's mother had taught her in Cooma twenty years before. Cooking wasn't the thing that brought her joy.

She had something that brought her joy and it had nothing to do with food.

'You know.' Vasiliki popped a cube of fetta cheese into her mouth. 'Speaking of forty-six. I've just realised something. I'm forty-six, too—I know, I know, I don't look a day over thirty—which is older than my parents were when they came to Australia. They left behind their entire families, both sets of parents, my *yiayia* and *papou* on my mother's side, and packed up as much as they could carry and left. They didn't know a word of English and uprooted their young family anyway and got on a boat. I still can't believe they did it, you know?'

'They were so brave back then. Everyone who came to Australia.' Frances stared at the platter. 'What's that?' She pointed to the pink dip.

'Taramasalata. Try it, you'll love it.'

Frances dipped a triangle of warm pita bread into it and took a bite. 'God, that's delicious.'

Vasiliki grinned. 'It's fish roe.'

Frances tried not to look shocked. 'Well, it's still delicious.' She dipped again and ate it hungrily.

'The thing is,' Vasiliki said. 'If my daughters did it to me, packed up and moved halfway across the world, I think I'd try to lock them in the house for the rest of their lives.'

'Is Aphrodite still living at home? She must be nearly thirty. I thought she must have moved out by now.'

'After the wedding, she and Peter will move into their house. They've had tenants in for two years and they've been saving, saving, saving to pay it off before the wedding. It helps when you both get to live at home and don't pay any board to your parents.'

'You're very generous. A wedding already.' Frances shook her head. 'You started so much younger than the rest of us. Having babies, I mean.'

Vasiliki's head shot up. She opened her lips as if she was about to speak but didn't say anything.

'You all right, Vicki?'

'I was just thinking back to when Aphrodite was born.' She stopped, took a deep breath. 'You're right. I was so young.'

'You know,' Frances said, feeling brave and picking up a meatball. 'The older I get, the more respect I have for the parents who did what yours did. And Elizabeta's and Iliana's and the three hundred and twenty thousand other people that went through Bonegilla before it closed. My father loved to remind me of that. Still does, in fact. And, to be honest, every migrant we have in Australia. It's fun to talk to my students about where their families are from. These days, it's not Greece and Italy and Germany but Malaysia and Vietnam and Cambodia and Laos and Lebanon. Everyone starts again looking for a better life. You know, I remember, back then, asking my father about it, why you all came out.'

'And what did he say?'

'"The war".'

Vasiliki met Frances's eyes. They were both thinking of Elizabeta and how her family had suffered. They had never forgotten what she'd told them about her sister. 'How do you think she's coping? After her mum's death, I mean?'

'It's hard to tell.' Frances shrugged. 'Elizabeta would never say it, but I think she's relieved in a way that her mother's suffering is over. When she called me to tell me about the funeral, she sounded … it's hard to find the words … as if a huge weight had been lifted from her shoulders.'

Vasiliki stared into the distance. 'I thought the same. Relieved isn't the right word but she had suffered so much. That whole family had.'

Frances put her hand up and waved. 'And here they are.' Seeing Iliana still gave Frances pangs of guilt. When she'd seen Massimo a few days before she'd left for Melbourne, he'd made her promise, once again, that she would never tell.

'I've kept this secret for ten years,' she'd said angrily. 'Since that night at my house all those years ago. Why do you think I would say something now?'

It wasn't unusual for him to be anxious when she saw him. He saw shadows everywhere when he was with her. Even when there were only the two of them in a motel room, alone with a Gideon Bible and a broken television.

Frances pushed back her chair and went to Elizabeta first. 'I'm so sorry about your mother.' She threw her arms around her friend and tried not to react when she felt skin and bones under her shirt. When she pulled back, saw Elizabeta's face up close, she saw hollows in her cheeks and clouds under her eyes.

'Thank you. That is kind of you.'

'Here, take a seat.' She ushered Elizabeta in next to her.

Vasiliki whistled. 'And look at you, glamourpuss.'

Iliana laughed. 'Thank you. The last time you saw me I was twelve months pregnant. Anything looks better than that.'

'How's Sonia?'

'Nine years old and all she wants to do is be a dancer on *Countdown*.'

'Oh, my girls loved that show,' Vasiliki said. 'Every Sunday night. We had to finish dinner by six o'clock or they would race from the table anyway and lie on the floor in front of the television. I understand about Sherbet and the Skyhooks and that John Paul Young. In my day, it was Johnny O'Keefe.'

'And the Easybeats and the Masters Apprentices!' Frances added.

Elizabeta smiled. 'I don't know who you're talking about. I never listened to that music.'

'The good old days, huh?' Iliana laughed.

Once the waiter had taken their orders, it wasn't long before more food arrived. Vasiliki seemed to have some influence, because bottles of wine followed and extra pita bread and more food than they would ever eat. Frances was glad of the distraction. As she ate barbecued octopus and grilled lamb and fish with garlic and rosemary, she went over and over what she was going to say. It had all been so easy in her head the past year. But now the Bonegilla girls were all together, she was suddenly nervous. She needed to tell someone and she couldn't tell their friends because they were all Andrew's friends, too.

She sipped her wine. 'I have some news.'

'God, you're not pregnant,' Vasiliki joked.

'No. Definitely not pregnant.' She steeled herself by taking a deep breath. 'Andrew and I are getting a divorce.'

The throaty roar of a car racing down Lygon Street drifted up to them on the balcony. Chattering voices from below filled the silence.

'Oh, Frances. That's terrible news.' Elizabeta looked heartbroken at the admission. She put down her cutlery, as if she'd suddenly lost her appetite.

'I'm so sorry for you,' Iliana said, crossing herself.

'What happened?' Vasiliki always dived right in for the truth.

'I don't know how to explain it, really. We've drifted apart over the past few years.' She looked at each of their faces, wondering who would judge her the most harshly. Surely it would be Iliana. She was a Catholic, a regular churchgoer, a believer. 'We've lost each other, I suppose.'

'Well, find each other again,' Vasiliki said adamantly. 'You can't do this to your girls. Divorced parents? You'll break their hearts, Frances. You owe it to them to work things out with your husband.'

'It's too late.' Frances couldn't care anymore if it would break their hearts. She had to preserve her own. Didn't she deserve some happiness in her life, after all these years, after all the secrets she'd kept that had slowly eaten away at who she was? In a few years she would be fifty. Old. Unlovable. And all that talk earlier about being a grandparent? It had sent shivers up her spine. She had given up so much already. She had decided to demand something for her own life for once, just like young women were doing now.

'It's never too late.' Vasiliki was angry. Frances couldn't figure out why.

'The truth is, I don't want to work it out. I'm in love with someone else. I have been for years.'

It felt to Frances like a moment from *Days of Our Lives*. She'd found herself immersed in the convoluted and extraordinary love lives of Salem's Bo and Hope and Marlena and John during the long summer holidays, when her girls were in their rooms listening to the radio or reading *Dolly* magazine; when it was too hot to do much of anything. There always seemed to be a dramatic moment just before a commercial, in which the camera would zoom in on a character's face and wait and wait and wait before cutting to an ad break for OMO or Pal-molive Gold.

She was in that scene right now. Her friends stared at her as if she'd gone mad.

Iliana leaned in, whispered fiercely. 'You've been having an *affair?*'

'Yes,' she replied, unashamed. Well, perhaps just the slightest bit ashamed.

'Who is it?' Elizabeta asked quietly.

'Someone I work with.' Frances lied to avoid Iliana's scrutiny.

'Is he married, too?' Iliana asked.

'Yes.'

'How could you?' Iliana's mouth twisted in a scowl and she crossed her arms over her chest. 'How could you do that to two families?'

'Don't be so harsh, Iliana,' Elizabeta said.

Iliana couldn't look at her and, in that moment, Frances knew Massimo had been right about not telling his sister. To her, adultery was a sin and divorce was also forbidden in her church. To a person with a happy marriage, it was easy to think in black and white.

'You're such a good person, Frances. You always were. What's happened to you?'

Without warning, tears were in her eyes. 'You know what happened to me, Iliana. You were there all those years ago. You were a friend to me then. A sister, actually. I hope you'll be there for me now.'

Iliana's face crumpled. 'Oh, Frances,' she whispered.

Frances turned to Elizabeta and Vasiliki. 'In 1958 I got pregnant and I had a baby. I gave him up for adoption.'

'*Gott im Himmel.*' Elizabeta slumped back in her chair.

Vasiliki's mouth gaped. 'You had a son?'

Something inside Frances split open and bled. 'And even though I never got to hold him, I think about him all the time. He would be twenty-five now. I could be a grand-mother already and I would never know.'

'I ... thought you'd forgotten all about the baby,' Iliana said quietly. 'You've never talked about it, all these years.'

Frances turned her pleading eyes to Iliana. 'That's what everyone told me I should do. The doctors. The nurses. My parents. But ... you're a mother. You must understand. How can a mother ever forget a baby?'

Iliana covered her face with her hands. 'I'm so sorry, Frances.'

'Wait a minute. You knew about the baby?' Vasiliki was incredulous.

'Yes. Frances came to Cooma when ...' Iliana stopped to let Frances tell her own story.

'When I had to hide, Iliana's family took me in. It was different back in those days. You all remember what they said about girls like me. We had to go away, disappear. Hide our shame. The Agnolis were wonderfully kind to me. I was in Cooma for about six months and when it was almost time, I went back to my parents and told them the truth. My son was born in Albury.'

'I can't believe it,' Elizabeta said.

'I have lived with that, with what I did, all this time. I need to do something for myself now. I had to give up my child. I've been a wife and mother for twenty years. You know, I think those feminists are right.'

'My daughter Stavroula is a feminist,' Vasiliki announced. There was a long pause. 'And ... a lesbian.'

Frances blinked. 'She is?'

Vasiliki waved a hand at a passing waiter. 'Two more bottles of wine.' She turned back to the table. 'I blame that university. She pushed and pushed to go and now she's doing something called Women's Studies. And she has a girlfriend. Who's not even Greek.'

'I think one of my aunties was a lesbian,' Frances said. 'My father's oldest sister never married and lived with her best friend her whole life. We used to call them spinsters back in those days.'

Iliana crossed herself again and said something quietly in Italian.

'Stop that with all the crossing,' Vasiliki snapped. 'Stavroula is fine. She's very smart and doing very well at the university. She's still my daughter. I don't understand this thing, and I can't say I like thinking about it, but I still love her. Steve … well, he's not so understanding. And her *yiayia* and *papou*? They can't even look at her.'

'They'll understand one day,' Elizabeta said. 'When they think about how lucky they are to have four granddaughters.'

'Do you sometimes wish we had been born when they were?' Frances asked. 'They have so much freedom, our daughters. They can do whatever they want.'

'I compare myself to her all the time. I couldn't even marry who I wanted to. And she gets to be a lesbian,' Vasiliki said. 'In 1956, we were two years out of Bonegilla and I was working at the milk bar in Bourke Street, the one my father and my uncle had back then. One Sunday, they introduced me to this man at church and that was it. We were getting married.' Her face fell. 'I didn't want to marry Steve.' She glanced at Frances and hesitated. 'I was in love with another boy.'

Frances remembered that day, ten years earlier, after she and Massimo had been together that first time in her sewing room. When Frances had walked back into the kitchen, she had seen the knowing look on Vasiliki's face and had realised immediately that Vasiliki had guessed her secret. And now, ten years later, Frances understood why she had never revealed it.

Because she'd had a secret, too.

'This other boy,' Elizabeta asked. 'Your family didn't approve?'

Vasiliki lowered her eyes to the empty plate in front of her. 'He was an Australian boy. A lovely boy. It would have broken our family apart if I told them. I couldn't do it. Greek girls didn't do things like that to their families back then.'

Frances laid her hand on Vasiliki's shoulder. They shared an understanding look.

'I'm glad things are changing,' Vasiliki said. 'It's about time. Can you imagine me these days telling my daughters who they should marry? We wouldn't think of doing such a thing.'

'Well,' Elizabeta sighed. 'It seems today is a day for sharing secrets.'

Her words were heavy between the four women.

She continued. 'We have been friends for thirty years. Will you all promise me something? Sometimes I worry that we will lose our friendship, that something will come between us, make us argue and not care about each other anymore. Or that we will let what we have slip through our fingers.'

The waiter arrived with the extra wine and clean glasses. They were silent until he left with a gracious smile.

'Iliana,' Elizabeta said. 'You don't agree with what Frances is doing but we must always be friends. I need to know that you will always be my friend. I need you all now more than ever.'

Frances reeled. The fragile bird who had turned up for their reunion lunch was stronger than any of them had realised. Of course she was. How on earth could she have survived everything in her life if she wasn't strong?

'I will need you to look after Nikolas and Luisa and Johnny if ...'

'If what, Elizabeta?' Vasiliki demanded.

'If I die. You see, I have breast cancer.'

Chapter Forty-two

Elizabeta blinked her eyes open against the bright ward lights after her surgery, and remembered her breast was gone.

There was a tightness where there had once been plump softness, and bandages now constricted her chest. She still felt thick-tongued from the anaesthetic and couldn't seem to move any of her limbs.

But she was awake.

And the first face she saw, leaning over her hospital bed, was her daughter's.

'You're awake,' Luisa said tremulously.

Elizabeta nodded. She tried to speak but her tongue and the roof of her mouth were stuck together, as if gummed up by cement. Luisa poured a glass of water from the plastic jug on the bedside cabinet and angled the straw so her mother could sip without sitting up. When she stopped, Luisa put the glass on the cabinet. She gripped the metal rail on the side of her mother's bed and watched her, her face half broken by the sight.

Luisa. Her lovely daughter. Elizabeta had tried to encourage play and delight and wonder in her children as a way to ward off what she feared lurked in them. What she'd seen in her own mother and what she suspected was in her heart, too. A memory of sadness and grief so strong that it washed up from its depths at times of its own choosing. Memories of trauma so fierce and overwhelming that Elizabeta thought they must be imprinted on her own DNA now, that they had set in the calcium of her bones.

And in her daughter's face, at that moment, she could see what she had so long feared. The ghost was there in her eyes. Elizabeta had tried so hard to kill it, to make it invisible, to fight it, but that had been to no avail. The knowledge that she had passed on her grief to her daughter hurt more than losing a breast ever would.

'How are you feeling?' Luisa asked. She quickly brushed the tears from her eyes and forced a smile.

You're so young to see your mother in such pain, Elizabeta thought.

Just like I was so young.

She wished she could excise the ghost in her daughter's eyes as easily as the doctors had predicted they would get rid of her cancerous breast.

'Not so bad,' Elizabeta croaked.

'Dad has taken Johnny to the cafeteria to get something to eat. I swear that boy has hollow legs.'

'That's good.' Nikolas was doing something good for their son, distracting him.

'And, there's a surprise for you,' Luisa said, and there was a cry mixed with a laugh in her voice. 'They're here.'

'Who is here?' Elizabeta rasped, her throat sore from the ventilator tube. She sounded as if she'd smoked for the past fifty years.

'The Bonegilla girls. Auntie Vicki's come from Melbourne and she picked up Auntie Iliana and Auntie Frances at the airport. They're waiting outside. Shall I tell them to come in?'

It had only been three weeks since she'd seen them in Melbourne.

She reached for her daughter's hand, her knuckles white on the rail, and held it. 'Tell them to come.'

Elizabeta felt greatly comforted by the presence of her friends. The girls she had known at Bonegilla now had girls of their own but in her eyes, at that moment, they were all sixteen again. Her eyes drifted closed again, and she heard the voice of the Bonegilla girls, chatting together as they roamed the vast camp, studying Frances's atlas at the mess, playing table tennis and watching the young men playing soccer. Her mind went back to the happy times they shared, not the grief since. She had hoped that the memory of the German would vanish; that he would become invisible, erased to history, too unimportant to ever be remembered by anyone. Remembering him only dignified his life, didn't it? When all he deserved was to be less than the dust on someone else's shoe? But life—and memories—didn't work that way. He was always there because he was her sister Luisa's father. The thought of it was still too much to contemplate.

When she'd been diagnosed Nikolas had asked her if she was scared. She had scoffed. How could she be scared of cancer? She had lived through so much worse. As soon as it could be done, she had wanted it gone, cut out of her, so she could forget it, too.

'Did it all go okay? The surgery?' Vasiliki clutched her hand. Her glossy black hair shone in the hospital lights. Tough, no-nonsense Vasiliki looked heartbroken. Her face was pale, her cheeks drawn, her bottom lip quivering.

'I spoke to the doctor just before you arrived,' Luisa chimed in. 'He says everything went very well. Mum will have to have some radiotherapy, just to make sure all the cancer cells are gone but, at this stage, no chemo.'

'That's a relief, isn't it?' It was Frances, on the other side of the bed, next to Luisa.

'It is, isn't it, Mum?'

Elizabeta felt tired. She had surrendered her body to the nurses and surgeons and anaesthetists and didn't want it back just yet. She needed to sleep, to find some strength, to find a future in the news that she would survive.

Iliana came forwards, leaned down, and kissed her on the cheek. She was sobbing.

'C'mon, Iliana. We'll get you a cup of coffee. Strong and black.' Vasiliki winked at Elizabeta.

She closed her eyes, gave in to the thick fog rolling into her head. She didn't want to see their pain as well as Luisa's. She'd been stoic for them all, for Luisa, for John and for Nikolas. For the Bonegilla girls.

Now she had to turn inwards, help herself heal.

There was so much scar tissue now.

Ten days later, when Elizabeta arrived home, the people who loved her most in the world were waiting.

Nikolas had picked her up from The Queen Elizabeth Hospital just before lunch, and they walked gingerly to the car, where he'd parked illegally in a disabled parking spot.

'You don't have a permit to park here,' she'd chastised him, refusing to get in the car. He'd put her hospital bag in the boot of the car and slammed it shut.

'You must be feeling better. You're already nagging me.' Nikolas smiled across at her and she realised then how much her illness had hurt him, too. They'd been married for twenty-five years. For half of their marriage, she had not loved him. They had drifted from each other, let each other go. But since her mother had died, they had remembered what they had loved about each other in the first place. And now, just when it seemed they might have some time for themselves, with Luisa and Johnny now twenty-four and twenty, a teacher and a carpenter, she'd been diagnosed. The trip they'd been talking about for years, a holiday back to Germany, was postponed. They'd planned to show Luisa and Johnny where Nikolas had grown up, in a town near the Bavarian Alps, and the place near Hessental where Elizabeta and her family had lived after they'd been deported from Hungary.

They'd saved for years for the airfares, not an easy feat on a single factory wage, but it could wait.

Elizabeta sometimes wondered, in those lonely hours in her hospital bed, in the rowdy night-time when machines beeped and there were too many nurses' footsteps and it was too light to sleep, if she had somehow wished her cancer on herself because she didn't want to go back to Europe.

She hadn't wanted to leave home; for, finally, Australia was home.

There was nothing about that part of her life that she wanted to revisit but she couldn't say that to Nikolas. He didn't know what had happened to her mother, what she herself had seen. There were some things best left unsaid in the hope that the memories would die out when she did.

Nikolas manoeuvred the car into the driveway and Elizabeta looked out over her front garden. The roses along the front fence were blooming in welcome and the lawn, which was John's weekly chore, was neat and trim. The lemon tree by the side fence looked shiny bright.

'Someone's been hard at work,' she said.

Nikolas turned the key in the ignition. 'Yes,' he smiled at her, tears welling in his eyes. 'Just you wait and see. Come on.'

Elizabeta took her husband's arm as she stepped up onto the front veranda and through the open front door into the house. The hallway was quiet. There was no evidence of Johnny's football boots outside his room, a regular sight. She glanced at Nikolas, who looked so happy she thought he might burst.

As they approached the living room, the glass sliding doors opened as if by magic and there they all were.

Luisa, Johnny, Nikolas's parents. And the Bonegilla girls. Her family.

A cheer went up and there was clapping. Elizabeta couldn't take it all in. Everything in the room had changed. A new plush green velour corner lounge sat elbowed around a new dark wood coffee table. In the other corner, facing the windows that looked out on to the street, a dark green leather recliner chair sat with a wide-ribboned bow around it. The walls had been painted a crisp off-white and there was a new framed photo of her family on the wall, something they'd taken for Christmas two years earlier and which had laid, unframed, in a kitchen drawer with pens and rubber bands and old bills. And on the main wall, there was a long wooden cabinet with a brand-new television set on it. It was the biggest screen Elizabeta had ever seen. It looked like something from the movies.

'What's all this?' she gasped. Luisa and Johnny were behind her, holding on tight.

'We used the holiday money,' Nikolas announced. 'What's the point of it sitting in the bank when you should be comfortable while you get better, huh?'

'Oh, my goodness.'

'And the chair in the corner there,' Luisa said. 'It's a present from the aunties.'

Open-mouthed, she turned to the Bonegilla girls. Had they performed this miracle for her?

They came to her with open arms.

'No one else sits in that chair but you,' Vasiliki said adamantly.

Frances whispered in her ear. 'We're glad to see you looking so much better.'

Iliana pulled away from the group embrace. 'Come and eat. I've made some lunch.'

They led Elizabeta to the dining table, which was filled with enough food for three times as many people.

This was her new start, she decided.

Her life was to begin again today.

Chapter Forty-three

1985

'So, my darling wife. How does it feel to be a *nonna?*'

Iliana thought over Vinnie's whispered question as she stared into the perfect face of her first grandchild. Bianca Iliana. The tiny baby was wrapped up tight in a blanket, only her face revealed. And what a beautiful face. Were there enough words in the whole world—in either Italian or English—to describe how much she already loved this little girl?

'It feels …' and before she could finish a sentence, Iliana burst into tears.

'Oh, Mum, don't cry. You'll make me cry.' Iliana and Vinnie's eldest daughter Anita lay in her hospital bed, exhausted but happy. Much like her mother.

'I can't help it. She's so … so …' Oh, this little girl was so *everything* that Iliana's heart was about to burst.

'Here's the prosecco.' Iliana and Vinnie's son-in-law, Michael, walked back into the maternity room clutching a bottle and four plastic glasses.

'See, Mum?' Anita said. 'He might not be Italian but we're brainwashing him into all our ways.'

So Michael wasn't Italian. He was Irish. But at least he was Catholic. And at least they were married. Iliana knew how things were for young people these days. Everyone now seemed to be living together and, much to Iliana's shock, having babies when they weren't even married. That was a bridge too far for her. She was happy and relieved when Anita had announced the year before that she was getting married, even if it was to an Irishman. A family was a family and Iliana could be Italian enough for them all. She was already planning in her head what she would cook for the christening party. They could have it in their backyard. It was big enough after all, and they could push back the doors of the shed, set up trestle tables and eat out there.

Vinnie took the bottle from Michael and poured out the prosecco. It fizzed in their glasses and Iliana carefully leaned sideways so she didn't dribble any on her beautiful grand-daughter. Bianca was only half an hour old. She and Vinnie had been waiting at home; well, Vinnie had been watching the football and she had been pacing, completely unable to concentrate on anything other than the pain her daughter was going through. While Vinnie watched, Iliana had called the maternity ward every ten minutes for updates on Anita's labour, presuming that she and Michael would be too busy to call them when, finally, she was told the baby had just been born. She'd pushed Vinnie into the car and they'd driven right to the hospital.

She wanted to meet her grandchild as soon as she could. If she could have flown there, she would have.

This little one nestled in her arms was reward enough for everything she had gone through to have her own children. She wished her own mother was still alive to see this. All the sacrifices her own parents had made in their lives, to see a future for their own children, had created life for their children and their children. A bedraggled, poor Italian family on a boat all those years ago had helped create this little girl. That was indeed a miracle. If they'd stayed in Italy, she would never have married Vinnie and never had Anita who would never have met Michael at the law firm and there it was, a history of a family. A story of a little girl born in Australia in 1985.

'Now, the christening,' Iliana whispered over Bianca's head.

Anita slapped her palm down on the sheets and turned to Michael. 'What did I tell you?'

Michael tried not to laugh.

'What do you mean, what did you tell him?'

'That you'd already be thinking of what next! She's only an hour old, Ma.'

'Well, I want to be ready.'

Vinnie patted her on the shoulder. 'Is it my turn yet?'

'Only if you promise not to drop her.' Iliana winked at Anita. 'You should have seen him after you were born. He was in the waiting room smoking a cigarette and he didn't hold you for a week.'

Vinnie huffed. 'It was different back then. We weren't allowed in to see the baby being born.'

Michael nudged Vinnie's arm. 'That might not be a bad thing there, Vinnie.'

Iliana carefully passed the tiny bundle to her husband. He held her gently and sat down in the plastic chair by Anita's bed. As Iliana watched him coo and whisper to Bianca, she felt her heart swell.

This life they had made for themselves was everything.

Chapter Forty-four

Vasiliki stared open-mouthed at her daughter. Aphrodite was clutching the skirt of her wedding gown, staring back at her mother. The two-thousand-dollar creation was so heavily beaded across the bodice that Vasiliki had to try not to look directly at it in case she was blinded.

'Did you hear what I said, Mum?'

Vasiliki pressed a hand to her forehead and felt beads of sweat there. Where was her handbag? She needed to blot. 'I need to sit down.'

'And I need to go get married. Aren't you going to say anything?'

Vasiliki closed her eyes, took a moment, tried to stay calm. 'I'm supposed to be happy that my oldest daughter is walking down the aisle and she's already pregnant?'

If God was listening, he would surely strike her down right there and then for her hypocrisy.

Aphrodite huffed and crossed her arms over her beaded bodice. 'Thanks for being happy for me.'

'Don't do that. The beads. You'll break them.' Vasiliki tugged at her daughter's arms and placed them by her side. 'What were you thinking, Aphrodite? Why did you have to tell me this right now?'

'Because I thought you'd be excited, that's why. For God's sake. *Now* you're going to get all Greek on me?'

'What's that supposed to mean, young lady?'

Aphrodite stomped her foot but the sound of it was buried in the massive skirts of her wedding dress. 'I'm twenty-eight years old! I don't want to wait until I'm thirty to have a baby. I'll be ancient. I honestly can't believe you're acting this way. One of your other daughters is a lesbian, for God's sake! I'm the one doing the traditional thing and you can't even be happy for me? What else do I have to do?'

Vasiliki put her head in her hands. Perhaps things were easier when parents sorted out their daughter's husbands. And speaking of which, perhaps she could choose another personality type for her daughter as well. Was this stubbornness from Tom? Is that what Aphrodite had inherited from him? She sighed. There was no use looking for blame somewhere else. Aphrodite had got all this temperament from her mother.

Vasiliki looked up wearily. 'What are your grandparents going to say when they find out?'

Aphrodite lifted a finger and speared it in her mother's direction. 'If they still think things were better back in the village, they can go back to Greece. This is the eighties, Mum. Things are different these days. I can't believe this. I'm marrying a Greek boy—someone I chose for myself, not like you—and you can't even be happy for me.'

Aphrodite spun around—storming out the door was out of the question as she would have had to walk into the inside vestibule of the church in front of all their guests—so she shuffled to the corner and huffed.

It was Vasiliki's job to calm her daughter's nerves. She had to pull herself together. Her own life had been a whirlwind in the past twelve months with her daughter's wedding preparations and her own two weeks in Adelaide to be with Elizabeta. Seeing her friend so weak and ill had given her a new perspective on many things, including making it a priority to look after her own health, but these insights were perhaps best not shared right now with her daughter, who seemed to be on the brink of a panic attack.

She took a deep breath and tottered over, trying to ignore the pain in her foot. She had a bunion on her left big toe from years of wearing heels like this and it was killing her. She smoothed down the skirt of her Carla Zampatti mother-of-the-bride suit.

'Aphrodite, come on.' She tried to calm herself. 'You took me a little bit by surprise. That's all. Phew. So, I'm going to be a grandmother, huh?'

Her daughter turned. Her eyes were glassy and her lips trembled. 'Yes. In about seven months.'

'Whoa.' Vasiliki breathed deep, tried to preserve this moment. Her firstborn was about to have her firstborn. And then a hurricane of memories rose up from her stomach and she could feel the bile in her throat. She felt dizzy.

'Mum, are you all right?' Aphrodite reached for her, pulled her to a plastic chair and pushed her shoulders down.

She wanted to strip off her damn wedding outfit and kick off her ridiculous heels and just be able to breathe. When she had conceived Aphrodite twenty-nine years earlier, when she'd spun a lie for the husband who had been chosen for her, for her family and for her daughter, she hadn't thought about what this exact moment would feel like. She should be happy—a wedding and a baby—but she felt treacherous. Like a giant fake and a liar. Her daughter was about to be walked down the aisle by the man who wasn't her father.

Who wasn't her birth father; she corrected that thought. Vasiliki's heart thumped. She had so many regrets about what she'd done all those years ago and the choices she'd made ever since to cover it all up. Australia had changed so much since then that it was hard to imagine what those days had been like for young women like her. Straight off the boat, that's what Australians used to say. And straight into Melbourne with as many Greeks as there were back home. She had become a part of this country, through hard work, through having children, through being a successful business owner with Steve. Did she feel Greek, still? She was Greek Australian. She held both countries in her heart. And her beautiful daughter, standing there pouting, was Greek Australian too, had been since the day she was conceived.

Vasiliki was convinced that if Tom knew about Aphrodite, he would be here. She knew it. He would be out there in the church, sitting with Frances and Andrew and Iliana and Vinnie, celebrating this day with the rest of the Bonegilla girls. She knew there was already one person missing—Elizabeta was still going through radiotherapy—but were there actually two?

She searched her daughter's face. There was so much water under the bridge now. What good would it do to find out the truth about who her birth father was? She loved Steve, adored him. And he adored her. He was her real father, had raised her, had loved her, had pushed her and encouraged her and protected her like every good father does. The truth about her genetics would be an explosion in the family that no one would recover from. It had been Vasiliki's choice to go into her marriage with that in her heart and in her belly.

Tom was going to be a grandfather and he would never know. And Frances? Her dear friend, Frances? She would be this child's great-aunt.

Vasiliki dropped her head between her knees.

'Mum. Mum,' Aphrodite pleaded. 'What's the matter? Oh God, should I call an ambulance? You look terrible.'

'No, don't.' Vasiliki said, her voice muffled by her skirt. 'I think … I'm having a hot flush, that's all. Stupid menopause.'

Aphrodite's hand was on her back, rubbing gently. 'Breathe, Mum. Breathe. I think I need to get Dad. God, where is he?' Her voice wobbled and broke.

You cannot let your guilt ruin her life.

Vasiliki sat up. She breathed deep. Found the steel in her spine. She gripped her daughter's hand. 'I need a tissue.'

'So do I,' Aphrodite sobbed.

Vasiliki clicked open her clutch. Inside was the handkerchief Tom had given her almost thirty years ago, in someone else's car down at the beach. The night Aphrodite was conceived. She stared at it, sitting neatly alongside her lipstick, compact, a comb, her purse and a packet of tissues. She had completely forgotten she had tucked it in there. She had wanted a little piece of Tom to be with her today. She took out the tissues and snapped her bag shut.

They stood together, two short women of the exact same height, elevated by their love of ridiculous heels, aided and abetted by Aphrodite's sister's job as the shoe buyer for a national department store, and fixed each other's make-up. Gently swiping the smudged mascara, reapplying foundation where it had been smoothed away, blotting lipstick and blushing cheeks. It took a few minutes, and some kind of calm was restored. From beyond the door, the sounds of voices and footsteps grew louder.

'I'm about to get married,' Aphrodite said, her eyes wide and scared.

'Yes you are, my beautiful clever girl. And I'm so proud of you.'

Mother and daughter held hands. There was no hugging with a dress that pouffy.

'Okay. Here's our plan,' Vasiliki said. 'I'm excited about the baby. Of course I am. But can this be our little secret for today? I can't tell your father. He'll have a heart attack. He's already stressing about the reception and the car parking. We invite two hundred people to your wedding and he thinks there are going to be no car parking problems. I'm surprised he's not out there in one of those orange vests directing the traffic.'

'Dad.' Aphrodite shook her head and smiled. 'He would if I asked him.'

'He would do anything for you, you know that.'

'I know it. Thank you to both of you for giving me this wedding. I'm sorry I told you this way. I'm excited, that's all. I wanted you to be the second to know.'

Vasiliki understood being excited about having a baby. She'd been through it four times. She would never tell anyone that her firstborn would always be her most precious. She clasped her daughter's hand.

In that moment, she decided.

She would never *skao to mistiko*. She would never burst the secret of Aphrodite. Never ever. She couldn't do that to Steve, who loved his daughter, or to Aphrodite, who adored her father. The past should stay in the past. What did the Australians say? That she should let sleeping dogs lie.

That's what she would do. That was her real wedding gift to her daughter. To gift her the life she already knew and a father who had raised her with all the love he had in his heart.

'Let's go.'

Chapter Forty-five

1989

'Do you think they're getting on?'

Frances sipped her Earl Grey tea and looked out at Elizabeta's back yard. It was a lovely home with a wide stretch of neatly trimmed lawn in the backyard, and beyond it fruit trees and a vegetable patch. A beach shade fluttered in the breeze, the kind made of green and white striped canvas, and under it sat four little girls. Elizabeta's husband Nikolas had been erecting it when they'd arrived.

'I don't want the girls to get sunburnt,' he'd said.

Her own granddaughter, little brown-haired Bethany, was standing by the small wooden table pouring cups of water for the other girls. Her two pigtails were bobbing up and down by her ears as she seemed to be instructing them in some way, judging by the finger pointing and the pursed lips.

'It looks like they're having fun,' Vasiliki said as she squinted over at them. 'If I had my glasses on I could be sure. I can't believe I left them in Melbourne. I know exactly where I put them too, on the kitchen table. I said to Steve just before we left for the airport, "Don't let me forget my glasses". So what did I do?' She threw her hands up in the air. 'I forgot my glasses. I was so excited about having a holiday, just Klio and me, that I didn't even think.'

'It was such a lovely idea to bring them along for a Bonegilla girls reunion,' Elizabeta said. 'Although it was very easy for me. I didn't have to fly anywhere. Luisa just dropped Sophie off and there we were.'

'Bianca couldn't wait. I don't think she slept for a week. She loved the flight over,' Iliana laughed. 'The air hostesses gave her a colouring book and a little pencil case. And she sat there the whole time from Sydney—what it is, two hours?—with her head down, scribbling.'

The four women repositioned their chairs so they could watch their granddaughters playing. Frances couldn't remember now whose idea it had actually been. There had been so many phone calls back and forth—from Sydney and Melbourne and Adelaide—that the original proponent had been forgotten in the excitement and plans for the weekend.

They were older now, the Bonegilla girls. It seemed ludicrous to call themselves 'girls' but the name had stuck and it gave them all a spring in their step when one of them said it. It invoked an instant smile, bringing back so many memories of what they had shared and now, what they would still share. Bonegilla had given them their friendship. Australia had given them a new life. And their daughters had given them these wonderful granddaughters to cluck and fuss over and spoil.

Thinking back now, Frances thought perhaps it had been Vasiliki's idea. Vicki, she should say. Frances had never managed to get used to calling her that, even after all these years. Vasiliki had called them all to lament that they hadn't met each other's granddaughters and the idea had sprung to life. A weekend away in Adelaide, the opportunity to give their own daughters a break, they suggested, and the idea had snowballed from there. They had chosen Adelaide for Elizabeta's sake. Since her own granddaughter had been born, she'd lost another breast to cancer and had gone through a punishing round of chemotherapy. None of the other Bonegilla girls said it out loud, but they knew money was tight for Elizabeta and Nikolas. Still only on one income, they made do, but there wasn't any left over to fly off to Sydney or Melbourne for the weekend. None of them minded. They had all sensed that Elizabeta was happiest when she was at home and were happy to come to her.

Over the years their reunions had been so important to them all, and now bringing their granddaughters along was a way of keeping that connection alive, of having something to talk about other than their aches and pains and their parents' illness and, sadly, deaths. Frances's parents had both died in the past year, so close together that Tom had flown out from London for her mother's funeral but hadn't been able to get back on a plane within two weeks to come home for their father's. Vasiliki's father had dropped dead from a heart attack in his fruit shop while unpacking rockmelons. Her mother lived with them now, frail and increasingly forgetful, with what little English she had fading fast from her memory.

As for Iliana, her parents had retired years before and during one of their annual trips to Italy, her father had died of a stroke. Her mother was still living at home, strong and independent.

'Look at them, will you?' Elizabeta laughed when her own granddaughter, Sophie, downed her glass of water, wiped her forearm across her mouth like a sailor might, and then ran across the lawn to the Hills Hoist. Elizabeta shook her head in amused disbelief. She seemed to know what was coming.

'What's she doing?' Iliana gasped.

'Just watch.' Elizabeta nodded.

Up Sophie scampered, finding purchase for her foot on the metal handle of the clothesline, and, like a little monkey, she was up on the frame, her knees hooked over one of the spokes, and hanging upside down by her knees.

'This is how you do it,' she called in her little-girl voice to the others. Bianca, Bethany and Klio ran after her and looked up at her, into the blue sky, as if she was flying off somewhere in a rocket. They reached high for her hands and held on, dragging her around in circles under the clothesline, running and giggling, their bare feet pressing lightly into the prickly grass, their laughter ringing around the backyard like the sweetest sound imaginable.

'Aren't you scared she'll fall off?' Iliana cried.

Elizabeta shrugged. 'She loves it. What can I do? She has a sense of adventure. My sister Luisa used to climb all the trees at Bonegilla. Just like she does. Like a little monkey. She was never scared. I think that's where she gets it.'

Frances understood why Elizabeta wouldn't want to take away her granddaughter's simple pleasure, why she would relish the look of pure joy and adventure in her little eyes when she dangled and spun and laughed and laughed.

'I like to see happiness in my family again,' Elizabeta said.

The girls knew why.

They had spent so many years worrying about Elizabeta, but something had changed in her. For the first time in many years, she seemed content with her life. It was there in her face, in the fullness that had returned to her body after the chemo the year before. The smiles they hadn't seen for such a long time. Was it too much to ask that all her suffering was finally over?

'What about you?' Iliana asked. 'How are you and Andrew going?'

Frances looked out to the girls, hesitant about answering the question. 'We're all right. We have our ups and downs like everyone else I suppose. We've been trying. That's all you can do, isn't it?' She'd been trying for a very long time to make her marriage to Andrew work. It wasn't his fault really. The problem was that no matter what he did, he wasn't Massimo.

'Are you glad you didn't leave him in the end?'

Five years before, on the day Elizabeta had told them she had breast cancer, Frances had made her choice. She was going to fly back to Sydney and see Massimo, tell him that she couldn't go on any longer the way they were, that she wanted to leave Andrew and be with him. Really be with him. Not in clandestine motels and in dangerous phone calls, but together, they way they should have always been. She'd had it all planned. She was at the motel early. She'd brought flowers and cheese and crackers and some other nibbles, the prosciutto he loved, and a bottle of wine, so they could talk and make plans. She'd found her bravery. She had decided what she wanted from her life and she had been determined to chase it.

She should have known when he didn't show up.

She'd waited and waited, sitting on the scratchy motel bedspread for two hours.

A week later, a letter turned up at work for her.

He wasn't ever going to be coming again. His wife, Domenica, had been diagnosed with multiple sclerosis. He was going to do the right thing, his letter said, and look after her. Francis had taken the letter to the staff toilets, read it over and over, and sobbed.

She went home that night, cooked chicken schnitzel and baked potatoes for dinner, and never mentioned to Andrew that she didn't love him anymore, that she had planned to leave him, that for almost fifteen years she'd been living a lie. *Another* lie. The truth of that didn't hurt her as much as she'd imagined it would. It was just another secret she had to add to her long list.

'How's Domenica doing?' Frances asked, careful not to hold Iliana's gaze for too long.

Iliana shook her head. 'Not so great. She's got the kind of MS that is terrible from the very beginning. She has the shakes quite bad and can't walk far. It's very sad. Massimo is so good with her. He only goes into work two days a week now that the boys have taken over the business. He's devoted to that woman.'

Iliana passed Frances a piece of Elizabeta's cherry strudel. It was her second piece; the flaky pastry and succulent cherries were irresistible. 'You won't regret sticking with your marriage. Marriages take work but it's what you get married for. That's what you promise God when you get married, to be with the same person for your whole life, to be happy together. To look after each other when you get sick, like Massimo and Domenica. To make a family so one day you get to love your grandchildren.'

Frances looked across the yard at Bethany. She did love that little girl. Perhaps she was freer to love her than she'd been to love her own children. She'd had Vanessa and Lyndall not so long after giving up her first baby. Too many times when they were young, she'd been blindsided by her grief about the adoption. All these years later, she could look at Bethany and almost not think about her son.

'She's just like you, you know,' Elizabeta said.

'Bethany's like me?' Frances replied, surprised.

Iliana, Elizabeta and Vasiliki laughed.

'Look at her. She's organising everyone. She's got that look on her face, just like the one you used to have at Bonegilla when you were teaching us English in the mess.'

'Did I?' Frances asked, surprised. She peered at Bethany. What was the look? Determination? Stubbornness? The look of someone who knew her own mind?

'You did. Exactly like her,' Vasiliki said. 'Look at her right now. That's it. She's trying to get Sophie to come down from the clothesline. She's trying to keep her safe.'

Bethany was beckoning Sophie, waving her little hand, pointing to the ground. Klio and Bianca were at her side, giggling behind their hands.

'I think they are going to be friends,' Frances said. 'I'm glad.'

There was laughter around the table and then a wistful silence descended.

'Aren't they lucky to be young girls now?' she asked.
'Think of all the things they'll be able to do, what they'll be
able to see. What will they be when they grow up?'

'Anything they want,' Vasiliki said.

'Astronauts,' Elizabeta said with a smile.

'Doctors,' Iliana said.

'And they'll be able to marry the person they love,' Vasiliki added. 'Except Stavroula. She can't marry her girlfriend.'

Iliana gasped. 'Your daughter wants to marry her
girlfriend?'

'One day, yes. Just like her sisters and your kids can get
married. It doesn't make me popular at church when I say
this, but why shouldn't they? She says people in Europe are
fighting to make it happen.'

'I don't know about that,' Iliana murmured, crossing
herself.

'I know, Iliana. It's a big change. It took me a long time,
too.'

The women turned to watch their grandchildren. Bethany was positioning the girls in a straight line and Frances chuckled. She was envious of the possibilities their lives
would offer them, of the jobs they would have, of the myriad choices they would sift through before they eventually
chose what path they would take. They had so much living
to do and so much time in which to do it.

'That's something I'll always regret,' she said wistfully.
'That I never got to travel. Remember that atlas I had at
Bonegilla? I used to study each and every page, imagining
all the places I'd go. All the things I'd see. The pyramids of
Egypt. The Eiffel Tower. Rome.'

'Well, why don't you?' Vasiliki was her usual blunt self.

'By myself? Andrew won't want to go, you know that. He's never been interested in going further than the New South Wales south coast to surf. Even after that knee replacement, he still drags out his bodyboard.'

'So why do you need him to go with you? Vasiliki popped an olive in her mouth. 'Your girls have left home. You must have that long service thing that government people have. Why don't you get on a plane? What's stopping you?'

'You could go and see your brother,' Iliana said.

Frances was taken aback. Talk was easy, but she didn't have the inclination anymore. It wasn't that easy for her now. Every time she'd stepped out on a limb, life had knocked her sideways. She didn't think she had it in her these days to take such risks. And how would she do it, travelling by herself? 'You know …' She laughed at the realisation. 'I don't even have a passport.'

Vasiliki wasn't going to let this one go. 'Then get yourself one.'

Frances shook her head and looked to Elizabeta and Iliana. They seemed to be in agreement with Vasiliki.

'She's right,' Elizabeta said. 'Go. Have your adventure, Frances.'

'You should,' Iliana added. 'Go to Italy and throw a coin in the Trevi Fountain for me, hey?'

Frances sat back in her chair. 'Well. You've given me something to think about.'

And in the moments that followed, when the fun and games of their granddaughters held their rapt attention again, Frances thought not of monuments or feats of human labour or waterfalls. She thought of her friendships with the Bonegilla girls. These three steadfast women, whom she'd met all those years ago when they had all seemed so young, when Frances herself had felt naive and innocent about the world, were now giving her the courage she needed, the strength that she had lost, bit by bit, throughout her life. The tables had turned, or perhaps the chairs had simply changed places. She had taken them all by the hand, guided them through the first months of life in a strange country and they had gone on their way, stronger, confident, with courage.

She could leave Andrew behind with a freezer full of meals and toss a rucksack on her back like the young ones did. Well, perhaps not a rucksack. She knew the bursitis in her knee would make that a painful journey. She had the time. Vasiliki was right in saying that she had long service leave—two lots of it, in fact—but she'd been cautiously saving it up as a retirement nest egg; for a time when she wasn't teaching anymore and when Bethany and her other grandchildren were grown up and she would be free to sit in her living room with a rug on her knees watching the midday movie and knitting booties for her great-grandchildren.

She watched Iliana, Elizabeta and Vasiliki laugh at their granddaughters. All four girls were now somersaulting and cartwheeling on the lawn, their legs waving in the air like arms at a concert, their laughter infectious.

This was what life was, Frances thought. Every choice she had made had led her to this moment. Good or bad, they were steps along the journey to the little girl with the brown pigtails who was learning to let go just a little, to not worry that her skirt was flapping and showing her underpants, that her hair was coming loose. Bethany somersaulted and popped up onto her feet.

'Granny!' she called, bouncing up and down, weightless, on her bare feet. 'Look at this!' She spun, threw her hands onto the grass and flicked her legs in the air.

Frances didn't need to travel to have an adventure to fill the holes in her heart.

She had to do one thing.

Find her son.

Chapter Forty-six

1990

Frances parked in the driveway and turned the key in the ignition. She stopped a moment, looking out over her front yard. It needed tidying. It always needed tidying. The bark from the gum trees had shredded like paper and tossed shards onto the dead lawn. The branch lost during high winds the previous autumn was still lying by the fence, looking now like a decorative feature rather than an accident.

The house was too big for her now. She really should move, but she hadn't quite been able to summon up the energy for something as mundane as cleaning and tidying and packing up a marriage's worth of possessions. Her daughters had moved out years before. Vanessa, her husband Bill and Bethany lived in Cronulla near where Vanessa taught; and Lyndall was still in the Northern Territory working as a nurse in an indigenous community.

Andrew was gone, too. He'd left six months earlier, having fallen in love with one of his colleagues at the private school where he was the deputy principal. He was fifty-two years old and had left her for a young woman of twenty-five. Karen. She was barely out of teacher's college. The last time she'd talked to Andrew, he'd told her he was going to try to have his vasectomy reversed so he and Karen could have children.

She had wished him luck.

Frances opened the car door, grabbed her bag full of books and marking, and remembered to check the letterbox before she went inside the house and thought about dinner. It too needed fixing. The flap on the back had broken off and when the postie shoved letters in through the slot on the front they slipped through the back and often fell into the shards of bark from the gum tree.

And that's where she found the envelope from the New South Wales government with the information she'd been waiting for.

She hurried inside, dropped her bag on the dining-room table and stared at her name on the front of the envelope.

Mrs Frances Coleman.

The words swam. All she saw was Frances Burley. The girl she was when she'd had to hide in shame, bearing the blame entirely on her own, the victim of a time and place in Australia that was thankfully now over.

She tore the end from the A4 envelope and pulled out forms and a letter addressed to her.

Earlier in the year, the laws around adoption in New South Wales had changed and during the debates there had been much discussion in the newspapers and on talkback radio about the whole issue. It was now the law that adopted people, once they reached eighteen years of age, had the right to know who their parents were. And Frances also had the right to know what had happened to her son. Born in Albury in 1959, he would be thirty-one years old now if he was still alive.

When Andrew had left to start a new family, Frances had decided that it was about time she was honest about her own. And, after months of waiting, she was holding the information in her hand that might help her. She shuffled the papers. She stilled when she saw the copy of her son's birth certificate.

The section marked 'Father' was blank.

And then in the box where she'd had to write the baby's name, there it was. His name.

Massimo Reginald Burley.

The papers shook and she couldn't focus. Something rose up in her, perhaps it was shock. Here was proof. He existed. She hadn't imagined her baby, the little one she'd never held or seen. He was real.

When she'd applied for the files on the adoption, she'd also had the chance to register a contact veto. She could prevent her Massimo—or whatever his name had been since the day he was adopted—from making contact. She hadn't ticked that box. And, it seemed, neither had he.

She wanted, finally, to know what had happened to her son.

She hadn't told the girls about him yet, nor Andrew. She steadied her nerves with a glass of wine from the cask in the fridge and then sat down in the hallway, on the chair by the telephone, and dialled Vanessa's number.

'Hey, Mum,' her daughter said breezily.

'Hi, sweetheart. How are you?'

'Good. Busy. What's up with you?'

Frances paused. She hadn't thought about this part, about how she would tell them. 'Can you come over? There's something I need to tell you.'

There was silence down the line. 'God, Mum, you're not sick, are you?'

Frances closed her eyes. 'No, darling, nothing like that. Will you come?'

'Sure. I'm on my way.'

Frances stumbled back to the kitchen table. She'd completely forgotten to open the other envelope.

She opened it. Inside it was her passport.

Chapter Forty-seven

1994

On a mild Wednesday in April, Iliana stood out front of St Fiacre's in Sydney and looked over the heads of the hundreds of people who'd come to mourn her sister-in-law, Domenica.

Vinnie hadn't left her side, and Anita and Sonia were there with their husbands, too. She had done her crying for her widowed brother already, in the quiet of her own home, and now she was trying to stay calm, to find comforting words to say to Domenica's family and all their friends, to be the support she needed to be for Massimo and his sons. His wife, their mother, had died too young. What else was there to say?

'He looks tired, Iliana.' Vinnie rocked back on his heels. He always did that when he was worried.

'He's exhausted. All those years looking after her at home and then visiting her every day in the nursing home. I kept telling him to take a break, but he wouldn't.'

'He was always a good husband to her. Always.' Iliana and Vinnie exchanged a look. She knew what he meant. Vinnie knew the truth about Massimo's wife. But today wasn't the place to voice those thoughts out loud, in honour of the dead. Wishing for things to have turned out differently was a road to nowhere. If Domenica hadn't married Massimo, Iliana would never have met her Vinnie at the wedding and married him. Life sometimes had a way of making things right.

'I'll be back in a minute,' Iliana told Vinnie. 'You go in. Save me a seat. The second row on our side, okay?'

He reached for her hand. 'Where are you going?'

'To Massimo.'

Vinnie pulled her close and kissed her cheek tenderly. She still tingled inside when he kissed her. Oh, he was a good man. A wonderful husband and father. He had made her laugh all the years they'd been together. She couldn't even put herself in the place to think about how she would be if it was his funeral today instead of Domenica's.

Iliana negotiated her way through the crowd of people, filled with so many familiar faces from the Italian community. The old ones looked as if they had just stepped out of the village; their wizened faces and stooped backs signs that their bodies had borne the scars of a lifetime of physical work. It struck her so vividly in that moment, in the faces of these people, that a whole generation was dying.

She slipped an arm through her brother's. 'You ready?' she asked quietly.

Massimo turned to her, his face stoic. He had hidden so much from her over the years that he was used to holding his face in such a way as to not give away what he was thinking. But she knew.

She squeezed his arm and he gave her a nod.

Then their younger brothers, Stefano and Giovani, were there too. Massimo and Domenica's boys, Joe and Sebastian, were enveloped in their uncles' arms.

This is a family, Iliana thought. 'Come on boys,' she said.

Iliana followed her brother and her nephews into church.

A few minutes later, the mourners were seated. At the head of the chapel, Domenica's coffin was laid out, a huge wreath upon it, made up of red and white flowers with green leaves underneath, creating a tableau of the colours of the Italian flag. A big white bow tied everything together, and right there in the bow the red blossoms of a flowering gum were tucked in tight. The light from the stained glass behind it spilled through, reflecting reds and greens and purples, as if heaven was right there just outside the window.

When the sombre music ended, the priest took his place behind the podium and waited, silently gathering his thoughts.

'It's hard for people to understand these days, especially the young ones,' the priest began his eulogy to a silent and respectful gathering, 'the struggles and deprivations that Domenica and her mother and father went through to start again in this country all those decades ago.'

There were murmurs among the mourners.

'Australia was the lucky country. Isn't that what you were all told when you came here? Domenica and her family and hundreds of thousands of people just like you all were the flotsam and jetsam of Europe, displaced, dispossessed, disrupted, people who simply wanted a better life for their families. You didn't know much about this country on the far side of the world. Our migrant communities are filled with people like you who took great risks. You were brave. You risked so much to make a good life here in this new country.'

There were nods of understanding and murmurs of agreement among the mourners.

'And look at what you helped create,' the priest continued, his voice rising. 'Strong families. Strong family trees with many, many branches. Children, grandchildren and great-grandchildren for some of you here today.'

Someone let out a sob.

Iliana looked over her shoulder to see who it was. It was Domenica's sister, in the second row, her head down, weeping.

But someone else caught her eye.

In the back row. It was Frances.

Afterwards, when there were cups of coffee and trays full of biscotti and cannoli and sfogliatelle in the reception room, Iliana found her friend. Respectfully dressed in a black jacket and trousers, Frances looked like the middle-aged schoolteacher she now was. Her hair was sensible and sat on her collar. She wore glasses, pale pink lipstick and a string of pearls around her neck.

'I'm so sorry about Domenica,' Frances said. 'It's such awful news.'

'Thank you for coming.' Iliana held her arms open and the two women hugged each other, a long history in their embrace.

When they finally let go, Frances searched Iliana's eyes. 'How are you all coping? It must have been dreadful for the family. For Massimo and the boys.'

'Oh, it's been very hard. The past two years when she was in the nursing home? Just awful. The boys are heartbroken. But,' Iliana said as she crossed herself, 'at least she's at peace now.'

'Yes, of course. And Massimo? How is he?' Frances asked quietly.

'Go talk to him. He'd like to know that you're here.'

'No, I wouldn't want to intrude. Not today.' Frances dropped her gaze and Iliana thought how useless it was to feel guilty about being in love with someone. If ever there was a time to tell her secret, this was it. She held out her hand and Frances put hers in Iliana's grasp. 'Frances, look at me.'

When Frances did, Iliana sighed. 'I know.'

Frances stared at her.

'Massimo told me.' Iliana slipped an arm through Frances's. 'Come for a walk with me.'

She led her out the big front doors and into the car park. They walked through the front gates and down Catherine Street. The sun was warm on their faces, the wind was at their backs. Frances clearly didn't know what to say, whether she was going to be accused and banished.

Iliana looked up the street and began her story. 'When Domenica went into the nursing home, Massimo finally talked to me. Really talked to me. For the first time ever in our whole lives. I think he was angry about her sickness, about what had happened in their marriage, about the boys having to go and visit their mother with dribble on her chin and people wiping her ... wiping her you know what.' Iliana shivered. 'It was a long story he told me, Frances, and you were in it.'

Frances met her friend's eyes.

'You were there at Bonegilla, at Cooma, and later. For all those years you were together and it was a secret. Even from me.'

'It had to be.'

'You know what's funny? Back in 1974, when we had that reunion at your old place? I asked Massimo to come, not because I thought I was going to go into labour or anything—remember I was about to burst with Sonia? I asked him along because I knew how unhappy he was. I thought seeing you again would make him happy. And then I find out all these years later what happened between you two.'

'You surprised both of us that day. I remember that. And Tom came. He's retired now, you know. He and Sally have moved to Bath. It's quite lovely.'

'Did you visit them when you were over there?'

Frances nodded. 'I stayed with them a week before I went to Paris and then on to Rome and Athens.'

'Did you throw a coin in the Trevi Fountain for me?'

Frances squeezed Iliana's arm. 'I did.' It hadn't been Massimo's coin, the one he had given her at Bonegilla. She still had it in her jewellery box. That was too precious to waste a wish on, one she knew would never come true.

'So, you see, I realised that if I hadn't invited him, nothing could have happened. So maybe it was my fault.'

'Oh, Iliana. You must think I'm awful. I do, you know? For someone who thought herself so smart, I've made some terrible choices. Keeping a secret from you was one of the biggest.'

'At first, I was angry about what the two of you did. But now, I'm older, I think I understand better. People are complicated. We do things for honour and responsibility and to keep face with people. And when you are lying there in your coffin, like Domenica ...' Iliana crossed herself. 'What does all that matter?'

'You and your family were so good to me all those years ago. I've never forgotten it.'

'You will always be part of my family, Francesca.'

Frances smiled at the memory of being called that. 'I loved him, Iliana. I really did.'

'And you still do, don't you?'

She shrugged. 'I never did figure out how to stop loving him.'

'Massimo told me that you said no to him when he asked you to marry him back in Cooma.'

'I didn't want to keep the baby. I couldn't have back then.' Frances lifted her chin up, closed her eyes to the sun. 'I found him, you know.'

Iliana turned to her, shocked. 'Your baby?'

'His name is Craig and he's a farmer near Albury. He's very happy. Married with a baby. He always knew he was adopted and had no interest in finding me until he became a father himself. He's lovely. A quiet country man.'

'Craig,' Iliana said. 'That's a good country-boy name.'

'I got to give him a name, you know, when he was born. That was one thing I was allowed to do. I named him after your brother and my father. Massimo Reginald. He asked me about that, the strange names on his birth certificate. I told him I named him after someone who wasn't his father, but who was a very good man. And he got a kick out of knowing his grandfather used to run Bonegilla. Can you believe he married a girl whose grandparents were there, in the camp?'

'Life is like a big circle sometimes, don't you think?'

The two friends stopped and Frances exhaled deeply. A lifetime's worth of secrets shared meant she felt lighter on her feet. 'The secrets we keep, huh?'

'So much wasted time for both of you. For everyone. So many years gone.'

Frances shrugged. 'I made my choice. I wouldn't make it the same way now. You know I wouldn't. But it was a different time. In some ways, it feels like ten lifetimes ago, not one.'

'It's not too late, you know,' Iliana said.

'For what?' Frances asked.

The two women stopped in the middle of the street. A car beeped its horn and they scuttled to the other side of the road. Iliana took her friend's face in her hands and looked at her, direct and true.

'He's never stopped loving you either, Frances.'

Chapter Forty-eight

2018

Twenty-five-year-old Sophie Greene parked her car in the neat, landscaped car park of the aged-care facility where her *oma*, Elizabeta, lived.

She swiped her access card at the front door, walked the long corridors to the lift and exited on the first floor into a light, spacious foyer. To one side, there were sofas arranged so residents could sit together and chat over a cup of tea or coffee in the warmth of the sun streaming in from the windows. On the other, there were sliding doors to a courtyard rooftop garden with a triangular sun shade.

Sophie always hoped she might see her *oma* sitting there, a smile on her face, her hands busy knitting, but Elizabeta had never walked these corridors. She hadn't ever sat on the sofas chatting with her fellow residents. She hadn't felt the sun on her face for two years now. She didn't walk. She couldn't talk. She was small and frail, a ghost of the person Sophie had known. Her *oma* had been going downhill for a couple of years before the crunch point had come. Her increasing forgetfulness and confusion had made her more anxious and angry, and Sophie's mother Luisa had finally decided Elizabeta needed more care than the family could provide. There were assessments and medical appointments and forms to fill in and, finally, a bed had become available. It was a lovely facility with kind and caring staff.

That didn't stop Sophie from wishing she'd never set foot in it.

She made her way down the corridor, past residents' rooms. There were names on each door to personalise these spaces and she whispered them to herself as she walked past.

'Mrs Gertrude (Trudy) Bierbaumer. Mr Miroslav Horvat. Mrs Bogdana Gwosdz.'

Had any of these people been at Bonegilla with her *oma*? Sophie smiled to herself. Wouldn't that be funny? To spend her last days living among the people she'd spent her first days in Australia with. Her *oma* had told her stories about coming to Australia. About Bonegilla. How strange the food was—'All that mutton'—and how her own father hadn't eaten lamb for twenty years after they'd left. Sophie had heard how cold it was, and how happy they were to finally leave and come to Adelaide. Her warmest stories were about her friends, the women Sophie's mother Luisa had called Auntie Iliana, Auntie Frances and Auntie Vicki.

Sophie found her grandmother propped up in her recliner chair, the kind with wheels and a vinyl covering, like a souped-up wheelchair, positioned near the windows overlooking the garden, so she could look out into the world beyond the glass. It could have been a brick wall instead of a lush garden. She wouldn't know the difference.

Sophie dragged a dining chair over to her and sat down. She reached for her *oma's* hand. Her paper-thin skin was so transparent Sophie could map out the veins.

'Hi, *Oma*. How are you going today?'

Elizabeta's face was wrinkled and pale. Her mouth was set in a permanent frown. Her hair, completely white now, was dishevelled and pushed back from her forehead, cut short so it wouldn't be a bother. She'd had such beautiful red hair when she was younger, everyone said. There was no physical response to Sophie's words or her touch. *Oma* didn't blink anymore; her eyes were barely open, as if letting the light in was painful. Her twisted feet were clad in multi-coloured socks to keep her toes warm, even in the middle of summer. A crocheted blanket, a gift from Sophie, covered her lap, and a small pillow was positioned by the side of her head to stop her head lolling onto her chest.

The staff who walked the floors in their silent shoes, who cheerily engaged other residents with their friendly chatter and small talk, still spoke to her, but Sophie knew they hadn't expected a response for twelve months now. But they talked to her anyway, which made Sophie so glad. It was as if they were holding onto the thought that even though a resident's body had failed them, their mind might still be active.

'Hi, love. Hi there, Elizabeta. Aren't you lucky to have a visitor today?'

It was Carol, the salt-of-the-earth aged-care worker who looked after Elizabeta on the weekends. Her blonded hair was pulled back in a clip and fluffed at the top. Her warm smile was always welcome.

'Hi, Carol. How are you?'

'Can't complain, Sophie. How is she today, the poor old thing?' Carol peered into Elizabeta's wizened face. Sophie held her hand.

'Her cheeks are a little rosy, I think. Don't you?'

Carol patted Sophie on the shoulder. 'They are. I think she likes seeing you and hearing your voice. If you need anything, let me know.'

Sophie watched as Carol walked away. She searched Elizabeta's face for a sign of something. There was nothing. But she had a little routine going with her grandmother. She came every Saturday afternoon and talked to her *oma*, filling her in on what she was up to, the gigs she had played that week, the weather. Perhaps this week's story would rouse her. Sophie cleared her throat. 'Well, *Oma*, I have some news.'

She waited for a reaction.

'You're going to be a great-grandmother. Or is that a great-*oma*. I'm pregnant.' Sophie held her arms up in the air in a celebratory pose. 'Yay, right? I'm so excited, but scared shitless at the same time. Bowen's tried to get me to rest in case anything happens but what's going to happen? I'm young. I'm healthy. I have excellent genes, thanks to you and *Opa*. And Mum and Dad, of course. Speaking of Mum, you won't believe how excited she is. Can you believe she's even started shopping for baby things? I think she bought a pram yesterday and I'm only twelve weeks.'

Sophie searched her grandmother's face. Her voice was a whisper. 'I wouldn't be here if it wasn't for you, do you know that? Sometimes I think about it and it makes my head spin. If your mum and dad hadn't decided to come to Australia all those years ago, I wouldn't exist. If you hadn't come, you would never have met *Opa* and Mum would never have met Dad and down it goes to me. And to my baby.'

Sophie pressed a hand to her stomach, still flat. 'Please, *Oma*. Just blink or something. Can you hear me?'

She wished so much that her grandmother would look at her one more time.

Sophie sighed and looked around the room. There seemed to be so few visitors. 'I went to Auntie Iliana's funeral this week. Mum didn't want to go to Sydney all by herself so I went too. It was … nice. Sad but nice.'

Was there a flicker just then, a blink of an eye, a breath?

'It was nice to see Bianca again, too. Remember Bianca? Iliana's granddaughter? The beautiful Italian one? I always wanted her big brown eyes. Anyway, she's a trainee diplomat in Canberra now. Very impressive. And Bethany was there, Frances's granddaughter. She's a travel agent. And, oh, how can I forget Auntie Vasiliki's granddaughter? Klio's making documentary films about refugees.'

Sophie's voice began to tremble. 'You're the last of the Bonegilla girls. Did you know that, *Oma*?'

There was so much she didn't know about Elizabeta Muller, Sophie realised. Why hadn't she been more curious about her *oma's* life when her grandmother would still have been able to tell all her stories? She'd never been interested until now, but it was too late. She reached a hand up to her *oma* and stroked her cheek, papery thin and creased as if it had been ironed that way. What did she really know about this woman, who had loved her, fed her, cared for her and fought for her throughout her entire life? There would be no more sauerkraut or cherry strudel or spätzle. There were gaps in the story of her grandmother's life that would now never be filled.

All Sophie had were potted family fables, disjointed remnants of memories: flour soup and picking wildflowers in the forest and a best friend who was in America and the long journey to Australia when a man in Egypt tried to buy her as his wife.

All the rest was a mystery. Sophie only existed because of this woman. Her history was Sophie's history. Her DNA was in Sophie and would soon be in her child.

If only she'd cared enough before now to ask, 'Who were you?'

Every day the old Greek man with the walking frame bustled over to her asking, 'No taxi today?' and every day she couldn't tell him that no, there was no taxi today or tomorrow or any other day for any of them.

Elizabeta didn't think about taxis or breakfast or lunch or activities like throwing and catching balloons or watching the midday movie or the traffic outside her window or the lush gardens of her aged-care home.

She smelled wild mushrooms, cupped in her hands, foraged from the earth, hidden under ferns, in a green, light-filled forest. She saw her basket filled with the white caps and promise of a delicious meal when she returned home.

She tasted her mother's flour soup and smelled her shampoo and her father's Old Spice cologne.

She saw her sister Luisa climbing gum trees at Bonegilla, crawling out onto spindly limbs, like a koala, her plaits looped over her ears and her face full of unbridled joy.

She saw a large book with pink and green and yellow countries divided by dotted lines and twisting rivers and mountain ranges.

She felt the cool waters of Lake Hume on her ankles and the pleasure of water splashing on her face.

She smelled the talcum-powder scent of her babies in her arms.

She tasted salty Greek food on her tongue.

She felt her husband giving her a ripe peach, the gentle furriness tickling her palm, and her granddaughter's silky hair, like ribbons between her fingers as she plaited it.

Frances. Iliana. Vasiliki.

A breath.

A husband. Photos. Friends. Rice.

Mushrooms.

Shampoo.

Old Spice.

Talcum powder.

A peach.

A breath.

About Bonegilla

If Australians have learned one lesson from the Pacific war now moving to a successful conclusion, it is surely that we cannot continue to hold our island continent for ourselves and our descendants unless we greatly increase our numbers. We are about 7 million people and we hold 3 million square miles [7.7 million square kilometres] of this Earth surface ... much development and settlement have yet to be undertaken. Our need to undertake it is urgent and imperative if we are to survive.

Minister for Immigration Arthur Calwell
Hansard, House of Representatives,
2 August 1945, pp 4911-4915

Arthur Calwell's 'populate or perish' policy changed the face of modern Australia.

More than three million refugees and migrants, 1.5 million of whom were British, came to Australia between 1945 and 1975, almost doubling Australia's population.

Between 1947 and 1971, more than 320,000 of them passed through the Bonegilla Migrant Reception Centre, a sprawling 320-acre ex-army camp on the River Murray in north-eastern Victoria, near Albury-Wodonga.

In the late 1940s, these people were Eastern European Displaced Persons from post-war refugee camps. In the 1950s, they were Assisted Migrants from throughout Europe looking for work and a new life. And in the 1960s and 1970s they were British migrants, or 'ten pound Poms'.

Bonegilla became their temporary home while they were processed and until they found work.

It was to become Australia's largest and longest-lasting post-war migrant accommodation centre.

One in twenty Australians have links to Bonegilla through migration of the post-war era.

Including me.

Author's Note

While *The Last of the Bonegilla Girls* is based in part on the experiences of my own family, it is a work of fiction.

The Bonegilla Migrant Reception Centre did have a camp director at the time my characters lived there, but Reginald Burley is entirely fictitious.

There are claims that up to 500 war criminals entered Australia in the post-war years. One of them, the Latvian Konrad Kalejs, arrived in Australia in 1950 and worked as a clerk at Bonegilla.

I would like to sincerely thank my mother, Emma Purman, and my aunt and godmother, Veronika Wassermann, for answering my many questions about their lives in Hungary and Germany, during and after the war, and their time at Bonegilla.

I wish I'd been more curious when my grandparents— my Oma and Opa—were alive so I could have asked the same questions of them but, sadly, even if I had, their English was not the best, my German only rudimentary and my Hungarian nonexistent. My fondest memory of them is a simple story they told me once about their lives before the war. They smiled and laughed as they remembered a party in Budapest at which they'd waltzed until the sun came up over the Danube.

They were brave, simple people who, like millions of others, had their lives forever changed by the war. They lost their home, were deported to Germany, and finally found their way to Australia. They raised their five children here and were still alive to meet all ten of their grandchildren.

There are now nineteen great-grandchildren and six great-great-grandchildren.

As always, much gratitude to my wonderful publisher Jo Mackay. Thanks, Jo, for having faith in me when I struggled to tell this story. To my editor Annabel Blay, my warmest thanks for your meticulous and constructive work on this book. And finally, thank you to the entire team at Harlequin and HarperCollins, especially the sales representatives who hit the road and talk to booksellers. Your support for Australian authors and stories is priceless.

Acknowledgements

A number of books were particularly useful for research for this book. I would like to acknowledge the many publications of Bruce Pennay, including: *Sharing Bonegilla Stories*, Albury Library Museum, 2012; and *Picturing and Re-picturing Bonegilla*, Specialty Press, 2016; as well as *Personal Stories of German Immigration to Australia Since 1945*, Ingrid Muenstermann (ed), XLibris, 2015; and *A History of Italian Settlement in NSW*, Ros Pesman, Catherine Kevin, NSW Heritage Office, 1998.

The Staff Rules in the Majestic Milk Bar were borrowed from Stratte Vellis (Vamvadelis) who operated three Tamworth businesses: the Capitol Sunday Shop, the Regeant Milk Bar and the Crown Face. They appear in the book *Greek Cafes and Milk Bars of Australia* by Effy Alexakis and Leonard Janiszewski, Halstead Press, ACT, 2016.

I would like to particularly thank the staff of the Albury LibraryMuseum for their assistance in accessing materials in their collection and archive.

LET'S TALK ABOUT BOOKS!

JOIN THE CONVERSATION

HARLEQUIN
AUSTRALIA

@HARLEQUINAUS

@HARLEQUINAUS

HQSTORIES

@HQSTORIES